Book of Days

Books by Deborah Grabien

The JP Kinkaid Chronicles

Rock and Roll Never Forgets
While My Guitar Gently Weeps
London Calling
Graceland
Book of Days
Uncle John's Band *
Dead Flowers *
Comfortably Numb *
Gimme Shelter *

The Haunted Ballads

The Weaver and the Factory Maid
The Famous Flower of Serving Men
Matty Groves
Cruel Sister
New-Slain Knight
Geordie *

Other Novels

Woman of Fire
Fire Queen
Plainsong
And Then Put Out the Light
Still Life With Devils
Dark's Tale

* *forthcoming*

Book of Days

Book #5 of the JP Kinkaid Chronicles

Deborah Grabien

Plus One Press
San Francisco

This is a work of fiction. All of the characters, organizations and events portrayed in this novel are either the products of the author's imagination or are used fictitiously.

Plus One Press

BOOK OF DAYS. Copyright © 2011 by Deborah Grabien. All rights reserved. Printed in the United States of America. For information, address Plus One Press, 2885 Golden Gate Avenue, San Francisco, California, 94118.

www.plusonepress.com

Book Design by Plus One Press

GRABIEN,
DEBORAH

Publisher's Cataloging-in-Publication Data

Grabien, Deborah.
  Book of days : book #5 of the JP Kinkaid chronicles / Deborah
Grabien.—1st. Plus One Press ed.
      p. cm.
    ISBN: 978-0-9844362-6-2
  1. Rock Musicians—Fiction. 2. Musical Fiction. 3. Murder—Fiction.
I. Title. II. Title: Book of Days
    PS3557.R1145 B66 2011
    813'.54—dc22

                                                    2011936081

First Edition: September, 2011

10 9 8 7 6 5 4 3 2 1

Raising a glass to those who accept adulthood

Acknowledgements

There's going to be all kinds of people who need thanking, here: WIP readers, musician friends, the people who gave me the soundtrack for this chunk of my life. But the truth is, it all pales behind the enormous shadow cast by the hard work Nic did on piecing this tour together.

A major tour is a juggernaut that runs on the tiniest of greased wheels; miss one small spoke, and bang!, down comes the whole damned thing. Nic didn't miss a thing. Thank you, love. Brilliant job!

I need to thank Charles Shaar Murray, for his sensational first novel, The Hellhound Sample. You should get it, and read it. His Mick Hudson and my JP Kinkaid have more than just the love of blues in common.

PS – thanks to Stephanie Lang, because she found the Arabic word for "lighthouse" for me. Trust me, it's relevant. Just keep reading. You'll see.

Book of Days

Prologue

From: Ian Hendry

To: mac@knifesharpe.co.uk; scorrigan@irisheyes.uk; lukeh@blacklightband.co.uk; calwil@bunkerbrothers.co.uk; jpkinkaid@blacklightband.co.uk; tmancuso@bombardiers.net; Carlafanucci@fanuccipros.com; Ops; Production

Date: 17 July, 2007

Subject: T-minus 200 days: Tour 2008 Prelim & Misc.

Greetings, all!

Here's the first production email for our 2008 tour. Full info will follow, as will the formal preliminary itinerary.

First order of business is welcoming Tony Mancuso to the family. Tony will be adding his considerable talents to the tour. This marks the first time BL has carried a guest performer for an entire tour since JP did it as a hired hand back in 1976, and we all know how *that* turned out.

So, Tony, welcome aboard! I've added you to the Band mailing list, and will CC you on everything sent to the Ops and Production lists, as well. If you start feeling overwhelmed, let me know and I'll ease up. For the moment, though, I do ask that you read them all. Full immersion in the way the band tours is really the most efficient way to get on.

I've got a shortlist you'll want, mostly department heads and the people you'll need for specific stuff. I'll send that as a separate email attachment, so you can download it and print it out. No need to clog up the internet. Now, on to business.

We've nailed the album release date: *Book of Days* will officially hit the street Monday, 15 January, 2008. We'll post up MP3s on the fan club website just before Christmas, so the kids have a nice present, while the radio stations are spinning the first single; the consensus has JP's song, "Remember Me," as the singles opener. Album art should be final by 15 December, so we'll have a month for manufacturing and distribution.

The tour opens Saturday, 2 February 2008, in Berlin. It's our standard: European leg first, American leg to follow. We're doing ice hockey arenas only, this time; the venue size has to do with the stage footprint and standardised floor plans. It'll cut down on load-ins and rigging, since everything should be the same from room to room.

First leg schedule runs through Sunday, 30 March, closing with two shows at the London Dome, which they promise will be ready. If it's not, we'll fall back on Wembley and add more dates to cover the headcount.

That's 27 shows total, 25 cities, 58 days. Heavier schedule than last time, but it's flexible, allows us to add dates if needed. The idea is to tour just enough to push CD sales to a top 10 position. Based on the last three tours, and the fact that this is a double CD, we have consensus that this is just about right for

Europe. We may get a carryover boost from the films, since both *Playing in the Dark* and *Good Evening, America!* are showing some legs.

Production begins at Shepperton on 17 December 2007, 7am call, Monday morning, Studio H. Nial's got the models done, and Ronan's happy enough with them. So, people, this is the heads-up to get into the touring headspace, and cross your fingers for a smooth ride.

Construction and tech is scheduled to go through 17 January, with the band in for first rehearsals on the 18th. Note to the band: Work out the set list before tech rehearsals, okay? We'll need every available day to get the blocking down. This is a huge build, and mucking with the running order and trying to relearn old stuff could slow us down. Thanks in advance.

We're out of Shepperton on 28 January. First rig leaves for Paris on the 21st, second rig leaves for Milan a week later. Moscow's opening a new arena and have specifically asked us to include them. The new place only has a 15,000 capacity, but it's good press and might sell some records in Russia. We're also playing St. Petersburg this time, so bring a heavy overcoat.

The rest of the leg is old news. We've played every venue before except the new dome in Amsterdam, so we've already got good tech in the library.

The US leg is essentially booked. We're just waiting on final confirmation from Glendale and Los Angeles. Right now, we're at 27 shows in 27 cities, spread out over 62 days, nice and relaxed. No shows on Mondays, as always, and no back-to-backs, unless we get some add-ons, but that's unlikely, unless we see a bump in demand. Kick-off on 29 April at Madison Square Garden, last show 28 June in San Jose. It's Bree's birthday, by the way, so we'll do something special for the dead dog party. A week at Tribeca for rehearsals again, starting on 22 April, so remember to pack for springtime in New York.

3

That's all for now. We'll be sending out the preliminary calendars and itineraries next week sometime.

Cheers, mates, and enjoy the rest of the summer!

Chapter One

"...007 Soundstage, Pinewood Studios—And, we're off! Welcome to my ongoing tour blog, *Virtual Days*.

I've been with Blacklight a long time now, and I'll admit, I'm superstitious about touring. At the start, this one had an 'oh, DAMN!' smell about it. We began with a possible logistics nightmare: the stage we'd designed was too large to fit anywhere but the 007 stage at Pinewood. That meant cancelling us out of Shepperton, and praying we'd be able to get in at Pinewood at ridiculously short notice. It could have been a complete cock-up, but it was averted by the nice people at Pinewood. Not sure who managed it, but someone pulled a large pink bunny out of a hat (or possibly out of somewhere else, but we won't get into that) and not only got us in, but got us in two days ahead of schedule, and bob's your uncle, off we go. It probably didn't hurt that both studios are owned by the same parent company.

As promised, I'll be popping round and posting up here, to give Blacklight fans a look at just what goes on. Fair warning, though, I may be AWOL for days at a time, so check back here—if I haven't updated, it means I'm up to my eyebrows in tech issues and build spec. Don't worry, I haven't deserted you.

The next two weeks are going to be about as difficult and concentrated as it gets. Most people think a big rock tour is all about sex and booze and glamour and mad partying, but the sad truth is, it's about work, work and more work, at least for the crew. My day began with a preproduction meeting at Pinewood at half five this morning, going over the weight capacity specs for the two side stages. More on that as we go along.

(If I'm being honest, I should probably admit that the likelihood of at least some mad partying is high. After all, Pinewood's got a wardrobe department, and the fancy dress rave-up is traditional. Last time we threw a studio party to kick off a tour, back at Shepperton in 2005, we invited half the studio staff, including their wardrobe lady. The highlight was getting a Nob Who Must Not Be Named into a Victorian corset...)"

"John? Did you say something?"

"Just reading Nial Laybourne's tour blog." I looked up from the laptop screen. Bree'd been doing a crossword puzzle or something in the paper; last I'd looked, she'd been glaring at a word she couldn't get, and I'd have bet on her being completely absorbed. I hadn't realised she was paying attention. Outside, the weather was doing what London weather likes doing best this time of year, which is pissing down icy cold rain. The windows in the house we'd rented for the trip were rattling with wind and water, and the way the temperature looked like going, we might be in for a hard freeze. "He's being funny, remembering the kick-off party at Shepperton, from the 2005 tour."

"Funny? How?" She set the paper down. "Because I wouldn't mind some funny. I'm so damned bored with being stuck indoors, you can't imagine, John. The weather service said it might stay this cold and crappy all the way through Christmas. This weather is like something out of a 1930's mystery novel, all about England never seeing sun."

"Well," I pointed out, "it *is* winter, Bree."

She shot me a look. "And the crossword is putting me to sleep. I know most of the answers, but I'm never sure how to spell them in British instead of American, and it makes me feel stupid. And UK phrases are just, well, weird. What in hell is a seven letter word for 'irritated', starting with a B, used with 'off'? Because it isn't 'browned.' Take my mind off cabin fever and not speaking British. How is Nial being funny?"

"It's this bit: *Last time we threw a studio party to kick off a tour, back at Shepperton in 2005, we invited half the studio staff, including their wardrobe lady. The highlight was getting a Nob Who Must Not Be Named into a Victorian corset.*" I grinned at her. "He's not about to go into detail—there'd be hell to pay—but the Nob in the pretty corset? It was Mac."

"What!" Her mouth dropped open. "You're kidding, right? They talked Malcolm Sharpe into a corset? A woman's corset?"

"A Victorian woman's corset. Satin or something, that shiny patterned stuff—what's it called, brocade. Hot pink, mostly." I was remembering, myself. "And he wasn't talked into it, he was muscled into it, by Luke and Domitra. He wasn't given a choice. I think there are pictures, somewhere. It was a killer party."

Bree burst out laughing. I was grinning myself, partly at the memory, but also at how relaxed Bree seemed. I mean, yeah, she was fed up being stuck inside for three straight days, and yeah, so, London isn't her favourite city, any more than New York is. What with missing our cats, hating the weather, and just coming off ten days of being stuck out in the wilds of Kent with nothing to do while the band spent ten hours a day in the studio finalising the set list for the tour, she'd been having her moments of being cranky and snappish.

But remembering our last visit here, that really brought the change in her into focus for me, you know? We'd come here on honeymoon not very long ago, and that trip had got sticky, to say the least.

See, when Bree's tense, it goes straight to her shoulders; she does the turtle thing, shoulders going up, head going down. She'd spent half our honeymoon with her shoulders hunched up hard and tight, not to mention the two bloody endless days we'd spent holding our breath, waiting to find out whether or not she'd been infected with HIV by a dirty syringe hidden in a pile of towels. And you'd think that was enough, but after that, we'd headed for the South of France, and things had happened too fast for her to really let up, and she'd got shot at, as well. Not exactly the sort of honeymoon you take pictures of and paste into scrapbooks.

This time, even though she was claustrophobic and chilly and whatever else, her shoulders were nice and loose, and they'd been that way since we'd got here. It probably helped that the rental Blacklight Corporate had got for us—a six-room mews house near Mac's place off Sloane Square—was decently spacious. I'd insisted on that. Also, the fact that I'd taken advantage of the rotten weather by taking every opportunity to pin her to the bed and get her eyes to roll back in her head, well, that couldn't have hurt, either. Nothing like massive amounts of sex if you fancy staying mellow, you know?

Bottom line was, she was relaxed. And it had taken me twenty-five years to get her to relax, because I hadn't had the wits or the willingness to see she was tense all that time.

Something else that was new this trip—she'd got used to going out and exploring the city on her own, or with Tony Mancuso's wife, Katia. Blacklight's new CD, a double disc we'd called *Book of Days*, was due out in a few weeks, and the entire Blacklight machine, band and roadies and crew and the whole lot of us, were gearing up to tour. I wasn't thrilled by the timing—no one wants to tour Scandinavia and Russia in February, unless they're off their nut—but this is how it works. This is my job. I'm a guitar player, my gig is playing guitar with Blacklight, and my gig meant that I was busy.

But, as a brilliant songwriter called Richard Thompson puts it, one door opens, another shuts behind. Since Tony was playing with Blacklight for the tour, taking the time away from his own band, the Bombardiers, to be here, he was busy as well, and he'd brought Katia with him. And that was a stroke of fantastic good luck all the way round, because Katia is Bree's best friend, and Katia had never been here before.

So my wife, who's got a nurturing streak so wide you could put traffic wardens and zebra crossings on it, had taken on the job of showing Katia the parts of London Bree herself had got familiar with during our honeymoon. And the situation with Katia had helped Bree get completely over her lingering squeamishness about blowing my money on anything that took her fancy.

Tony's not poor, but he isn't rolling in dosh, either. The Bombardiers aren't Blacklight, not in any sense, fame, money or anything else, except for talent and longevity. But touring with Blacklight meant that Tony was entitled to an equal share of a guaranteed minimum, and the number Ian had quoted, back when we'd made Tony the offer, was up near three million dollars.

I don't handle the money stuff in our house. I've been a member of Blacklight so long that I barely notice the finances, and anyway Bree does all that, at least the parts of it that Blacklight Corporate's accounting department doesn't cope with for me.

But Tony noticed it, all right, and Katia, yeah, well. The first meeting with Maureen Bennett, we'd gone over the way we handle tour finances, and Katia had just sat there with her mouth open and her eyes popping. Whatever she'd been expecting, it

9

apparently hadn't been two credit cards, one with a ceiling in the mid-five figures, the other with no ceiling at all. And those were above and beyond the per diem Tony was entitled to.

Katia does all of Tony's finances, the same way Bree does mine. She'd said something about their monthly mortgage payments being less than the per diem Blacklight was handing out, but that was ridiculous—she had to be exaggerating. Of course, they'd bought their house years ago, so maybe the mortgage payments weren't all that high, you know?

Thing is, when it comes to money, the per diem's like anything else about Blacklight tour finances: the money is there, and it's guaranteed. Once Tony and Katia managed to wrap their heads around that, it wasn't hard to convince Katia to go buy something to wear at the kick-off press stuff we'd scheduled. She, and Bree as well, were going to need plenty of new gear, because the CD kick-off wasn't the only thing coming up. We were a few days away from Christmas, about to move to a hotel on the Pinewood grounds, in the wilds of Buckinghamshire. Since the band had taken the entire hotel for our use, there was definitely going to be a do or three happening. Not only that, I'd heard mutterings about a major party down in Kent, at Luke Hedley's farm at Draycote for New Years Eve. Both Bree and Katia would probably empty Harrods and Harvey Nichols, buying up party gear.

"I think I need new boots, if this weather is going to keep up." Bree had got up. "I also think I need more caffeine first. Another one for you?"

"Ta, love." I passed her my cup, and splashed a few drops of coffee onto the table. *Shit.* My hand was shaking, a hard little tremor.

"John?" Of course she'd seen it. Bree doesn't miss anything, not when it comes to my health. I've got multiple sclerosis, and a heart condition, MVP with arrhythmia, as well. She's spent her entire adult life looking after me, making my life possible, and she's a doctor's daughter, as well. "Are you okay? Do you need anything?"

"I'm fine, Bree." It was true. The MS had been laying back for a few weeks, hardly giving me any trouble at all. I'd had a full MRI before we'd left San Francisco, the usual miserable annual suckfest of being injected with dye and slid into a metal tube and screamed at by a snotty little brat of a tech, and the results had shown no real changes from the previous year's suckfest. "Just a bit of shake, is all. I'd lay odds it's the cold weather's doing it. Seriously, love, I promise I'd tell you otherwise. I feel fine."

"...I've had some questions, through the Ask The Band link, about what the band does during the staging builds and production ramp-ups. Mostly, they rehearse. Luke Hedley has one of the best-equipped mobile studios in the UK, down at his farm in Kent, and it's set up especially for Blacklight. So the band and their families congregate down there, and the boys spend dawn until dusk working out the set lists, and getting the kinks out of the songs they're going to do live. This time has been quite work-intensive, what with the new CD being a double, and having Tony Mancuso joining us for this tour, on keyboards. One thing they don't do is hang about at the soundstage during the build. They'd be very much in our way...."

I closed out of the Blacklight website, and turned off the laptop. I was still fumbling with it; the whole computer thing, that's all new to me. I'd come to it late, but it's handy for keeping up with the world outside. As a bloke who loves his morning news, I've got to admit that I like having different sources right there, without having to stack up and recycle actual newspapers. I'm not particularly interested in the tech side of it—Bree's the geek or nerd or techie or whatever in the family, not me. Thing is, I don't like looking like an amateur, so I was making it my business to get as comfortable with it as I could, as fast as I could. "You off shopping, then? And by the way, that word you wanted? Try 'brassed'."

11

"What word I—oh, you mean the crossword? Seven letters, starts with B, et cetera? Brassed off?"

She reached for her pen. Funny thing about Bree, something else I'd only come to notice recently: she does her crosswords and acrostics and whatnot in pen, not pencil. She says she's been doing it that way since I met her as a teenager, and for some reason, my brain hadn't bothered to register that, much less retain it. Most people use pencils with rubber erasers at the tip, in case of mistakes. Bree, though? She just doesn't fill in a word unless she's certain she's got it right.

"Yep, that's it." She set the pen down, and stretched. "Brassed off. Great phrase. Here, let me get those dishes. And yes, I'm heading out in a few minutes, unless you want me underfoot all day, being a bitch over the weather—I'm supposed to meet Katia at the Covent Garden market. She wants to get Tony a silver bracelet for Christmas, a good-luck thing for the tour. Oh, wait, I forgot, you've got that band meeting at the offices. They're going to give you lunch, right? Are you home in time for dinner? Should I hit the food hall at Harrods and get something, maybe some chops or fish? Or I can make some pasta…"

Nice peaceful morning, just before the holidays. I rinsed dishes at the sink, she loaded them into the dishwasher, and all the time, we were making the sort of small talk that the people who read Nial Laybourne's tour blog wouldn't have believed for a minute: what a bummer it was that Bree's mum wouldn't be able to get the time off from her medical practice to fly out for Christmas. Natter about the fact that Luke Hedley, Blacklight's other guitarist, seemed to have finally found himself a honey to play with, after nearly twenty years of being a widower, and that he was being secretive about it. Whether or not Luke's daughter, Solange, was ever going to stop arsing about and choose from the list of colleges and universities around the world who'd queued up to get her as a student.

All good, basic stuff, what anyone might talk about after breakfast, doing the washing up. Just a placid middle-aged couple, if you ignored the fact that the next few months were going to involve private jets, making five-star hotels our home base, playing to screaming delirious fans in Europe and America.

There was one thing we weren't discussing, though. It was sitting right there, just waiting for one of us to bring it up: we hadn't talked about the one piece of London real estate I owned. That was the house I'd bought when I was still married to my first wife, Cilla, the house I'd handed over to her to live in when I left her for Bree, and for America, when Cilla had chosen heroin over me: 18, Howard Crescent, London, NW1.

Nice part of town, nice neighbours, nice house, and really bad memories. It was definitely the white elephant in our marital living room, right now.

First time Bree'd seen the place, it was a few months after Cilla'd died. We'd walked in the front door and nearly had heart failure, both of us. The house—where Cilla'd lived on her own for twenty-five years—had been like some twisted sick shrine to the days when she and I had been a couple: Pictures glued to the walls, my gold records dangling off nails, even my clothes from thirty years earlier. It was as if Cilla had tried to make me a ghost she could summon, to hang on to me somehow, hang on to our time together, all those years ago.

I'd decided the best way to deal with it was to offer the house to Bree, so she could make it hers. Sensible, yeah? I still think the core idea was quite sound, but the problem was, I'd been really clumsy about the timing, and Bree flipped her shit over it, and everything had got completely ballsed up.

There's nothing Bree isn't willing to do for me if she thinks it'll make me happy. Hell, the girl's spent basically half her time since she was sixteen trying to sort out what makes my life easier, and the other half trying to make it happen. But by the time she'd been inside the front door for half an hour, 18, Howard Crescent was already looking like too much for her to deal with.

Then she'd managed to puncture her hand on some leftover works of Cilla's, hidden behind some towels for God only knew how long, and there was that whole HIV scare I mentioned. That pretty much put a tin cupola on it. So, yeah, I wasn't surprised that she'd taken a scunner to the place.

We'd gone back at the end of the trip, and buried Cilla's wedding ring under a tree in the back garden—that was something we'd planned on, and hell, Bree had been the one to suggest it in the first place. A lot had happened between visits, and Bree seemed to have come to some sort of mental truce with the house. As for me, I was quite happy to see the back of it, and buy us another house, or a condo or a tepee or a luxury tomato crate in Hyde Park, if that was what Bree wanted. But for some reason, neither of us seemed ready to bring it up, I wasn't sure why.

Bree headed out to meet Katia for what she kept calling "a few hours of serious power-shopping." I kissed her goodbye at the door; she was bundled up to the teeth in the coat I'd given her as the groom's gift to the bride, last time we'd been here. The damned thing was the same colour green as her eyes, was made of pure cashmere, and had cost enough to set off every guilt trigger she had left over from the Cilla years, about letting me blow my money on her.

We'd nearly had a row over me buying it for her, right in front of a gaggle of Harvey Nichols shopgirls, but the net result had been good all the way round. She'd got a coat she loved. The not-quite-row forced me to tell her why I thought it was time she lost the triggers, and let me convince her that I did understand why she had them in the first place. She decided it was okay for me to give her things. I got to finally even up for the fact that the bride's gift to the groom at our wedding had been a custom guitar; the groom, who'd eloped the first time he'd got married and knew sod-all about wedding traditions, had got the bride nothing at all. Plus, at the end of the day, I'd got some brilliant sex out of the deal, the sort that blows the top of your head straight off. Like I said, all good, you know?

David Walters, who does the Euro operations for the band, sent a car round to get me about an hour after Bree'd left. That's one of those perqs I take for granted, not having to ring round for a car, or wait for a taxi; I don't drive, and even if I did, I wouldn't, not in London. David may not be Carla Fanucci—Ian had once brought down the house by wondering out loud how she'd react to kryptonite—but he's damned good, and he never forgets the small stuff.

Blacklight Corporate has its headquarters in a nice little terraced house, right at the western edge of the Kings Road, where Chelsea meets Fulham. We actually outgrew the place a long time ago; these days, the bulk of the band's business is handled from two floors of a building at the other end of town, right off Tottenham Court Road, near the Post Office Tower.

But we all love the old offices, and besides, our brilliant manager, Chris Fallow, had paid pennies for it, and now the place was worth a bloody fortune. Chris died back in 2006—he'd been ill a long time. Chris being as canny about money as he'd been, I don't know whether he'd have been chuffed or cross as hell to know that we'd paid the Royal Borough of Kensington and Chelsea a metric fuckload of dosh to officially name the office Fallow House, but we'd done it, and it had made his widow, Meg, mist up. The staff at Fallow House handle some of the core stuff, including the band's charities.

Full-on band meetings and press stuff are also handled out of Fallow House, and today, I was damned glad about it. One thing I love about the old place is the conference room. It used to be the combination front room and dining room, but now it's got a conference table that holds two dozen or so people running the length of it.

What's really cool is that the far end has its original fireplace, a sodding huge marble thing, with angels and whatnot carved into it. You're not allowed to burn real fires in London anymore—my mum used to talk about the London fogs, which were really killer smog from all the coal fires people burned in the winter—so we had it wired up as a nice realistic gas fire, complete with flickery fake flame, oversized fake fire logs, and very real heat coming off it. On a day like this, that fireplace was a godsend.

Bree'd been right about them feeding us. There was a nice spread laid out on the conference table, designer sandwiches and soups in chafing dishes and whatnot, waiting for the band and the design crew. I got there right round the same time Cal Wilson's car dropped him off out front, so we went in together.

It was a good meeting. Mostly, these pre-release dos are a drag, people going on about cover art and promo copies and all that, a lot of stuff I have no stake in and no say on. That kind of thing comes with the gig, same category as soundchecks, back in the old days before Ronan Greene took us digital; there's no avoiding it. Generally, I use the time to catch up on kip.

One thing that happened was that I finally got a look at Luke's mystery girlfriend. Luke's wife, Viv, died from ovarian cancer when Solange was still in nappies, and except for the occasional one-nighter on the road, Luke seemed to have basically shut it down. The occasional bit of sex, to keep him healthy and sane, that was one thing. But that was all.

Bree had once surprised the hell out of me by saying that when Luke had lost Viv, he'd taken out his heart and put it somewhere, and then forgot where he'd left it. That had an odd effect on me, her saying that, because she'd nailed it. He liked women, he had women friends, he'd give a hottie a good long look and occasionally take one back to the hotel for the night after a gig, but I

16

never once saw him as being in any danger of investing his heart.

But recently he'd changed, and once I sussed out why, I was prepared to cheer him on. Thing is, he'd been really secretive about her; all anyone knew was that her name was Karen, that we'd possibly met her, and that her daughter had been at school with Solange. Even Mac, Luke's closest friend, didn't know much.

That last bit of info, about this mysterious bird having a grown-up kid, had got a sigh of relief out of Bree, once I'd passed it along. She said it made Mysterious Karen at least an adult, that it meant Luke hadn't gone arse over teapot for a girl thirty years his junior, the way some blokes tend to do when they get into middle age. I thought about teasing Bree for that one—after all, I fell in love with her when she was still in her teens and I was in my late twenties—but of course I didn't. No need to stir those particular coals.

I sat down in the window seat, my back to the street. My legs had gone trembly, not bad, just a small shake, typical of the MS. I don't do fake macho, because toughing it out does sod all except make it worse. So I headed for the window seat with a plate of food, with our bassist, Cal Wilson, right behind me. I don't need to explain to my mates; they know about the disease, about the tricks and shortcuts I use to keep it from nailing me.

We'd been talking about the new stage design for the tour, but I'd barely got settled when Cal suddenly stopped, and stared out the window over my head.

"Blimey!" There was real interest in his face. "Here's Luke, and I think he's got his bird with him."

I swung round in a hurry. They were both out of the car, standing on the street. The rain had tapered off into a hard cold drip, and Luke was holding a brolly over both of them. She was shorter than he was, but that's not hard, Luke being a bit over six feet. He bent over and kissed her, and out of nowhere, I suddenly felt guilty, sort of perverted, you know? I'm not much for voyeurism. As I turned to look away, I caught a swing of what looked like auburn hair, fading the way Bree's was beginning to fade.

Then she was back in the car, pulling off into traffic on the Fulham Road, and the rain started up again. The front doorbell rang, the opening buzzer sounded from upstairs, and Luke came in, looking about as happy and relaxed as I'd seen him since before Viv got sick.

It was a productive meeting, nothing major except for the news that the tour dates Ian had told us about had got switched round, and we'd be starting off the Euro leg of the tour in Paris. That made me happy, because what had been done bumped the really cold parts of the tour by a few days, and that gave me at least a better shot at having it be a degree or two warmer. The MS doesn't care much for icy weather.

"That's all for now." Ian was wrapping it up for the day, and various cars were queuing up out front. "One more thing—Luke's got something to tell us, and then we're done for the day. I'll send an email covering everything, itineraries, hotels, rehearsal times at Pinewood once the tech is set up and production has the stages ready. Luke? Over to you, mate."

Everyone's head swivelled. I think we were all expecting some big announcement—*bloody hell, I'm getting married!* The only one of us who wasn't looking expectant was Mac, but Mac probably knew that wasn't it.

"Just wanted to invite everyone here down to Draycote for New Years Eve." Luke's a skinny bloke, very lanky, but also very fit—he doesn't eat crap food and he takes care of himself. He got into the habit of doing that because he had to, after Viv died; he'd been left with a frightened toddler on his hands. Solange was barely two years old, she'd been done out of her mum and she was scared shitless she'd lose her dad as well. Luke hadn't been about to let that happen. He's a really good parent, even when it couldn't have been easy. Solange always came first.

But there was something new about him, more than just the normal feeling of health; he seemed a lot more mellow and at ease with himself than I could remember him being. "I'm having a party, friends and family. Be warned, it'll be dry except for champagne, so if you need a booze-up, that's not on. But nosh and music and ringing in the new year. Anyone not able to make it, let me know, all right?"

On the way out, climbing into the hire car, I got another look at Mysterious Karen, a much better look this time. She was Bree's age, or maybe a bit older. I'd been right about her being a redhead, another dark auburn, very much like my wife's hair. She looked very pleasant, a bit shy, as if she didn't really feel comfortable being seen by Luke's mates just yet. I found myself wondering if that was what this New Years Eve party was in aid of: introducing her to his world, letting her know she'd be welcomed, letting her know she didn't need to stay invisible.

Somehow, I couldn't shake the feeling I'd seen her before.

The party at Luke's place ended up being a whole lot more than just your basic New Years Eve rave-up. Turned out there were all sorts of things going on backstage, as well.

We went down to Kent in a hired limo. Christmas had been a nice quiet day, a little bit of everything we both enjoy: Bree cooking a brilliant breakfast, a nice long snog in front of the telly with the sound turned all the way down, a walk round the north side of Hyde Park, past Marble Arch and down Park Lane, stopping in for a high tea at the Dorchester. It was a wet day, but not that cold, really; Bree was wearing her new boots, high heels and all. We held hands like a couple of teenagers.

We'd gone about halfway, and had just reached Speakers Corner, when Bree floored me. She suddenly reached out and did just what she'd done at the Cow Palace near San Francisco, the

19

first time we'd met, nearly thirty years earlier: she put her hands on my face and pulled us together, a long warm kiss, tongue tip to tongue tip.

"Wow." I came up for air, and found my arms had gone round her. Her eyes were as bright a green as they'd ever been, a sure sign she was going to pounce on me the minute we got back to our rented digs. She tasted just the same as she had all those years ago, of strawberries. "What was all that about, then? Was that a Christmas prezzie?"

"I just wanted to, that's all. Can I help it if you make me feel sixteen again?" She was smiling, but her eyes had gone cloudy, tears down there somewhere. "Just—looking back, that's all. Being grateful we're here. We so easily could have been elsewhere, or dead, or something."

"You've got that right, lady." She did, too. Addiction, heroin, booze. I could have stayed with Cilla, gone down that road, died years ago, become the stereotypical rocker statistic, had mediocre musicians I'd met maybe once writing sappy tribute songs about what an influence I'd been on them, probably lyrics about me having a gig in Heaven with Jimi and Janis, all that bullshit. "But we're here, you know? You and me. Light's still on, right?"

"Always on." Her eyes were wet. "Always burning. Let's get some hot scones and clotted cream, okay? Katia said Tony took her to the Dorchester and she was in hog heaven over it."

So Christmas was nice and peaceful, a very good day and an even better night. Bree hit the after-Christmas sales looking for new gear, and came back in a taxi. She came in to get me— turned out there was so much to carry, she needed a roadie. It looked like she'd officially got over that whole 'mustn't spend John's money on myself' rubbish trip she'd been on so long.

Luke's party was supposed to begin right round seven, so we'd packed overnight bags, and headed out mid-afternoon. Bree knows how to dress for display—interesting, that is, because she'd spent so many years perfecting how to be invisible around my mates, the bad years when I'd stayed married to Cilla out of inertia and being a lazy sod. But these days, when she dresses for a show, or a party, or a press do, anything to do with my job, she's dressing to be the woman on the rocker's arm, and that means flash gear, all the way.

So her dress for Luke's do was a surprise. She came out of the bathroom where she'd gone to get dressed and do up her hair and her makeup, and I looked up from packing.

"John?" She turned slowly, giving me a full rotation. "What do you think?"

I opened my mouth, and closed it again. Bree doesn't do that whole stereotypical thing. You know the old jokes, yeah? Woman asks her bloke if something makes her look fat, he gives her the truth, she either cripples him or bursts into tears. Because, see, according to the old joke and all the sitcoms on the telly, women want to be reassured, or lied to. Bree doesn't. If the girl asks my opinion, she wants to know.

"John?"

"Yeah. Hang on, I'm just sorting out what I think."

The dress was gorgeous—no problem there. She's five foot ten and your basic dark redhead, and she likes dresses in what she calls jewel tones: ruby and emerald and sapphire. Green's her big thing, usually, because her eyes are green, and so's the emerald in the engagement ring I'd given her.

This was—I don't know, a jewel tone, but not quite. It was a bit darker than usual, the colour of a Christmas tree, not a precious stone. The fabric was stiffer than her usual choices, heavier, not as much movement, somehow. The dress had buttons— Bree's button-mad, the more the merrier, and always has been— but there seemed to be fewer of them than I'd have expected. The neck and back were both higher up than usual; she's curvy, Bree is, and likes to show that off.

21

"Don't you like it?" *Shit.* I'd been silent a fraction too long, and now she was nervous. Not what I was going for, damn it. "Should I change it? Does it not work?"

"No, it does. Here, hold still, let me have a proper look."

She stayed where she was, and I did the walking. Her hair was up, tucked into a shiny copper thing, a sort of mini-hood; snoods, I think they're called. The dress was long, but I caught a glimpse of black heels. New Jimmy Choos, or maybe a new pair of Christian Louboutins; she'd been cooing over those recently. My wife's got a jones for shoes, a whole closet at home full of them, the higher the heels, the better...

"John?"

"Got it." I'd figured it out. "Took me a moment—sorry, love. Yeah, the dress works great. It's more toned down than you usually do, though. The whole look's toned down. Formal or muted, or something. *Grande dame.* Were you trying for that?"

"More adult, you mean?" She let her breath out. "Yes. Everything I tried on that I'd usually wear to a party—I don't know how to explain it, John. It just suddenly looked a bit pathetic on me. Too young, or something. I think I'll let Solange do the Hot Young Thing. After all, when you come down to it, I'm not the Hot Young Thing anymore, I'm in my forties. And anyway, it's Solange's party, right?"

So we'd headed off to Kent in the limo sent by Blacklight Corporate. Bree had a split of champagne in a silver cooler, I had a cold bottle of mineral water, we shared some chocolates and off-season raspberries. Halfway down, I decided that being too adult for too long was a stone drag and a bore; I got a hand up under her skirt and spent the rest of the ride down being a randy teenaged boy in the back seat of the car, snogging with the hottest woman on earth. Judging from the glaze in her eyes when we pulled through the gates at Draycote, and how unsteady she was on those high heels, I'd hit all the right buttons. If Bree has a limit to how much of that she can take, I haven't found it and I hope I never do. The driver kept his eyes on the road the whole time and anyway, I drew the privacy curtains.

We weren't the first there; when the limo pulled up in front of the main house, there were quite a few other cars, lined up and waiting to be parked round back, out of the way. Luke had hired some of the locals to valet, but of course the limo didn't need it, because the bloke wasn't waiting. Our driver held the door for me, waited until I'd helped Bree out, took the tip I slipped him, got back behind the wheel, and glided off into the night. No idea where the bloke and his posh car were spending the night, and didn't care. He'd be back tomorrow to pick us up.

"JP! Oh, man, I'm glad you guys made it down. Bree, you look wonderful. That's a killer dress." Luke met us at the front door, and he wasn't alone. At his side was the pretty redhead I'd seen outside Fallow House. Now that I got a closer look at her, she was even more familiar than I'd thought.

"Bree, JP, let me introduce someone." Luke was unbelievably relaxed. I felt a pang, a tug of history at the heartstrings; the last time I'd seen him this way, he and Viv had been newlyweds, so deep in love they barely saw anything that wasn't each other. "This is Karen McElroy. JP, I think you may have met Karen before, at Chris Fallow's funeral. She's the lead designer for the band's website. Karen, this is JP Kinkaid and his wife, Bree." He smiled suddenly, easy, happy. "Redheads, unite!"

"Right." I shook hands with her. Now he mentioned it, I did have a vague memory of someone who might have been her at the funeral. But there was something else pinging me, and I couldn't sort out what it was. Whatever it was that was familiar about her, it wasn't that. "Great to meet you. Sorry—I just can't shake the feeling we've met elsewhere. My God, how rude does that sound? Problem is, my memory is crap, so if I've put my foot in it…"

"It's a pleasure." She smiled back at me, and at Bree. She had a wonderful voice, as good as a massage. Nice clear hazel eyes, and damn it, they were familiar, as well. Where in hell had I come across her, and why was it making me edgy? "And you aren't being rude. I'd remember if we'd been introduced, and I don't, so we haven't, and how's that for rude? I'd never come to a show before, not backstage, anyway, even though Solange always assured me I could come to any show I wanted."

"Solange?" Something had suddenly made my nerve endings tighten up, I wasn't sure why.

"Well, yes—that's how Blacklight came to ask me to work on the website design. My daughter was at school with Solange. They've been good friends for years." She laughed suddenly, a happy noise, genuine. This was a nice woman, a woman who was enjoying herself hugely and what was more, I'd have bet money on her being honestly in love with Luke. Right that moment, with the penny dropping good and hard, she was a lot happier than I was. "I'll admit, I've always been more of a jazz lover than rock. I leave all the backstage networking stuff to Suzanne. She's a huge Blacklight fan."

Oh, bloody hell.

I had it now, why she looked so damned familiar. I'd never met Karen McElroy before, she had that bit right. But I'd met her daughter, back at the end of the Euro leg of our 2005 tour. She'd been backstage with Solange, dancing in the wings, making a hot and heavy pass at me, asking me straight up to take her home with me and do her. A pretty girl, with long legs and her mother's red hair—or Bree's red hair. She'd reminded me of the first time I'd met Bree, a world and a generation away.

Of course I'd turned her down. I don't cheat on Bree—I never have and never will. But this was looking to be a masterpiece of an example of Sod's Law. Of all the rotten coincidences, this one was going down in the record books.

24

"John?" Bree'd picked up on something. Of course she had; when it came to me, she'd been tuned in for most of her life. "Is something wrong?"

"No, nothing at all."

Maybe the girl would have forgotten about that incident. Maybe there wouldn't be any awkwardness; hell, I was only a couple of years younger than her mum's boyfriend, and surely she'd have got over that crush by now. Besides, I live on the other side of the planet from Draycote. It wasn't as if I was going to have to deal with her on a daily basis, or anything.

We'd moved indoors now, out of the cold. And here came Solange, blonde and slender, looking like her mother's clone at the same age, and she wasn't alone: right behind her was a girl, with pair of long legs, red hair in a chic little ponytail. The girl stopped a few feet back and stood there staring at me, not saying anything, letting Solange surge forward and hug Bree, taking our coats....

Her eyes were hazel, not green. Just like her mother's eyes, easy as hell to read.

Suzanne McElroy hadn't forgotten a damned thing. And unless I'd lost my mind, she hadn't changed her opinion that me taking her home and showing her what an aging rocker could do for her was just what the doctor ordered.

"...going to be such fun." Karen McElroy's charming voice brought me back to full attention. I jerked my head, and caught Bree's eye. Had she noticed?

Oh, hell yes, she'd noticed all right. Her face had gone mask-like, her smile was fixed in place. She was staring at Suzanne McElroy the way Cilla had once stared at her, backstage at the Cow Palace in San Francisco all those years ago the night I'd first met Bree, and Suzanne McElroy was staring at me as if I were lunch, or maybe the Holy Grail. As for me, I was doing my best not to meet anyone's eye, and wondering if it was possible to slip out a side door and walk back to London....

"We're going to be roomies, on the Euro leg." Solange hadn't noticed anything. She was happy and bubbly and probably a bit tipsy on champagne. Inside, the party was at full swing. "Just like at school. Isn't that fantastic?"

"Fantastic." Suzanne McElroy's voice, high and clear, came out as a deliberate drawl. She stepped forward. For a moment, she caught Bree's eye, and my heart went straight down like an express lift. I may be dim, but I know a challenge when I see one. "For the entire Euro leg. I can hardly wait."

Chapter Two

"007 Studio, Pinewood—welcome back to *Virtual Days*, boys and girls. *Book of Days* just hit the shops, and we're a day or two off from welcoming the band to the build here. I know you're probably all tired of me being such a tease about it, but the staging on this one is not going to be like anything you've seen before, not from Blacklight or from anyone else.

Let me just say, the entire Blacklight family is quite pleased about the reception the new disc is getting from the fans. *Book of Days* actually debuted in the UK charts at #4, which is the best start since *Jubilation City* came out, back in 1997. And it's at #26 with a bullet, over in the States, so good job, all you people who spent the extra pennies for a double disc!

Here's something else that's new: If you've been paying attention, or had a radio on anywhere in the First World for the past couple of weeks, you already know that the lead single from the double CD is 'Remember Me.' And you're all saying right, song, yeah, whatever, mate, what's new about that?

Well, this is the first song—words and lyrics alike—to be written entirely by JP Kinkaid. Up until now, everything Blacklight has done has had the lyrics written by Mac; JP's done some music composition before, and so have Cal and Stu, but until now, it's been mostly music by Luke Hedley, lyrics by Malcolm Sharpe, even though the entire band gets co-author credits on everything. Book of Days has songs with lyrics and music by JP Kinkaid, ditto Luke Hedley, and even one written by Tony Mancuso, the brilliant piano player for San Francisco-based band The Bombardiers.

I'm going to do my very best to get JP up here to guest blog for you all, about the circs under which he wrote 'Remember Me'—I was there, and trust me, the way that song came about is a story, all by itself. I can't make any promises, because JP is a very busy bloke these days and he's about to be even busier, but I'll do my best...."

After all these years of playing in Blacklight, all those albums, all those tours, the whole bloody grind of the music industry machinery, I ought to have got a whiff of something new and different about Book of Days a lot sooner than I did.

Truth is, I've never paid much attention to the charts and the sales figures, not since the first tour, when I was the new kid. I play, I record, I tour live with the band to promote whatever the thing is, but watching the numbers, that's not my thing. I leave that up to Bree at the home end, and Blacklight Corporate at the other.

We've got a brilliant crew running things. Chris Fallow was a superb judge of character and talent, and he almost never put a foot wrong, not when it came to the proper person for a job. He'd handpicked Blacklight's head accountant, Maureen Bennett, back in 1988, and she's been here ever since. Ian, of course, had basically saved our arses, all the time Chris was dying, and Chris had handpicked him as well.

So I don't pay much attention to things, because the best manager who ever drew breath made sure I don't have to. And that morning, reading Nial's blog, was actually the first I heard about the CD debuting at #4 on the UK charts, and #26 in the US.

We were at breakfast at the Notting Hill house, two days away from checking into the hotel out at Pinewood for a week's intensive rehearsals, getting used to the new stage. None of us had even seen it yet. I must have made a noise, because Bree, who'd been checking her email on her own laptop across the kitchen table, looked up.

"What's up?"

"We hit the UK charts in the four-spot." I was aware of a moment there, just how nice it was to say something without having to pick every word I said. "And climbing in the US charts. Best release numbers in eleven years."

Things had been iffy for a couple of days after Luke's party, to say the least. When Bree gets angry about something, or upset, she gets distant, you know? Remote. Not half an hour into the party, turning a corner and finding her in a huddle, talking furiously to Katia, I'd known I was in for it, in a major way, especially when Katia gave me one of those looks, the kind that basically translate into "unclean!" or "you rotten heartless bastard, how could you!"

Of course, this was all in aid of me not ever having mentioned the existence of the little redhead whose mum looked set to keep Luke warm for the next several years, at least. And really, that was beyond silly and into completely insane; I'd never mentioned Suzanne McElroy to Bree because, honestly, I'd basically forgotten the girl's existence as soon as I'd turned my back. She was a kid who'd made a pass at me. I'd been kind about it, since she really had been very young and a friend of Solange's besides. I'd told her I didn't cheat on my old lady, and I'd left. Nothing to tell.

But here was the reality, this kid coming back and now about

29

to be underfoot twenty-four/seven. And the kid wasn't a kid, she was an adult, and she'd looked at me in a way that might have been designed to hit every button Bree's got. It really hadn't helped that the first thing Suzanne had done after that challenge to Bree had been to offer me a hand, and a smile, and ask—in this intimate little voice, like we had some kind of history, or something—whether I remembered her.

So, yeah, Bree was furious. She'd gone distant and remote, and that hadn't given me any opening at all, to tell her that no, the kid was projecting or playing games or something, and the only reason I hadn't ever mentioned Suzanne McElroy was that there wasn't anything to mention.

I'd let her sulk a few days, mostly because—okay, right, Johnny, might as well be straight about it. I just don't fancy rows, you know? I don't let the world blow up around me to avoid them, the way I used to do, but I loathe fuss and noise and mess and I especially don't want to deal with it when the person I'm rowing with is Bree. So I stayed quiet, thinking *right, let the girl get over it, then we can talk.*

Yeah, well, not my brightest idea. She can hold a grudge for years, Bree can. Three days of it, while I got less and less comfortable, until I finally decided I'd had enough of it, and I caved, and told her just what had happened three years back.

And of course, there wasn't any row, after all. I told her what had happened, why I'd never mentioned it, and she got it, straight off. So those three uncomfortable days, they'd been no one's fault but my own.

"John –"

She stopped, closing her mouth hard. I'd been about to get up, offer a hand with clearing the table, but I stayed where I was. The table could wait; she had something on her mind, and I'd have to have been completely dim not to know what it was. Best to let her say it her own way, though.

30

She started again. "John, listen. About that girl…"

She stopped again. I lifted an eyebrow at her.

"Yeah, I figured this had to be about her. Bree, love, just dish, yeah? Are you wondering how to cope with her? Or are you wondering how I'm planning to cope with her?"

"Do you have a plan?" She looked hopeful, and she wasn't joking, either—she really was rattled by it, and I was damned if I could see why. "Because I can't see any way for me to deal, John. I mean, shit, what is there? Her position is pretty much bulletproof. I can't get security to toss the little groupie out the backstage door and onto her ass. Neither of us can take Luke aside and explain that his squeeze's brat has ambitions to get naked for his married bandmate. Hell, I can't even get her in an armlock and forcibly explain that the size of the guitar and the size of the organ are not the same -"

"Oi!"

"Not necessarily the same." She'd caught my mock outrage and responded, but she wasn't amused, not really. "I can't bitch-slap her into the next century. And anyway…"

There went her voice again. Ah. Here we were, whatever it was. Finally getting to whatever was making her feel so helpless. Bree doesn't do helpless, not as a usual thing. Valkyries don't, much.

"Anyway? Anyway what, love?"

"I don't want to bitch-slap her." She looked up at me, and I jumped; her eyes were full of tears. "Or, I mean, I do want to, but I shouldn't want to. Because this is my karma coming back, or something."

"What –" I blinked at her. "What in hell…?"

"Jesus, John, don't you get it? She's me. She's doing to me just what I did to Cilla. Who am I, to hate the little brat's guts? I've got no right to hate her guts. But I do. I'd like to deck her, sock her one, right in the jaw, knock her on her young pampered pretty little ass. God, I am such a fucking hypocrite."

31

"Hold it." Right. Maybe I'm getting more observant in my old age, or something, but this time, I'd actually sort of sniffed out what she was going to say, and I was ready for it. "Hang on. Put Saint Bree d'Arc back in her cubby half a mo, love, will you? Tell me if I've got this right: you're equating what you did when you first saw me with what Suzanne did and is still apparently doing. That it?"

"Of course it is."

"Well, yeah, right, except that you're nuts. Either that, or my memory's gone. Because the way I remember it, you said you couldn't help yourself, you kissed me, you apologised, and you disappeared. I was the one who rang you, remember? Not the other way round. Not quite the same thing as Suzanne's little game, which looks like throwing out a challenge to my wife, like a dog in heat. And I'll tell you what, I don't much fancy being cast to play the bone in that particular fight, so let's make sure it doesn't happen, all right?"

She was quiet, her teeth sunk into her lower lip. I reached out an index finger, bent at the knuckle, and chucked her under the chin with it. It's an old gesture, one I don't use very often, but it has a meaning for both of us: *stop being so silly.*

"Not the same," I told her, and got up. "Not even close. For one thing, you and I, we were a couple from that first look, even though it took me a while to suss that out. Want to help me clear up in here? Oh, and as for that girl? I'm planning on being polite and acting like an elderly uncle. I doubt that would work for you, but not to worry. Whatever you decide to do, I've got your back."

The first morning the band actually walked in the huge doors of the 007 soundstage at Pinewood, we all took a butcher's at what Nial and Ronan had come up with, and went slack-jawed. Right, well, I did, anyway. I was gobsmacked. The scope of the thing took my breath away.

It was the middle of January, and we'd been talking about the staging for this tour for months, dozens of emails and phone calls, concepts and fine details, what would work, what wouldn't work, how big was too big. So it wasn't as if I didn't know, as if we all didn't know, what the boys had put together.

But reading words on paper, or hearing someone going on about it over a telephone, that's not the same as walking into a soundstage that's nearly four hundred feet long, a hundred and sixty feet wide, and about five storeys tall, and seeing a pair of identical layouts for where you're going to be spending all your working hours for the next half a year at least.

"Bloody *hell*." Mac, leading the way in, stopped so suddenly I nearly walked straight up his back. "Sorry, Johnny. But that's— right. This is going to take some getting used to."

I got around him, trying to sort it out. The build was huge, just fucking enormous. They'd built two of them, mirror images, and looking at the damned things, I saw why we'd needed the biggest soundstage on the planet for this one.

The main stage, by itself, would have been impressive enough. I knew from the endless stream of production and tech emails how big it was, but seeing it on a computer screen as words, that doesn't really paint the picture accurately in the head, you know?

As if the size of the main stage wasn't enough, each one had two side stages, one at each end, one step down from the main stage, shaped like huge wooden peanuts. They jutted out even farther. Off behind the main stage was a ramp that reminded me of an airport runway. Nial gave me the actual stage dimensions later, everything except the ramp: the damned thing was nine feet high, sixty feet deep, and a hundred thirty long. Bloody hell, that's half a football stadium.

But once I got past the size, there was another couple of weird bits to deal with. For one thing, I'm used to stages being made of

33

wood; my whole working life, that's what they've been. And these didn't look to be wood, except the ramp.

For another thing, they were black. Every inch of the damned things were black. They looked like someone had dug out Darth Vader's swimming pools, turned them wrong side out, and given them to our production team, on loan...

"Oh, good, you're all here. Nial! Ready to get started?"

Ronan Greene always wears a kilt. It's not affectation; he says a kilt is the most comfortable thing he's ever worn, that it's perfect for climbing about up in the rigging, checking the bits and pieces. He has his kilts custom-made for him, complete with a shitload of pockets, all different sizes to hold his gear, and all with zippers. Chris Fallow had insisted on the zippers after a heavy wrench fell out of one of Ronan's pockets while he was checking something forty feet up and nearly brained Stu Corrigan during a soundcheck in Manchester, about three tours ago.

Nial had come up to meet us, and he and Ronan were talking, but most of it went straight past me. I was too busy blinking at the stage setup. I'd accepted the scale of the damned thing, I'd accepted the blackness of it, and I'd accepted that, whatever they'd rigged this up from that wasn't wood, they weren't about to endanger our lives by using something iffy for us to play on.

What I hadn't wrapped my head around was the emptiness. The stages were totally bare. There was nothing on them.

It shouldn't have been a surprise, much less a shock to the system. After all, I'd read Nial's most recent email, and he'd talked about it, about what he envisioned the opening sequence of the live show being. This setup was totally new to us; Ronan had gone completely over to line arrays and he was flying the entire thing. If you don't speak music tech, the plain English translation is 'no amps at all onstage, no monitors, nothing'. It was a bare stage, with all the gear that sends the music out into the audience hanging above, tuned so that there wasn't one corner of the building the system would miss.

And that was just the beginning of the weirdness. Not only were there no amps onstage, there were no instruments, either. While everything at the delivery end of the music was above us, everything we used to make the music was below us, under trap doors. So yeah, I'd seen it talked about and even asked a few questions myself, but seeing it, that was different.

And then there was the video aspect. Previous tours, we'd used damned near everything out there at the time: lasers, big screen, the whole lot. The bloke who handles all the video stuff for the band's live shows is called Paul Ivey. This time, while we were apparently still going with the big screen TV stuff hanging high, Paul had added something brand new. From the looks of it, we were going to have something that might have every major act touring after us copying the set-up. It was something Paul had christened the video veil, a sort of curtain thing we'd have hanging. But it wasn't a fabric curtain. The thing was made up of thousands of tiny light elements. Brave new world, in all sorts of ways. Everything about this CD and tour was new.

We'd had the conference call about the video stuff, the entire design team, management, the band. Paul had described the concept by saying it was like the netting they put up around hockey ice, to keep the ball or puck or whatever from flying out into the crowd and braining someone; for the most part, the net's invisible. With this new tech product, they could use it as a video screen. Of course, since I know fuck-all about hockey and care less, I hadn't got a clue what he'd been on about, but the rest of the band seemed quite happy about it, and I went along. Looking up at the thing now, I got it, all right.

Ronan and Nial led us up to the nearer of the two stages, back around to the ramp, up and onstage. Right; this really was a whole new world, top to bottom. Maybe it was because there was nothing on it—no guitars, no piano, no mics, no drum kits, nothing at all—but, whatever the reason, the oval felt even bigger standing on it than it did from below.

"Bloody hell, what's this thing made of?" Mac bounced a few times, and I was doing the same. I'd been right, this wasn't wood. "It feels like foam, or something."

Nial explained. I'd been right to think that the framework for the stage wasn't something they'd just bodge up and trust; the surface was really a kind of grid, made mostly of aluminium, with bits of carbon fibre and titanium where that was needed for weight savings, and strength. What the build team had done was, they'd used open-cell foam, and painted the entire thing matte black. The foam was almost completely transparent acoustically, and fantastic as a way to avoid the fatigue that we always seemed to get from a carpeted wooden stage.

"So what's the story, Ronan?" Mac had walked to centre stage, and was looking around. His voice was echoing and curling all over the place. The acoustics in here were bizarre, which wasn't surprising—the place was a barn. "How does this work? I know we talked about it, but seeing it, that's different."

"Well, we start out bare." Nial had come up. "From the time the audience enters the arena right up until the performance starts, all the audience sees is a completely empty stage. Then Mac—we'll have you stageside on the ramp, ready and waiting for your cue—just walks out to centre stage with the houselights still up full."

"Right. Let's run through it." Mac was already into it, seeing the theatre potential in it. He's a brilliant frontman, is Mac, and this is one reason why: he sees it all as theatre. You can't make a frontman. They're born, not made. "So I've strolled up the ramp and out onstage. The houselights are up. The audience has probably sussed out that it's me, and they're buzzing and hooting and all that, not to mention wondering what in hell is going on. What happens next?"

36

"You greet the audience." Ronan waved a hand, one of those gestures you always see the Queen doing. I had a mad moment of thinking he was taking the piss, but you never can tell when he's having you on, and when he's serious. He hasn't got a lot of humour, not while he's working. "Meanwhile, Luke starts playing an old acoustic blues number offstage—you've got something in the set list from your old days as Blackpool Southern, right? Your last email, you said something about a twelve-bar from the first album."

"Right. 'Home Cookin' Blues,' it's called. Covered it on the first Blacklight album, too." Luke hummed a snatch of melody. "Good song for a long vamp. JP, you know it, right?"

"Yeah, I think so. If not, I'll get it down—just a bit of work." Spanning forty years, I thought. Then and now and everything in between. It was suddenly there, you know? Right there, obvious and just so damned cool. *Book of Days* was about us as grownups, adults, still alive and not addicted to anything except making music. This one, we were covering it all. "No worries. So Luke's offstage, acoustic jamming. And…?"

"And he walks onstage via the main ramp. Mac, you join him on harp as the houselights go down, leaving the pair of you in isolated spot lighting."

"Cool." Cal had been wandering the stage, looking at the floor, at the flies, back at us. "You lot planning on a rhythm section in there somewhere?"

Ronan didn't even bother answering that. Like I said, he doesn't have much humour or patience with cheekiness either, especially when he's being full-on tech genius. "From full dark, a spotlight picks up Cal—it tracks him as he walks on from the main entrance to his spot onstage. So we've got three spots in the dark house, Mac's wailing away on harp, Luke's on acoustic guitar. Third spot, Cal bends over and knocks on the stage floor."

"What?" Tony was blinking. "Knocks on the *floor*?"

"On the floor. You can't tell now, because the lights are up, but there are floor lights embedded in the foam—they'll show you the way in the dark, before the full stage lighting goes on. So, Cal walks over and knock on the floor, a trap opens, and his bass—on its stand, of course—rises from the underworld. The instruments, all the props, that stuff isn't on foam, obviously. All the traps are solid wood platforms, to support the weight."

"Bloody hell." Cal's a very unemotional bloke—he leaves the temperament to Stu Corrigan, who's got enough temperament for the lot of us going on—but he sounded enthused. "So what goes on after that?"

"You strap up and join the jam. Of course, all you lot are preset for wireless." Ronan was snapping his fingers, something he does when he's concentrating. "By the way, everything you're doing is clearly visible to the entire audience. There's no backline onstage. They can all see."

"Glad to hear we've got bass." Stu was grinning, and bouncing on the balls of his feet. He's a little bloke, Black Irish and with a lot of energy. He was getting into it. "What's on next, then? Drums, or JP, or Tony?"

"Drums." Nial nodded at him. "Stu, you walk out, go to a premarked spot, and knocks on the floor. Step back beyond the ring of floor lighting, a couple of larger traps open, and the kit rises from beneath the stage. You sit down and start up."

"I can hardly wait," I said. I meant it, too—I wasn't cheeking them. The picture was coming very clear in my head, and I was getting some of the excitement I'd felt during the recording sessions back. "Who's up next, me or Tony? Or both?"

"You are." Nial grinned at me suddenly. "Actually, we've worked out a funny bit of business for you, JP, and I hope you're all right with it, because it'll knock them dead."

"Funny?" I felt one eyebrow go up. "Want to clue me in, mate? What sort of funny are we talking about, here?"

"Slapstick, almost—just, well, very humanising. You walk out, knock on the floor, and wait. Except that, in your case, nothing happens. You act puzzled—visibly, I mean, so that there's no chance the audience won't get the gag. Play to the gallery, the lot of you. Luke mimes a long, loud whistle, you look up, he points to a different spot on stage. You go there, knock again. Still nothing. Cal points to yet another spot on stage. Third time's a charm—this time the trap opens and your guitar is handed up to you by a roadie—or, really, a roadie's hand." He grinned suddenly. "Like the old Charles Addams cartoons. Just the hand and arm."

"And the crowd only sees his disembodied hand?" The more I looked at it, the better this thing looked. It was more than just a damned funny bit of business. It was brilliant, pulling the audience in, making them insiders, making us human. "Nial, Ronan, this is bloody superb, is what this is. Cheers, mates! Then what happens?"

"You give the audience this 'what the hell?' look." Nial looked relieved. I wondered if he'd thought we'd get shirty over the idea, but if he thought that, even for a second, he didn't know us as well as he ought to, after all this time working for the band. "Conspiratorial, sort of, bringing them in on the joke. The hand points back to the first spot. You go back to the first spot and stamp your foot—a little bit of temper tantrum in there, a little bit Spinal Tap. A trap opens and that stool you use rises into position. At that point, you park yourself on it, start playing, and the band kicks into full gear."

He turned to Tony. "And last but not least, we've got the piano to go."

"I can hardly wait." Tony was dead serious; hell, he was damned near holding his breath. "What do I do?"

"You play." Ronan had stopped the finger tapping. "The crowd hears the piano joining the mix, but they don't see you, because

39

you're not there yet. That might puzzle some of the fans for a minute, because they're used to any piano being played by Mac, and he obviously isn't, this time. The last traps open and presto! Up comes the piano setup, rising out of the underworld. You're on your bench, playing away on 'Home Cookin' Blues.' And there we are. Showtime."

"And once the whole band's onstage, the show's going to shift gears, isn't it? Shift straight up?" Luke sounded young again, enthusiastic in a way I hadn't heard him sound in much too long. "We've got the crowd in the palm of our hand and we're taking them along for the ride. And this time, they're coming along as part of the show? Nial, Ronan, cheers, mate. Well done."

"Brilliant. God, I fucking love this! I can't wait to see Ian's reaction to it." Mac was dancing; if I hadn't been playing with him for thirty years, I would have thought he was either burning off energy or just being blissed. Thing is, I do know Mac, and I knew just what he was doing: measuring out how many steps he had in each direction, before running out of floor or into one of our patches. "What's on the docket for starters, Ronan? Learn our marks…?"

I don't remember a first-in rehearsal like that one, not in all the years I've been with Blacklight. There was something about it, something in the air, something about having Tony along to provide the killer piano we hadn't known we were missing, something about the CD itself maybe. Maybe it was about the way we'd suddenly grown up, gone from singing about sex and good times and all the stuff you deal with when you're younger, to suddenly realising that we were adults, and not only copping to it, but actually digging it enough to sing about it. I'm damned if I knew what it was, but whatever was doing it, we all seemed energised, fresher than we'd been the last few tours.

We got an incredible amount worked out, that first run-through. I mean, granted, we'd been down at Draycote, hammering out day after day of high intensity setlisting, but doing that in a studio is different from being surrounded by the crew, onstage; you have to pay attention to where you are, what the acoustics are about, how to deal with the wireless, all that. Usually, the first day's run-through rehearsals are about as productive as a session of Parliament during an election off-year. People digging their heels in, people being narked because they don't think their sound is balanced, not enough drums in the monitor, on and on.

This, though—yeah, well. It was all the way different. It was just like everything else to do with this new double CD so far; everything we touched or did seemed to have something new about it, going back a year and more, to me actually writing lyrics for this thing. I'd never done that before. The staging, the songs, the addition of a world-class piano player, the sense that everything about us had suddenly got this massive infusion of freshness and energy, you just couldn't miss it. It was right there, every chord we played, every note Mac sang.

Another thing that was different about this one; first-ins tend to drag, go on forever, lots of little time-out calls to adjust the small stuff. Not this time, though. We flew through it, ran through the opening, saw how the traps worked, worked that part of the business out, got completely gobsmacked by how perfectly Ronan had balanced the overhead setup. Once we had that down, we had a good laugh about cool it was, especially watching Tony come rising out of the floor with a grand piano in front of him, and then we went on to cover the first five songs off the set list we'd put together for Paris.

And yeah, that was one more thing that was different: we were taking a break and doing two sets, instead of one long one. I was quite chuffed about that. The past few tours, ours shows had generally run about two hours twenty, including the short break between the show closer and the encore. Standing about with a ten-pound guitar in my arms, even sitting on my usual stool play-

41

ing, for that long without a break, was no fun at all. I'm in my fifties, I have multiple sclerosis and an iffy heart, and I get tired a lot more easily than I used to do....

"Right, gents, it's just gone seven." Ian Hendry, our manager and road manager, wandered over to the foot of the stage. He'd shown up right around the time we'd been getting silly with the roadie's disembodied hand. The set was no surprise to Ian, he'd seen it before, but I thought he was as surprised and pleased as the rest of us at just how fast we'd taken to it. "Cars are outside. Everyone ready to pack it in for the night? Lovely. Have a good night's sleep, and we'll see everyone back here in the morning."

Chapter Three

"2 February 2008—Bon soir from Paris, France, and the kick-off show of Blacklight's Book of Days European tour.

We've actually been here a few days, getting settled in and set up. Yesterday was full rehearsal at the venue—the Palais Omnisports de Paris-Bercy—making sure everything worked. Today was the usual show day deal: soundcheck at one this afternoon, getting the feel of the new stage setup. Lucky for us, we've done Bercy before, so we've got actual audio files of how a show sounds here when the place is full of 19,000 fans.

I'm not going to say much about the whole stage thing. We've kept this pretty locked down until kick-off tonight. The press, even the usual suspects, weren't let in ahead of time. This thing has been kept to a "no one sees this beforehand except the band and the crew" minimum. So, for those of you lucky enough to hit opening night in Paris, the media is going to be just as surprised as you are...."

"You ready for this, JP?"

I turned. Tony had come up next to me, looking like he had butterflies the size of condors in his stomach.

We were standing at the foot of the ramp, toward the back. It was five minutes to eight, on a very cold Saturday night in Paris, and the houselights were still up. The audience was getting restless and of course, pretty much every show by every major act they'd ever seen, the houselights going down was the signal to go nuts, because it meant the band was hitting the stage. That wasn't going to be the way it worked, not tonight, but of course, they had no way of knowing that.

"Yeah, about as ready as I'll ever be." My own nerves were actually humming like a leaky capacitor, they always do on first nights, but if Tony was as spooked as he looked, me looking calm was a good idea. "When do you head down to do your Phantom of the Opera thing?"

"Me for the underworld in about two minutes." He swallowed hard. "Man, this is way different from Bombardier shows. And it's another fucking galaxy from what we do with the Fog City Geezers. Jesus, listen to that audience!"

"Getting restless." I craned over his shoulder, looking for Bree. During that last tour of the States in 2005, when she'd come along for the first time, I'd got into the habit of not feeling comfortable unless I could see her, dancing in the wings. That wasn't going to be possible this time, not with the new staging, but the entire area out front of the stage was reserved specially for people with the special gold and green laminates, the ones that simply said "Family" on them.

So yeah, she'd be out front and not off to my right, but I still wanted to see her, most of all before I went on. She'd got into a nice little habit on that last tour, of reaching between my thighs and giving me a quick squeeze, just to send a bit of sex out into the air with me.

"Hey."

She'd come up the other side, with Katia in tow. They were both dressed for opening night, Katia in a dress that probably cost enough to give her nightmares.

Bree, though—what she'd put on made me jump, and do a double-take, and swallow hard. I'd have expected her to have hit Chanel or something, but instead, she'd opted for a dress I'd seen before, blue velvet and buttons all the way down her back. She had two of the same one, actually; she'd worn the first one the first night we'd been to bed together, and she'd worn the second one, an exact copy a size or so larger and without the side zipper, as her wedding dress, a bit over two years ago. Tonight, she was wearing her wedding dress.

When she'd asked me to do up her buttons back at the hotel, I'd done it with my fingers trembling slightly; the dress has that effect on me, every damned time. And of course, she'd noticed.

"It's for luck." She'd lifted her hair free of her neck, and held it there. There were faint laugh-lines at the corners of her eyes, and with her head tilted at this particular angle, I noticed small lines making brackets around the corners of her mouth, as well. This was the first time I'd ever noticed them, but I didn't bother wondering how long they'd been there, because it didn't matter. Truth is, they made her even more beautiful to me, somehow: experience, those little lines were, and I'd been there for every minute of it. "This dress always seems to bring us both luck. Doesn't it?"

"Always burning," I told her. I pulled her back up against me, kissing her neck, nibbling a bit. "I'll tell you what, you look better now than you did the first time you wore this, and that's saying a lot."

"Well, the first time I wore it, you couldn't wait to get it off me." She was smiling, but she wasn't relaxed. There was some tension in those shoulders of hers. They wanted to hunch up and

45

she wasn't letting them. I couldn't imagine why; she never sweats opening nights. It's the one thing she knows she can't affect at all, except by letting me know she's there. That particular set of circs is beyond her control, so she does what I do about everything else: she goes very Zen. Nice to know one of us is being calm at all times, at least on paper.

I got a clue as to what the tension was all about, while we were standing about in the hotel lobby, waiting for our ride from the hotel to the venue after dinner. Ian always sets up a full band dinner on show nights. It makes sense—that way, he knows where we all are between dinner and hitting the green room backstage for wardrobe and makeup and whatnot. But what with me having MS, I do sometimes stay at the hotel and rest, instead. And last tour, when I'd had a heart attack, Bree had stared Ian down and told him in no uncertain terms that my health came first. Of course he agreed.

Tonight, we'd opted to stay in and have a meal sent up. It had been a long few weeks of rehearsals, and I was more tired than I liked, certainly more than Bree liked—also, the weather was very cold and damp, and that doesn't help the disease. Truth is, the MS was laying back, not being too noisy, so I suppose we could have gone out to the band dinner. But Bree'd suggested we have an extra hour of quiet, me able to rest instead of moving about, and I'd gone for that. Made a lot of sense, any way I looked at it; we had one of the Presidential suites, which is about as posh as it gets, and the hotel has quite nice food. Why go out in the cold until we had to? It wasn't as if I needed to see the band. I was going to see more than enough of them over the next few months.

The limo that took us over also had Tony, Katia, Luke and Karen. We'd all met in the lobby of the George V, looking out into the dark, waiting for the car, talking, Tony trying not to be nervous about the opener. He and Katia had actually caught the lift down with us—Katia was in a state bordering on ecstasy over the posh digs, and had been since we'd checked in a few days earlier—and we were standing about talking, when Tony looked over Bree's shoulder.

"Here comes Luke and his girlfriend." He peered. "And the girls. Holy crap, what is that kid wearing? Or not wearing?"

Of course, I turned. So did Bree. So did quite a few heads in the lobby, most of them male. It wasn't hard to see why.

Suzanne McElroy was wearing the shortest skirt I think I've ever seen. I had a moment of wondering what her mum was thinking, letting the girl out in that. I mean, I'm not exactly a prude, you know? But if that had been my daughter, she'd have been marched straight back to her room and told to put a bottom half on. The girl might as well have worn a sign round her neck that said *Roadie Snack*.

"Nice dress she's almost wearing." Katia sounded about as nasty as I'd ever heard her, and I saw Tony flinch. "That puts a brand new spin on 'I see Paris, I see France, I see Suzanne's underpants', doesn't it? Assuming she's bothered to put on underpants, which considering that dress, I doubt."

"Yeah, well, if she catches pneumonia, that'll be a prime case of Darwinism at work, won't it?" I heard my own voice, amused and a bit bored, and felt Bree relax next to me. It seemed a good moment to put my arm around her, so I did, and a bit more tension went out of her shoulders. "Better her than me. I wonder if she realises how cold it gets in a theatre? Sod it, not my problem. Katia, that looks to be a nice warm coat—did you get that in London...?"

We left the girls waiting in the lobby with Mac and Dom. That actually did take a bit of load off my mind. I mean, I didn't really think the kid was going to get dragged off and rogered behind a potted palm in the lobby of the George V, but if they were going to the show with Domitra Calley anywhere near them, there was nothing to worry about. Any would-be rapist stupid enough to not recognise a trained martial artist who loved nothing better than finding trouble to stomp on when he saw one deserved the arse-kicking Dom would give him.

So here we were, ready to get on with it. Right about now, at every live show the band had ever played until tonight, the houselights would be flickering. Every other show, we'd be waiting for the recorded voice, the announcement: *Good evening, Chicago! Bon soir, Paris! Buona sera, Roma! Guten abend, Berlin!*

Not tonight, though. The audience had no way to know it, but we were all on brand new territory.

"BlackLIGHT! BlackLIGHT!"

Eight o'clock. Bree leaned in, slid a hand between my legs, gave me a quick squeeze, and kissed me.

"Play a good gig, baby." Her eyes were bright. "I'll be down front, mostly, but if not, Cyn Corrigan said she'd hold a seat in the reserved gallery next to the ramp. Barb Wilson's already up there. I'll see you backstage during the break."

She was gone, disappearing into the mass of bodies heading for the family-only guest section, down in front of the main stage. Mac breezed past me, limber and ready, adjusting his headphones and tiny ear-clip mic, his harmonica in one hand. The rest of the band was right there, getting into position for their own entrances, waiting for their cues.

Right. Showtime.

"Eight o'clock," Mac said, and laughed. "Let's rock!"

There's something about opening nights.

Right, I know, I've said it before, but it's always true, and this time, with so much that was new and so much on the line, there was something that felt like raw electricity in the air.

It went off beautifully, just the way we'd hoped, right down to the audience reactions. Mac strolled out onstage, dressed very

48

differently from his usual spandex and flash gear; he was in tight black jeans and soft flat boots and an oversized fisherman's jersey. When I'd found out what he planned to wear, I'd told Bree that I hoped the disappointed howls from his female fans wouldn't drown out the band, and she'd looked at me as if I was dim, or speaking a foreign language. I couldn't suss out why, but when Katia'd seen him walk out of the Green Room in that gear, she'd whimpered and said something under her breath, so it looked like Bree'd been right, as usual.

And he'd walked out onstage to the edge, waiting a moment for the audience to recognise him, giving them just a second, but not longer than that. He had his harp out, ready and waiting for guitar music.

And here came Luke, his old Guild acoustic slung round his neck, miked and ready to go. And here it came, right on cue: just as the first members of the audience realised who was standing there under full house lights, Luke went up the ramp, playing the twelve-bar cheeky grit of "Home Cookin' Blues." Just as the first gasps and the first cheers of recognition rippled through the crowd, Mac grinned and lifted the harmonica and they were wailing together, Blacklight's two original founders.

The houselights went down now, full dark, and of course the crowd went totally bonkers. Mac and Luke kept it up, and the crowd quieted down, because they aren't stupid, our fans, and this was new, something they hadn't seen, and it was pretty obvious there was more to come.

And here came Cal into the blackness, following his cue. The spot found him and focused, drawing the crowd's attention his way. He squatted down, knocked on the floor, and here was the second big surprise of the night, the bass on its stand rising out of the blackness. Then Stu, following on, watching the drum kit on its risers, the crowd cheering and yelling and stamping while all the time, the band, four members strong and onstage in the same order in which they'd become members of Blacklight in the first place, were jamming away on one of the first songs to ever carry the imprint "Blacklight" on the vinyl, on the record sleeve.

And now it was my turn. It went like a charm, everything just the way we'd rehearsed it. I surprised myself, a bit; I've always thought I was a piss-poor actor, but that night I got into it, hamming it up, getting the crowd to laugh at me and with me. The entire place erupted, laughing and cheering and hooting, first with my pantomime of exasperation at the supposedly malfunctioning trap doors, but especially when the disembodied arm—it was actually one of the local crew, with his upper arm in a black sleeve and a black mask over his face—popped up and pointed. Me and my Martin, and a bottleneck, the entire band the crowd knew and dug, all jamming hard.

But the roar that went up when the piano came up—that was something special. I mean, right, it was impressive, a grand piano rising out of the stage with a bloke there and playing some stellar barrelhouse runs, but there was a sort of completeness to it, you know? Just perfect. It was as if they knew the night was about to really kick into high gear.

We went through that first set in a state of rapture. Yeah, I know, it sounds barmy, but I talked to the rest of the band about it later, and they said just the same: everything that happened onstage that night was the stuff you wait your whole bloody life for, moments of perfection, all the old stuff that your earliest fans never thought they'd hear again, all the new stuff that was already pushing *Book of Days* into the top tier sellers, and everything in between. Besides, I don't have to take anyone's word for it; the entire tour was being filmed. It's all there, every bit of byplay, Luke swapping his Guild for his PRS, me knocking on the floor and watching the Martin sink into the stage while my favourite stage axe, Little Queenie, slid up out of it, Cal and Stu locked up in a roaring rhythm, Mac just hitting it out there, fronting the band he'd founded, making damned near every woman and probably a goodly number of blokes want to take him home.

One cool thing was the reaction to the video net. We'd rehearsed with it, but not very much—the video crew had still been compiling some of the historic Blacklight footage they wanted until just a few days earlier. Besides, as impressive as it was, you couldn't really tell what sort of effect it was going to have on a paying audience.

Gordon *Bennett*, it was astonishing. Just fucking amazing, you know? What looked to be a million tiny lights, basically invisible, suddenly became this moving shimmering mirror of another Blacklight, me in flash gear, Mac in the days when he'd worn his hair long with a black flapping ponytail, Stu drumming in a bomber jacket. It was so powerful, it was unsettling.

Another really cool thing was watching Tony get a chance to shine. We finished the first set with "Liplock," a hot dirty thing that had been mostly written by the late lead singer of the Bombardiers, who'd got his head bashed in with his own guitar. Tony wrote most of the music on this one, and we'd covered it on the new CD; Mac had actually done the vocals for the Bombardiers' last CD, so he knew the song inside and out. As Katia put it, Mac had made "Liplock" his bitch.

But the real driving on that one is a three-way deal: Mac's vocal, my snarling spitting guitar, and Tony's killer piano. The bass and drums hold it down hard, a thrust like a man's pelvis, just brutal; Luke uses his Strat and gives it a nice twangy rhythmic counterpoint. We'd figured it would be perfect to close a set with, and since we were going to close the show with the single, my song "Remember Me," the first set closer looked to be ready-made for "Liplock."

Did it work? Oh hell, yeah. It took Mac nearly three minutes to quiet the crowd down enough to tell them we were taking a break, and we'd back shortly.

Instruments back on stands, everything back down into the underworld, houselights up. We headed off for a twenty-minute break, rehydrating and heading for the loo, grabbing some food, towelling down, Mac changing clothes—he was soaked through.

There was no press backstage, not yet. We'd arranged that for later; Carla, and David Walters, had told them up front that between the first song and the last encore, there wasn't going to be any media access. Afterward, yes, but not before and not during. The press got to stay in their own area, where there was a nice buffet table and buckets of liquid for their use.

So it was all friends and family and crew, and a nice relaxing break. Of course, there were people there I didn't know, faces I couldn't have put a name to; the entourage for this tour was already bigger than anything we'd ever had before.

Little things stand out from that break: Bree bringing me a folding chair and a bottle of mineral water, kneeling next to me, with her head resting against my thigh for a minute. Luke talking to Solange, who was wearing one of her mum's vintage designer things; he gestured at Suzanne, just a tiny jerk of the head, but he looked a bit worried, and I found myself wondering if he'd finally noticed what she was wearing.

There was one very weird moment, at the buffet table. There was a gorgeous spread set up—no shock there, we travel with our own catering services, something that amuses Bree. After all, she's a caterer herself. The theme that night seemed to be Greek or Turkish or something; I was standing there, trying to decide between two plates I couldn't sort out, when someone giggled next to me.

"You should eat that." It was a girl, long black hair, designer gear, and a sort of headscarf affair, spangled and pretty, but somehow it didn't go with what she was wearing. Made me think vaguely of church, for some reason. She was a little thing, probably no older than Solange, or not much older. Her eyes were even darker than mine. "It is very, very good."

She giggled at me. Right—bit weird, that was, but whatever, she was probably attached to one of the crew. I smiled down at her, and she giggled again. I don't care much for gigglers—they creep me out.

"Yeah." I reached for one of the plates at random. "Ta. What is it, do you know?"

"It is called *sabzi polow*." The other voice came from the other side of me. I turned, and nearly jumped out of my shoes; for a second there, I thought I was losing my mind, that the bird had somehow moved faster than I could turn my head. Took me a moment to realise they were wearing different headscarves, that I was looking at identical twins. "It is very tasty, isn't it, Azra? Our father's chef was trained in Paris, but he learned how to make this for us sometimes, because we both like it. It has dill in it."

"Yes, it's yummy yummy food." The girl called Azra giggled around the front of me, at her sister. "But Paksima, many people don't care so much for eating dill."

She put her hand on my arm. Another touch, light as a feather, against my other hand; her sister had done the same.

I don't tend to think of myself as anything to write home about, you know? I mean, middle aged, happily married, skinny bloke with some serious health issues. I'm not naive—I do get that for some people, sex and fame are the same thing. But I began as a session bloke, not a rock star, and I'm never going to see myself as someone famous.

So trust me, if a bird is hitting on me, it's got to be pretty damned blatant for me to know that's what it is, straight off. And this time, there was no doubt at all.

Suzanne McElroy had told me she thought I was hot, that she didn't care if I was married or had an old lady, just take her home with me and take her to bed. Compared to the vibe I was getting off these two, she'd been subtle.

53

They were both peering up at me, identical heart-shaped faces with black hair done up by experts. Short skirts, high heels Bree would have salivated over, and those headscarves. They were both smiling, dainty little dimpled smiles, eyes about as upfront bold as any streetcorner hooker. What the fuck…?

"Um, excuse me."

Bree's voice, cold and sharp, came from right behind me. She was seriously narked, not at me, and thank God for it, because I was getting pretty damned tired of having to be polite to children who wanted me to roger them. Bree was my wife, damn it. Let her deal with them.

Both girls let go of me, and backed up fast. Bree, at that moment, was about six foot two, and she had a look in her eye that was just about as scary as anything Domitra could summon. The twins, whoever they were and however randy they might be, apparently didn't have a death wish, because they both cooed and fluttered off, in search of fresh meat.

"Bitches," Bree muttered. "John, is this going to happen every damned night? Skanky little hos, hitting on you?"

"Christ, I bloody hope not." I handed her a plate. "Here, what is this stuff, anyway…?"

Back out for the second set. I'm not going to go on about it, not too much; you can always read Nial's blog for the details. But we began the second set with Mac's "Hammer It Home," and he actually sang a chunk of the most political bits in French. Of course, that enslaved the few remaining members of the audience who hadn't been at his feet already.

The show closer—yeah. We did the single, the song I'd written in my head onstage at the anti-racism benefit we'd played at Frejus two years ago: it's called "Remember Me" and at the time, I'd been staggered by it, the way it came out, no halts or pauses for thinking, just there.

We got to the penultimate verse—*we never know just what*

54

might happen, we never know how high to fly, maybe we get to keep each other or lose it all in the blink of an eye—and the crowd was singing with us. That surprised the hell out of me, because the single was only just out, but all these people seemed to know every word of the song. Bloody hell, English wasn't even their native language, you know? And they were singing with it, nineteen thousand strong. Amazing.

By the time we got to the final verse of it—*And now I lay me down to sleep, you're everything I want to keep, if you should wake and find me gone, feel free to live, and carry on, so much to do, so much to see, I only ask one thing:*—the crowd was waiting, holding their breath.

Mac held the vocal, one beat longer than we'd rehearsed or recorded. Didn't matter—all of us held it with him, knowing from the gut what he was going to do. The audience, all nineteen thousand of them, came in right as Mac did:

Just, remember me.

"*Merci*, Paris!" Arms around each other's waists, bowing deep, turning four times, bowing to every corner, every watching eye. "*Bonne nuit!*"

55

Chapter Four

"5 February—Hello from Virtual Days, Nial here. This is going to be a blog and run, I'm afraid. The Book of Days Euro tour just crossed borders, having finished up strong in Paris and moved on to Milan. Tomorrow is a show day, so today means working like ants to get everything ready at the venue, the Forum di Assago. Luckily, you can always find a good fast meal in Italy…"

"John?"

Bree's voice sounded peculiar. I'd been going back and forth between sorting out my meds—it was that time again—and reading Nial's current blog. I stopped, and lifted an eyebrow at her.

"What?"

"Have you seen this review?"

She was sitting at the fancy little writing desk in our suite in the Milan Four Seasons. Nice thing about a top of the line chain is, I know what to expect from each one. Not a lot of difference, and not much new to have to learn. Thing is, we rotate which band member gets the best suite that isn't given over to Black-light Corporate as an ops centre, and sometimes, we pull the best of the lot at a given hotel. This time, luck of the draw, we'd pulled the posh digs.

"No—haven't seen any of the reviews yet, actually."

"Well, it's from one of the London dailies. This guy was at the Paris opener, and—well—you should see it, John."

"We're getting our first look at the reviews of the "bare stage, flying arrays" design, as well as the new material, or will be, as soon as some-one translates them for us. Personally, I don't have any French beyond how to ask for coffee and the loo. But from the noises the head blokes are making, the tech reviews at least are straight through the roof..."

"Right." I glanced away from the screen and back at the small pile of pharmacy bottles. Bloody hell, where was the big stash of anti-spasmodics? It had to be somewhere... "Can you read me a paragraph or two, Bree?"

"You bet." She cleared her throat. "It's by someone named Corbett, and it starts out, 'As a member of the senior circuit my-self—I was at the first Isle of Wight festival, and what's more, I actually remember it—I've had my expectations raised by the rockers I've gone into middle age with too many times to count. The bands are many and varied. Their names are legion. We all know how it works: there's hosannas and over-the-top PR and early sneak release info, they trumpet that the new CD, their fortieth or whatever number it is, is Groundbreaking! New! A first in their Long and Distinguished Career! Unfortunately, the one thing they all seem to have in common is that, in the end, the hype is never supported by the music.'"

"Bloody hell." I straightened up and stared at her. The meds could wait. "This is Corbett? Right, okay, carry on. How bad is it?"

"Bad?" Bree blinked at me. "Who said it was bad? Here's more of it: 'So, when I settled into the press area at the Omnisports Bercy in Paris Saturday night, I was expecting the usual: a decent show, nothing really new. I went in well-armoured against disappointment. After all, you can always count on Blacklight to give you a good show, but *good* and *great* aren't synonymous. And before I get too deep into it, let me say right up front that talking about Saturday night, neither word works: the only thing that comes to mind is *transcendent*. Or, if you want something with fewer associations, try *astonishing*.'"

"Gordon *Bennett!*" I'd suddenly stopped worrying about my meds. "Go on, Bree, will you?"

"My pleasure. Where was I? Oh, right. 'From the opening moments—rock's cheekiest and most cheerful frontman strolling onstage and jamming with Blacklight co-founder Luke Hedley on a song none of us ever thought we'd hear again in this life—through an intimate use of genuinely innovative staging, they did more than deliver what the advance PR had hinted at. *Book of Days* is a journey, from the band's earliest work through what Blacklight is today. Listening to the incandescent humanist burn of Mac Sharpe's "Hammer it Home," to "You Never Kissed Me Goodbye," Luke Hedley's loving farewell to his late wife, to "Remember Me," JP Kinkaid's heartfelt homage to his generation's faults and virtues, it became clear to those of us fortunate enough to be bearing witness that, with *Book of Days*, Blacklight has done what few long-lived rockers have managed without some degree of self-parody: they've come to terms with coming of age.'"

I opened my mouth, and closed it again. Truth is, I don't think I could have talked right that moment. I was gobsmacked.

"There's more. He says he didn't know whether he was glad or sorry he wasn't there for the Sunday show, too, because Saturday was so perfect, he was afraid Sunday couldn't have measured up." She folded the paper open, and set it on the desk. "John, I don't think I've ever seen a review of a Blacklight show like this one. I mean, good reviews, yes. I've seen plenty of those. But..." Her voice died away.

"Yeah, I know what you mean. And by the way, that 'someone named Corbett'? That's Digby Cole Corbett, one of the greats. There's journalists and reviewers, and then there's Corbett." I turned my suitcase over on its side, and dumped everything out on the bed which, since this was the Visconti Suite at the Four Seasons, was about the size of a swimming pool and looked like something one of the Borgias used to host house parties on. "Good, there's the pills. Thought I'd lost them. I need to take meds and have a piss, but I want to check my email, see if anyone's seen Corbett's thing yet. Because yeah, the CD reviews have all been fantastic, but this is the first tour review I've seen—heard, rather."

"Good idea." She shivered suddenly. "God, I'm tired of feeling cold. For some reason, I can't get warm right now, and since we've got the fireplace going, I want to stand there for a couple of minutes and toast. And my eyes hurt."

"Cold?" I turned around and looked at her. "Bree, love, aren't you feeling well? Bloody hell, here, let me get all this rubbish off the bed—you get under the covers, I'll ring down to the desk and make them send up something hot to drink."

"No, no, I'm fine. Just cold. And I think I need new reading glasses—the ones I have don't seem to be working right. This ageing thing sucks." She wandered out into the living room, and went to stand by the fire. The suite had nice big windows—the Milan Four Seasons used to be a monastery or something, and it's all very posh and antique and whatnot, but just at the moment, you couldn't see a damned thing because the windows were streaky with icy rain, right at the edge of being actual sleet.

Most people think of Italy, they think of sunshine and olive groves, a sort of eternal summer. You know, like old Fellini movies, all *la dolce vita* and Vespas, or Sophia Loren in a print dress and stomping on grapes. The reality is, Italy is just as cold and nasty as the rest of Europe come winter. Bree wrapped her arms round herself. "Is that someone at the door?"

She was right—someone was out there, banging on the door. Annoying, since there was a perfectly good buzzer. "I'll get it. You just stay there and warm up, lady." I shot her a look—*don't argue with me, Bree*—and she turned back to the fire, rubbing her hands.

Right, so I was being fussy and silly, worrying over her. I couldn't help it. Truth is, I hate any sign that she isn't completely invincible. The laugh lines don't bother me, I quite like them, but her looking tired, or fine-drawn, or just not feeling well, that always does a number on my head. I haven't forgotten her bout with cancer, a couple of years ago, just how scary that had been.

It was Mac at the door, with Domitra right behind him. He was holding the paper with Corbett's review, and he had this odd, concentrated look on his face. Taut, you know? If any of his female fans had been there to see it, Domitra would have had her hands full—well, okay, full of body parts, but still.

"Johnny, have you seen this yet?" He came in, caught sight of Bree at the fire, and headed over to join her. "Corbett wrote us a brilliant review—I swear, the next time I see him, I'm going to kiss him. Bree, angel, you're the colour of an Etruscan grand-mother's tomb effigy. Have you caught a bug, or something? Shall we ring down to the desk and make them send you up you a toddy, or something? Or maybe some grappa or a nice *vin santo* or a bowl of chicken soup?"

"I'm fine. No need for people to fuss." Mac was right, she looked pale and tired. I hadn't liked that effigy comparison much, but he wasn't wrong. She wasn't moving away from the fire, ei-ther. "Hey, Dom. Busy day?"

"Are you joking? In Italy?" Dom shook her head and snorted.

There was no sign of a smile. "Always. At least these women are nice and upfront about wanting to climb my boss. No one ever accused Italian chicks of subtlety."

"Johnny, look." Something had to be up—Mac wasn't big on interrupting people, especially Dom. "What's your feeling about Ian's suggestion? Because Luke says he's all in favour of it, but we need agreement all the way round before we say yes. And why are you looking at me like that?"

"Because I haven't got a clue what you're on about. I haven't checked my email yet." There was another knock at the door. Blimey, the Visconti Suite was beginning to feel more like the Victoria Station Suite, or something. "All right, what's Ian suggesting? And hang on, let me get the door."

It was Stu this time, with Cal and Tony at his heels. Everyone had this sort of intense look and vibe about them, except for Tony, who was looking completely freaked. I just held the door open and waited, and about thirty seconds later, I heard the private lift stop, and here came Luke.

Bree slipped into the bedroom and came out with a nice warm sweater on, and an offer of refreshments. Well or unwell, this was her turf, and invited or not, these weren't just my mates, they were our guests. So of course, she had to play hostess. I glared her back over to the fire, and took over. After all, this looked to be band business: my problem, not hers.

"Right." The suite had two enormous leather sofas across from each other, both within range of the warmth of the fire. "Okay. Everyone comfy, then? Good. Now. Someone want to tell me what the fuck is going on?"

"I'm guessing you haven't checked your email." Stu had a glass of something he'd brought with him, but he wasn't drinking it, he was swishing the liquid round and round. "Ian sent out a group note. It's marked urgent—he's waiting to hear back from us. I think you ought to go look, JP."

61

I stared at him for a moment. Then I headed for my laptop. The email was there, top of the queue.

From: Ian Hendry

To: Band; Production; Ops; tour crew

Date: 7 February 2008

Subject: Book of Days charting progress US/UK, tour extension, Japanese offer, URGENT

Welcome to Milan. Great shows in Paris, btw. Updates on a couple of things:

CD update: *Book of Days* is the #1 UK album. It's at #9 on the US charts. "Remember Me" is sitting at 8 & 22, UK/US.

Tour update: This is getting serious, people. There's a lot of pressure on, to extend this leg of the tour as much as we possibly can. It's coming from everywhere. I'm heading back to the office for a few days to get some stuff in order; I'll rejoin you next Tuesday, in Vienna, before the show. But I'll want to talk to you all before tomorrow.

The big news: we've had an offer from Sapporo Motors, in Osaka—they're pleading with us for the privilege of kicking in about £18M to get us to play a Japanese tour. I've pushed back and stalled so far, but the total gross is looking huge. A back-of-envelope says a gross of over £90M for 20 dates in 7 cities.

As discussed before we left Paris, I went ahead and doubled up the Prague, Munich and Cologne shows. Carla will have the hotel changes later this afternoon. With the howl that's gone up from the promoters, we're probably going to want to double up the rest of this leg, but I'm not doing that without a solid yes from you lot. You need to decide by tonight, so I'm asking that you talk it over, get the consensus if possible, and let me know fast. Short notice, but this CD is shaping up as being something we haven't seen before. That happens, it'll take the tour right along with it. So we've got decisions to make. Cheers, Ian.

I just stood there, blinking like a badger. The numbers Ian had come up with, for the Japanese thing, those were enough to explain why Tony was looking glazed and freaked; after all, ninety million quid is a big enough number to wrap your head around, and that's even before you remember that the pound is worth more than the dollar, and that ninety damned near doubles when you convert it.

But honestly, the money wasn't was what I was thinking about. It was the other numbers—what the CD and single were doing on the charts—that were leaving me speechless. When I took those numbers and added them to Corbett's review, I felt something move down my back...

"I think we should do it." Luke couldn't seem to sit still; he was pacing. He'd parked on one of the sofas, but in the past two minutes, he'd got up, sat down, and got up again. "My own feeling is, doubling up this leg is going to be tiring, but it's short-term and not much brain involved, really. Ian wants a consensus, so let's get this one out of the way first. Show of hands, mates: Anyone see any reason to not double up on the Euro leg? If you think we should do it, hands up. And Bree, we'd keep Monday nights open for JP, so no worries there."

Everyone lifted a hand, except Tony. "Tony, you don't think we should? Why not? What are we missing?"

"Oh, I'd love to do it. And I checked with Katia, before she and Karen went out." Tony put his hand up, but he looked a bit unsure. Unusual for him, that is. He's got that whole Italian-American thing of being emphatic, hardwired into the genes, or something. "But I'm just guesting on this tour, guys. I didn't realise I got an equal vote on the bigger picture. I feel like the Musketeer who wasn't one, Whatsisame."

"D'Artagnan?" Mac grinned. "Tony, anything to do with this tour, you're an equal member with an equal vote. One for all, all for one, mate. It's how we work, and it's the way we've always worked. So we're unanimous on the doubling for the Euro leg?

Good. You do realise we'll probably need to extend the US leg as well, right?"

"Yeah, that seems obvious." Stu was up and pacing now, as well; the whole band seemed restless. Good job the suite was so roomy. "Okay, we've got that out of the way. What does everyone want to do about a Japanese tour? Do we tell Ian yes, explore it at least? Because if Sapporo is offering that kind of money in a sponsorship deal, the demand is there, and it's serious. Even a short tour would be huge—what did he say, twenty dates? Quick vote, people, just on telling Ian to check out the logistics of a short one. Yea or nay?"

Hands up, every one of us. This time, there was no hesitation from Tony, either. He seemed to have got that he was a full member of the band for all these decisions, and about time, you know?

"We're on, then." Luke headed for the door. "Bree, love, sorry to vote and run, but Ian needs to get started on this. And I must say, quite a nice way to balance out what happened after the Sunday show."

"What?" It was Bree, from behind me. "What do you mean, Luke? What happened after the show? I didn't hear anything. Was there some kind of problem?"

"One of our crew died." Mac sounded regretful. "JP, you met him—French kid, Alain Descarres. He was the one who provided the disembodied arm for your bit of business at Bercy. The local cops found him early Sunday morning, near his place near La Defense—we had the crew staying at the Sofitel, but he hadn't wanted a room. It was a hit and run driver, apparently—I only found out about an hour ago. There was a phone call from David Walters. Bree, angel, you ought to go have a long lovely hot bath, and take the chill off. We'll see you at dinner."

We stayed in Milan, parked in our posh suite at the Four Seasons, all the way through that week.

One nice thing about touring Europe: if you've got gigs set up in countries bordering each other, you don't really have to pick up and move hotels for every show. We played the one show in Milan and one in Bern, across the border in Switzerland—we went by air, Milan to Bern, and it took all of half an hour. Carla had got into the habit of arranging things with as few hotel changes as possible almost from the day she came on. It saves a lot of stress.

The Milan and Bern shows went off brilliantly, no problems at all. We kept the intensity levels up, and honestly, it wasn't what I'd call hard work—that just seemed to be happening, every single show. Yeah, I know, early days yet and probably too soon to know whether it could be this easy for the rest of the tour, but so far, so good.

We'd told Ian to go ahead and double the dates, and when we were handed the updated schedules, I expected Bree to be fussing over it. After all, she does that, worrying about whether my health is up for it. But she stayed quiet, and that got me worrying instead. Mac had made that crack about her being pale as an effigy, and now I looked at her, he was dead right.

I didn't really have any space to bring it up with her until after we'd got through the first week. We were actually set to play two cities in Switzerland, Bern and Zurich, but the thing is, Zurich was being followed by the Vienna gigs, and geographically, it made more sense for us to settle into the Vienna hotel before we played Zurich.

By the time we checked into the Grand Hotel Wien, I was worried as hell. In less than a week, she'd gone quiet, she couldn't seem to stay warm, she kept rubbing her eyes when she thought I wasn't watching, and—scariest thing—she'd lost weight. That's what scared me most, because it was visible; her clothes were loose on her. Losing enough weight in a week for it to be obvious, that's not supposed to happen.

Plus, she'd begged out of the Zurich gig. She said she wanted to stay back at the hotel instead. And considering how edgy she'd been about all the groupies backstage, something was definitely wrong. I could put it aside while we were playing—in fact, I had to, no choice—but I was freaked out, getting more freaked every day, and prepared to come the heavy husband and flip my shit over it, if she argued about it.

So we hadn't even unpacked in our suite at the Grand in Vienna when I sat her down on the bed, planted both feet in front of her to keep her there, and unloaded.

"Bree. Look, love." She sat there, quiet, tired, pale, just looking up at me. I felt my heart do a quick stuttery thing. "I'm worried half off my nut. You're ringing a doctor, and no arguing with me, Bree. You're not well and I'm not having you get sick, okay?"

"I wasn't planning on arguing." She sighed, a tiny little noise. "Why would I argue? It's a good idea. I was planning on doing that anyway, John. I called my mom and she gave me a couple of names and numbers. She knows doctors in Vienna."

"You rang Miranda?" That sent my heart stuttering again, and I took a couple of deep breaths, trying to steady it. The arrhythmia is scary stuff. Thing is, if Bree was sick enough to ring her mum, then she was serious. Miranda's a surgeon. "Glad to hear it. Does she have any ideas? Opinions, about what it might be, I mean? Or is she doing that whole silent-ethics thing doctors do? And you know, Bree, we do have a doctor along for the tour— we'd be nuts not to, what with our combined age being about four hundred years old."

"She had some ideas, yes." Bree's hands were calm in her lap, and her shoulders were relaxed. "She wasn't sharing them, though. Her feeling was that I should get hold of some of her buddies here and get a check-up, and probably some blood work. That's one reason I didn't talk to the Blacklight guy. He's not set up for blood tests, is he?"

"No, not really." My stomach had joined my heart in doing little flip-flops. "Bree, talk to me. What's wrong?"

"I don't know." It hit me suddenly, she was scared, maybe not as scared as I was, but definitely scared. It was there, just a small bubble at the back of her voice. Her shoulders were relaxed because she was forcing them down. "If I had to make a guess, or describe it to a doctor, I'd say I think I'm anaemic. I've had anaemia before, and this feels like what I remember, just worse. They'll probably give me some shots of iron, or something. I hate those. They hurt like hell."

"You've had anaemia before?" Bloody hell, all I seemed to be able to do was the whole 'answer in the form of a question' thing. That was a sure sign I was rattled. I sat on the bed, and got both her hands in mine. "Your hands feel like Norway in January. I don't remember the anaemia thing, not at all. When was it, Bree? Was that an official diagnosis?"

"Yes, but it was a very long time ago." She wasn't meeting my eye, but she wasn't actively avoiding it, either; it was just that her own stare seemed to be looking back, a long way into the past. "You weren't with me—it was when you were in London, taking care of Cilla."

Shit. Bad memory, that is, one of my worst: my first wife ringing me in San Francisco, with suspected ovarian cancer, begging me for the help that I didn't think I had any right to refuse giving her. Me leaving Bree to go take care of Cilla, seven months, her surviving the cancer, me hating every minute of being there, drinking too much, Cilla never letting go of her crack addiction.

I didn't know then, hadn't known until Miranda had told me back when Bree had gone in for her own cancer surgery twenty five years later, that Bree had been in hospital herself, while I was AWOL in the UK. She'd been rushed in by her mum, had her stomach pumped out after she'd decided she didn't want to deal with being alive without me anymore, and had taken an entire

bottle of my pain pills and washed them down with a fifth of te-
quila. She'd been barely nineteen.

"I'll call tomorrow." She'd read my face, known I was remembering the time in London, with Cilla. Once, that would have
hurt her, knowing I'd gone down that road, but not anymore. She
can look at the past a bit more easily these days; that's one of the
side effects of the wedding ring, knowing that the history is just
that, and won't happen again. She smiled suddenly, a real smile.
"Because I don't like feeling this way. And besides, if I'm curled
up in bed at the hotel like an old crone, Suzanne gets a clear shot
at you."

"Yeah, I need the protection." I was grinning. "You never know
when she might drag me off and ravish me behind a Marshall
stack, or something. Truth, though? If you want to worry about
me being dragged off, worry about the Persian Princesses doing it.
There's two of them to my one."

"Oh my God, the Tahini Twins!" Bree rolled her eyes. "I'm sure
you'd struggle and scream for help. I can just see Phil MacDermott whisking them out of the place, or maybe even Dom. I'm
just surprised they aren't doing their little dance of the seven
veils for Mac. Are they just terrified of Domitra?"

"Damned if I know. Probably." I'd got her hands between mine,
and was rubbing them, trying to get the blood flowing. The skin on
her hands felt odd—not just cold, but dry, a bit papery. "Now I
think about it, he really doesn't seem remotely into it, not with
those two. Weird, that is, you know? Because I'd have thought a
nice little threesome would be right up Mac's street. Big dark eyes,
cooing and giggling, clearly complete horny little minks, and anyway, two little starfuckers for the price of one. He could have a
brilliant little orgy. And it's got nothing to do with ethnic issues—
when it comes to sex, Mac's about as equal op as it gets. You've
heard him on the subject of what he'd like to do with Dom's sister
Savannah. But he isn't interested, not this time."

68

"Smart man." She looked wistful. "I don't suppose there's any chance Suzanne will switch from you to Mac…?"

"Crikey, don't I wish." I gave her a final rub, and got up to finish unpacking; we were checked in at the Grand for nearly a week, using it as our home base while we did gigs in Zurich and Budapest, as well as right here in Vienna. "But that would be seriously creepy. I mean, that girl is Solange's best friend, and Mac is Solange's godfather. That's way over the top half of daytime telly, all the way into sleaze."

"Well, I personally think the idea of her chasing you in the first place is seriously creepy and all the way into sleaze. But that's just me." She reached for the hotel phone. "Time to bite the bullet and do what the doctor ordered. Yes, hello, is that the front desk? *Guten tag.* I was wondering if I could have an outside line, and the local dialling code…?"

So she got her appointment made for the next day, and that perked her up so much that she decided to come along to the Zurich show that night. She seemed to have some trouble wrapping her head round the fact that, even though we were flying to another country to have dinner and play a show, it was a quicker flight than San Francisco to Seattle would have been. Plus, we were coming straight back here to the hotel when the show was done with. It's that "Europe at each other's doorstep" deal. Besides, we had our own jet for the tour—Blacklight Corporate had leased us a private business jet, a very tarted-up 737—so it wasn't as if we had to hurry or be told we'd have to take a later flight.

The show was just as strong as the earlier ones. You can't always count on that, with the Swiss or Viennese or Germans—if you don't measure up, they can freeze you, really bloody quick. But we had a new disembodied arm for me, and whoever it belonged to must have spent a few hours watching old clips of the Addams Family, because he had the gestures down, and the place was roaring with laughter. I did think that gag was going to get

69

old after awhile. It was something to bring up with the braintrust and the band, how to keep it fresh.

Backstage during the break, I walked in and spotted Bree, sitting on a folding chair and deep in conversation with Karen McElroy. That surprised me, a bit; what with the whole Suzanne situation, Bree hadn't seemed very comfortable being around Karen. She's pretty damned blunt, my wife is, and I suspect she was afraid she'd open her mouth to say something like "that's a nice dress" and what would come out would be "would you please tell your tarty little daughter to keep off my husband."

I headed over. On the way, looking around through the crush of people, I saw Suzanne McElroy, looking really fed up and cross, glaring at either her mum or Bree, possibly both. She wasn't alone, either; she had one of Phil MacDermott's security people just a few feet off her elbow, but I don't think she realised he'd been detailed to keep an eye on her. After all, it wasn't as if she had any reason to get that, as family, she was being covered and kept out of harm's way.

I did, though. I know I miss a lot, not paying attention when I ought to, but I'm not dim and the way he moved when she did, that was a dead giveaway. And of course Solange had to know, after all these years of hanging with her dad's friends. She probably took it for granted by now; she'd had a band bodyguard so long, he was probably invisible to her.

What was really funny was that the Persian Princesses, Azra and Paksima, were hanging out and whispering to each other, with their heads together, staring at a group of blokes across the room. They were only about three feet away, but didn't seem remotely interested in Suzanne—I wasn't even sure they knew or cared she was there. But of course, they probably weren't all that interested in other women at the best of times.

"...ashy. Just, kind of dry, as if -" Bree saw me over Karen's shoulder, and broke off what she'd been saying. She got to her feet. "John! Here, I saved you a chair, and some mineral water. Sit."

"Not yet, ta." What in hell? I'd interrupted something, that was obvious; women get a look to them, when they're talking secrets or about stuff they think the men around them are too dim to follow. I leaned in, and kissed her hard. "Bree, tell you what, why don't you keep the chair warm a minute longer, and I'll get us both a plate of nosh? No, don't argue with me, and don't tell me you're not hungry, because I don't care and anyway I don't believe it. You barely ate anything at dinner."

She sat back down, her face even paler than it had been. That was a dead giveaway, all by itself; Bree doesn't blush, unless she's furious. Anything else, she goes pale.

I spent the rest of the break picking at my own food, a good healthy plate of carbs and protein, bullying her into eating some of the veggies on her plate. Luke had come up, to get a fast kiss off Karen. It was nice, seeing the two of them getting closer as the tour went on. That's a make or break deal, a major tour is. If the woman can cope, you've got something there. If she can't, or if she's there for all the wrong reasons, you know that pretty fast, as well.

Back out onstage, opening with the huge, slamming build that leads into "Hammer It Home," the audience holding its breath and then going nuts. Closing with "Remember Me," some fantastic bits of back and forth with Cal's bassline; Stu and Tony had worked out a thing where they held the beat down for a dozen or so bars, leaving me and Luke and Cal, strings and nothing but strings, throwing it back and forth. Then Stu came in, drumbeat like jackboots marching, and Tony, thundering on the deep end of the piano's soundbox...

Encore, goodnights, bows, houselights up, band and family into the limos at the backstage door. Not out quite as fast as we would have liked—the crowds of fans at the backstage door

71

seemed to be getting larger with every show—but back to the airport, eighty-five minutes in the air back to Austria, and into bed for my weekly interferon shot and some kip, with a day off on Monday.

And whether Bree knew it or not, whether she liked it or not, I was coming along for that visit to her mother's doctor chum, and I wasn't taking no for an answer.

Chapter Five

"...*You know, these days, I don't post anything sensitive in my blog without an okay from the band and management. So I checked with them, and it's okay for me to announce in advance that 'Hammer It Home' is going to be the second single released from the Book of Days CD...*"

"John?"

I turned. The house lights were full up in the Wiener Stadthaller, and there we were, standing at the foot of the stairs up to the ramp. This time, though, nearly twelve thousand people knew what was up; the reviews from the tour were all over the press, and all over the net.

She smiled at me. I wanted to smile back, she needed it and deserved it, but I hadn't really been able to smile since yesterday, and nothing that had happened today had left me anywhere close to smiling.

…Also, thanks to a huge demand, we've basically doubled our tour dates for America, so if you've been reading this from a Starbucks or something in Los Angeles or Atlanta or San Jose, here's hoping you were able to score tickets. The word is, we sold out two nights at the Staples Center in Los Angeles—that's 20,000 per night—in eighteen minutes. Lucky for you, we've added two more shows there, and two in Anaheim, as well, at the Honda Center…

"It's going to be fine." Bree had on a brand new dress, gorgeous thing, ruby silk with a plunging neckline and basically no back. Pure jewel tones, this time, and no nonsense about wanting to be *grande dame*. Sod that. The dress was killer and it looked fantastic on her, but I didn't think I was ever going to be able to look at it without bad associations.

"Yeah." She got the smile from me this time, but I hoped to hell she didn't know what an effort it was. "I know it is. Could have been a lot worse."

So, I said it, nice and reassuring. Trouble was, I didn't believe it.

We'd gone shopping, the two of us, straight from leaving her blood samples at the lab that morning. The doctor who'd seen her yesterday, a nice competent bloke with some kind things to say about Miranda, had wanted blood work, but he'd wanted it the following morning, after she'd fasted all night. We'd done that, and right after, I'd told her we were off to Hotel Sacher's cafe, because she was having a hot chocolate, and that she was by God going to eat a slab of the torte they're famous for.

All these years, it's always been me getting diagnosed with shit, and Bree sitting there melting down, you know? I'd missed every damned major medical thing of hers—somehow, from day one, I'd managed to be elsewhere when she'd had a health crisis. The only exception was getting the good news about her not having caught AIDS from one of Cilla's needles. I hadn't even known about her miscarriage until recently, and when she'd got her cancer diagnosis, I'd been in the studio with the Bombardiers and hadn't found out until she'd already been set up for surgery. I'd already decided that, whatever was going on, I was going to damned well be there this time.

So we'd gone to the lab together, after we'd fasted together the night before. She didn't like that, me not eating, but she wasn't getting a vote. We'd gone to the lab and she'd had too much blood for comfort taken, and come out of it shaky and pale, and ready for food. We'd eaten breakfast and split a big gooey pastry that was almost too rich for either of us; it was so dense and sweet, it made my teeth ache and made her sleepy. We'd gone straight from that off shopping, to buy her something to wear to tonight's show. They'd weighed her at the doctor's office, and from what she told me after we'd hit the street, she'd lost about ten pounds in the last week.

So yeah, I was right there, holding her hand, taking her shopping, insisting she eat, fussing over her like a furious nanny. And yeah, I was scared shitless.

And I was with her, early afternoon, when we walked back into the suite at the Grand, and saw the red light blinking on the hotel phone. *Blip, blip, blip*, just blinking away. There was a message for one of us.

I sat down next to her on the bed. She seemed very calm, picking up the phone, following the recorded instructions, going through the song and dance to retrieve the voicemail. I remember she had a notepad, one of those little engraved things they give you at the better hotels, and I remember that I saw her hand crunch it a bit, tightening as she listened, but that she relaxed the hand right away.

She put the phone down, finally, and took a breath. It seemed to take forever.

"Bree?"

"It's what I thought." She looked at me; I couldn't tell whether she was relieved or freaked or what. "Diabetes."

I reached out and got both arms around her. I wasn't saying anything, not yet. She'd tell me how bad it was, or wasn't. She's a doctor's daughter, and sometimes that helps.

"My fasting blood sugar should have been right around 95 to 100." She snuggled up to me, still calm. "It was about 265. I've been nonstop thirsty for a while—that's a dead giveaway. But I thought it had to do with it being winter. And my feet—the skin was really dry, sort of ashy and peeling. I thought that was because of the cold, too."

"Bree." There was a shake in my voice. Ridiculous; I'd got the MS diagnosis in total calm. "Details, please, lady?"

"I got lucky." She smiled up at me, a real smile. "It's okay, John, honestly. This isn't the Big Bad version, the insulin shots thing. This is type two. Should be controllable with diet, and pills. I'll need to work out what I can and can't eat, and see about monitoring my blood sugars. But I got off light. It could have been a lot worse. Reminds me, I ought to tell Karen McElroy. She'll want to know she was right."

"Right?" I knew sod-all about diabetes. I was going to know a lot more, once I had half an hour to sit down with the laptop and look it up. "What do you mean, Bree? And when did you chum up with Suzanne's mum?"

"Karen's a Type One diabetic. She guessed." Bree suddenly turned all the way around, and pulled my face to hers, and kissed me, long and deep. "Do you have a soundcheck to go to? Because if not, give me a reason to need a good hot shower in about half an hour, okay…?"

"BlackLIGHT! BlackLIGHT!"

"Here we go." Mac was dancing in place, but he stopped suddenly, and gave Bree a hard fast hug. "Karen told us the news. If I tell you I'm glad it wasn't worse, don't thump me. And will you stop getting sick, please, the pair of you?"

"Do our best, mate." There was a knot at the back of my throat. I love these blokes, the lot of them. You couldn't ask for better friends. "Showtime. Off you go."

…There's also early word that we're going to be adding a third leg to the existing tour: twenty dates in Japan. That's always a fun trip, especially loving sashimi the way I do…

"Do a good gig, baby." She was behind me this time, speaking straight into my ear; the house lights were full up, and the audience was roaring, seeing Mac, the harmonica starting up, Luke coming up the ramp. I wouldn't have heard her had she been any further away. "Oh, and by the way?"

"BlackLIGHT! BlackLIGHT!"

She snaked one hand between my thighs, but this time, she made me jump. It was a grip, nothing symbolic about it. She had the family jewels in the palm of her hand, and she wasn't letting go. Her chin was resting on my shoulder, and she was looking straight ahead.

I focussed my eyes and realised that Suzanne McElroy was standing about ten feet away, staring at us, staring at Bree holding on to me, staring at me.

Right. I stood where I was, nice and relaxed, completely trusting my wife. Whatever she was going to do, I was playing along. She'd never done a damned thing to make me not trust her, with my bollocks or anything else.

"*Mine*," Bree said, or maybe she simply mouthed it. Whichever it was, Suzanne McElroy turned on her heel and stormed off. One of Phil MacDermott's people, a different bloke from the one at the last show, slipped away behind her.

"Heard the news, Bree." Domitra, with Mac safely onstage, was making the rounds. "Sucks, but it could have been worse. JP, dude, aren't you up next? Is Bree going to give you back your nuts…?"

77

Another brilliant show, this time with the video veil getting a workout. The team had gone deep into the archives, and had come up with clips from the Frejus show we'd done after the Cannes festival two years ago, Mac with his arm in a sling after he'd been shot by a white supremacist called Terry Goff, the crowd then and the crowd today seeming to somehow blend together.

They ran that video, flickering and shimmering as the video veil waved from all the air generated by people dancing, while we were doing "Hammer It Home." They ran it again for "Remember Me," but this time there was added footage, that made me jump a bit: shots of the party at the Bellagio in Las Vegas, after Bree and I got married. It made the song really intimate. I'd given blanket permission to use anything, of course, because I trust our staff. I just wondered if Bree was smiling up at it from wherever she was at the moment.

Bows, goodnights, limo back to the hotel; I had an arm around Bree the entire drive back. I'd got into the habit of leaving the laptop plugged in, doing its rest mode thing. Bree checked at the front desk, with the concierge; she'd arranged to have the first round of the meds she'd be taking for the rest of her life delivered to the Grand, and of course, they were there, waiting for her, along with a little device for poking herself in the finger and reading her blood sugar levels. You've got to love a good hotel, yeah? Comfort and competence.

Bree settled down on our enormous bed, sorting out the different pills, reading the directions, reading the labels. I flipped open the laptop and went straight to my email.

From: Ian Hendry
To: Band; Production; Ops; tour crew
Date: 12 February 2008
Subject: Various
Quick update: I've gone ahead and begun the preliminary

talks with Sapporo Motors, for the Japanese tour. They want it soon, but I've told them that at least a month's rest after the end of the US leg is not negotiable. We're waiting to hear back on that, but I can't imagine there's going to be any problem. The money they've offered is solid, and they aren't trying to hide how much they want the Japanese leg to happen.

The US tour has also been extended, and thanks for not wasting time on getting back to me about it. We haven't seen anything like this kind of demand, not since the *Pick Up The Slack* tour, and this looks to outstrip that, easily.

We've got the remainder of the Euro leg booked up pretty tight, as well, but you've got a few more shows on the old schedule—we don't begin doubling until Prague. So relax while you can. It's going to be a busy month.

Also, on a less cheerful note, Blacklight management has sent flowers and all the appropriate condolences to the families of Alain Descarres and Gregory Maltin, in all of our names. I know that having two crew members die so soon after each other casts a shadow over what is shaping up to be the best tour ever.

The new chart numbers will be in from SoundScan Wednesday night, a day in advance of publication. I'll let everyone know just how good or bad the CD and single's legs are…

"John? What is it? What's wrong?"

I jerked my head. She was sitting there, a drop of blood on her finger, staring at me.

"We lost another crew member." Bloody hell, why hadn't I heard? Greg Maltin had died, and no one had mentioned it. "One of the lighting crew. Nice kid, very smart, very eager, loved his job. You met him, Bree. Back at the party at Pinewood, he was the kid with the apple juice and the pennywhistle, playing that Irish jig Mac was singing against, remember? Christ, he was in his twenties! What the hell could have happened? Too late to ring anyone now, but come tomorrow, I'm checking it out."

"Wow." She was sucking her fingertip, wincing a bit. "I remember him—he was really young. That's two people dying in, what? Nine days? What's up with that?"

"I don't know." I closed up the laptop, heading for my own meds, a good long cuddle, and some kip. "I just hope this doesn't mean we're in for a run of bad luck."

We did one show in Budapest, headquartering at the Grand in Vienna. Then it was on to Prague, and the tour hitting the vamped-up schedule with its double dates. And the whole time, niggling away at the back of my mind, was the reality of two deaths that shouldn't have happened.

I may not be the most observant bloke out there, but I'm not dim, either. Maybe I'd spent too much time around sudden death during the past couple of years, or maybe I'd just spent too much time dealing with our annoying detective chum, Patrick Ormand. Whatever the reason, those two deaths, Alain Descarres and Greg Maltin dying, had all my red flags at full hoist.

Like I said, I'm not dim. You've got to expect things to go wrong, especially on a tour this size, where the set has a major footprint. There's a lot going on physically, you know? People fall, they break ankles and arms; when you have to hire local people to help out, you add to the risk.

Blacklight's got a fantastic safety record. Hell, we'd gone three or four consecutive tours without a major injury on the part of our union crew. So two deaths in basically the first week of the tour, that just had all my nerves prickling.

We played two sensational gigs in Prague, back to back. That distracted me for a bit, because I'd mentioned my concern about my stage entrance bit getting stale, and of course that was a no-brainer, and everyone agreed.

The new routine Nial came up with involved a fake cock-up with Tony's piano. The plan was, he'd be sitting there, with just his head sticking up, and the blokes running the equipment from the underworld would stop it right there, make it look as if the entire piano had got itself stuck, you know? We'd all turn round and glare at him, waiting for it to work.

That took some rehearsing, getting the timing right, but once we got it down and premiered it, it brought down the house. Most of the audience had to be reading the reviews, or else they were reading Nial's blog, because they were obviously expecting the bit with me and the pointing hand. So when it didn't happen, but the piano looked to get stuck halfway up instead, the crowd went nuts, laughing and cheering. And the reviewers loved it, as well.

The morning after the Vienna show, I rang Ian right after my second cup of coffee and some room service breakfast. The news about Greg Maltin, about him being the second member of the crew to have died, was right there in my frontal lobes, and it wasn't going to let me relax, not until I'd had a couple of questions answered. Ian was the bloke who'd know.

Bree curled up on the bed next to me, snuggled hard against my left arm. I punched Ian in on my speed dial, and waited for him to pick up, in the suite down the hall.

"JP?" He sounded tense, but he usually did. Ian doesn't ever relax, not really, especially when we're in mid-tour. "What's up? I heard about Bree. How's she doing?"

"Hey, Ian." Bree was quiet, curled up. She'd taken her first meds for the diabetes, and I knew what she was doing: listening to her body, waiting for a difference. Me being here, up against her, she seemed to be digging that, and I wasn't going anywhere. "Yeah, it's JP. Bree's fine—she's right here, in fact. We're coping. Look, I want to ask you something. I saw the thing in your email, about Greg Maltin dying. What the hell happened, mate? Accident at the show? Because this is two crew members gone in a week."

"I know." He yawned; I could hear him do it, and it must have been a jaw-cracker. "Sorry, JP. It's been a long week. And yeah, I'm with you—two of our crew gone in a week, that's not good. But neither happened anywhere near the band or the venue. Both things happened the morning after the show. Nothing to do with us. Do you want more on what happened?"

"Yeah, I do." Outside, the weather was clear and gorgeous, but cold as hell. I wasn't looking forward to going out in that, and Russia was likely to be worse. "What have you got?"

He gave me some details. I kept my arm round my wife, rubbing her shoulder. She was warmer than she'd been, and a lot more relaxed. I caught her eye, blew her a kiss, and listened.

It turned out that the French kid who'd played the part of the pointing hand on opening night had been knocked down by a hit and run driver, sometime in the small hours of the morning after the show. Ian hadn't followed up—he had no grounds for asking the Paris police questions, and having dealt with some of the local *gendarmes* in the South of France myself, I couldn't see him fancying pushing it. But they'd come round and asked him some questions, after they'd found Alain Descarres dead by the side of the road a few blocks from where he'd apparently lived, out near La Defense.

"Okay." I was mentally sorting out a map of Paris in my head. "That's nowhere near Bercy, is it? That's out in the western bit."

"That's right." I heard a murmur in the background, a female voice. Right—this was Action Central for the tour.

"Is that Carla I'm hearing? Say hello to her for me."

"Yeah, I will. Anyway—from what I remember, the local cops told me he was probably hit by this car around six in the morning. Whatever he'd been up to, he was on his way home from something else. It had nothing to do with the show."

"Good." For some reason, my nerves were still tingling, on high alert, and I don't mean anything to do with my multiple sclerosis, either. "What happened to Greg Maltin, then?"

"He drowned."

I think my hand, the one resting on Bree, must have tightened up or something, because she went taut as a drumhead and there was no way in hell she could have heard a word Ian was saying. I made myself ease up—*come on, Johnny, pretend it's an MRI, all about the Zen, you can do it*—and waited for her to relax along with me.

"JP? You still there?"

"Yeah, still here, Ian. Details, please."

The story—I didn't know if it had hit Ian this way or not—was too much like the first one for my peace of mind. Same deal: long after the show, this time in Zurich, different part of town, no one saw what happened. All anyone seemed to know was that Greg, a bloke who was sharp and funny and dedicated to his craft, had been spotted by a local couple out for a sunrise jog along the east bank of the Limmat, Zurich's river. He'd been floating face down, well beyond any help. No one knew how he'd got into the river. No one had seen a damned thing.

"Right." I heard my own voice, and took in air. *Zen, Johnny. Just go Zen.* "This was off the Niederdorf? The east bank? No one saw what happened?"

"That's what the cops told me. They seemed to think he'd been high or something, that he put a foot wrong and fell in the river. Might have frozen, might have banged his head."

Right then, I got a major shock; Ian's voice was every bit as careful as mine was. Only reason I could think of for that was that maybe he didn't want Carla getting into this, didn't want her guessing that something was off. Of course, if the cops were right, there was nothing for anyone get into anyway, so why were we being so damned cautious?

The answer to that one was there as well, staring me straight in the face, not letting me wriggle off the hook. Greg Maltin had made his living crawling around catwalks that were thirty, fifty, seventy five feet off the ground. He'd been one of the people handling the lights at our live shows, high above the arena. He was as easy up there as a tightrope walker.

But apparently, we were supposed to believe he'd been dodgy enough on his feet, from booze or tiredness or just basic clumsiness, to have slipped off a nice wide riverbank into the icy water, and drowned there. I bit back what wanted out: *try it on the dog, mate. Not buying a fucking word of that. That's pants, rubbish, bollocks.*

Even if the incident had been isolated, Greg and just Greg, I wouldn't be buying that. It was crap. But he wasn't the only one; he was the second death.

Early morning hours, after a show. Two members of the crew, not senior members, but still, people who worked with us, for us. Two different shows, two different countries.

Shit does happen on the road, there's no way round that. We'd got a huge crew together for this tour—I didn't have exact numbers, but it was over a hundred people and maybe closer to two hundred. So yeah, the chance of something happening to someone was there. That wasn't what was making me edgy.

And I didn't know what was getting at me. Maybe it was because the two deaths seemed similar, somehow. Maybe it had to do with what a waste it was—those had been two young blokes, less than half my age. Dead in an alley in Paris, with your own apartment windows a block or so away, that was no way to die. And freezing to death, or choking on icy river water, that was just as bad, or worse. Death is a drag, no matter how or when it goes down. But this was just a pointless waste, you know?

I hadn't been close to either of them, but that didn't matter. They were with us, two of ours. They were Blacklight. They were family. That made whatever this was, if there was anything going on, our business and maybe our responsibility.

"JP?"

"Yeah, sorry. I was thinking." Bree had got up, and headed for the loo. She turned in the doorway, and smiled at me, and I mouthed a kiss at her. Soon as the door shut behind her, I heard my own voice change.

"Ian, look. I'm not happy about this. It smells all wrong to me—no, don't interrupt, Bree's gone to the loo and I don't want her worrying, she's got enough of her own stuff to deal with. If you hear anything else back from the cops, in Paris, in Zurich, wherever, keep me in the loop. Email me, leave a voicemail, something. Just between us, yeah?"

"Yeah, I will." The scary thing was, he didn't sound surprised. Maybe his nerves had been tingling, as well.

"Good." I heard the toilet flush. "Look, I have to go. See you at dinner, and remember, let's keep this quiet, all right? I don't fancy upsetting Bree, or anyone else. Not yet."

"You got it." He hesitated a moment, just a moment, but it was right there, and I knew I'd been right. He wasn't happy about any of this either. "Unless something else happens. That goes down, I've got no control over it."

"Something else?" The loo door was clicking open, and Bree was washing her hands. "What's that supposed to mean, mate? What are you on about? Such as?"

"I don't know that, do I?" His voice had flattened out. "With any luck, nothing at all. But this tour's already shaping up to be different from anything else we've seen. So who knows? See you at dinner."

Chapter Six

"...Good morning, welcome to Virtual Days, a happy 6 March to Blacklight fans and bloggers out there, and hello from beautiful (and really cold!) Stockholm. Sorry I've been so random these past few blogs, but crossing borders with a mass of trucks and personnel is always a major production.

Anyway, we've been getting the arena together for two shows here in Stockholm, and we still have what's probably going to be a long conference call with management and the band later on. Timing this stuff is tricky when we're in three separate countries, but thank goodness for conference calling—anyone ever wonder how we did this in the days before the internet and immediate telecommunication and all that lot? Anyway, it seems there are major doings afoot, so stay tuned..."

Prague, Munich, Mannheim, Cologne, Hanover, Moscow, St.

Petersburg, Helsinki. It had been one hell of a run, so far.

"Should I call down for more coffee?" Bree was emptying the last of a pot of good dark stuff into her cup. Room service at the Hotel d'Angleterre in Copenhagen had sent us up a nice healthy breakfast, but either they'd decided "healthy" meant that caffeine was bad for us and skimped on the French roast, or else we'd sucked down more of it than we thought we had. My money was on that option; like I said, we'd just had the hell of a run. We were all completely fragged out.

"I'll get to those major doings in just a minute, but first, I've been asked to thank every last one of you who went out and made your feelings about Book of Days known at the retail outlets and the radio stations too. Cheers, mates, and thanks for a job well done! Right now, for the first time since I've been with the band, we have the number one and two spots locked up on the UK singles charts: 'Remember Me' has a lock on the top spot, but 'Hammer It Home' debuted at #3, has already moved up to #2, and looks set to give 'Remember Me' a run for its money. We've got a pool going, taking bets on what 'Liplock' does. Pull up a chair, pass the popcorn, it's a Kinkaid-Sharpe deathmatch! Well, all right, not really—but the band sends its thanks, and so do we. And by the way, check back later this week as we announce the three winners of the 'Backstage With Blacklight' contest..."

"Yeah, more coffee would be good. Now I think of it, you might want to tell them to send up a few gallons of it. Everyone's coming up here for that conference call thing."

I stretched both legs, trying to be casual about it. The truth is, I ached from heel to hip, and there was a nasty little jolt running up and down my left side; the MS, after hanging back for the better part of three months, had suddenly remembered what it was all about and hit me, good and hard.

It wasn't quite bad enough to make me let Bree know about it, though. Adjusting to the new schedule—already packed solid for the rest of the European leg, and with the US leg looking to be jammed up as well—had been nearly as hard on her as it had on me. I was distracted and busy and my time was mostly booked up; Carla had us scheduled for press interviews, plus the shows and everything that went with them. No matter what I was doing, though, one corner of my attention seemed to have got my wife's name permanently hung over the door.

She'd been having trouble adjusting to the meds, which was worrying. They'd put her on something called glucophages, and some other meds, as well. Something about the pills was playing hell with her digestion. She watched her diet, and took her blood sugar readings—the numbers were coming down, which was a relief—but she still got dizzy and groggy at odd times.

I'd rung my mother-in-law back in San Francisco about it, and got snubbed. Miranda told me Bree seemed to be responding well, did I remember how long it had taken me to adjust to the anti-spasmodics and the heart meds, not to worry, Bree was very sensible and anyway she was a trained chef, so go play your shows, dear, and see you when you get home.

The conversation with Miranda had actually led to a funny moment. Her reminding me that Bree was trained to understand food gave me what felt like a brilliant idea; I got hold of Carla and got the name and location of the bloke who headed up our catering staff, who turned out to be a Frenchman called Sylvain Pantall. I rang him up, and we had a long conversation about Bree's diabetes, and how I wanted to make certain she'd be properly fed, and what did he suggest, and all that. Well, right, not a conversation, really, more like me rabbiting on, and him listening and agreeing. When I mentioned it to Bree the next day, I found out she'd had the same conversation with him three days ago, and with the head chef as well.

Anyway, we were tired, and stressed, and ready for home and a good long kip in our own beds. And we still had twenty-two dates left to play on the Euro leg, alone.

Room service showed up with a tray full of caffeine and nosh within five minutes of Bree ringing downstairs. Good timing, that was; the band showed up all together, this time with all the women in tow, as well. Ian had emailed us to let us know he wanted everyone in on this thing, families as well, so yeah, major doings, whatever it was.

It's funny how our suite always seems to wind up being the one place everyone fetches up in. It hadn't used to be that way; back when Bree was avoiding the public parts of my life, the band hadn't gravitated to any particular place. But since she'd started coming with, everyone seemed to want to come to us.

I mean, take that morning: our suite at the d'Angleterre was exactly the same suite the rest of the band had. But no one even suggested we congregate down the hall in Mac's suite, or Luke's, you know? No discussion or planning, or any of that; they all just headed straight for us, and they always do, now. It's a mystery.

One exception to that had been the Hedley-McElroy extended family. Luke and Karen, they came to us all right, but the girls didn't seem to fancy it as much. That was actually fine with me. I'm cool with Solange—I've known the girl since she was in nappies and I'm just as protective of her as the rest of her crazy rocker uncles are—but the idea of having Suzanne McElroy within arm's length of my bedroom put me off. And even though Bree quite likes Solange, I got the feeling she was just as happy to not have to be polite to Suzanne, either.

The entire band, wives and all, showed up right behind room service, settling in, perching on things, waiting for the extra chairs from downstairs. We'd arranged with Ian, who was back in London being mysterious and negotiating a few things, for a three-way conference call; Nial and Ronan were in Stockholm doing set-up with the crew, we were here in Denmark, Ian was at his own desk.

I don't know, now, what I was expecting off that call. Ian's pretty hard to faze, which is one reason he's such a fantastic choice as a manager. Also, he's been our road manager damned near forever, and he knows just how much we value our days off. It takes something major to make him set something like this up on a rest day, even on a more traditional relaxed tour schedule. Asking for it with the blocked-up schedule we were on, this had to be a huge deal, you know?

He didn't waste any time about getting down to it. He ran the roll call, band and personnel. He made sure everyone was there and listening. And then he dished.

"Look. I've got some news for you lot. I'm going to want input, and I need it pretty damned fast." He sounded almost shaken, and that made me sit up and take notice. I wasn't the only one, either. We all know our Ian.

"Come on, Ian." Mac let his voice carry, pitched it just right. Of course, he's a singer. "What's going on, then?"

"We've sold out all the American dates." He sounded more than shaken—he sounded stunned. "I just got off the phone with the Los Angeles promoter. They sold forty thousand tickets for the Staples Center in eighteen minutes. *Eighteen minutes*, guys. We've tacked on two more LA shows after San Jose—I told you were going to do that, right? Well. Those shows just sold out in twenty-four minutes. We could play three weeks solid just in LA, and sell out every show."

I opened my mouth, and closed it again. There was noise, people making little sounds, but I wasn't saying anything, not yet. No words, no breath. Was he joking…?

"And it's just as nuts everywhere else." He wasn't joking. Bloody hell. "Here's some numbers for you to try and wrap your heads around. San Jose: sixty thousand tickets in just under an hour. Glendale, thirty eight thousand tickets went in ninety minutes. That's bloody Glendale, in Arizona. New York, we knew about; those tickets went out ten days ago. Sixty thousand sold out in seventy five minutes. We snuck in one more show, and sold it out in half an hour."

"Are you serious?" Cal Wilson sounded as if he thought he'd just fallen down a hole in Wonderland. "Ian, what in hell is going on?"

"Chicago, three shows, seventy five thousand in an hour." I had a moment of wishing I could reach through the phone and shake him; our unflappable manager sounded like an old-fashioned vinyl record with the needle stuck in a single groove. "Want more? Guys, it's fucking nuts. I've never seen anything like this, and that's including the *Pick Up the Slack* tour. *Book of Days* is everywhere. "Remember Me" is still #1 in every damned market on the planet. "Hammer it Home" is in the top 3. Hell, "Liplock" just debuted at #7 in the US. Connie, over at Sound-Scan, says we'll have the 1-2-3 slots locked up in the US, UK, Japan, Australia, Germany and Italy by next week's charts. All of them, a clean sweep. That's ever been done before, and I mean never. Not the Beatles, not the Stones, not U2, not Elvis. Never."

He stopped. It suddenly occurred to me: *bloody hell, Ian's hyperventilating...*

"Ian, breathe. Breathe, and listen a second. I want to run some numbers out here. Tell me if they synch with yours." Carla had her little electronic palm device in hand; trust her to keep it grounded. It was a damned good thing someone could, because the rest of us were sitting there like a bunch of storefront mannequins, mouths open. Katia looked to be whispering something to herself under breath—*I don't believe it, I don't believe it.* Karen McElroy looked bewildered and out at sea.

"Do it." Ian still sounded punch-drunk. "I could use some good sensible corroboration on this one, Carla, believe me. Because what I'm looking at, the sums I came up with, I keep thinking, that can't be right, not possibly. Hit me with it. What's your math?"

"I make it ninety million in gross ticket sales." How in hell could she sound so calm, coming out with those numbers? "That's pounds sterling, of course, not dollars. Is that right? Does that jive with yours?"

"Oh, good, so I haven't gone completely off my nut." He swallowed hard, a thousand or so miles away. I had a quick mental image of him, in his office at Fallow House, door locked, trying to keep it together, not wanting to let the staff see him flipping his shit. "We're still seven weeks away from New York. And we've sold over eight million tickets."

"Crikey." Mac was up and out of his chair. "You said you needed fast input. What on? What's the problem?"

"Live Nation wants us to do another US leg over the summer, stadiums this time. I said fuck no, not a chance, the band is going to be wasted and we've already had to extend the tour, we're not in our twenties anymore. The bloke I was talking to damned near burst into tears. I was still on the phone with them and my other line went off—a cold call from somebody in the National Football League head office, for Christ's sake, offering us twenty-five million dollars for a partial sponsorship, if we do a package 'NFL Tour'."

"Holy shit!" Tony had found his voice, right round the same time he'd lost all the colour in his face. He's got your basic Italian olive skin thing going on, but right then, he was the colour of uncooked pasta. "The NFL wants to sponsor this?"

"Don't sound so surprised, Tony." Carla was clicking away at her palm thing, talking as she clicked, not even looking up. She's so damned competent, she scares me, sometimes. "My guess is, they've seen what we did for the hockey venue sales. They're not idiots—they want to leverage the exposure by putting us in football stadiums, and they're ready to pay for the privilege. Is that it, Ian? What did you tell them?"

"Yeah, that's it. I said I'd get back to them, I had to talk with you lot first. I'm afraid that if I say no, they'll offer us part owner-ship of a team, or something."

"Well, if they do, I have dibs on the Raiders." Bree sounded more amused than anything else. "Ian, you know I don't usually get involved in anything to do with the band's business. But this time, I have the feeling you really won't be like the manager in 'Spinal Tap' and wave a cricket bat at me if I put my two cents in. Because you're about to propose turning this into a mega-tour. Aren't you?"

"I'm not proposing anything, Bree, not yet. I'm just letting everyone know, and hoping you can all think about this, nice and fast. Once someone tells me you've hit a consensus, I'll propose something, for real."

He stopped. I wondered if he realised what a load of old bol-locks that was; of course he was proposing a mega-tour. I thought about saying something, but he'd moved on.

"We shouldn't be making this kind of decision right now any-way. Normally, I wouldn't even be bringing it up yet. But they're not letting up. If we decide to say yes, and tell them within the next three weeks or so, we can probably book every NFL stadium we want, and most of the larger Canadian sheds, as well. I worked up a rough after Live Nation rang."

"Good." Luke was on his feet, pacing. I caught something out of the corner of my eye, red hair moving; it was Karen, watching him pace. Gave me a warm feeling, that did, knowing there was someone there caring, worrying about what Luke did. He's been one of the best mates I've ever had, and he'd been alone and without anyone for a damned long time. "Because I've got a pe-culiar feeling of inevitability about all this, and I'd be curious to hear the roughs, Ian."

"So would I." It was Nial's voice, and I jumped; the production boys had been quiet this entire time, and I'd forgot he and Ronan were listening as well, out there in Sweden. "Because we'd have to build and adapt the concept to the larger venues. What kind of numbers are you looking at?"

"Early numbers?" Ian cleared his throat. "Just as a rough? Call it three months, between thirty and thirty-six cities, and as many shows as we feel like playing. If we double-stack the tour, it'd be around 50 shows, allowing for JP's Mondays off."

"What about the money?" That was Katia, and I caught Bree's eye, and grinned. "Is it okay to ask that?"

"You'd be an idiot if you didn't," Ian told her. "Besides, I was just coming to that. Suggestion? Everyone might want to sit down for this: If we stay with the same general ticket scale, it's an insane amount of money. I don't even believe it myself, and I did the calculations."

"Define 'insane', would you?" That was Cyn Corrigan, who usually left the business end of Blacklight entirely to Stu. Nice to hear the women putting their tuppence in.

"At least a hundred and sixty million." He waited for someone to say something, but no one did. "Probably closer to a hundred and eighty million. And that's pounds, not dollars. Today's exchange rate was about a dollar seventy to one pound."

"Gordon *Bennett*!" I heard my own voice, but my brain didn't seem to be driving it. "That's—Ian, are you serious?"

"Two hundred seventy million dollars, or right around that. The down side, of course, is that we swore we'd never do a mega-tour again, not after the Jubilation City, back in 1997." He paused. "I just want to make sure everyone's clear on the ramifications of this. If we do this, we'll have no excuse to not do Japan, and if we do Japan, we're going to be under massive pressure to do Australia and South America, and that would probably mean adding a stadium tour in Europe next year. We could be signing up for a death march, touring this beast into the ground until next Christmas or something. Two years on the road is a hell of a lot to ask. Don't think I'm not aware of it. The kids in the crew can do it, but us geezers might run out of gas at some point. It'd take every trick in the book to keep us going."

We'd gone quiet, all of us. Ian was right.

We'd been on the road a bare month, and I was already longing for a break, home, the cats and the San Francisco foghorns in the distance out under the Golden Gate, waking up in my own bed with Bree next to me, maybe staying fresh with a pickup Fog City Geezers gig at the Fillmore or Great American Music Hall. I'm not the kid I used to be; I'm in my mid-fifties, and I'm in iffy health. The other blokes didn't have anything serious wrong with them, but they're even older than I am. The idea of two and half bloody years of this made my stomach knot up; what Ian was talking about was a monster in the making.

Thing is, it wasn't as if he was pulling this out of thin air, you know? The tour he wasn't quite proposing was looking to be a monster because the CD itself had turned into a monster— something about it had hit a nerve somewhere, struck home across the board. Ian couldn't have predicted that happening. It's one of those things, it happens or it doesn't, no control over it. He was doing his job, showing us the situation, looking down the road at what was waiting down the long end of it.

"Give it some thought." He'd got the silence, what it meant. "I'm not pushing anyone to do anything at all, except to think about it. When you've done that, talk to each other, and then talk to me—Ronan, Nial, that includes your lot, as well. Have a great gig in Stockholm tomorrow night. I'll be back in time for Oslo."

Five minutes of eight on a rainy Wednesday night, and the houselights were still up in the London Dome.

"John! Are you ready for this? Three guitars! You and Luke and even me! Isn't this the coolest of cool things? I can't find anything that could be cooler. And I love all the noise coming

95

from this crowd, the hum, all of it. They are also ready. Are you ready? I'm ready!"

I turned round to look at Winston Dupres. He's one of the nicest people out there, especially for being a musician: killer good guitarist for Traitors Gate, Jamaica by way of South London. We'd met last year, at the Hall of Fame ceremony in New York; right now, he was bouncing even more than usual, which is saying something. Even his dreadlocks looked to be moving on their own.

"Yeah," I told him. "Absolutely ready. And yeah, I love the vibe off this audience, as well. Last night of the leg, that's always got some extra edge on it. You know that as well as I do. But if you think it's noisy now, wait until we open the second set and they see we've got guests."

He grinned, and as knackered as I was, I had to grin back. He's got this amazing smile, Winston has—he smiles at you and you've got to respond to it somehow, even if you can see nukes dropping out of the sky over his shoulder. But as much fun as this gig was likely to be, and as much love as was coming off that crowd out there right now, the day after tomorrow, ten hours on a plane and home to San Francisco at the other end of the ride, couldn't come fast enough for me. I was so damned tired, I could barely think straight. And this wasn't going to get any easier, either, not with what we'd told Ian to sign us on for. I just hoped a month off between legs was going to make a dent.

"Showtime." Mac had come up beside me, with everyone but Tony queueing up for their entrance. "Winston, great, you're here—Greg's back in the dressing room, sucking down vitamin water. You know Dom, don't you? Jamaica rules!"

If you want to know whose idea it had been to get Traitors Gate's lead singer and guitar player in to guest on "Hammer It Home" that night, I couldn't tell you. They'd been recording in Amsterdam during our gigs there, and stopped by during the first show. We'd had a nice reunion, all the way round—Gregory Carver, their lead singer, is as fierce about his politics as Mac is, and Greg had heard about Mac translating some of the angrier bits of the song into French, opening night of the tour in Paris. One thing led to another, and all of a sudden, there we were, adding some extra rehearsal time to a pretty tight schedule, so that Greg and Mac could work out how they wanted to handle a dual vocal, while Winston and Luke and I worked two guitar parts into three.

"Such nice things, last nights." Winston was bouncing, right along with Mac. "I love them, but do you know, I love the sleep the next morning even more. And is it true we might see Mick Hudson play tonight? Did I say a wrong thing?"

"Just touched an old memory, that's all." He really had. My head had gone back nearly thirty years, visiting my old friend Jack Featherstone, parked in his wheelchair in his London flat, wasted out, basically helpless and days away from dying. He'd had multiple sclerosis, the worst kind, rampaging through his system like a four-alarm, unable to walk, unable to play...

I flexed my fingers. "Don't know where that story came from, but it's the first I've heard of it. I haven't seen Mick since the eighties—he came along to see an old mate of ours, session bloke, brilliant bassist. Gorgeous jam we had. I wonder what old Mick's been up to these past few years. He's gone dark—hello, love."

"Hey, babe." Bree had come up next to me. "Did you remember your afternoon meds?"

"Yeah, I did. You look fantastic, Bree—did I tell you that already?"

She really did. She was dressed to the nines, but no surprise there—this was a closing night. She hasn't done much touring with Blacklight, but between the 2005 American tour and the Cannes thing, she'd got the last-night vibe down, and gone shopping to deal with it. It turned out Karen McElroy had a few quiet little shops out near Kensington High Street up her sleeve, places that catered to women rather than girls, and that worked out quite well, what with both of them being redheads. "Missed you this afternoon," I told her.

"You had time to miss me? Wow." She had her hair in a nice casual ponytail, which somehow made the dress—it was a bronze-coloured knee length thing that looked to be spray-painted on her—look even sexier. She'd got a bit of her normal body weight back, now that the diabetes was under control; it was nice to see some curves again. She was a head taller than I was right then, me being in nice sensible shoes for the gig, and her in four-inch killers. "Even though you were buried in rehearsal stuff? I'm flattered."

"Damn right I missed you." I got an arm round her waist and pulled her closer. "Oi! Bring your ear down here, lady, will you? I fancy a nibble. What are you staring at?"

She didn't answer, and I followed her look.

Solange Hedley, dressed down for a change, was hanging out near the dressing room door. Suzanne was with her, or rather, nearby. I'm not the world's most observant bloke, there's a lot I don't notice, but even at this distance, it was obvious there was some sort of tension in the air. Solange wasn't looking at Suzanne, and Suzanne, for once, didn't seem to know what to do.

"There they are again." Bree was still staring at the girls, Solange not smiling, seeming to ignore her friend and potential step-sister, Suzanne looking awkward and uncertain. "Does anyone actually know them? Who are they with, anyway?"

"What?" For a mad moment, I wondered if she'd lost her mind. Then Suzanne moved, out and away from the dressing room door, and I saw who Bree had been looking at, over her shoulder. I caught the flutter of headscarves, not quite matching, embroidered with sparkly beads, and a pair of identical faces, curly dark hair, big dark eyes and designer gear. "Oh, right. You're talking about the Tahini Twins. Got it."

"Well, duh!" She turned to stare at me. "Who else?"

"Doesn't matter." I watched the twins ooze out of the dressing room—there really doesn't seem to be a word that covers how they moved, those two. One of them said something to Suzanne; the girl tilted her head, looking after Solange, but Solange had sauntered off alone towards the family section, not looking back. I saw Suzanne flush, and put her teeth into her lip; the other twin laid a hand on her arm. Suzanne nodded, as if she'd come to a decision about something, and the three of them moved away, disappearing into the crowd.

"Ah, the Doe-Eyed Darlings of the Dressing Room." Mac had watched them go; I couldn't tell from his voice or his face, either, what he really thought about them. "You know who they are, don't you? Daughters of a certain oil baron potentate from a luxury resort area of Arabia? All Gucci heels and micro-skirts and modest little head coverings. I've met their dad a couple of times—he was at my school. Good devout Muslim, if you ignore his taste for pricey cigars and fifty-year-old cognac."

"Oh, bloody hell, is that who they are?" That explained it, all right, at least if Mac meant who I thought he did. "That's the bloke who's opening that island place out in the Gulf? I remember reading about that, back before we opened the tour."

"That's them." Mac reached behind his head and rolled his neck, limbering and loosening. "Very weird, them wanting to hang out backstage with a bunch of geezers, but it seems to be what they want. And what daddy's little girls want, they get. Rumour has it the old man dotes on them."

"Mostly, they get what they want." Domitra had been talking to Winston, dancing in place, stretching her hamstrings, getting ready to move. "Not always. Mac, you heading onstage? It's eight o'clock, dude."

That show was brilliant, one of the best we'd done in a tour without a single humdrum performance so far. Between the last-night energy and the sheer uproarious boost of having Greg and Winston playing with us, we damned near blew the roof off the London Dome. The new bit of business we'd come up with at the beginning of the show—Stu, waiting for his drums to come up on a riser from the underworld and having only a stool and then some drumsticks come up instead—went off perfectly.

The first set was killer, as good as we'd played, but that second set was fantastic. Mac always has a bit of extra sparkle on closing nights anyway, but when we opened the second set, the relentless noise of the instrumental that leads into "Hammer It Home," and the audience realised we had guests, that half the personnel of Traitors Gate were coming up out of the underworld and sitting in, things went straight into overdrive, and stayed there for the rest of the night.

Arms around each other, bowing. Mac spraying the audience with champagne, something he hadn't been doing on this tour, but he did it tonight, and the crowd loved it. Out for an encore, and then a second one—we only do one, usually, but again, that's the prize the fans get if they score tickets to a closing gig, the band throwing everything out there. After all, with a month off beginning as soon as the house lights went up, there wasn't any reason to hold anything back.

"Am I off my nut, or is it not nearly as crowded in here as usual?" We were in the dressing room during the break between the first and second encores. I was towelling down and sucking down mineral water; next to me, Luke had splashed his face with cold water and found a bottle of juice. "I mean, nice to be able to move without banging into someone, but where is everyone?"

"Probably still in their seats. It's pretty obvious we're giving them another encore tonight. Where's Bree?"

"You just missed her." I finished the water, and reached for another one. Both legs were shaky enough as it was, I'd spent most of the second set on the stool, but not staying hydrated, that makes them even worse. "She came in for some water, and went back out again. What's wrong, Luke?"

He was looking across the room, at his daughter. Solange had come in, and she was on her own. Luke muttered something under his breath.

"Girls not getting on well?"

"Damn. No, they're not." He turned round and looked at me. "I think they've had some sort of row. Don't seem to be talking to each other much. And I'll tell you what, JP, this is one of those times when I really haven't got any clue what to do. Truth is, Suzanne's a handful. She and Solange have been friends since they were kids, and I wouldn't say this to Karen, but Suzanne's pretty spoiled. Only child, dad died early, and she's all Karen had for a good long time. But Solange isn't spoiled, is she, JP? It's a damned miracle, considering how useless I was as a dad most of the time, but she just grew up real."

"Useless?" I stared at him. Ian was in the doorway, which meant we were about to be booted back onstage. "Oh, please, mate, you were a superb dad. And Meg Fallow helped, Luke, no denying that—Solange would have grown up very different if Meg hadn't been there. But…"

I stopped. *Shit.* Suzanne McElroy, that subject was something I really felt uncomfortable talking about at all, especially to Luke. Thing is, it had just occurred to me that he didn't know…

"What?" He'd set the empty juice bottle down, and was looking me straight in the eye. "But what?"

"I really didn't want to hassle you with this." Right. If I had to talk to him about it, might as well keep it lightweight, you know? "Just my own shit, Luke, really not a problem. I'm dealing, Bree's dealing. Thing is, Suzanne's hit on me a couple of times. She did it first time I met her, back in 2005—yeah, I know, she was a schoolgirl. Shocked the hell out of me. But…" I trailed off again.

"Go on." He sounded grim. "But…?"

"She did it again, down at Draycote. That was at your New Year's do. And she did it in front of Bree—gave me a couple of bad days, there, but Bree knows me. I've never cheated on her, and she knows it. Not a big deal, Luke, not really. Just let it go, yeah? We did."

"Why didn't you say something?" Bloody hell, he was furious. "Did she stop?"

"Well, we didn't want to hit you with that, not when you and Karen were so new. And Suzanne was rooming with Solange. Besides, she pretty much stopped. Bree and me, we're solid, and that shows, doesn't it? And Suzanne, she's not dim. She threw the glove down, my wife nailed her, end of story." I laid a hand on his arm. "Relax, Luke, okay? There's no damage done."

"Maybe not, JP, but I wish you'd told me. Bree's had enough to deal with, without having my stepdaughter making it worse." He shook his head. "I'm worried about that girl. She's getting into bad habits, hanging with people she'd do better to avoid like the plague. I don't know how to bring it up to Karen."

"Your what?" Ian was waving us out, and the lights were flickering—*showtime!* The noise from the arena was building to where we could barely hear each other. "Luke, what did -"

"We got married in Amsterdam." He grinned suddenly, huge and wide and relaxed, and I couldn't help it, I grinned right back at him. "Mac knows, and Dom. You're the only other person who knows, and yes, don't even ask, of course you can tell Bree. Just—keep it quiet for now, will you? We're going to announce it when everyone's home, at the end of the week. Just a quiet little thing, no big deal. Both girls, Mac was best man, he and Dom were our witnesses. We'll have the party for it down the road sometime, when we're done with this tour."

"Gordon *Bennett!*" We were at the door to the dressing room now, and the crowd noise was a wave, breaking over everyone, nearly knocking us backwards. There were points of light all over the London Dome; ten years ago, the fans would have been waving their lighters, but these days, the lights are mostly the screens on cell phones. "Right, no worries, I'll keep it quiet. But congratulations, mate. I'm damned glad to hear it. Karen's great. It looks like you've found your heart again, after all these years."

"Nope. I lost it, once I found Karen." Up the ramp, out into the roar and the darkness, the bare innovative stage with its rows and circles of lights set into the floor. Above our heads, the light trusses rotated, the computer fixing the spots, changing colour. We paused, just a moment, before we headed off to our own circles of light. "What's wrong, JP?"

"Nothing." It was a lie, but the kind it's okay to tell. Truth was, just for a moment, I'd remembered Greg Maltin up there, careful and smart, agile as an acrobat or maybe one of our cats. "Here we go. Showtime. Let's put this leg to bed, and head home."

Chapter Seven

"…Hey there, Blacklight fans! Sorry I've been neglecting this blog for the past week, but now that we've actually got a few weeks' rest between tour legs, I took the opportunity to actually sleep in and put my brain in snooze-mode. Of course, when I say 'a few weeks off,' I'm talking about the band. For the production and build teams, it's closer to a week. And even that only came after we'd worked out what modifications were going to be needed for the newly announced US stadium leg."

"I don't know, Mom—let me check with John, okay?"

I looked up from the laptop screen. Bree was on the phone, I was at our big kitchen table reading Nial's Virtual Days blog, and all three cats had set up what looked to be security checkpoints in the kitchen: *right, don't try anything, we know you're up to something but we've got our eye on you, you're not leaving again for a bit, not without getting past us first.* It was still foggy outside, at ten in the morning, but that was going to burn off, I could tell. Nice basic April morning in San Francisco. I was damned glad to be home again, even for a little bit. And I was exhausted.

It was ten days into what felt like the most welcome rest break I'd ever had in my life, ten days of sleeping in my own bed, ten days of eating Bree's cooking and hanging out at home, at 2828 Clay Street. I hadn't done a damned thing that required any particular energy since we'd got home; about the most work I'd had to do was scooping catboxes. And that was just as well, because that was about the upper limit of my energy.

It was nuts. There was no reason I could think of for being this knackered, unless it was age catching up to me. I mean, okay, so we'd doubled up on the Euro tour dates. We'd played a lot more shows than I'd psyched myself up for doing. I'd known I'd be coming home tired. But I wasn't recouping nearly as fast as I needed to. We were due in Boston for four days rehearsal in less than three weeks, and right now, I didn't even want to leave the house.

I wasn't going to get a vote on that one, though. Tomorrow was going to be a total drag, and I knew it; the day was due to start out with a full-scale MRI. I was going straight from there to my cardiologist's office for the usual battery of heart tests. And, as if that wasn't enough, we'd be fetching up with my regular doctor for my annual physical. In a moment of what now looked to be complete insanity, I'd decided to get all the annual medical shite taken care of in one day. Yeah, I know. But it had seemed bright at the time. And at least the cardio bloke and my doctor were in the same building. Poor Bree, who drives me everywhere, was in for a long day…

"Mom wants to know if she can buy us dinner tonight." Bree had her hand over the mouthpiece. "Don't say yes if you really don't want to, okay? I can always just cook something, if you'd

105

rather hang out here. But we haven't seen her since we got back, and, well…"

"Yeah, sure—love to see her." It wasn't one of those marital fibs people get into the habit of telling, either. I quite like Bree's mum; she's been right there for Bree for as long as I can remember, no matter what the deal was. And there'd been too many times, early on, when Bree'd needed her because I hadn't been there for her. "Tomorrow's looking to be pretty grim. I could use something special by way of dinner tonight, you know? I don't mind who cooks it, you or a restaurant."

"*…catching up on some shoutouts, now that the heavy lifting part of getting ready for America is done. We've never done anything quite like this before, jumping straight from hockey arenas to football stadiums with a month to gear up, so we had to take a good long look at how to accommodate certain aspects of the stage set-up—the biggest issues were how to hang the video veil and fly the line arrays in a building without a roof. Good thing I'm surrounded by clever people, and we got it done with some time to spare…*"

"Mom says, how about Angelino's? She'll drive."

"Sounds good. Actually, it sounds better than good. I could fancy some seafood." I bit back a yawn. For all that I can't stand dealing with the medical stuff, I was glad I was seeing my various doctors tomorrow. I suspected a lot of my tiredness had to do with the change in the way Bree and I ate; with the diabetes, she'd begun going much more toward veggies and grains, and there seemed to be a lot less meat in the diet. Maybe I was short on a vitamin, or something. "Or a plate of that braised beef thing they do, with the noodles. Or no, sod that, I think a nice big steak. Something with a lot of blood in it, anyway."

"*If you're reading this, you probably already know that not only is Book of Days topping the charts worldwide, we've also locked up the three top spots on the US and UK singles charts. Here's a small way of us saying thanks for supporting the band: if you've registered as an*

All Access fan club member, click the prompt next to your password next time you log on, to receive a free ringtone of "Hammer It Home" for your cell phone. This is for phones that support realtone technology, and isn't going to be made available anywhere but here…"

"Have I been shorting you on the B12? Are you feeling anaemic?" Bree sounded worried, and I glanced up. Damn. She was worried, all right. "I know I've been focussed on adjusting the diet, but damn, I didn't think about whether you were getting enough of what you need. John, why didn't you say something?"

"Oi! Bree, knock it off, all right?" There she went again, obsessing over stuff. "All I said was, I could do with a nice steak. That's a comment, love, not a complaint. I'm a big boy. If I want something, I'll ask for it. And actually, that whole less meat deal is probably just as good for me as it is for you. Last I looked, my cholesterol was okay, but with an iffy heart, I'm probably better going without, or at least with less of it than I used to eat."

She wasn't looking convinced. I leaned across the table and knuckled her lightly under the chin.

"Bree, love, look. We're not babies, you and me. You've got the diabetes to cope with, I've got the MS and the heart and who knows what else. And we *are* coping—you're doing a brilliant job." I grinned at her. "Truth is, I'd have been meat myself, without you there looking after me."

"Just so long as I can trust you to tell me if you want something." She wasn't smiling. "Promise?"

"I'll tell you. That's a promise."

I went back to reading Nial's blog. Bree, rinsing the breakfast dishes and putting them in the dishwasher, was singing under her breath: it sounded like "Can't Buy Me Love," a Beatles song that had topped the charts when she'd been a toddler.

"For those of you who like to keep up with what the band gets up to offstage, the big news comes from Luke Hedley: I've finally been given the go-ahead to officially announce that Luke and his girlfriend,

Blacklight web design consultant Karen McElroy, were married in Amsterdam during the band's European tour. While Luke and Karen's daughters have been friends for many years, their respective parents only became aware of each during the past year..."

"Anything new and interesting going on?" Bree was scooping dry food into the cats' food dish. "Anything we don't know?"

"Not really, except that they finally made the public announcement, about Luke and Karen. Oi!" Something was bumping into my ankles. I reached down and scratched Simon, our youngest and dimmest cat, behind the ears; he was giving me a *feed me, I'm being forcibly starved* look. "No good sucking up to me, mate. Go talk to Bree, she's the one with the tin opener."

"Were you heading down to the studio?" Bree sat down next to me. "Because if you're going to be downstairs and you don't need me for anything right now, I ought to get some groceries and cat food and whatnot. We're low on everything. And tonight we're going out, and tomorrow's booked solid."

"Yeah, you go shop, or get a massage, or whatever, love." I opened my email, and began tagging spam to delete. "I've got some new stuff I want to record. I promised Luke and Mac I'd send it along. Anyway, I've got an itch to play the Byrdland."

"Okay—John? What is it?"

I'd said something, muttered, exclaimed, whatever. I'd been staring at the computer, but I looked up at Bree.

"Someone's gone missing."

I hadn't really given too much thought to those two deaths back in Europe, not since we'd got home. Out of sight, out of mind, all that rubbish—I just hadn't been thinking about that, because there wasn't any reason to.

But I suspect it was probably sitting there at the back of my head the whole time, just waiting for something to hook my attention straight back into it. And the hook had just shown up, halfway down the list of unread emails: *Sender, Phil MacDermott.*

Subject, Urgent request for info re missing staffer.

I clicked on the email, and opened it. Bree settled in next to me, reading along with me, squinting because her glasses were across the room.

From: Phil MacDermott

To: mac@knifesharpe.co.uk; scorrigan@irisheyes.co.uk; lukeh@blacklightband.co.uk; calwil@bunkerbrothers.co.uk; jpkinkaid@blacklightband.co.uk; tmancuso@bombardiers.net; Carlafanucci@fanuccipros.com; Ops; Production

Date: 13 April 2008

Subject: Missing Security staffer

I've just been rung up by the police in Manchester. Apparently, one of the local people we hired on as supplemental security for the Manchester shows at the end of March has been officially listed as a Missing Person, and the family has asked the police to open an investigation.

The missing staffer is a local Mancusian, name of James Morse. He lives alone, so it took awhile for anyone to realise he'd gone missing, but it now appears he never made it home after the 28 March show at the Evening News Arena.

I've promised the Manchester police full cooperation with their investigation. I'm taking this situation as seriously as I am taking it personally, so if anyone has any information, or can help by offering any information about Morse's whereabouts after the show ended, I'd appreciate it. Phil.

Shit. Another one.

"But -" Bree was tight up against my right arm, and there was trouble in her voice. "John, wait a minute. Does this make three times in a month that someone had something happen to them after a Blacklight show? Or am I losing my mind?"

"You're not losing your mind," I told her, and nearly jumped at how grim I sounded.

Another one. Small hours after the show, nowhere near the

band; hell, we'd walked offstage and straight into limos. The limos had taken us to Manchester airport, we'd got on our jet—two jets, actually, because the larger one we'd wanted had been booked out by someone else and we'd had to take two smaller ones, leaving in shifts. We'd strapped ourselves in, flown south to London, and slept like babies at our posh digs at the Four Seasons Canary Wharf, on the Isle of Dogs.

"Yeah," I told Bree. "This is three. And I don't like it, Bree. I don't like it at all."

"No. No, neither do I."

We were staring at each other, and it suddenly hit me: she'd been smelling something wrong about this, just as I'd been. Somehow, the whole issue had got lost in the cracks of being on tour, finding out about her diabetes, adjusting to meds, getting home. And yeah, I know I miss things sometimes, but this wasn't anything I'd have thought about anyway.

One death, that first one in Paris, that might have been just bad luck, you know? Like I've said before, shit does happen on tour. But Greg Maltin dying had put my warning lights on high, because even if Greg hadn't been about the last bloke on earth to get drunk or stoned and stumble into an icy river, two in two weeks was a bit much to swallow.

Now this made three, and there was no way in hell I was believing this was coincidence, or bad luck, or whatever. Not a chance. It was the same deal, all over again: show's over, band's gone, nothing to do with us except that these people were family, even the ones we'd hired for a night or two. They were there because of us. And that meant I couldn't just shrug my shoulders, ignore it, act as if it was nothing to do with Blacklight. Three people were dead, and they'd worked for us.

Hold on a minute, Johnny. Just hold on. How do you know this Morse bloke is dead?

I got another shock right then, realising that it never occurred to me he might still be alive somewhere. Phil's email, that said missing, not dead. But after Alain Descarres in Paris, and Greg Maltin in Zurich, I'd have taken any bet right then, laid any odds, against James Morse still being among the living.

"John?" Bree was watching me, waiting. "Look, what do you think we should do? Is there anything we can do?"

"Yeah, love, there is." I don't know when the idea had hit me, or if it had just been sitting there, waiting for me to get round to noticing it. "I'm thinking an expert opinion might be just what's wanted. Can you put off the shopping for a few minutes, please? And I need to use your cell."

It had been over a year since I'd had any contact with Patrick Ormand, homicide detective for the SFPD, and I can't honestly say I'd missed him much.

There's history there. We'd always been a bit sniffy round each other—okay, right, truth is, the sniff was mostly on my side, but it's not like there aren't reasons for it, you know? Our first encounter with the bloke, back when he was with NYPD on the other coast, he'd tried nailing Bree on a murder rap. He'd used every cop cliché he could dig up to do it, too: lying about what he knew, setting traps, the lot. He hadn't missed a trick.

So I really didn't have any immediate plans to pencil his name in on my Top Five People I Want To Hang Out With list. I'd won that first round, because of course Bree never killed anyone. But that first encounter, that had set the tone. The bloke was a hunter, a predator, and he was never going to be anything else.

We'd had a lot of interaction since then, most of it official, some of it personal. He'd got bored with New York—he was a bit of a job-jumper, was Patrick. Anyway, he'd changed offices and coasts, a couple of years back. I hadn't been especially pleased to find him in charge of the investigation into the death of the lead singer for the Bombardiers, but I have to admit, having him around had been useful to me since then. Whatever I thought of his trustworthiness on a personal level, I did trust him to hunt down facts and hand them over, without adding a lot of rubbish to the basics.

Besides, he'd let Bree off when he could have put her away on an accessory charge. But the fact that I owe him doesn't mean I was ever going to like him.

So hearing that official-sounding little snap in his voice when he picked up the phone and told me that he was Ormand and I was ringing homicide, that was always going to have this nasty effect on my nervous system. It didn't matter why I was ringing him, might have been to invite him to a party or ask after his mum, assuming he had one—it didn't matter. I always felt my nerves tighten up, heard a little voice whispering at the back of my head: *look sharp, Johnny, here we go, there's another pissing contest about to happen, and you can't let him win, you need to come out on top.*

"Homicide, Ormand speaking. Bree? Is that you?"

"Right. Hang on a mo, will you?" I cleared my throat, and put the phone on speaker, so that Bree could hear. I'd forgotten that her name and number showed up on his caller ID. "Hello, Patrick. It's JP, but Bree's here, too. How are you?"

"Fine." He wasn't usually quite this terse, but after all, he was at work, and considering his work, I'd probably taken his attention away from sticking bamboo under someone's fingernails to get them to confess, or measuring a corpse's nose hairs, or something. "How are you both? I thought you were on tour, JP."

"We are. This is the rest break between the first two legs." I stopped for a moment—the way it came out, I wondered why that phrase never sounded if I was talking about pornography before. "The Euro and US legs, I mean. We're back out in a few weeks, starting rehearsals in Boston for the American leg." I took a breath. "Look, would it be possible to get together, for maybe an hour? There's something come up, and Bree and I both thought a professional opinion would be good. Can we give you lunch? Are you busy?"

"No, I'm not busy. I wish I were." He sounded as if he meant it. "Sounds intriguing, whatever it is. Not another research project for me, by any chance?"

His voice hadn't changed, but I found myself tightening up for a few seconds. I knew what he meant. He was talking about the favour he'd done me last year, researching the truth behind the story of the man whose work was the main reason I'd ever picked up a guitar in the first place. Long story, but a boy had died, who shouldn't have died, and that had worried me enough to ask Patrick to use his professional connections to get me the truth, to hunt down the facts.

Well—he'd had got the truth for me, all right. And the truth had been bad enough. Thing is, Patrick didn't know how bad, and he wasn't going to, either. We knew something Patrick didn't, me and Bree. Besides, that whole thing about not killing the messenger? You might get it with your head, but that doesn't stop you wanting to bash the bloke who delivers the bad news...

"JP? Are you still there?"

"Yeah, I am. Sorry." I shook it off. This was business, but it was going to be on our turf. That made it easier. It's what Bree calls the home field advantage, and it's a lot different from sitting in the reception area at the cop shop, waiting on his convenience. "Soon would be best, if we can synch up the timing. Problem is, tomorrow I've got medical bullshit all day and I don't know how the day after would -"

"What about today?"

I opened my mouth, and shut it again. Across the kitchen table, Bree was looking at me, her own mouth half-open. I met her eye, and saw she was thinking the same thing I was: for a busy homicide detective being dragged away from his desk in the middle of the week and the middle of the morning by an ageing rocker who didn't much like him, Patrick Ormand was pretty damned eager to accommodate us.

Still, it was up to Bree, since she was the cook around here. I mouthed the question at her—*all right?*—and she nodded.

"Yeah, today works." Right. If he was going to be this helpful, I was damned well going to take advantage of it. Besides, I was curious, about why he sounded so restless. "Half past twelve work? Or would later be better...?"

He rang the front doorbell at just before one. With a good two hours in hand between Patrick ringing off and me opening the front door to let him in, Bree'd made a fast run on the local market. She came back with stuff for lunch, and put together a salad with about eight different kinds of meat and fish in it—the market's got a pricey deli section, so everything Bree needed was right there, and she knew what she wanted and where it was behind the long glass counter. She never messes up, not when it's a matter of a good meal.

When I let Patrick in, he was standing in full sunlight, and I had this bizarre sensation, really peculiar, that one of us had got stuck in time, or something. He didn't look older, or different. It was like someone had put him in a glass box for a year, like someone in a fairy tale. Or maybe cold storage, one of those body-sized freezers down there at Homicide HQ.

I couldn't see a damned thing that showed he'd aged at all since the last time I'd seen him. He's got those sort of looks anyway, where it's tricky even guessing age within five years, but even his damned hair didn't look to be receding. He wasn't even human enough to be showing grey.

"Hey, JP." He was on the doorstep, looking at me. He can do the one-eyebrow-up trick, same as I can, and he was doing it just then. "Something wrong?"

"Not a thing." There was no way was I going to give him the

satisfaction of telling him he looked fantastic, especially when I knew damned well I was showing my age. The little pouches under my own eyes had gone puffy with tiredness, and I'd actually lost a bit of weight I couldn't really afford to lose. Touring is hell on the body, no matter how much luxury you're allowing yourself—standing onstage and producing two and a half hours of music takes a lot of energy, and when you're changing time zones, it gets a lot worse.

I held the door open, and stepped aside. "Come on in—there's lunch ready on the table. There's a pot of coffee ready, as well. Bree put everything together already—we didn't know how long you could stay."

"As long as I need to." He followed me down the long hall. "No one's going to get on my case if I'm gone a couple of hours. Where—ah, there we go."

He stopped behind me. Farrowen, Bree's Siamese, had wandered in from the front room to investigate; she was busy sniffing Patrick's trouser legs, and making the sort of little deep-voiced shirty noises in her throat that Siamese all seem to do. So of course, Patrick being a cat fancier, he spent a couple of minutes giving Farrowen her due, getting two fingers under her chin and scratching her, getting her to stretch out her neck. Ten seconds of that, and the purring was rattling the walls. Him fancying cats, that's one of the few things I actually like about him. And all three of ours quite like him, as well. That probably means he can't be as bad as I think he is. Either that, or our cats are piss-poor judges of character.

"Patrick! Long time, no see." Bree offered a hand. "I don't know about you two, but I'm starved. You know, I really thought this whole thing about having to eat a lot of tiny meals during the day instead of three normal ones was going to make me crazy, but it isn't. I guess that means the diet is working. That's a good thing, right?"

"Diet?" Patrick, waiting for me to finish loading my plate with salad and bread, took a good long look at her, head to toe. "Why in the world would you think you needed to go on a diet?"

I took a deep breath. *Right. Mustn't bash the nice copper, Johnny.* That was one thing wasn't changing any time soon—he could tell me he didn't want to get into Bree's knickers until he ran out of breath, but those particular hackles were always going to stand to attention. And what's more, the bugger knew it. He'd just given her the full laser beam thing he does, as if he could see straight through to her skin.

"I'm not dieting to lose weight—this is doctor's orders." If Bree'd noticed that look of his, she wasn't copping to it. She explained about the diabetes, and of course, that was five minutes of Patrick sounding horrified, and asking questions and all the rest of it. Yeah, he doesn't fancy Bree. Right.

"So, what's going on?"

We'd finished lunch, and cleared away. Bree suggested we go sit in the garden, so we took our coffee and headed out of doors. It was a good call; the fog had burned away and the weather was nice and soft.

"We're not sure. That's the problem." I'd been turning the whole thing around in my mind, wondering how to get what I needed, what to ask. "Basic thing is, we've had two deaths on this tour so far, and this morning I got an email from our head security bloke—you remember Phil MacDermott from back in New York, yeah?—saying one of the locals we'd hired for the gigs in Manchester had gone missing."

"Two people died?" Patrick's eyes are the colour of dirty ice, and when he concentrates, they go scary as hell. He was concentrating now. "And a third's missing? Wow. Is that level of loss usual on a tour?"

"Usual?" I blinked at him. "Of course not. Why do you think we rang you? Possible, yeah. But it's not so much the numbers that are hitting my buttons, it's that all of them seem to be so much alike."

"How?" Oh, bloody hell, now I'd done it, pushed him into full hunter mode. You couldn't miss it. He was practically baring his teeth. "Can you be more specific, JP?"

I gave him the story—hell, this was why I'd asked him to come in the first place. He sat there, listening, not saying anything. I've got to give him that—he's a fantastic listener, but of course, that's part of his gig. And he's one of those people that listens with their whole body. It's not so much that he's hearing information, more like he's absorbing it straight through the pores.

"Okay." He was tapping two fingers on the table, *rat-tat*, a fast little drumbeat in four-four timing. "You know, JP, I see why your buttons were pushed—I'm just surprised more people haven't picked up on something, here. The MO in those first two are close enough to send the odds of it being coincidental up into the stratosphere. Is there any way I could get some more details about this? Right now, I'm particularly interested in this missing person case. That's Manchester? England, right?"

"Yeah, England, up in the northwest. I haven't got anything particular about the two deaths—what I got sent was just the notice, that the band as a family sent flowers, condolences, whatever. But if it's the Manchester thing you want, yeah, I've got Phil's email about it. You can have a look at that." I got up. "Computers are inside. Bree, no, you put those down, damn it! We can carry our own cups. Hell, we'll be your roadies—you relax, love, all right?"

"Okay." She smiled at me, one of those smiles, the kind she only ever gives me when we're sharing a moment that no one else is likely to get. No clue why I was getting one just then, but I'll take it, whenever she wants to offer it. I gave her smile right back again, and we headed inside. I was thinking it was funny, that look of hers, that moment just between us, seems to happen mostly when Patrick Ormand is on the premises.

She rinsed cups while I opened my email. There were new messages, but nothing Patrick needed to see. I found Phil's email, brought it up, and stepped aside to let Patrick read it.

He read it, all right. He read it through at least three times. Maybe I'm getting more observant in my old age, but whatever— I could actually see what he was doing, as he did it. First time he read it, I saw him reach the end, stop, process a bit, go back up for a second look-through. That time, he was a bit slower about it, and his lips moved just a bit. *Memorising*, I thought, and then I saw his eye go back to the top of the screen and read it one more time. Don't know what that was all about, unless he was extracting what he wanted from the lot.

"All right." Apparently, he'd got what he needed; he turned away from the screen entirely, and focussed on me. "I don't know anyone over there to talk to, not on a professional level, but I can call Pirmin Bochsler at Interpol, and ask him if he's heard anything. But you said you wanted an opinion. An opinion of what, exactly?"

"Of the smell." We'd locked up eyes again, staring at each other, but this time, for a change, we were on the same side of the divide and there was no reason to dance about. Just for once, we weren't being sniffy, or pissing on trees; there wasn't any need. "Could be I've spent too much time hanging round with a copper and his mates, but I've been twitchy since I heard about that kid dying in Paris."

I stopped. Something was there, wanting me to look at it. And if it was anything I didn't want to look at, there was a damned good chance Patrick Ormand was going to make bloody sure it was pushed right up in my face.

"Somehow, I don't get the feeling it's the guy who died in Paris that's setting your alarms so high." How in hell he does it, I don't know, but he does it every damned time. If he wants to know something, and you don't even want to think about it, you're in deep shit. "And the missing person case is still just that, although I agree with you, it reeks to high heaven."

I was quiet. He looked at me, one eyebrow up.

"What is it, JP? The second death?"

"Yeah." I swallowed hard. "Greg Maltin."

There it was, right in my face. No more twisting to get away from it. I'd just remembered, just realised, what had set me on this particular bit of rocky road in the first place.

"He was one of our regulars, you know?" I was talking it out, slow and careful. "On the Blacklight payroll for the 2005 tour, and this one as well. Spent most of his life up in the rigging. Ian Hendry told me the Swiss police said they thought he must have been drunk, or high. Lost his footing, fell in the river, the river was ice cold. He'd have been dead within a couple of minutes if no one had helped him out." I stopped, took in some air. *Shit, shit, shit.* "Or if someone made sure he couldn't get out."

"Why are you so sure?" Patrick's eyes looked like slits in concrete right about then, grey ice in grey stone. "Because you are, aren't you?"

"Yeah, I'm sure. Greg didn't drink." I'd remembered, all right, and it had taken me far too long to remember. I couldn't lay that one at Patrick Ormand's doorstep—it was my own mention to Bree, me reminding her that she'd met him at the Pinewood party, that had done it. I'd said that days ago, weeks ago, and I was only just making the connection now. Maybe I'm dim, after all. "Not a drop, Patrick, not even beer. He didn't smoke pot, either. I remember, I actually cracked a line about it, during the kick-off party, about me and him and Cal Wilson being the only dry guests at Pinewood that night. He was drinking apple juice. He said…"

I stopped again. My own throat had gone dry as a bone.

"That's right. I remember." Bree was very pale. She reached

119

out suddenly, and I got hold of her hand and just hung on to it. Her fingers were chilly. "I was standing next to you and he said something about being able to do booze or being able to do heights, but not both."

"Yeah." I was rubbing her fingers. "And he was the same about drugs."

"So what you're saying is, this guy, Greg Maltin, was someone whose job description basically said, sure-footed and sober." Patrick's eyes opened all the way, and I jumped; he had damned near no pupil. Scary bastard. "And he knew that, and never touched anything that would interfere in any way with his ability to perform that job requirement?"

"Yeah, that's it. You got it. No drugs, no booze, climbed like a cat or maybe a monkey." I took a good long breath. I hated having to say it, but I'd rung Patrick, and here he was, and I had no right to push an idea away from me, just because I didn't fancy looking unpleasantness in the eye. "And I don't believe for one second that Greg lost his footing, stone cold sober, and fell in the river and couldn't get out. That's bollocks, all right? I don't believe it."

"No." Patrick's voice was matter-of-fact, but it was quiet, and there was an edge to it, now. "If what you're telling me is accurate, I can see why not. So you believe he was killed?"

"Yeah." I reached out a hand. Bree got hold of it and moved up close, warm and supportive. "I do. Don't ask me why anyone would kill him. I haven't got a clue. But I think someone did."

"Then you have to understand something." His voice was quiet. "If you're right, and the second death was deliberate, there's a high probability that the other two incidents, that missing person and the death in Paris, were also deliberate."

"But -" Bree turned to me. She was chalky. "John?"

"Yeah." I swung her hand gently, keeping it as light as I could. "I wouldn't mind being wrong about this. Because if I'm right, it would mean we've got someone stalking the tour."

Chapter Eight

"…Happy Monday, campers! Here we are in Chicago, just past the midway point of the first part of the US leg. Today is a rest day— unlike the rest of the world, Monday's the one day of the week where we know we don't have to work.

I have to say, it's been an absolute kicker of a tour so far, mostly thanks to our American fans. You might not know this, but every member of Blacklight gets jazzed when they know they're going to play in the US. For fifty years, Americans have had the reputation for being the most enthusiastic rock fans in the world, and you've earned it…."

"You know, this is one gorgeous view."

"Yeah, Chicago's got a nice skyline." I glanced up from the laptop, one fast look up out the window, one quick smile for my wife, and back again to the computer. From where I was sitting, all I could see was sky, really, but I wasn't just nodding and grunting—I knew that view, even if it was new to Bree.

Our suite was right up near the top of the hotel, and no matter which direction you looked, the lake and the skyline were stretched out. The Four Seasons chain gives all sorts of goodies for your money, and that includes views. Even though I had no clue what sort of deal Carla'd put together with the hotel, it still wasn't going to be cheap.

I was glad for the little luxuries. That wasn't on my own behalf, it was for Bree. I hadn't used to give a damn about the views, or the bubbly, or the rest of it. I'd spent so many years on the road that my feelings about hotels had got pretty basic: a hotel is where I sleep when my job keeps me from sleeping in my own bed, period. Views, comfort, fancy little touches—I take all that for granted.

So I hadn't really stopped to think about it before. But I was just beginning to notice, this tour, that I liked the posh touches, not having to worry about privacy, being able to take the services for granted. That was all about Bree, of course. With my wife on the road with me, I felt like I'd brought what meant home to me along, as well. The way I thought about touring, what I expected along the way, seemed to be changing.

"...*The first winner of the Backstage With Blacklight contest, David Echols of Parsippany, New Jersey, claimed his prize on opening night. (Click the Rogues Gallery link for photos.) Turns out David's an up and coming bassist—his band, The Stickers, has played some local gigs at David's own school in Connecticut. So he got to have a good long conversation with Cal Wilson, about what it takes...*"

I'd just had one of those moments with the computer, the kind that still make me jump. I'd been looking at the band's website, and I'd hit the refresh key, right as Nial's blog was being posted. Very weird, that is.

"...*from our new Ask The Band section, here's a question from*

Ally, in San Antonio: Hi! I'm a Blacklight newbie—I heard the band for the first time when Book of Days was released, and now I'm totally addicted. I was actually at the last show at the London Dome, with my mom. It was so awesome! The way the second set opened just blew me away! I love that instrumental piece, the one that leads into 'Hammer It Home.' What's it called, and which album is it from?

I gave this question to Luke Hedley, who wrote it. He says: "Hello, Ally—The instrumental lead-in is called 'Aftertouch.' It's only ever been recorded once so far, on Straight and Narrow, our live CD from 1998. That version is much shorter, and will probably sound less dense and layered. The version we're using now is expanded to make it a perfect lead-in for 'Hammer It Home,' and with Tony Mancuso along for this tour, we were able to significantly add to the structure of the piece...."

I adjusted my readers on my nose, and peered down at the screen. That's one thing I hate about the laptop, how small everything is. I'm still fairly new at this internet thing, and computers in general. Sitting in on some recording sessions with Tony's band, the Bombardiers, a few years back, I'd got a first-hand look at what you could do with digital recording, how easy it made things. That had been an eye-opener for me.

Funny thing is, that part of it, I'd got down with no trouble at all. Actual computers, though, laptops and whatnot, I was still fumbling about with those.

"...*The indoor arena segment of our North American tour wraps up in Anaheim on 5 July. After that, the band gets a decent break, and they've certainly earned it. We'll be heading up to Canada, to work on the final preparation for shifting this tour from indoor arenas to outdoor stadiums...*"

"John?" Bree'd come up behind me, and was rubbing my shoulders. That got my attention, all right; I could ask the front desk for a masseuse, but I'd rather have Bree do it. "Can I talk to you?"

"Hang on—let me turn this off." I turned round, and looked up at her. She was looking—I don't know, wistful, or something. Out of sorts, in a way I couldn't pin down. "You're looking like an Aunt Sally someone's left out in the rain. Forlorn. What's up, love?"

"Nothing, really." She knelt down, and leaned her cheek up against my knee. "Except that—no, never mind."

"Never mind what?" I'd got one hand, rubbing her arm. "Talk to me. What's going on, then?"

"Nothing. It's just -" She stopped.

"Right." I stood up, got hold of both her hands, and got her up, as well. "That's enough of that. I said, talk to me. What's this nothing? My job driving you off your nut?"

"No—not your job." She was leaning against me, and I got one hand on the small of her back, and slipped it up under her shirt. There was nothing sexy about that; the small of Bree's back is where she keeps her temperature sensor. Too hot or too cold, and I get worried. Right now, it was the same temperature as the rest of her back. "And I don't want to sound like some rocker's whiny wife."

"Ah." I lifted an eyebrow at her. "But…?"

"Well…" She bit her lip. "I feel like I'm actually seeing less of you than when I used to stay home."

"Yeah, I wondered about that. Let's have a sit-down, okay?"

The suite in Chicago had two bedrooms and a full living room. Perfectly good comfy sofa, but I never even glanced that way; I just headed straight for our bedroom, and she came right after, no argument. Not sure what was going on in her head, but I know what was going on in mine: the rest of our digs were just another hotel, but our bed, well, that's ours. It doesn't matter which bed, either, which hotel, which country. There's only ever been once that either of us haven't felt that way, and that was back at the Omni Hotel in New York, back in 2005. A very bad week, that had been.

But that was then and this was now. A lot of water had gone under more bridges than I want to bother about counting. I sat down on the end of the bed, let her settle herself next to me, and tilted my head at her.

"Right," I told her. "I'm listening, Bree. What's on your mind?"

She told me. It was pretty much what I'd thought it might be; I hadn't actually been through this myself, because Cilla would have eaten rat poison before she'd let me do a major Blacklight tour without her, but I knew about it happening.

Thing is, this is my job. I'm a musician. I know most of the world thinks this is all about glamour and exciting shit happening and fantastic meals and all the shiny sparkly stuff that comes along with this level of success. And yeah, of course there's a lot of that. Me sitting in the Presidential Suite of the Chicago Four Seasons, saying *bollocks, it's no different from sitting in an office or taking orders at a restaurant from six until midnight*, I wouldn't have much cred, you know?

You get down to it, though, and any musician will tell you the same. Session player, garage band, jazz trumpeter, steel drum player, busker, rock and roll superstar: it doesn't make any difference. If the musician is for real, music's what they are. But if they make it their life as well, it becomes their job. And doing it properly, as a job, that takes a weird, heavy focus. You've got to be willing to give it all of you, while you're doing it, and that's hell on your sweetie; it takes a very particular person to be able to cope with it. It's a wonder any of us end up in relationships lasting more than six months. Musicians are no fun at all, not while we're in full focus mode.

I pulled her up close, shutting my gob, letting her talk. That's something I'd had to learn to do. A few years back, that same bad week, the one that had ended up with her thinking she had no right to her own bed, she'd gone missing on me. I'd been a wreck, not knowing where she was, or why she'd left. When she'd finally checked in, she'd said something that stayed in my head: she'd told me I didn't really listen to her, and that was okay with her. I hadn't ever thought about it until then, but she was right, about me not listening.

She was all wrong about it being okay, though. It wasn't. Not good, not fair, and definitely not okay. And bloody hell, living with a musician's tricky enough—she didn't need that added to it. So I'd taught myself to listen.

She was snuggled up close, not meeting my eye. It probably would have been easier on her if I actually had interrupted, but I'd stayed quiet, and she'd dished. Once she stopped talking, I gave it a minute, making sure she'd said what she wanted to say. "Okay. Let's see if I've got it. You're tired, you're missing your own kitchen and the cats, and you feel as if you're getting less sex than you did when you stayed home and waited in San Francisco for me?"

"Not less sex. Just—not as intense, I guess. But that's only a little part of it." She sniffed a bit. Crikey, this really had been tricky for her to talk about, if she was in tears over it. "I know this tour is bigger than we thought it was going to be, John. I get that. I know you can't help it if Carla's got all your free time booked up with press stuff, and photo shoots, and PR appearances. I know you're working, that this is all part of the job. But..."

I stayed quiet. She'd lifted her face to where I could see it, finally, and I was right, her eyes were damp.

"I feel extraneous. I feel as if I'm in the way, almost. I feel like a piece of pretty furniture that you have to bring with you, along with the guitars, except I'm not as useful as the guitars and anyway, you've got to drag me along yourself. You can't even get a roadie to carry me around." The words came out in a rush. "And I know that's just stupid, you don't have to tell me. I know it's bullshit, I know I'm your wife, I know I'm not just a drag or an ornament, I know you want me here and you aren't actually wishing I'd go away and let you do your thing. I know all that, in my head, anyway."

She stopped, swallowed hard, and I watched her stop trying to control it. "Oh, *goddamnit*," she said, and burst into tears.

"Right," I said, and gathered her in. Maybe I'm getting some sense in my old age, I don't know. Whatever, I just knew that letting her cry herself out and just being there for her while she did it was the best move right then.

After a while, she pulled back in my arms. "Sorry." Her face was a mess. "Need tissues."

"Here you go." I stretched out and pulled over one of the marbleised boxes of tissues the Four Seasons puts on each side of the bed. "Have a good blow, love."

She did. It took three tries before she got it under control and stopped sniffling, and then she hiccoughed, which for some reason was about as touching as it could have got, right then.

I leaned over and kissed her.

"Bree. Listen, love. I'm going to be straight with you—I can do that, right? Because this is us."

"Okay." Shit. I'd scared her—I couldn't help it, but it wasn't what I'd been trying to do. "Yes."

"Gordon *Bennett*, Bree, don't look so traumatised! I just want to say, I know how boring this has to get for you. Thing is, I did my first big tour with Cilla, and she wasn't letting me out of her sight. I haven't got any way of measuring it, yeah? So I need to ask you: Do you want shore leave?"

"Yes." She had the hiccoughs for real, now. "No. I don't know, John!"

"Here, hold your breath a minute, get rid of those shakes while I talk. Right. Better? Good. Now listen. You aren't furniture, trust me. And yeah, my head's elsewhere, a lot of the time—it's got to be, to do my job. We've got a month off coming up, so there's that, but that's not for a few weeks yet. I'd miss you every minute you weren't here, at least every minute we weren't actually on-stage playing, and the only reason I wouldn't miss you then is that with this damned stage set-up, I can't see you anyway. So—shore leave? Do you want to take the rest of this leg off, and head home?"

"No." She meant it, this time. I was glad I'd been upfront with her. She'd needed that space—that had let her sort it out in her mind. "No, I'm being a whiny bitch. It's a few more weeks and then we'll be home for a month. I might just fly home for one or two shows, to check on the cats and make my mom dinner. But I'm just being stupid. I'm sorry, John. I didn't mean to add to it."

"No, it's good." I brought over a wastebasket. "Here you go—drop those tissues in here, and we'll let housekeeping wonder which of us had the crying jag. You know, what with me being a selfish, spoiled, pampered bloke, I'm glad you're staying put. The bed's too big without you—doesn't matter which bed. But you need to not be afraid to say John, look, I need to not be in a ho-tel, I need to be doing stuff that isn't shopping or hanging out with the band wives, I need to get away from all this for a day or two. Okay?"

"Okay." She was up and moving, putting the wastebasket back where I'd found it. The hiccoughs were gone. "At least this time, if I did take a break, I wouldn't be worrying about some skanky little groupie trying to climb into your lap while I wasn't there."

"True." I ginned at her. "This leg's been a lot calmer, hasn't it? And thank God for it."

It really had been. Even though the actual number of people backstage here in North America was higher than Europe had been, it was less fraught, somehow. There was always the occa-sional bit of road nookie wandering about—good thing, too, be-cause that was one of Mac's perqs on the road, and he'd have been very cross about not having anything soft and horny and female to play with after a show. The standing joke with Mac was that the road nookie backstage ought to have been part of the contract rider. But what Katia called the "skanky ho factor" was lower.

We'd said goodbye to a few people for this leg. Solange and Suzanne were both gone; Solange was off on one of her endless rounds of looking at universities and trying to settle on one. I had no clue what Suzanne was up to, and didn't much care; so long as what she was doing wasn't bothering Luke, I was happy she was elsewhere. A few regulars, hangers-on who somehow managed to get backstage for every European tour leg we'd done in recent years, had melted away. And a double handful of staff, people we only worked with in Europe, had stayed behind while we used American union crews.

"Occurs to me, love, we've got the day off." I'd wandered over to the window, taking a good long look at that view Bree'd mentioned earlier. Bright sunny skies, maybe some rain off in the distance, across the lake, but right now, it was quite nice outside. "I haven't got a damned thing I need to do today. Let's take this one just for us, yeah? What would you like to do?"

"Guess."

That got my attention away from the window and straight back to Bree. Her eyes had gone jade-coloured, except jade's not nearly that shiny, mostly. That meant she was serious; if I fancied some mind-blowing sex, all I had to do was say so.

"How many guesses do I get?"

"You need more than one?"

"Ah." I pulled her up close, and got one hand up under her skirt. "What do I get if I guess right..?"

"Anything you—oh, damn! Is that your cell?"

"Yeah, and I'm not answering it." I was ignoring it. "Sod the phone. Whoever it is, they can wait. Right now, Little Miss I Feel Like A Useless Ornament, I've got a job for you. Go put the Do

Not Disturb sign on the door, and lock it behind you. And then get back in here, lady, and get your knickers off."

She turned and headed for the door, her eyes getting greener by the second. Getting out of my own clothes, I heard the cell give its little triple-beep that means someone's left a message. Right now, it could wait. If Carla or anyone else thought they were getting their hands on me right then, they could sod off. The only person getting a hand on me was Bree.

We had an afternoon, all right. Maybe my ego had got poked by that whole talk about the sex being less intense recently. I'm damned if I know. All I know is, she blew the top of my head off, and I was right there with her, returning the favour.

"Hello, darling." Maybe she'd been right, about the intensity thing—it was taking me longer than usual to get my heart rate back down, and it was a good thing I was on my back and not my feet, because my legs felt shaky. I breathed in, breathed out; next to me, Bree, sweet and salty, rolled up close and licked the base of my throat. "Are you having a good time?"

She made a noise. I breathed in, exhaled, felt everything steady down and become less hectic. Good.

"You know, Bree, you just lost your shot at going home and leaving me here." The pulse in my throat, under her tongue, was slowing down to normal. "Not parting with any of you, lady."

"You silver-tongued devil, you. You say the nicest things, some-times." She had a hand resting on me, but just resting, not doing anything to start up a second round. Good job, too, since right then, I'd done for the moment.

I turned my head, and looked at her. Her eyes were still cloudy and just coming back into focus, and the rest of her was still rip-pling. That made me happy. Whether I was up for a second round of belly-bumping or not, it was good to know I could al-ways take her places.

"What do you want to do between now and dinner?" She'd sat

130

up, cross-legged and naked. "Besides check your messages? No, don't glare at me, I promise I won't mind. You know as well as I do that if you don't, it'll bug you all day. And that's no fun."

"Yeah, well, the damned phone can stay in my trousers pocket until I've got them on again. And that's not going to be for a bit. Oi! Where do you think you're going, lady...?"

We stayed in bed for most of the day. If she'd seriously been thinking I was losing interest in sex, I knocked that little notion out of her head. We even got back to a place she'd taken us last year, when she'd decided she wanted to experiment a bit, and I'd said right, let's do it. A year later, we even both remembered the safe word. It was brilliant. And we followed up by ringing down to the desk and getting a couple of in-room massages, and sent down to room service for a good lunch. A nice day, just me and Bree.

Right around six, we'd been talking about dinner, when my phone went again. Since neither of us had bothered putting clothes on, we were lounging in the Four Seasons' posh robes, and I had to scramble for my gear before I found the phone.

Turned out it was Luke, wanting to know if we fancied going along with him and Karen to see a blues combo that was playing across town. Bree gave me thumbs up, so I told Luke yeah, we'd meet him downstairs at eight, but I wasn't going to make it a late night, tonight being my weekly shot night. That reminded me to take the interferon out of the suite's fridge; you don't want to be shooting yourself up with cold meds, believe me.

"So was there a message?" Bree stretched, and I heard her joints cracking. She always says it feels great, doing that, but it makes me edgy. "I seem to remember that your phone rang, about twenty orgasms ago."

"Yeah, right, and you called me the silver-tongued devil in the family?" I grinned at her, and glanced back at the phone. "Three messages, actually. Hang on, let's see who wants me to go where, and when."

Carla, letting me know that refills for my heart meds would be waiting for me next week, when we checked into the Ritz-Carlton in Dallas. My guitar tech, Jas, letting me know that he'd had got a call from a rep for a new guitar string maker, and would we be willing to try them out, maybe endorse them…

"John?" She was sitting up, staring at me. "What? Is something wrong?"

"No, not wrong. I don't recognise the third number, that's all." I didn't recognise the country, either. Europe, somewhere—not England, though. Different country code. "Hang on, let me see who this is, and what it's about, yeah?"

"(beep)…Mr. Kinkaid? This is Pirmin Bochsler, from Interpol. Patrick Ormand told me that you wished for any information about a missing persons case in Manchester, in England, a man named James Morse. I hope you were not good friends—if you were, I am afraid I am the bearer of bad news. James Morse's body was found three days ago, near an unused factory fifteen kilometres south of Manchester. At the moment, the local constabulary are treating this as a suspicious death."

As much as I wanted to talk to Pirmin Bochsler about that message of his, it didn't happen, at least not right away: my attention got sidetracked. And Bree missed an entire week of shows for the same reason. We'd barely got ourselves settled in at the Vancouver Four Seasons when Sammy, our housekeeper and cat sitter, rang up and scared us both; Wolfling, our oldest cat, was listless and off his food. Of course, Bree had the next flight back to SFO booked within ten minutes.

So she missed the entire Canadian leg, all the gigs in Edmonton, Vancouver and Calgary. That was a damned shame on a couple of levels; she'd never seen Canada, for one thing, and for another, the shows she missed turned out to be fantastic, or at least the reviewers thought so.

I was worried as hell about Wolfling, myself. After all, I was the one who'd found him. He'd been a tiny frightened tabby kitten, about a month old, abandoned and left in a cardboard box in the parking lot of our local market, and don't even get me started on what I'd fancy doing to people who do things like that. I'd brought him home, tucked under my jacket, me getting odd looks from people walking by because I was talking to myself, Wolfling alternately purring and making small frightened *meep* noises, all the way back to Clay Street.

Wolfling was my baby, and he was thirteen years old, and sick. And yeah, circle of life, we get old and we die, but that doesn't mean I have to like it. Obviously, I couldn't leave or do one damned thing about it, and that meant Bree had to cope.

I'd kissed her goodbye at the hotel, told her to ring me the moment she knew what was going on, and got her off to the airport. At least we were in the same time zone; between that and knowing when the shows were, she wasn't going to have to worry about waking me up or getting my voicemail during a gig.

Bree rang me the day after she got home. The news was, Wolfling had crystals in his urinary tract. That sounded dire, and I was just about to flip my shit over it, but Bree said no, the vet had told her male cats, especially older ones, get it—it had something to do with not enough wet food in their diet. Wolfling also had a minor infection.

"The vet says the crystals thing is actually pretty common," Bree told me. "So don't worry, John. The vet isn't worrying. Oh, and the whole desk staff said to say hi—they've all got tickets to San Jose, up in the nosebleed seats."

"Yeah, right, don't worry." I was getting ready to meet the rest of the band for dinner; we actually had two days off, no show until we did Edmonton tomorrow. That back to back rest, that had become a rarity on this tour, and yeah, I was digging it, but there was also a part of me wanting to sulk, not having Bree there to dig it with me. "Try that on the dog, lady. Of course I'm worried. What's the fix, then? Not surgery, is it? He's elderly for that."

"He's on special dry food—costs a fortune, but it's supposed to fix the urinary tract thing. And just for once, we got lucky with how finicky the beasties are—both the boys like it, but Farrowen took one sniff and tried to bury it."

"What about that infection?"

"Antibiotics. I swear, John, the vet says he'll be fine." She sighed. "Seven days' worth of pills, and it's the same deal as human antibiotics—he has to have the full course, or you risk the problem coming back, worse than ever. Poor baby, he took the first pill without any struggling—just let me shove it down his throat. Definitely listless. The vet says we should see improvement within a couple of days. If not, I'm supposed to bring him back. But he's already a little more energetic. I think it's working. And of course I'm not about to ask Sammy to try and stuff pills down Wolfling's throat."

"Yeah, not without getting Sammy to sign a waiver. Wolfling gets his strength back, he'd rip Sammy to small bloody strips." It was my turn to sigh; it was pretty obvious where she was going with all this. "So. You're staying home and giving him his drugs until the cycle's done? That's, what, seven days?"

"Six left. He's had his first two doses already." Her voice sounded far away, and it occurred to me she'd put the speaker on and set the phone down. I heard water running, and suddenly, there was the picture in my head, so sharp and clear that it made me a bit dizzy: our kitchen, with its six-burner stove and the enormous Sub-Zero fridge that Bree and I had rowed over buying, and the cats' dishes in the shadow under the window to keep the sun from drying out their food, Bree moving about, making herself tea, with the kitchen overheads making her hair look even redder, and the fog curling in from the Pacific off to the west. "I'll give him the extra day, to make sure there aren't any

134

problems. If the vet says he's okay, I'll be on the next plane after that. That's—where are we in a week? Is that LA? Anaheim? Because that's only an hour in the air."

"Yeah, probably—depends on the day, but we'll hook it up. Ring Carla when you're ready, love, will you? Let her book it and make sure you've got a car waiting when you get here. I don't want to worry about you trying to save a few dollars, flying coach or any of that rubbish. Okay?"

"Okay." She hesitated. "John—listen. Can I tell you something? Nothing huge, not a big deal, just something I want to say. Is that okay?"

"Of course you can—anything you like, any time. You don't ever need to ask me that." I'd gone taut, suddenly, all my nerve endings talking to me. Her asking me, wondering if it was okay to say something, worrying I didn't want to hear her, didn't want to listen to her? I thought we were well past that rubbish. "What's up, Bree?"

"It's just that I realised something, last night." Her voice was close again, so the phone was probably back up next to her ear. There was something weirdly intimate about that, her voice coming suddenly close to me again. "I was thinking about all those times when I stayed here, when I wouldn't go out on the road with you. Some of that was because I thought everyone would think I was a tramp, because of Cilla. I was convinced of that, that all your friends despised me because I'd come between you and your wife."

"I know, Bree." I did, too. I hadn't always understood, but these days, I saw a lot more than I used to. "They didn't, though. You know that, right? They really didn't."

"I do now. But back then, I just couldn't get rid of this picture. Every time you asked me to come out on tour with you, that came into my head: I just kept seeing all your friends and all the wives, cutting me dead. It was this nightmare thing, that they'd all look right through me, or be polite because they felt they had to. I don't know which one would have been worse."

"Bree -"

"No, let me finish, John. Please?" She took a breath, and I stayed quiet. "That wasn't the only thing. The other—oh, man, this is hard. Okay. Here it is: I was always scared to death she'd show up. I know you think that's stupid, but she might have, John. She could have walked in the backstage door any time she wanted. She had a right to be there. She was your wife."

"I never said I thought you were being stupid, Bree." I was keeping my voice steady, but my hands had gone sweaty. Christ, we were coming up on thirty years, and even now, talking about my first wife was still tricky, at least for me. Yeah, it was easier than it used to be, when even mentioning Cilla's name was like this automatic signal for Bree to lose it, build walls to hide behind. But if she still felt she had to brace herself to even say Cilla's name to me, we still had a good long way to go. "I never thought that, either. Truth is, I didn't think much about why you wouldn't do it. I was too busy being pissy about it happening at all. Go on, love. There's more, yeah?"

"It's about what you said, back in Chicago. You said the bed was too big without me, any bed. Remember? Well—I thought about that last night when I was climbing into bed. I got in and I rolled over and you weren't there. And I just looked at your side of the bed and it felt like, holy *fuck*, how big is this damned thing? Because without you in it, it's like the size of one of those stadiums you're going to be playing. And how weird is that? Because I had all those years to get used to it, and I always thought I was used to it. But I was wrong. I hate being in different beds. And now I seem to be making up for lost time, because I keep looking back at all those times when you wanted me to come out with you, and I wouldn't. And I just want to kick myself. What was I thinking?"

136

"Bree—oi, are you crying?" I had a lump at the back of my own throat. "Don't cry, love. Yeah, I don't exactly enjoy being elsewhere, myself. Keep your chin up—it's less than a week. It's okay. Look, I've got a band meeting in about ten minutes, so I'd best ring off. Leave the light on for me?"

"Always on." Her voice was shaking—that phrase has a lot of meaning for both of us. Hell, I'd had it engraved on the inside of her engagement ring. "Always burning."

Edmonton, Calgary, Vancouver. Those were killer shows, the ones we did in Canada that week. Those nights, I had an edge and I took it onstage with me. It bled into the music, right there in the guitar. I was missing Bree, the way she slipped one hand between my thighs before I went onstage, knowing she was waiting for me backstage. I was missing her at the window, admiring the skyline. I was missing her next to me, day and night.

All that stuff, being frustrated and anxious and tense, that got into every note I played. Of course the band picked it up and went with it, Mac using it to punch the vocals, Luke's guitar work going mean and tight. Good stuff.

And I'd surprised myself: I realised just how much I missed our suite being the place people came to hang out. Because they didn't, not without Bree there to make it feel hospitable; we had three band meetings during that stay at the Vancouver Four Seasons, and they were all held upstairs in the corporate suite. Without Bree there, my room was just another room.

The last two days she was gone, it turned into a "misery loves company" thing. The morning of the Vancouver gig, Barb Wilson got a call; turned out her mum, who was well into her eighties, had broken a hip and gone into hospital in Lancashire. Carla had her on the next flight to the UK, and that meant me and Cal were grumpy bachelors again, roughing it until our old ladies got back where they belonged, and generally whingeing and moaning. Pathetic, really.

137

So we were hanging out together, probably driving the rest of the band bonkers, when I got the shock of my life. Turned out I wasn't the only one who'd wondered about those three deaths.

Cal had come up to my suite to hang out. The official reason was that he and Stu, working as the Bunker Brothers, had produced a CD for an old enemy of mine, and Cal wanted to get my opinion of it. But really, he was bored and lonely and he wanted to hang out. Thinking back on it, I couldn't remember him doing a tour when Barb wasn't there with him.

So yeah, we were cranky and pissy. Two geezers, deprived of their birds. He brought his MP3 player up with him, and asked me to give a listen: Bergen Sandoval's comeback CD.

It wasn't great, but it was quite good. That wasn't a surprise—the bloke in question is one of the great bassists out there. He's also a mean, mingy little shit, something I'd found out when I spent my nineteenth birthday skint in a ratty B&B in Leeds with two bandmates, panicking because we couldn't pay for our rooms. Bergen hadn't coughed up the wages for the backing band of session players he'd hired.

I found out later he'd build up quite a reputation for doing that, you know? He made a habit of screwing the people who were helping him. But at nineteen, thick as a brick and naive as any virgin, I'd been flattered that a great session bloke like Bergen Sandoval wanted me along. Yeah, right.

"I'm not completely happy with it." Cal was wandering about, picking things up, setting them back down. "It's missing something. Stu agrees, but neither of us can put a finger on it. What do you think, JP?"

"It's okay, but yeah. Not great. Thin, I'd say—there's something, I don't know, underfed about it. Hang on, let me give it another go." I listened, and took the earbuds out. "It could use some backup vocals, or maybe just some decent piano. I'm hearing some synth in there, and honestly, Cal, it doesn't work. Too lush, too much contrast, especially with how lean the rest of it is. Just my take—this is your baby, yours and Stu's. Oh, and of course, Bergen's. What's he got to say about it?"

"Do you have to ask?" Cal rolled his eyes. "It's perfect, it's fantastic, it's the best thing ever recorded, he's a genius. You know Bergen as well as I do, maybe better. He's not just a pain in the arse, he's a world class pain in the arse."

"Yeah, I know. And Christ, what a mean shit he is, too. Well past greedy and all the way into pathological about money. You could offer to sign the Royal Mint over to him and he'd try to do you out of the money for the ink in your pen. I hope you and Stu got paid upfront."

"Oh, hell yes. Stu told me the drummer on this—you know Seamus Clancy?—said they'd all demanded cash on the barrel. It's Bergen's own fault. He comes by that rep honestly." Cal was staring out over Vancouver. "It's been a fun leg, hasn't it? I haven't wanted to say anything to anyone—well, just to Barb— but after those three deaths on the Euro leg, I was really spooked."

"Three?" I was staring at his back. "Cal—how did you know it was three, not two?"

"Because I checked." He turned around and looked at me. Cal's a long, skinny bloke, with a very bony face. He doesn't show much, but right then, there was a lot of shrewdness there. "Like I said, I haven't really wanted to say anything. Hell, we all get superstitious when people die on tour. Not something to talk about, is it? No one likes talking about bad luck on a tour. But two deaths, one right after the other? That's hard to miss, JP. When Phil MacDermott sent that group email out, about the missing security bloke, I subscribed to the online version of the Manchester papers. They reported the story, when his body was found. Why are you looking at me as if I had two heads?"

"Not two heads. Just a mind that works a lot more like mine

139

does than I ever thought about it doing. Look, have you got a couple of minutes…?"

I told him everything, from my first moments of feeling uneasy about Greg Maltin falling in the river, right through my ringing Patrick and the call from Pirmin. By the time I'd finished, the boot was definitely on the other leg—he was the one staring at me as if I had two heads.

"…and I haven't rung Pirmin back yet, or Patrick either. Wolfling getting sick pushed everything to the side, you know? He's like my kid, that cat is. But I'm damned well going to ring them back, especially now. Cal, mate, say something, would you please? You're looking at me like you'd never seen me before."

"Sorry." He looked round for the nearest chair, and sank into it. "It's just that you're the last person I'd have thought would be curious enough about a situation to do something about it. You never used to let stuff touch you. But that thing about Greg not getting stoned or high? That clinches it, for me. If that's true, nothing will make me believe it was an accident."

"No, I'm with you. So's Bree, and so's Patrick Ormand." I was smarting a little, and I didn't know why, but something about what he'd said, how he'd described me, had stung: …*the last person I'd have thought would be curious enough about a situation to do something about it.* "Patrick was the one who pointed out that we had to look at the whole picture—that if Greg's death was murder, the others likely were, as well."

"But that doesn't make sense!" That bony unrevealing face of his was tight with concentration. "That kid in Paris wasn't one of ours—he was a two-night hire. We'd never worked with him before. Greg was Greg, one of the family. And the dead bloke up in Manchester, what was his name?"

"James Morse." I was trying to sort it out, looking for common ground where things could possibly touch, and I wasn't finding much. "He was temporary security staff, just for those shows. Cal,

I can't get this to fit together anywhere. One hired French stage-hand, one of our own guys, one local security bloke. All they had in common is that they worked for us, so far as I can see. So what the fuck? Why would anyone take them out?"

"You're asking me? I'm not a copper. I don't know either." We locked stares, and I got it—he was just as worried as I was, and just as out at sea. "JP, I don't like this. It has to be someone close to us, doesn't it? Assuming we aren't crazy paranoiacs? Because otherwise, how would whoever is doing this know these blokes, and where to find them?"

"I'm not a copper, either," I pointed out. "But Jesus, Cal, that's ugly. I can't wrap my head round that. One of our own people, killing crew members? Why…?"

"Yeah, this is seriously fucked up." He got up. "You said Bree was suspicious, as well?"

"Yeah, she didn't like the smell of it. She was there when I rang Patrick Ormand about it. That was back in San Francisco—hell, she gave Patrick lunch. But I haven't got a clue about what to do next. I mean, I did my thing, rang our connection at the local cop shop, he rang his connection at the international cop shop, and now we know that yeah, we were probably right about the smell. And if Pirmin rang me, then he rang Patrick first—fair to even odds on that. So they may be checking it out even as we speak, or they may not. But what do we do now?"

"Nothing, yet." He looked surprised. "What can we do?"

I stared at him. He shook his head at me.

"Look, you said it yourself—the cops are probably burning up the wires, figuring out what's going on. That's their gig, not ours. Besides, no one's died on this leg, right? At least, no one we know about. So maybe we just had some local nutter, part of the temp crew for that first leg, someone with a screw loose or a grudge or something. I'll admit, that would surprise me, considering how good Ian and David are when it comes to screening people. But no one's perfect."

"Yeah, that's true. But at the very least, we ought to run this by Ian and Phil, see what they want to do. Those deaths, they all happened in different countries, and that may mean no one's really connected the dots yet. Ian should have a list of the entire staff, and it wouldn't do any harm to pass that along to the people in charge, right?"

"Probably not." He wasn't looking convinced. "But I think we ought to talk it over with the rest of the band at least, before we do anything we can't take back."

"We've got that photo shoot in about twenty minutes. We're supposed to meet upstairs, in the corporate suite." I got up, looking at my watch. "So you think we ought to basically sit back and wait? Because nothing's gone wrong since we got to America, it was probably a freak on the Euro leg? Is that it?"

"Not wait—talk it over. But with us, not the cops, not yet. Ian, Carla, Phil, everyone else. Shit, JP, we aren't some little cabal. If something's wrong, they're affected as well."

He followed me out, watching me lock the suite doors behind me. As we waited for the lift, he gave a huge sigh.

"Barb's supposed to be back the day after tomorrow, unless her mum has complications. When's Bree due back?"

"Also the day after tomorrow. She's flying down to LA, meeting me there. Why?"

"Just wondering. I talked to Barb about being worried, and Bree's in on this, as well. And that got me wondering if we were the only ones who were thinking this way."

"No idea." Into the lift, up one flight, into the corporate suite where Ian and Carla and the rest of the band were already waiting, along with two photographers. "Tell you what. Let's talk it over with Bree and Barb. After that, maybe we can get Ian aside for a quiet word."

Chapter Nine

From: Ian Hendry

To: mac@knifesharpe.co.uk; lukeh@blacklightband.co.uk; scorrigan@irisheyes.co.uk; calwil@bunkerbrothers.co.uk; jpkinkaid@blacklightband.co.uk; tmancuso@bombardiers.net; Carlafanucci@fanuccipros.com; philm@blacklightband.co.uk

Date: 23 June, 2008

Subject: Conference Call

Reminder: we have an all-hands conference call at 6:00 pm tonight, in re the deaths of three Blacklight crew personnel members during the Euro leg. For anyone who's still unaware of what's been happening, two of the three deaths have been confirmed as homicides. Please have your cell phones ready at that time. We're using our usual conferencing service. When prompted for the conference ID code, please enter 4645478.

That conference call—well.

I'm not about to forget it, not anytime soon. I mean yeah, I was tired as hell, and looking forward to the last few gigs of the arena leg. As good a time as we were having, there was one bit of me that kept wanting to just be done with it, get home, curl up with Bree, check on Wolfling and make sure my wife hadn't been blowing smoke when she told me my cat was over his infection and healthy again, eat brilliant food at my own table, and sleep for about a week.

But tired as I was, I was there for that conference call, there all the way, I mean. After all, the whole thing being dumped in Ian's lap? That was my fault, with backup from Bree and Barb. Cal actually needed some convincing, even after we'd talked it into the ground.

I hadn't rung Pirmin Bochsler back, in Marseilles. He's a good bloke, Pirmin is—precise and careful, not much of a shock considering he's Swiss, but very pleasant. And being high up at Interpol, he hadn't been under any obligation to ring me up and tell me a damned thing. But he had, and I owed him a phone call.

We'd got to the Beverly Wilshire from Vancouver after one in the morning, and Bree and Barb had both got to the hotel at breakfast, so all four of us were a bit off our games. If either of them was surprised at being sat down for a discussion about murder in our suite over a room service breakfast, they weren't showing it. Like I said, we all could have been better; between worry over her mum, a three-hour layover in New York, and the eight-hour time lag between California and the UK, Barb was the worst off, and she wasn't talking much. Cal seemed to think we ought to ring Pirmin and hand it off to him; his take was that this was Pirmin's gig, and us getting involved, all it could do was get under the experts' feet and complicate the tour.

It was right round that point that Bree, who'd been picking at her breakfast, pushed it away entirely and spoke up.

144

"So you guys are going to call Pirmin? Just go straight to him?" That got my attention—there was an edge to her voice. "Do I get a vote? Or do I sit here and smile and look nice?"

"Of course you get a vote," Cal told her. "So does Barb, once she shakes off the cobwebs. What's on your mind, Bree?"

"What's on my mind is that when I fed seafood salad to Patrick Ormand, and John and I asked for his opinion, it was unofficial. The only thing we were going on was the feeling that something just wasn't right." She emptied half a cup of coffee. "But that was before that poor man in Manchester was found. We were going on the fact that three incidents were a lot to swallow as coincidence, especially because they seemed so much alike. And anyway, it was Greg Maltin's death that John was really thinking about. Wasn't it, John?"

"Yeah, it was." Barb and Cal were both watching me; Barb looked to be getting a second wind. "It was remembering that he didn't do any drugs or booze that pretty much put the lid on it, you know? We were supposed to believe he'd fallen in the river and drowned. I thought that was bollocks, and still do."

"Barb and I discussed this at the time, JP. We agree with you. Greg was practically an acrobat. He never fell in the river on his own." Cal couldn't seem to sit still. "And now we know that bloke in Manchester was a homicide. So what do we do about it? We've got some options. We could talk to the rest of the band, get everyone in on this. We can put Ian and Carla on it, and not worry anyone else. Or do we just say sod it, and play copper's nark? Go straight to the blokes with the badges, tell them what we think, and say over to you and best of luck with it? Because I've said it before and I'll say it again—why worry Ian with this? It's not his responsibility."

"Oh for Christ's sake, Cal! Will you listen to yourself?" Barb must have been thoroughly knackered. She's usually nice and calm, but just then, she sounded irritated beyond endurance.

"This isn't a 'pick one and run' thing—we're talking about murder. Of course we need to talk to the band, and if you don't tell Ian and Carla as well, I swear I will. It's looking like someone who works with you is a psycho. Bree, for heavens sake, a bit of backup, please?"

"All the backup you want, Barb. I'm with you." Bree was on her feet. I thought for a moment that she'd gone as antsy as Cal was, but no—she was just being Bree, gathering up the dirty cups and plates. "The whole band is affected if we're right, and Ian and Carla need to have all the information we can give them. But let's face it—Carla and Ian are the two most capable people in the whole organisation. So if I really do have a voice here, I say we tell Ian everything, and let him decide how to use the information."

"Yeah, well, what information is that, Bree?" Cal wasn't being shirty; he genuinely wanted to know. "What do we know that Ian doesn't? Tell Ian, sure, all right—I'm down with that. But you realise he's probably going to get everyone together and turn the floor over to us. What in hell are we supposed to tell them?"

"Patrick told us that if one of those incidents was murder, we'd have to consider that all three of them could be murder." She was watching him, very steady. "And now we know that one definitely was, and one probably was. Did you want to put odds on that first one just being some kind of coincidence? Because I'll take the bet, and walk away with your money, Cal. We're talking about three deaths. *Three.*"

We were all quiet, watching her. She wiped a damp patch off the table with a used napkin, and sighed. "I don't want to be pushy. But at the very least, I want input before John calls Pirmin Bochsler back. It's our asses in the sling. We're the ones who got Patrick over and stuffed him full of lunch and asked him to call Pirmin. It's on us. And I'm damned if I'm going to have gone this far with it and then hand it off to the cops without a word to the band, and look surprised when everyone wants to kick my ass. No way."

"She's right. You know she's right." I lifted one brow at Cal, and watched him purse his lips and let off a good hard exhale of frustration. "Look, let's just do it, Cal, yeah? Get it over, get Ian on the phone, tell him what's happening, let him sort out what happens next. Honestly, mate, dealing with anything that might look like turning into a shitstorm, that's what we pay him for."

With the others there as backup, I'd rung Ian, and given him just what had been happening; I'd also told him that the call on what we did about it was his to make. Of course, I hadn't actually wondered whether he'd think it needed handling, and I was right. He went terse and tight and started talking in as few words as possible—*I'm on it, check your email in half an hour.* That meant he'd flipped his shit over it completely.

So I wasn't surprised to get the email, or the ID code for a conference call. That led to a funny moment because of course, Bree being back, everyone decided to gather in our suite. Since we'd actually got one of the smaller ones this time—we rotate who gets the bigger suites, and this time, the Hedleys had pulled the really luxe digs—it made for a major crush.

Turned out the only reason we even needed the phone part of the conversation was because Nial and Ronan had actually gone ahead to the Hilton Suites in Glendale along with the rest of the crew, making sure everything was set for the Arizona shows. Ian and Carla were both right there at the Beverly Wilshire—Carla actually lives in LA and has her production office on La Cienega, but she was staying in the corporate suite, same as she did on the road. So instead of all these people in different places, ringing in from different places on different phones, we just put Mac's fancy phone on the dining table in our suite, and everyone except Nial and Ronan crushed in shoulder to shoulder to share the speaker.

Of course Bree went into complete super-hostess mode, sort of hospitable massive control freakery, that left me shaking my head at her. It also left me wondering just how much she was missing her catering business; I may be spoiled rotten, but listening to her on the phone, pressing details with the hotel housekeeping staff, I suddenly got how much she was digging it.

Bree was on her mettle, trying for as close to perfection as she could get; this time, we had not only Domitra along, but also the band's official head of security for the past twenty years, Phil MacDermott. Looking at him, you'd pick him as a bus conductor, or an accountant, or maybe someone's personal assistant: anything that wasn't security, because he just didn't fit the picture. He's a little bloke, for one thing, actually a bit shorter than me. He's also completely bald, and has been since he first joined on, but he's got a bristly little moustache, the kind my mum used to call a soup strainer.

This was the first time he'd come along to see us for any reason at all, and of course Bree made a fuss over him, making sure he got a comfy chair and a glass of beer. Phil's usually so busy being buried under making sure no one's getting damaged, or sending his hired crew all over the venue and the hotel and wherever else they're needed, he's almost invisible. Anyway, he wasn't used to being put in the limelight, so when Bree called him by name and asked him if he wanted a bottle of pale ale, his ears turned bright pink, and he stammered something.

Looking back, I don't know what I thought was going to come from that call. Going on past history, it could have gone any number of ways. Cal told me later he'd personally been expecting a communal meltdown. He was wrong, fortunately. What blew my mind was the fact that no one seemed surprised, no one at all. It turned out there wasn't one person in the room with us who hadn't already been uneasy over it.

Ian didn't sugar-coat it. He just made sure Nial and Ronan were at the other end and paying attention, and then announced flat out that the Euro leg had ended with three members of the Blacklight crew, one regular and two temporary, dead under suspicious circs. He had a couple of details we didn't; he'd rung the Manchester police himself right after he'd got off the phone with me, and got the details on the James Morse killing. They weren't pretty; the autopsy on Morse had shown that he'd died from a blow to the side of the head. When Domitra asked him what that was supposed to prove, Ian met her stare, and held it.

"He was missing for three weeks, Dom." He was as curt as I've ever heard him. "It rained quite a bit—you went to school in England, you know how wet English springtime gets—and he'd been dumped out of doors. So the body was in rotten shape. But they told me their ME had found signs on his wrists that he'd been tied up. There were rope burns."

"What the hell?" Stu, our ruddy-skinned Irishman, had gone yellow. "Damn. That's just ugly, Ian. What else do we know?"

"About James Morse? Nothing, nada, zip, fuck all, or at least that's what they were willing to share with me. No known reason, open case, any information please ring, blah blah."

"What about that kid in Paris?" Ronan's voice crackled over the speaker; he sounded angry, right on the edge of being outraged. I could see that feeling reflected in faces all round that table. No one was about to let this drop. "And what about Greg? Because if someone was killing off members of our family, I want to nail the fucker. It's unacceptable. What are you planning on doing about it, Ian?"

"If you'll give me a moment and let me finish, Ronan, I'll tell you what I have." Bloody hell, they were snapping at each other. "About Alain Descarres, I've got nothing. The French police pretty much told me to sod off. I've got no official cred with them, and they're not telling me a damned thing. I'm hoping I can get the gen by going roundabout, and hooking up with Pirmin Bochsler, that bloke from Interpol. If anyone has a better notion, I'm open to it. If you think I find this situation acceptable myself, you're fucking hallucinating."

"What about Greg, Ian?" Luke's voice was a shock—he was furious. "Are the Zurich police giving you the runaround, as well? Greg was one of ours, damn it. And I, for one, am willing to hire someone to make them talk with us. If someone laid a finger on Greg, I want them caught. I don't give a fuck how much it costs or what it takes, I want them caught."

"Okay. Everyone want to calm down, please?" Oh, bloody hell. That was my own voice I was hearing. "Luke, half a mo, yeah? I've actually got a message in my voicemail from Pirmin. Bree and I had Patrick Ormand to lunch, right after Phil told us James Morse had gone missing. We were already worried about what happened to Greg. Patrick made it pretty clear that it was all or nothing—one murder meant it was probably three. Turned out Cal and Barb had already talked it out. Anyone else? No, don't tell me, too many voices at once. Just a show of hands, yeah?"

Everyone. There wasn't a single hand down. I caught Bree's eye, and took a long deep breath.

"Ronan? Nial? Your turn. This come as a shock to either of you? No? Right. Then here's my suggestion. Pirmin rang me up, and left me the message. That puts it on me, doesn't it? So I'll ring him back, a conference call, with Ian. I'll tell him we've got a consensus, that we want it looked into, that if he needs resources or cooperation or whatever, he's got it. He gets to confab with Ian over it, and Ian can keep the rest of us up on what they find. That work for everyone?"

"No." It was Phil MacDermott. "Not quite. I need to be in for as much of this as Ian is, JP. And I wouldn't speak for Domitra, but from the way she's nodding, I'm guessing she and I are on the same wavelength. Think about it a minute, will you? It's my job in the end, isn't it? I'm head of security—keeping you lot alive and well is on me, except for Mac. If someone close to us is kill-

150

ing people, I'm going to have to find a way to do my job. Do you really want me assigning someone to you, or Solange, or Cyn Corrigan, who might be a nutter?"

Of course he was right. No one said a damned thing. Phil turned to look at Ian, and waited.

"So we're all agreed?" Ian got up, looking at his watch. "JP makes the call and sets up the liaison, with me, Phil, and Dom. Carla, you ought to be in on this as well. It's a quarter of seven. Bochsler's where? Marseilles? Nine hour difference. JP, I know Monday's a shot night for you. I'm thinking we can get together around half past eleven tonight, and make the call then. It shouldn't take more than a few minutes. Bree, do you want us down here, or should we plan on doing it upstairs...?"

"...Welcome back to Virtual Days. Sorry for the long break, but here we are, about two weeks in on the stadium leg of the North American tour. We're having a rest day in sunny Manhattan—very rare, getting a Friday night off. Tomorrow, Blacklight's playing the first of two sold-out nights at Giants Stadium, across the river in East Rutherford. The locals swear it won't rain, so we're hoping for two splendid shows. So far, this leg's been fantastic—even the weather's been good. Nearest thing to a problem was that odd little lightning show Mother Nature threw at us during the set break in Foxboro...."

"Wow."

I turned round, and looked at Tony. He'd come up behind me, staring out at the empty stadium. He looked gobsmacked, and I didn't blame him. I'd played stadiums before, but even used to it, an empty stadium looks the size of the Sahara—just huge.

It had been a quiet couple of months. We'd done what we'd planned, linking Ian and our security staff up with Pirmin and his staff. After that, we sat back and waited.

Nothing had happened, nothing at all. We finished the arena leg with no one so much as breaking a fingernail. I'd gone into a huddle with Carla and the staff at the Four Seasons Silicon Valley, and thrown a surprise party after the San Jose show on Bree's 46th birthday; we'd got Miranda down from the City for that, and we'd had a nice little surprise for Bree, baby pictures of her on the video veil during the show, while we were doing a song I wrote, called "And You Left The Light On." Didn't mean anything to the audience, of course, but it did to Bree—she was in tears. The party afterward, with Mac singing Happy Birthday and me helping her cut the cake, just frosted her completely. We'd even got the cake made with sugar substitute.

"...*Our second Backstage With Blacklight winner, Lisa McCaffrey of Robesonia, Pennsylvania, has opted to claim her prize at the show tomorrow night, rather than at either of the Philadelphia shows. Turns out she has a collection of vintage harmonicas, which she'll get to discuss over a private dinner with Mac Sharpe. As every Blacklight fan knows, Mac is a serious fan of Sonny Boy Williamson, and plays harp whenever he can...*"

No deaths, no injuries, no calls in the night to say anything had happened to anyone. And no news, either, at least about those three dead blokes. We'd had Patrick over again, but that just as one guest as part of a larger party, and no real conversation went down.

I'd been right about Bree missing her own gig, catering things. I'd felt guilty enough about that so that, even with my MS giving me a bad time, I'd gone along with her wanting to have a party at Clay Street. Ian did send out the email confirming the Japanese tour, and letting us know that South America was also on the cards; a handful of promoters were apparently getting into a bidding war to see who could book us down in Rio and Sao Paulo and Buenos Aires.

And *Book of Days*, well, it just kept going. It was ridiculous, the legs this CD was showing. It had been out the better part of nine months, and it wasn't slowing down. We'd cut two videos for VH-1, and both of them had shot to the top of the charts. The first three singles were still way up in the charts, and we were deciding which was likely to be the fourth.

"...For fans writing to Ask The Band from Australia and New Zealand, I'm hoping to have some good news for you in the not too distant future. Blacklight loves playing in the Southern Hemisphere. We haven't forgot about you, I swear..."

We had a month to recoup and get ready for the stadium leg. The production crew had worked out the logistics of how to fly the line arrays and hang the video veil in stadiums—not as easy as it sounds, since an outdoor stadium hasn't got a roof to hang things from. We'd done a few days of extensive rehearsal in Montreal, opened the show, and we were off again, this time playing to seventy thousand people at a time.

It was nice, you know? It had been a good long time since we'd played gigs this size. There were things about it I quite liked, and I fell straight back into the routine. But it wasn't a routine for everyone.

So there we were, on a nice afternoon, heading toward a muggy evening at Giants Stadium in Rutherford, New Jersey. I'd been shirty about Ronan dragging us out for a soundcheck on a rest day, but I'd lost my bad mood when I realised they'd be filming it to use as the basis for the "Liplock" video. That meant we were going to save a full day in a studio somewhere.

Mac was going all out with the sexy stuff. Right now, he was about ten feet away, waving his hands about and explaining the concept behind the video to a talking head from one of the New York TV stations. The talking head was in her early forties and had obviously dressed for the event—I'd have bet she'd bought the shoes she was wobbling about on in a fetish shop somewhere. Mac was inches from charming the knickers off her, and he wasn't even trying. Hell, I wasn't even sure he knew what she was up to...

"JP—have I said thanks, yet?"

That got my attention off Mac and back to Tony. He'd come up behind me; at the back of the stage, his piano was going up and down on its riser, the crew discussing things, and two blokes with Steadicams getting it all down for posterity or MTV or something.

"Thanks?" He'd sounded dead serious. "For what?"

"Come on, man, don't be coy." He waved one arm out and around, a sort of circle, taking in the entire stadium. "For this. For getting me in on this. Because I know damned well it would-n't have happened without you. I don't want to embarrass you or anything, but shit, I'm not stupid, and, well—thanks, JP. In case I didn't say it already."

"You're not serious, are you?" I caught my guitar tech's atten-tion, halfway across the stage. "Hang on a minute, I've got some-thing I want to get over. Oi! Jas! Can you get me Little Queenie, please? And ask Ronan to power me up for a moment—oh, we are? Ta, mate."

"Fuck yeah, I'm serious." Tony meant it. "You think I don't know I wouldn't be up here, playing with you guys, if it wasn't for you? Dude, I'm not retarded, okay? There's a shitload of good piano players out there. If Blacklight wanted a piano, they could have asked anyone. I'm here because you and me, we're friends. So thanks, JP. I've been playing music all my life, but this is a whole different deal."

"Yeah, well, you're welcome, but the thing is, you're also wrong." Jas had come up, and brought my guitar with him. I slung the strap over my shoulder, and turned her master volume on. From up in the line array, I heard the hum, and saw a few of the crew glance up at the array, and then up at me. "It wasn't just me, mate. The whole band thought it was a brilliant idea—if you want the truth, I don't even know who came up with the idea first, of you coming along. Luke, probably, or Mac."

He wasn't looking convinced. I grinned at him, and checked Queenie's tuning. Perfect, of course. Jas is always spot on.

"Seriously, Tony." I glanced down and out, across what looked to be an endless sea of grass. The official number of people we'd be playing to tomorrow night was right round eighty three thousand. Right now, there were maybe thirty people out there, including half the video film crew, some of Phil's security crew, and Bree. For whatever reason, she'd opted to come along for the soundcheck, and I was damned glad of it. She had Katia with her, and Karen Hedley, as well; Barb Wilson and Cyn Corrigan had stayed in the city. "I don't suggest that kind of major deal, not when it's Blacklight, and I don't make those decisions. I leave that up to Mac and Luke."

"Why?"

"Because it's their band. They just let me play with them." I heard myself say it, and stopped. "Wow. Bloody hell."

It hadn't ever occurred to me, not once in over thirty years of being the second guitarist for Blacklight. I hadn't ever asked myself the question, and until just then, no one had ever asked me, either. I hadn't thought about it, ever. So the answer had just popped out, and it was true.

Thirty plus years, and I still saw myself as the new kid, the add-on. And I hadn't known it.

"Whatever you say." Tony was grinning at me. "I'm just glad you were along for the ride, the day Blacklight came up and played the Hurricane Felina benefit. It's been a good thirty years, JP. Pleasure to know you."

"Right back at you, mate." There was a lump at the back of my throat. "Hang on a minute, will you? There's something I want to do."

I reached down, cranked the volume up as high as she'd go, and hit an A, serious power chord, full on.

There's something about an empty stadium. If you ever play

guitar in one, you'll get what I mean: the acoustics are like nothing else on earth. You hit a note and the sound wave travels out there, it goes and goes and goes until it finally hits the back wall. And then it bounces back and travels back to you, ripples and echoes and feedback and it's fucking perfect, a sensation and a sound you just won't get indoors, or when the stadium is full.

Of course, everyone reacted. Down on the grass, Bree and the other women looked about ready to jump half out of their shoes, and the video team were right with them. Even Tony, standing next to me, looked startled for a moment. Then he caught on, and streaked for the piano.

"Whoo!" Luke, a few feet behind me, was laughing. He had his PRS custom all ready to go—gorgeous guitar, that is. He immediately hit the major for the A I'd played, the C sharp, and let the wave hit the back wall and ride back. I hit another A, a seventh this time, perfect bitchy blues chord. They echoed together, both of us grinning like idiots.

Of course, that did it. Cal played the underlying A note, a single note, pure thunder, on his Alembic. Mac turned his head to watch, dancing in place, swaying. Next to him, the talking head mouthed something; he dropped his arm around her shoulders and pulled her close to whisper an explanation into one ear, and I watched her practically puddle up.

The cameras were on us, four Steadicams and a couple of smaller ones, and of course we were recording. A, the seventh, the thunder of the E, Stu stamping on the bare stage to get them to send up his drum kit, and then there was Tony, both hands flying over the keys, the vicious evil barrelhouse run that's the underlying signature riff of the song.

And then there was Mac, singing, and he had the talking head in the circle of his arm, tilting her back and singing it straight at her: *Mama, pretty mama, honey lock your lips on me, slide 'em down lower, I'll be yellin' like a banshee...*

I had Little Queenie in full-on growl now, and Luke's PRS was wicked and hot. Tony was running the piano high in the mix, and it worked, but most of my attention, at least the bit that wasn't locked up hard with Luke and Cal, was on the impromptu of Mac seducing the talking head by singing a song about oral sex straight into her eyes. *Lock 'em on me low, there's a fire down below, lock me down, honey, take it deep, take it slow....*

Gordon *Bennett*, it was funny. She had this moony smile on her face and her legs were wobbling. I swear, I thought she was going to take the lyric as an invitation, and do him right there on stage. Mac had one arm round her, a hand sitting just off her bottom on one hip, and he wasn't letting go. Sixty years old, and her twenty years younger, she was ready to climb him. It was nice to know he hadn't lost a damned thing to age. He was hamming it up for the cameras: *Just a little nibble, honey, just a little touch, don't bother sayin' that I want it too much, lock me up, lock me down, you got me in a liplock...*

We wrapped it, letting the last notes scream out over the empty field and bounce back again. Mac gave his armful a nice little pat on the hip and let go of her; before she could say anything, he'd got hold of one of her hands and raised it to his lips. The cameras were still running.

"Indecent, isn't he?" Luke, standing next to me, jerked his head toward Mac. He was trying not to laugh. "You know what he's doing, don't you? He's sweet-talking her into making sure she signs a release to appear in the video."

"Yeah, I figured. Right old snake oil salesman we've got there." The video crew had swarmed onstage, up the ramps, taking their shots, powering down, all of them nice and enthusiastic. I heard bits of phrases: *did you get the angle front of house during the second bridge, we can edit that to get the drums in the shot, what about a fade.* I looked out over the edge, hunting for Bree, and found her. She was heading away from the stage, across the grass, behind

Karen Hedley. "Luke, mate, were you expecting your daughter? Because unless I'm off my nut, there's Solange, just walked in."

It was Solange, all right, with one of Phil MacDermott's people at her back. She gave Bree a hard hug, gave her stepmum a smile and a much lighter hug, and headed up the ramp towards Luke, who'd handed his guitar off to the tech and was waiting for her.

"Oi!" There was nothing short or distant in that hug; they've always been a solid little family unit. "I thought we weren't seeing you until Miami! Everything all right, then?"

"Everything's fine. I just got bored looking at schools. Besides, I've narrowed it down to three." She looked older than she had a few months ago. Funny, the way that works; the older I get, the faster everyone else seems to age, except for Mac. "So I checked into the Four Seasons early. The concierge told me the band had two empty rooms reserved, and we cleared it with Carla. I wanted to see the show tomorrow. That's okay, isn't it?"

"Of course it is." We were powering down, done for the day. "Where's Suzanne, love? She back at Draycote?"

Solange made a face. At least, I thought that's what she was doing. It took me a moment to realise that she was just looking uncomfortable. I wondered if Luke noticed it—you'd think he would, knowing her so much better than I did, but I know sometimes parents don't see that stuff. I've always wondered if it's part of not wanting to know what your kids are getting up to when you aren't looking.

"No—I don't think so." She wasn't meeting Luke's eye. "She said something about being invited to go hang out with some friends she made this spring. She said they—she—was going to be here in time for tomorrow's show, though."

Luke opened his mouth, and closed it again. Much as I like Solange, I was really glad, right then, that Bree hadn't wanted to do the parenting thing. It was pretty obvious Solange knew Suzanne had got up to something her parents likely wouldn't take

158

well, and didn't want to rat out her new stepsister. And Luke knew it, all right, but he didn't have the first clue about what to do about it. As for Solange, well, she isn't used to keeping secrets from her dad, and it showed.

"John?" It was Bree, waving at me from the edge of the ramp. Good timing, that was; standing there with that vibe going on onstage, that was pretty uncomfortable, and yeah, so, I'm a coward, but I was glad to escape. "You have a phone call."

"Ta." I got to her, and got a good look at her face, and my comfort level went straight down the toilet. She wasn't smiling, and she seemed to be having some trouble just swallowing. "Who is it? What's wrong?"

"It's Ian." Now I looked at her, I could see how pale she was. "He wants you. He says he has some news."

I stared at her for a moment, and around at all the outsiders, video people, stadium personnel, the lot. Then I got her by one hand and headed off down the ramp and away from all those eyes and ears, so fast she damned near stumbled trying to keep up. We were halfway across the pitch before it felt like a safe distance for any sort of privacy.

When I took the phone from Bree, I nearly dropped it, my hands were that sweaty and slick. It wasn't raining, but it was wet anyway; the air had gone that miserable dense humidity you get on the east coast, this time of year. I remember thinking the locals who'd told Nial it wasn't going to rain for the shows must be used to living in a swamp. I'm lucky mosquitoes don't much fancy me, since there were little clouds of them swarming, and I remember Bree slapping them away, trying not to swear.

"Ian?"

"JP, yeah, it's me." He sounded about as grim as I'd ever heard him. His voice was stretched as tight as one of Stu's drumheads. "Listen, I'm going to send this out in an email to everyone, but you were my liaison with Pirmin Bochsler, so I wanted to let you know. We've got a problem. We were right about Greg Maltin's death not being an accident. The Zurich police rang Pirmin, and he rang me. Some bloke came forward to say he saw someone's body being thrown in the river by two men in a black car, and they think it was Greg."

Chapter Ten

Looking back, I think it was that day at Giants Stadium, taking that call from Ian, where I began to realise that stuff was going on in places I'd never have thought to look.

"JP?" I must have gone quiet a few seconds too long, because Ian sounded even closer to snapping. "Say something."

"Right." It was bizarre, the way I was reacting. I wasn't surprised to get it confirmed that Greg hadn't just slipped and fallen—in a strange way, knowing I'd been right about him was validating—but I was shocked. Never occurred to me you could be both, unsurprised and shocked, at the same time. "Still here, Ian, just processing. When did Pirmin ring you?"

"About twenty minutes ago. I'll talk to Phil MacDermott as soon as we're done here. He and Dom are going to need to know all about it." He paused for a moment. "Not that there's much to know about."

He sounded bitter. I caught the look on Bree's face, and remembered that she couldn't hear Ian's end, just mine. It was obvious how anxious she was, and I pulled her up close to me. I wasn't about to hit the speaker, though, not with a video crew and reporters hanging about. Those people have bloody radar, or something, especially if they smell other peoples' trouble.

"Ian, talk to me, will you please? What did Pirmin say? Because that thing the Zurich police said, a witness seeing two blokes throw Greg in the river? I don't think I buy it. I mean, what the fuck is that about? Someone saw two men throwing a body in the freezing cold river and only just now decided to mention it to the coppers, oh by the way, I saw a murder? That's pants. Greg died months ago."

"It's not that simple. Turns out the bloke who saw it was wanted in a different canton for burglary, and he knew it. So he wasn't exactly leaping to do the right thing. They only got the story because they popped him for something else, and he spilled. Probably hoping for a reduced sentence in exchange for valuable information about a crime, or something." He took a deep breath. "JP, the guy described what happened, and he described Greg, at least what Greg was wearing that night. Pirmin said it matched the description the Zurich cops have in their files. I don't know about you, but I'm convinced. There wasn't much in the local press, at the time—they thought it was an accident, and Greg was a crew guy. It's not like he was famous. So, making this up? How? Why? I don't see it."

"Damn. No, you're right." I was quiet for minute, digesting it, rubbing my hand up and down Bree's arm. "Okay. Did Pirmin have any real gen to share? Details about the two blokes, about the car, anything?"

"Not yet, or at least, not to me. Give him a chance—the Zurich cops rang him around eleven tonight, his time. Not much he

162

could do, that late. One thing he did say, there's probably going to be an exhumation order requested—Greg's body was sent home to Kent, to his parents. He's buried there. They're going to talk to Greg's family, and ask for cooperation."

"They're going to dig him up?" I felt Bree, pressed up against me, stiffen up. I kept my voice even, which wasn't easy; for some reason, the idea hit every button I've got. I felt a few sharp little tremors run up my right arm and leg, and bit back wanting to swear; I'd been standing in place too long, and that always kicks the MS into high gear. "What in hell for?"

"Because of the Manchester case, and what happened to that French kid, the morning after we opened at Bercy. They're going to look for signs of a blow to the head, and if they find any, we're looking at a pattern here. Pirmin says he's going to talk to the Paris police as well, and that works for me, because I've had fuck-all in the way of luck getting them to talk with me. All I got was *oui monsieur, mais non monsieur, bon jour, bon soir, d'accord*. You can translate all that to *piss off, who the hell are you to be asking us anything, then?* They won't talk to me, and the Manchester police weren't keen on talking to me, either. And if I push it, tell them they've got to keep me informed because I'm Blacklight's manager, we're into high risk territory, because it links the deaths with the band. One leak, one local employee of the Manchester cop shop without enough sense to connect the dots, and the headlines will go ballistic. It's a real possibility. Because…"

He stopped. I stayed quiet, waiting him out. It's the same technique I used on Patrick Ormand; it was pretty clear he had something else to say, and he finally said it.

"Those three deaths have some things in common." He hated saying it; I could tell from his voice. "What cops call the MO. We talked about this, remember? All early morning hours after a Blacklight show, all three on their way to or from somewhere, long after the gig was over. And the victims have something in common, as well, and it's pretty obvious."

He stopped again. This time, though, I wasn't waiting him out; I finished it for him.

"They all worked for us. That what you were going to say? Us, the band, Blacklight, we're what they had in common. Yeah, fairly obvious, Ian. And of course, three deaths in three different countries, that gives Pirmin and his lot at Interpol an all-access pass into this. Shit. I don't like this."

"Yeah, well, why would you? There's nothing to like." Here it came, whatever it was he really hadn't wanted to say. "And I've been kicking myself for not putting my mind on this, when Greg died. Busy, yeah, I've been busy as hell, but that's no excuse. Staying on top of things is what you pay me for. I should have seen it earlier, and I didn't. I let myself get distracted by what the CD was doing, the Japanese thing, South America, the NFL of-fer, all that. I cocked it up, JP, and don't think I don't know it. If we weren't in mid-tour, I'd call a conference and propose that you guys officially sack me."

"Oh for fuck's sake, Ian, knock it off, will you?" Bloody hell, he was serious. "Did you hit anyone with a car? Throw Greg in the river? Tie up that poor sod in Manchester and dump his body? Because if you didn't, you're talking bullshit, and we've got enough to cope with without you beating your chest over what you think you should have done. So stop, please."

"Okay. Thanks." That did the trick; he was back to his usual Ian-voice, tight and gruff, but not flipping out. "Look, I'll be straight with you: maybe I'm paranoid, but I'm not sure Pirmin Bochsler is telling me everything he knows. Do you think he'd tell you more than he'd tell me? I mean, you know him better than I do; Bree fed him, back in Cannes. I can't read him well enough to decide whether he gave me the lot, or whether he's sitting on information because he's got no reason to trust me with it. Can you talk to him and see?"

"Yeah, I will. What time is it? Half past twelve in the morning in France? I'll ring him back before we go to bed tonight. And I'll let you know—what, tonight, or should I wait until tomorrow morning?"

"Tomorrow's fine, unless he tells you something you think I need to know tonight." He blew out his breath, a hard little rasp into my ear. "Thanks, JP. I don't want to sound like a bloody schoolboy, but fact is, I'm seriously freaked. If it turns out someone close to us is doing a V-for-vendetta on the rest of the crew, we're in deep shit. Hell, even if we get lucky and it turns out it was just a barmy local hire with an itch, there's going to be a media meltdown over it. Just thinking about the aggro is giving me an ulcer. Anyway. Whatever. I need to go find Carla. Cheers, and thanks again."

He rang off before I could say anything. I still had Bree snuggled up against me, but the truth was, I'd forgotten about her and everything else for the moment. My brain was doing the sort of dance moves I can never seem to keep up with.

What Ian had said, about the media having a field day with it, that was true. After the sleazy little shit who'd appointed himself Blacklight's biographer had got his throat bashed in with my guitar stand in a Madison Square Garden dressing room few years back, we'd got the full press treatment, reporters everywhere, doing hatchet jobs on us, our families, our friends. It had been as close to group hell as we'd ever got.

So yeah, Ian had that right, and no shock, since he'd been our road manager during all that. He and Carla had coped with the bulk of it, but even with them shielding us from as much of the shitstorm as possible, it had still been zero fun.

The problem was, he hadn't thought past the potential media nightmare. I had, though. And we had something a lot scarier to worry about than just the media circus.

If a Blacklight employee, or a member of our family, had done this, we had no idea who was safe and who wasn't. Hell, for all anyone knew, no one was safe. There didn't seem to be any motive, and that meant that any one of us—band, wives, crew, management, whoever—could be on this nutter's hit parade...

"John?" She sounded worried. "What's happening?"

"You pretty much heard it, love, except the bit where Ian thinks Pirmin is keeping gen back. Oh, and the bit where Ian thinks we should sack him for not noticing this before. He's doing the guilt thing." I kept my voice down. Ridiculous, really; the nearest people to us were well out of earshot. "Local burglar got nabbed by the Zurich police and told them he'd seen a murder. They seem to think what he saw was Greg Maltin being thrown in the Limmat."

"You mean, Greg was alive?" Her eyes were wide and one hand had gone to her mouth. For a moment, I thought she was going to black out. "The burglar actually saw someone kill Greg? They weren't just dumping his body—he drowned? Oh, John!"

"Bree, love, breathe, please? This is ugly, yeah, but there's sod-all you can do about it, so it's no good you imagining the worst, and I'm not having you make yourself ill over it." I reached up and tilted her chin down. "Come on, lady, take a breath. Good. Right. Do it again. Anyway, I don't know whether Greg was alive or not. Only one way to find out, yeah? I'm ringing Pirmin."

"Now?" Her shoulders had hunched up hard. "Not in the morning?"

"Now. Sod it, he's a law enforcement bloke. He's used to having his phone go off at weird hours."

I got the cell back out, and scrolled through old messages. There it was, country code for France, no caller ID listed.

"Here we go." I hit the "return call" option. "Anyone comes too close, wave them off, all right? I don't need an audience."

The phone hadn't done its little double-ping twice before I realised that the number I was connecting to was likely Pirmin's office, and that the chances of him actually being there to pick it up and talk to me were small to none. But of course, he picked it up at the third ring.

"This is Pirmin Bochsler." He sounded the same as always; if he really was one of those Patrick Ormand-level obsessive nutters who basically sleep at their desks, he'd probably sound the same if the world was ending. Nearest I'd ever seen him to being shaken off balance, the world pretty much *had* been ending, and all he'd got was more organised. Maybe it's a Swiss thing, not a cop thing. "How may I help you?"

"Oi, Pirmin, it's JP Kinkaid. I'm surprised I got you—middle of the night there, isn't it?" I glanced up. No one was coming closer, but there were a few people looking our way. Right. They could be curious all they wanted, so long as they stayed where they were. Bree was scratching at her arms, looking miserable. "Look, I'm out of doors and poor Bree's being eaten alive by mosquitoes or gnats or something, and anyway, this isn't the smartest place for this sort of conversation, you know? Let's keep this short. I just got off the phone with Ian. He told me what's happening, but is there anything you didn't tell him? Because he's been getting the brush-off from the Paris police, and getting snubbed by the Manchester coppers as well, and I think he's feeling paranoid."

"No, there is nothing, not as yet. I have conference calls already arranged for the morning, with the authorities of all three cities." Bloody hell, he was doing it again: faced with a multi-city border-crossing murderer, all he got was even more competent. "Please assure Mr. Hendry that he will be the first person to hear any details from those conversations."

"Yeah, I will. But hang on a mo, will you? I need to ask you one particular question, all right?" Bree was watching me, her shoulders still up around her ears. "I've got a very tense wife over here, with a really vivid imagination. She heard my end of Ian's

167

call, and I'd bet a stack of Euros that if I don't get an answer, she'll be awake half the night, imagining all sorts of horrors. Bree's waving hello, by the way."

"Send Mrs. Kinkaid my greetings, and high regards." He sounded a lot more human, suddenly. "I have not forgotten that she made me welcome at her table. And I have no wish for her to harrow herself, so tell me, what do you wish to know?"

"It's about Greg Maltin. Ian told me about some burglar telling the Zurich cops he'd seen two men throw Greg in the river, and now Bree's thinking he was awake and alive, and drowned. Was he?"

"That, I don't know, as yet." He answered me without even one moment's pause. "But please tell Mrs. Kinkaid we think it unlikely. Apparently, there was no struggle. And in any case, if there had been obvious marks of violence on Mr. Maltin's body, there would have been an immediate suspicion. The Swiss police are very thorough."

"So he was probably already dead, then?" There were people headed toward us, Tony and Katia, with Luke and Karen behind them, and Mac and Dom just a few steps back, Mac talking to Solange. "Pirmin, there's a bit of a mob here—bad place for this particular conversation. Ring Ian when you've got news, okay? I'll let him know we talked."

"Yes, certainly I will. As to your question, only a pathology report would confirm that. But please, reassure Mrs. Kinkaid: at the very least, he was unconscious. It is extremely unlikely that he knew what was happening to him. And accept my hope that your show tomorrow night—it is a very large show, is it not, and an important one for your group?—is a success. Now I must try to sleep; it's very late here. Good night to you."

"...Hello again, Blacklight fans! Nial here, with a fast update from the East Coast. We're at showtime minus three hours (that doesn't

168

include the dinner break) for the first of two sold-out shows at Giants Stadium, here in New Jersey..."

"Holy crap, it's a mob!" Tony was sounding spooked. "Who are all these people, anyway?"

"...Rumours have been flying fast and thick about a Very Special Guest (or guests) for either or both Jersey shows. All I can say is, that may or may not be true. You'll just have to wait and see..."

I turned round. The show was due to start at seven; it was ten of, and we'd just come out of the green room, beginning to line up at the foot of the ramp. Our special guests—yeah, there were going to be two of them, just for tonight's show, during the second set—were still all the way backstage, staying well out of sight until they were ready to slip under the stage.

We'd actually worked this out down to the last detail, under a hard lockdown during the initial stadium rehearsals, back in Montreal. The plan was that Mac would make a chatty remark to the crowd about New Jersey, the crowd would respond, catcalls and hoots and all that. At that point, our guests would come up on risers, along with their instruments: one guitar plus vocal mic, one saxophone.

And of course, the crowd would go berserk. Hell, for these particular guests, any audience anywhere in the known universe would have gone berserk, but this was their home turf. There's nothing like having your local legends sitting in to rock the crowd, you know?

"Wow, it's crowded." Katia had joined us, with Bree right behind her. "Who are all these people?"

"Haven't got a clue. But if they're in here, they were on the list. Phil's got the security locked down tight."

He really did. Pirmin had rung Ian directly after his conference with the various coppers. I hadn't been privy to that, which was fine with me, but Ian had rung me to say thanks, he and Pirmin were on the same page now, I could go back to just doing what I

169

do, playing music, leave the rest to him and Phil and Dom. I said right, sounds good, cheers, and did my best to not wonder what in hell was going on in Zurich and Paris and Manchester. But he'd called it: not my job.

Whatever Ian had said had sent Phil into the kind of protection mode I didn't think anyone who wasn't on the Secret Service presidential detail ever did. There were already security cameras in place backstage and over all the gates in—that was standard. Tonight, though, everyone not only got a brand new laminate, they also got their ID checked and their hands stamped with a nice inky Blacklight logo: left wrist for in and out backstage access, right wrist for everywhere that wasn't full backstage. If you fancied a wander anywhere outside the secured backstage area, you had to jump through some flaming hoops to get back in. I kept expecting to see Dom muttering something about "liberty moving" into a radio disguised as a lapel pin, or something. It was nuts.

There were security people at every door. Every warm body going in or out was getting checked. Anyone stupid enough to get shirty about it with Phil or his staff found himself face to face with Dom. So far, people were behaving; I hadn't heard much muttering, even from the people who'd been allowed full access before but were being denied it now.

Phil had also made sure that every member of the band family itself—band, wives, kids, immediate relatives—had his personal 911 code programmed into their phone. He'd been making the rounds since before we'd left the hotel, checking everyone's cell except Mac's: *show me your phone, right, good, you know that in an emergency, day or night, you just hit the panic code and we'll take care of whatever it is for you, just do it.* It was completely barmy and over the top, or at least I hoped it was; as I say, I didn't know what Pirmin had told Ian. I was out of that loop, at least for the moment.

Just then, I was waiting for Bree to get behind me. I knew

what she was going to do, slipping that hand in, the light squeeze to send a little sex onstage with me. It had become a ritual, these past few years, and I'd come to want it. But Bree hadn't moved; I was getting a nice view of her back.

"I see Suzanne's here." She was scanning the crowd. "And there are those three guys who were at most of the Europe gigs. That guy in the green jacket, wasn't he at the Pinewood party? And the Tahini Twins, oh joy, oh rapture. Heads up, Katia! I'm officially raising the Skanky Ho Alert level to bright red."

I snorted. Bree heard it and turned around, looking over her shoulder at me. I raised an eyebrow, and jerked my head a bit, and she came over and got behind me.

"That's a fantastic dress." It really was. I can't tell fabrics apart, mostly, so I go by the colour and the way it hugs. This one was new, the colour of an Abyssinian cat, golden-orange, and yeah, it hugged, all right. If we hadn't been where we were, I'd have been tempted to lift the skirt over her head and see if I was right about what she didn't have on under it. "Gorgeous colour on you, too—damned if I know why you don't wear it more often. You know, Bree, if you wore jewellery, I'd have to buy you something to go with that. Is it new?"

"Yep." She bit my right ear, a tiny little nip. Crikey, she hadn't touched the really sensitive bits yet, and I was already turned on. "I got it at Armani, this morning. Tony's going to shoot me—I bullied Katia into buying some new stuff. She was moaning over this one, so I made the guy come over and wave some pretty shiny clothes at her. Once we revived her after she saw the price, she decided she needed it. Doesn't she look hot?"

"Probably. My eyes are rather full of you at the moment, so you'd have to ask Tony."

"Damn, I love you, John." She slipped a hand between my thighs, cupped, squeezed; she made a little noise, probably realising what she was in for later. "Wow. Do a good gig, baby."

171

"You got it." Noise, suddenly, eighty thousand people's worth of noise; Mac had hit the stage. "I'll do my best."

It was a brilliant show. Technically, it wasn't the US opener—we'd done that in Foxboro. But it had that sort of energy to it, and of course, when Mac chivvied the crowd about New Jersey and our guests emerged out of the stage, you could have heard the reaction in Boston. It was amazing.

Show closer, with the video veil dancing and shimmering, alive with graphics and photos and subtle little light displays. Backstage to towel down and rehydrate. Mac grabbed a bottle of champagne, Luke grabbed another one, spraying the first few rows of the crowd off each of the stage's two wings. Encore with an oldie, "Heart Attack," and of course the crowd loved it.

Lights up, show over, arms round each other for the goodnight bow. Just a few minutes to unwind and get ourselves into the limos, along with a police escort to get us to the New Jersey Turnpike, so that we didn't have to spend what was left of the night sitting in a solid traffic jam, eighty thousand people in cars. I was ready for a nice tumble with my wife and a good night's sleep. After all, we were going to have to come back out and do this all again tomorrow…

"Solange? Suzanne?" Karen sounded a bit edgy. "Aren't you riding back with us?"

We were waiting for our six-seater limo back to the hotel. Mac and Dom, the Wilsons and the Corrigans had all settled into the first one; the liveried driver was closing the doors, and ours was right behind it. Phil had asked us to not wander off, please just wait for our ride to pull up to us. Apparently, that made his job, keeping an eye on all of us, a lot easier.

We were supposed to be heading back with Luke and Karen and the girls, or so we'd thought, but Tony and Katia had come up, and were waiting with us. The limos seat six people, and eight into six doesn't go.

"No, we're not, Karen, but thanks." Solange leaned up and gave her dad a peck on the cheek. "There's some private party down in Tribeca somewhere, at an art gallery or something, and we got invited. We've got a ride. See you in the morning?"

There wasn't much conversation in the limo. It was mostly Bree and Katia, just a bit of chatter. Me and Tony and Luke, we were all knackered; besides, the noise levels at any gig are intense, but this leg, we'd basically quadrupled all that, and we were still getting used to dealing with stadium levels again after a good long time away. Maybe that's why it took me as long as it did, to realise that Karen Hedley wasn't saying anything. She was completely quiet, that ride into Manhattan.

We got back to the Four Seasons before midnight, and I did both things on my list: pinned Bree to the overstuffed mattress, and got a decent night's sleep. But again, I must have been seriously tired, because I was all the way down in REM sleep when the real world came crashing in on me. Someone was shaking my shoulder, good and hard.

"John? John! Wake up, please wake up…"

I opened my eyes. That took a few moments, but when I got them open and managed to focus on Bree's face, quite a few things got through the leftover sleep haze, and into my brain.

She was grey-faced. I could hear voices, confused and muffled, coming from the suite's outer room. The door between the rooms was shut, but those voices were still getting through. Mostly what I heard was just the edge, but one word suddenly came through, clear and sharp, Ian's voice: *Police*.

I woke up, then. Not completely, there was still some fog in the brain and over the eyes, but enough to get a coherent thought stream going: *it's morning, something's happening, come along Johnny, get on with it, you've got visitors and something's wrong, wake up.*

"Okay. I'm awake." I swung my legs out of bed, and bit back a

173

yelp. I hadn't done my usual first-thing stretch, hadn't checked on what was likely to hurt, hadn't adjusted for it. Instead, I'd just put both feet down on the floor and stood up, and really that was bloody stupid, because my legs always get the worst of the MS, and this morning both heels were on fire. "What time is it?"

"Not quite seven." She swallowed. "John -"

"Wait, Bree, please. Damned disease is acting up. Half a mo." I gave it a couple a seconds; the pain in both legs got a bit less excruciating, and I got a good long breath in there. "We got one of those nice plush robes handy? I need the loo and I can't deal with whatever's going on naked. Just—get me a robe and give me a moment, yeah?"

"Here." She'd already found mine where I'd dropped it the night before, and draped it over my shoulders like a boxer's manager, or James Brown, or something. Her hands were trembling, but she was still Bree, and her first concern still seemed to be me, thank God. "Do you need me to get you your meds? Anything?"

"Ta." I knotted the belt, and looked at her. "Okay. Tell me quick, and then do me a favour, get back out there and tell them I'll be out in a few minutes. What's going on?"

"Phil MacDermott's dead." Her lips were almost as grey as her face. She got the words out, but I'm damned if I know how. "Someone killed him, John. Someone killed Phil."

Chapter Eleven

Most mornings, I just deal and forget, once they're done with. I've got my routines: stretch, label the bad bits, out of bed, try to keep the pain to a minimum, into the loo for meds, shower, dressed, coffee and breakfast. When the bad mornings do hit, I'm usually too sick to remember anything.

But I remember everything about the morning Phil was killed. Not only what I did—everything I felt, everything everyone else said. I'm damned if I know why.

I remember that I stood there, just staring at Bree. My feet were yelling, every nerve telling me to sit down, and get the weight off them, please. The bladder was being just as noisy. I was ignoring the lot, standing there like a shop window manne-quin, staring at my wife.

"What?" Nothing came out, just a scratchy nonsense. Just beyond the closed door, people were talking. I could hear the voices, not the words, but the tones were very clear. "Bree? What did -"

I cleared my throat, and tried again; I was dry as a bone. "Bree, what in hell…?"

"I—that's all I know." She began to shake, shudder really, and I wasn't even aware of doing it, but suddenly I had both arms around her, holding on. "All I know," she said into my hair, and started sobbing. It scared me half off my nut—I'd never heard that sound from her before, harsh and raspy and dry, sounding as if things were tearing inside.

"It's all right." Yeah, I know, stupid thing to say—it wasn't even close to all right, but that's what came out. I couldn't take it—I had to make her stop, somehow. We couldn't be flipping our shit, not now.

I turned us both around, back toward the bed, and sat her down at the end of it. "Love, wait for me. Two minutes. We'll go out together. Stay put, yeah? Meanwhile, breathe. Do a bit of that yoga stuff you do, whatever it is. Get your breath back. All right?"

"Okay." She closed her eyes. "Yes. I will. Okay."

It took me closer to ten minutes, because everything hurt and I was short of breath. I thought about the shower, decided *sod it*, and got dressed. I nearly didn't make it; there was a half-minute of shakes so bad, I didn't think I was going to be able to stand, straighten up and zip up my trousers. I sat down hard, waiting for the legs to start working, waiting for the ataxia to let go and give me a fucking break. The whole time, I was gritting my teeth and giving the legs a silent lecture: *come on, stop assing about, your timing needs works, stop it, come on, right, hurt if you need to but you've got to hold me up*….

So it took longer than I'd told Bree. But the extra time gave her some extra time; when I got back out into the bedroom, those dry sobs had stopped completely. I suppose I must have looked pretty shaky, because she got a hand on my arm.

"Ready?" I asked her, and she nodded. "Right. Let's do it."

We opened the doors and walked into what sounded like one of Blacklight's rowdier audiences, waiting for an encore: it was really loud in there. The suite's main room was SRO, wall to wall: the rest of the band, all the wives, Domitra, Luke and Karen's girls, Ian, Carla. There were also three members of the hotel's staff, wheeling in carts loaded with food and coffee. I thought the hotel must train their people to look blank, no matter what…

"Johnny, thank God, there you are." That got my attention. Mac was right on the edge of losing it, and that's something he doesn't do often. I could see it in his face, hear it in his voice. I saw one of the hotel people, a woman, glance up at him, and then away, smoothing out that fast flicker of curiosity. "Here, have some food, get something in you. Did Bree tell you what was happening?"

"Yes, Mac, I told him." Out of nowhere, there was my old lady, Bree doing her thing, remembering that I'd been dragged out of sleep, that my MS was being iffy, that I was being expected to cope before breakfast, that my well-being was her business and no one else's. "Um, will everyone just shut up and hang on and let John get some breakfast? John, could you pass me a cup, please? No, no toast, just coffee. You eat."

That quietened everyone down, all right. I don't think any of them had heard that tone from her before, except maybe Tony and Katia. I saw Suzanne's head jerk up—she was hiding behind her hair, something Bree used to do when she was about Suzanne's age and shit was just piling on too high and too hard for coping—and her eyes went very wide. Then she realised she was being looked at, flinched, and ducked her head again. I found my-self wondering just what she was hiding from, wondering just what

177

she thought that swinging curtain of hair was protecting her from.

I grabbed some food and poured a cup. Cyn Corrigan herded the hotel staff out, and shut the door behind them. It had just barely clicked shut when Ian spoke up.

"Bree, sorry, but I'm going to talk while JP eats. We don't have much time—NYPD's going to hit the doorstep pretty much any minute, now." Ian was standing, his shoulders hunched as hard as Bree's get sometimes; he was rocking, swaying really. He sounded beyond grim, into lifeless, and I thought, *my God, he's in shock*. "I want us all on the same page when they get here, and there are things that need explaining. All right?"

My mouth was full of scrambled egg, but I nodded. He took a deep breath. *Showtime*.

"Here's what I know. I got woken up at right round half past five this morning. It was Jamil Corbin, one of the guys Phil hired for this leg—I don't know how many of you are aware of it, but Phil handpicked every member of the leg security team, and they're all on for the whole leg. So Jamil is staff for the next three months. He was ringing from a homicide cop's office, downtown: Phil had been found dead on a path in Fort Tryon Park about an hour earlier. There was no sign of his car." He swallowed hard. "Jesus. Phil's gone. He's really gone."

He sagged suddenly. Carla moved, but Bree got there first.

"Sit." She pushed a chair under him, and watched him sink down. He was grey-faced.

"Ta." He was trying to hold it together. "Anyway. Jamil gave me some gen. He said Phil had assigned him to Solange and Suzanne last night. Apparently, there was some sort of do, a private invite-only party at the Lazy Eye Club, down in Tribeca, after the show. He had a problem—right around half past two, Solange had come out on her own, and looked around for a cab."

"Solange?" Luke was looking at his daughter, and she met his eye. "Want to tell us about it?"

"Not really." She gave herself a little shake. Her voice was chilly, and suddenly, out of nowhere, she looked and sounded just like Viv. I saw Mac's mouth twist a bit. "But I will. It—just, it wasn't my kind of party, that's all. I was expecting something very different. I didn't like where things seemed to be headed. I'm not a fan of what everyone was getting into. So I said goodnight, and left."

"Rough sex?" We all jumped, I think; Mac's voice was living up to his name. He could have faceted a diamond with it, it was that sharp and hard. Someone in the room, one of the women, made a tiny noise that might have been a whimper. "Or just hard dope? Talk to us, Solange. Phil's dead. Sex, or dope?"

"Both." She hated saying it, and I wondered why. We were all staring at her, except Suzanne, and she flushed. "I don't like orgies and I don't like opium. So I said goodnight."

"Ian, where's this security bloke?" Stu looked as tired as I felt. "Why not let him speak for himself?"

"He can't. He's downtown at the cop shop." Carla had both hands on Ian's shoulders, rubbing, making him wince. It reminded me of Bree, working on me. "Let Ian talk, Stu. He has all the details. Pretty much everything Jamil's telling the cops right now, Ian is telling us. Just let him talk. We need to know as much as we can, right now. What else, Ian?"

"One security tail, two girls, minor problem." Ian leaned back into the shoulder rub. He looked like he needed it. "They hadn't thought about what to do if the girls left the party at different times; after all, they'd gone together. Phil told Jamil to tell Solange to wait in his car, Phil was on his way. He'd take over and cover Suzanne, whenever she wanted to leave."

"You stayed on at the party, Suzanne?" Luke's voice was blank, very careful, but it wasn't working; I saw Karen Hedley's face, and wished I hadn't, not when I caught the look she shot her daughter. The look she gave Luke right after was even worse; it

179

brought back a picture, a memory, Bree, damned near thirty years ago, asking me not to leave.

"I—yes…" Suzanne looked at her stepfather, not at her mum. I wondered if she'd seen the pain in Karen's face. "For a while. I didn't want to be rude—I wasn't sure if -"

She stopped. Everyone in the room was staring at her, except for Ian. He had his eyes closed. He waited a minute; when it was clear she'd stopped, he started talking again.

"Anyway—Jamil followed orders, and Solange came and sat in the security car. Solange, could you say how long it was, you waiting for Phil? Can you tell us what happened?"

"After Jamil rang Phil? It was ten minutes, maybe fifteen." She spoke up straight off, and I thought, *right, she's been sorting it out in her head, she knows she's going to get asked about this, she and this Corbin bloke, crikey, last people to see Phil alive, maybe.* "He showed up pretty fast. And he came over to check on me, make sure I was all right, and I said yes, I'm fine, Suzanne was still inside hanging out with her friends, but I was tired and I wanted to go back to the hotel and go to bed." She glanced at her stepsister, and then away. "He asked, was I sure Suzanne was still there, and I told him yes, she was. But he wasn't paying much attention by then."

"What?" It was Katia, of all people. "What do you mean, he wasn't paying attention? Why not?"

"Well, he was looking at this car, parked up the street from the gallery. It might have been a small SUV, or an estate wagon—I don't know, I'm not particularly interested in cars. Biggish, anyway, and black. I hadn't noticed it before, but of course, I'd only just come outside when Jamil came over. Phil told Jamil he wanted to talk to him for a minute. Jamil got out of the car, and they sort of huddled. But if I have to say, then I think it was all about that car. Something about it—I don't know. They were waving their hands, and nodding towards it."

She yawned, a huge gulp of air, just pure tiredness. She might be twenty years old but she was also jetlagged, partied out, and she'd got dragged awake and out of bed just as early as everyone else. Three hours' sleep is going to leave you yawning, I don't give a toss what your age is.

"And...?" Luke wasn't being quite so careful to hide his feelings, not talking to Solange. He was pissed off, yeah, but not at her. "What happened after that?"

"I don't know, do I, Dad?" You'd have thought Luke was dim, from the tone of her voice. "Jamil drove me straight back here."

"Okay." I put my plate down, and got up to shake my legs; they'd gone pins and needles, all over. "So Phil stayed to cover Suzanne, and I'm guessing we're about to ask Suzanne just what went down at this little orgy, or whatever it was. Sorry, Karen, not trying to be rude, but I've been in rock and roll a good long time, and we've seen it all, pretty much."

"You're damned right we're asking." Luke was so narked, it was scary. If I'd been Suzanne and Luke had been aiming that tone at me, I'd have gone looking for a hole to crawl into. He had cold steel in his voice. "Suzanne? We're waiting."

"Don't bully her, Luke."

We all jumped at that. Luke's voice had been cold and pissed off—he was in full Furious Dad mode. But he couldn't hold a candle to how cold Bree sounded, or how fierce. "Can't you see she's scared?"

She walked straight up to Suzanne and got a finger under her chin, tilting her face up, locking eyes, making her look at the world. It was the same gesture I've been using on Bree since she was a teenager, every time I felt she needed reminding about how young she was.

Something in my stomach tightened up and then let go, but whatever it was, it left me wanting to boot everyone out and hold on to my wife. It's not as if she had any reason to be kind to the girl, you know?

181

"It's all right." If it had been anyone but Bree, I'd have thought it was a fantastic acting job, she sounded that gentle. But this was Bree, and she wasn't putting it on. "Just tell us, Suzanne, okay? No one's going to yell at you or get on your case or hate you, but here's the thing: you have to stop hiding. You can't pretend you're invisible, not with a murder. It doesn't work. Believe me, I learned that the hard way. Just talk to us. We're here for you. We've got your back."

Of course, that did it. Suzanne started to shake, first the shoulders, then the rest of her. Bree looked at Luke, and jerked her head. It was a very clear message, that look: *get your bum over here, now.*

And then she stepped back and out of the way, because Luke and Karen were right there, holding on to Suzanne, letting her cry it out. It would have been a very pretty little family moment, but Solange stayed out of it. Whatever had been going on between the girls, Solange wasn't offering any hugs.

"We went to this party." Suzanne had got hold of one of Karen's hands, and was hanging on for dear life. "It was invite only, and I thought it would be sort of posh, and exclusive. I thought it would be like a couple of parties I went to in Paris last month, a DJ and music and dancing and some really cool people, just hanging out. But it wasn't like that at all. It was different."

"Oh, bloody hell. Yeah, I bet it was." Mac shook his head. "I know that kind of party. What did they trot out for this one, Suzanne? Threesomes with blindfolds? Ropes and gags? Some meth to get everyone in the mood, maybe rohypnol or something for the girls who didn't fancy playing rough? Some toys from the fetish specialists, maybe some handcuffs, that lot? The girls waking up with a few deliberately inflicted scars to not remember the party by? An opium pipe for a chaser, after the boys have done the rounds? I hear that's the in thing right now."

"Jesus." Tony looked sick. "Man, that's seriously fucked up. I'm glad I'm not a parent.""

"Was it like that?" Luke had an arm round Suzanne. If he was still narked, it wasn't at her.

"Not at first." Suzanne looked up, finally. Her face was a wreck, clogged with tears, and she had the hiccoughs. "It was just the way Solange said. I knew some people there, just a few, from the Euro tour. I felt sort of isolated—my friends went off to hang with some other people. But later on, a few of the guys from backstage showed up, crew guys, I mean. They waved at us, and the DJ was spinning some good techno, and everyone was dancing. So I started having fun. It was a really cool party, for a while. But…"

"Go on, love," Luke told her. "But…?"

"But then it all went wrong." She bit her lip. "Two guys came over, and asked if I wanted to go out back with them, smoke a joint. I said no, not really, I just want to dance. But they kept trying to push me out toward the back of the club. They sort of boxed me in." Suzanne sounded about twelve years old, remembered panic in her voice. What she was saying wasn't half as vivid as what she wasn't saying. "I didn't know what to do."

"Oh, God." Karen had one arm round her daughter, and her voice was unsteady. "It's all right, darling, you're safe. No one's cross with you. Tell us what happened."

"Well, it was really crowded, too crowded. I looked around for my friends, and I saw them with one of the guys from the crew. I looked for Solange, but I couldn't see her anywhere." She glanced across the room at her stepsister, but Solange very carefully wasn't looking back. "So I thought she'd gone."

"You must have been scared." Dom had been watching and listening. "You have a phone with the security code in it. Why didn't you ring it?"

"But—I did!" Suzanne was gawking at her. "And Phil rang me right back, I mean, just the way he'd said he would, if we needed to ring him. He told me to wait, just outside the front door. He told me our detail had taken Solange home but he was going to send someone back to come get me. So I went outside, and waited, and Jamil came back and drove me home, back here."

"Did you see Phil?" Dom's eyebrows were about the deepest vee I'd ever seen. "I'm not getting this. Doesn't make sense. Where in hell was Phil? Ian, dude, don't glare at me. This is security's business, all the way. Phil was the one who came up with the procedure. If he told Jamil that he'd cover Suzanne—and Jamil is a professional bodyguard, he's good at what he does—then where was Phil, and why did he detail Jamil to do it? Something to do with that car, maybe, but the point is, he was breaking his own protocol. Does that sound like Phil to you?"

"No, it doesn't." Carla had obviously been thinking, something she does better than most people, and a lot more quickly, as well. "Dom, you're right. We need to talk to Jamil when he gets back. For one thing, he told Ian that Phil's body was found in Fort Tryon Park, and that's the other end of the city from Tribeca. I want to know what he was doing up there. But right now, I need to raise an issue, and it's major."

"They're all major." Ian opened his eyes, took a deep breath, and closed them again. "What's the issue?"

"What have you got in mind as a replacement? Because we've got a breach in security now that's about the size of the Holland Tunnel, and I can't think of a worse time for it."

"Fuck!" It obviously hadn't been at the forefront of his mind, but it was now. Carla's good at that, yeah? She makes you focus, like it or not. "No clue, not one. Brilliant, just bloody brilliant. Carla, can you get me a list? I need names, anyone who might be up for a huge contract, really complex, involving travel, at a moment's notice. Can you think of anyone?"

"If she can't, I can."

I heard myself say it, but I didn't believe it. Of course, they all turned round to look at me.

"You do?" Ian actually sounded hopeful. "Dish, JP, please?"

I don't know where the idea came from. Maybe it had been sitting at the back of my head from the moment Bree'd told me about Phil, or maybe it just popped in there, right then. Either way, I had one of those moments: my memory opened up, and there I was, asking, *are you busy?*, and the answer, restless, bored, discontented: *I wish I were.*

I heard my own voice. With the half of my brain that wasn't involved in talking, I was asking myself if I'd lost my mind.

"Why don't we ask Patrick Ormand?"

That was one of the longest days I've ever gone through, not to mention one of the busiest and oh, yeah, one of the weirdest. For one thing, the way everyone reacted to me suggesting Patrick Ormand for security, you'd have thought I was the Pope, or something. They damned near picked me up and carried me round the Four Seasons on their shoulders.

"Bloody hell, mate, that's brilliant!" Cal was on his feet. "Show of hands? Consensus?"

"Johnny, you ought to be sleep-deprived more often, if this is how your brain works when you're asleep on your feet. Bree, angel, make a note of that, will you please? Wake him up every two hours during a crisis." Mac was pouring himself more coffee. "Seriously, Johnny, that's a fantastic idea. I mean, it covers everything, doesn't? Get the Human Bloodhound out here and we not only solves the security problem, we get someone who can talk to the cops—hell, he *is* a copper. He probably still knows most of the people at NYPD Homicide. And the best of it is, if he's working for us, he can't set traps for us to fall into. A bit too much bite-the-hand, that would be. I say we ring him. Oi! Johnny! Got his number? What time is it in California? Never mind, I don't care, just wake him up. And when he says yes, hire him a plane or a flying carpet or the space shuttle, or whatever will get him here fastest, because this is going to be a damned nightmare and we need him."

Oh, bloody hell. Of course, having opened my damned mouth, I couldn't just turn round and say, *wait, never mind, bad idea, forget I said it.* Bree was already hunting out her cell phone.

"Bree, no, don't give it to me, love." Fuck. What in hell had I done? Why couldn't I have just kept my mouth shut? Patrick Ormand was possibly the last face on earth I wanted to look at, day in and day out, never mind trip over in my hotel, day after day. As for him guarding anyone's body, I still remembered him covering Bree when the bullets were flying in France a couple of years ago. Yeah, all right, I admit it, he probably saved her life, but that doesn't stop my teeth grinding whenever I think about him rubbing up against my wife. "Ian makes that call, not me. He's the one with the details."

"Here." Bree handed Ian her phone. "Just hit 'contacts' and scroll down. He's number nine or ten, or something. Press 'talk' and the autodial kicks in."

"Ta." He looked around at us. "Anyone not want me to make the call, anyone not okay with me doing this? Better tell me now, because I've got fuck all else."

Nothing. The only person in the suite who seemed to hate the idea was me, and I'd suggested it in the first place. Ian flipped the phone open, scrolled down, found what he wanted, and clicked on the speakerphone.

"*(beep) You have reached the voicemail of Patrick Ormand, San Francisco Police Department, Homicide.*"

"Shit!"

"No, hang on. It's all right." I shook my head at Ian. Of course, Patrick wasn't at his desk, not at half past five in the morning. I was remembering my own frustration when I'd gone through this exact little dance myself, ringing him from Cannes when Bree had been taken off to jail by the local gendarmes. "It'll give you a code to punch in—but you've got to listen to him go on for a minute, first."

"If you need immediate assistance, or wish to report a crime in progress, please hang up and dial 911. To have this call forwarded to my cell phone, please press seven three six, followed by the pound key. (beep)"

So yeah, we woke him up. Sod it. It wasn't the first time he'd had a panicky rocker waking him up at the crack of dawn, and it probably wouldn't be the last.

"Patrick Ormand speaking." He sounded groggy, but only for a moment; he must have had caller ID on his home phone, because he got where the call was coming from straight off, and he woke up a lot faster than I'd done. "Bree? JP? What's wrong?"

"Actually, neither. This is Ian Hendry, Blacklight's manager, ringing from New York. Sorry to wake you, but we have an emergency."

He spelled it out. It took him less than three minutes and the way he summed it up was so clear, it might have come straight from a police report. Ian's very good at what he does. He's not the only one, though; Patrick is the best listener I've ever come across in my life, and while Ian was talking, Patrick was listening. The whole time, I was glancing at the clock. At some point, the room phone was going to go off and the desk staff was going to tell us that Detective Whatever of NYPD Homicide was on his way up...

"All right. I think I've got this, at least the bare bones of it." Patrick was awake now—he had his full Crisp Smart Copper voice on. "You do understand that I can't do anything about the official investigation until there is one, and even then, it could be tricky. The best I might be able to do is buffer you from the worst of it. I can also probably be useful in keeping the communication channels open. But right now, if you don't mind, I'd like to make sure I have one thing clear. Did you just make me a job offer?"

187

"Yes." Ian didn't even pause for breath. "As head of Blacklight security for the rest of this tour, however long it ends up going. Right now, it's the next three months in North America, then a rest break. After that, Japan is definite, South America's being negotiated, and Australia- New Zealand generally follow, if we're doing Japan. There may be a Beijing show, maybe not. Nothing definite there. We're likely to end up with another European leg, stadiums this time. We're talking about another year on the road, probably more. It could be closer to two."

"So, we're not just talking about a leave of absence from SFPD." It was starting to get up my nose, how calm Patrick sounded. "I'd have to give them formal notice, and that would leave me without a job when the tour was done. Right?"

"Wrong. Hi, Patrick, how are you? It's Carla." She had her little palm device out and ready. "What Ian's offering is the same arrangement Blacklight had with Phil, for the past twenty years: flat salary as retainer, plus a share of the tour net, as a bonus. Then there's the retainer during the down times, so that you're guaranteed a base income, but you're free to do other business, if you want. Essentially, you become an employee of Blacklight Corporate."

"Sounds lovely." Took me a moment to get that he wasn't entirely believing it. "But you guys don't tour all the time, do you? So you'd be paying me to do nothing. Why would you pay for what you aren't using?"

"The fact that you'd be paid a retainer—that's an annual base salary, entirely separate from tour bonuses—means that Blacklight comes first." Carla sounded patient. "That's my exact arrangement, if you're curious. Fanucci Productions, Beverly Hills, handles a dozen regular clients, everything from PR to full travel to, well, getting diplomatic backup."

"I know." He sounded amused. After all, he'd been the recipient of that diplomatic backup, back in Cannes. He'd told me

188

then he was surprised we weren't bankrolling her for a run at the White House, she was that capable. "Believe me, I know."

"But Blacklight comes first," she told him. "If I'm in mid-project with another client and Blacklight needs me, I delegate the client. Blacklight has dibs. They're my number one."

"Ah." Still not convinced. Either that, or he was playing it close, which was quite possible, the cagey bastard. "Well. Since you're proposing that I leave my job and take one with you, let's talk numbers. Ballpark's fine. What's the offer?"

I turned around and grinned at Bree. Yeah, I know, it was petty, but I really wished we had visual two-way with Patrick Ormand just then; I would have written a sizeable cheque for the privilege of seeing his face when he heard the answer to that little question, the smug git. Nice thing was, she grinned right back at me. She knew damned well why I was smiling.

"The formal offer would be for the same deal we had with Phil." Carla passed Ian her palm device; he squinted down at the screen. "Got a pen? Here's the numbers: annual retainer salary, whether the band was touring or not, $150K—that's dollars, not pounds, and that's not ballpark, that's firm."

"A hundred and fif –" He stopped, and I thought I heard him swallow. Right. Might as well just enjoy for a moment; he's not the easiest bloke in the world to get a reaction from. "Sorry. I didn't mean to interrupt."

"No problem. Then we come to the tour bonuses, but these are going to be rough estimates, I'm afraid. I can't give you hard totals, because you'd be signing on after the first two legs of this beast are already done. Phil was in for just over two-tenths of a percentage point of the net, point two-one actually. If we estimate and say that roughly three-quarters of that should make up the rest of the net, your share would be roughly $1.8 million. Again, dollars, not pounds."

Silence. I took a look round the suite, and discovered that

Bree and I weren't the only ones digging that something had finally managed to rattle Patrick Ormand; Dom, who doesn't do much in the way of smiling, had a mean little grin on her face. I wondered if she was grinning for the same reason I was: having deprived that smooth chilly sod of breath, even for a moment.

Actually, that was going to be interesting, Patrick having to work with Dom; there was history there, Patrick having got Mac shot in France. Dom's job is the protection of Malcolm Sharpe, and she doesn't take well to anyone messing with that. She hadn't been too pleased with Patrick over that shooting. She'd shown it by leaving Patrick's eye looking like hamburger.

"Wow." Yeah, we'd shaken him all right—all the smugness had gone out of his voice. "Okay. Since I'd have to be an idiot to say no to that, and since I like to think I'm not an idiot, I'm obviously not going to say no. Ian, Carla, someone—two things I need to know. First, what exactly does your head of security actually do? I mean, what's the job description? And how soon do you need me there...?"

So it was as easy as that. I mean, yeah, there were details that needed sorting out, but they weren't my problem, that was Ian and Carla's thing, and thank God for it. I only hoped I wasn't going to end up wanting to kick myself for coming up with the idea in the first place, but looking it at now, I've got to admit that, at the time, it was the right call.

They worked it out. Carla would book Patrick a first-class seat on the red-eye from San Francisco, with a limo to meet him at Kennedy; that would get him here tomorrow morning, after the second Giants Stadium show. Seemed like short notice to me, but he seemed to think that was plenty of notice to his bosses. Carla gave him the room number, and something cold went down my back—the room had been Phil's, until a few hours ago. I was glad I didn't have to do that, change Phil's name on the reservation to Patrick's. I don't do well with morbid.

So for the next little while, everyone was thumping me on the back and telling me I was brilliant, and the whole time, I was trying to turn the subject and wondering where I could find a time machine, go back, and not suggest it. And then, of course, I remembered that Patrick's mates from NYPD Homicide would be stopping by, and I found myself wishing we had that magic carpet Mac had mentioned, to get Patrick here sooner.

The media was going to get the story, any moment now. Every reporter or talking head out there was going to remember opening night of our 2005 tour, when Perry Dillon was murdered backstage at Madison Square Garden. Even with Ian and Carla bearing the brunt of it, it was going to be a logistical nightmare, and a stone drag. After all, we had a show to do that night, in Jersey, and no chief of security until Patrick got here.

Bad as it was for the rest of us, it was likely to be worse for Luke and Karen. There was nothing they could do about the cops; everyone was going to have to do the interview thing with Patrick Ormand Rev.2, and the girls were going to be high up on the list, since they'd been the last members of the band family to interact with Phil. When Carla said that none of us were to answer any questions, or allow ourselves to be provoked into saying anything to anyone at all except "no comment," Luke nearly put his neck out, nodding.

"And that's not only the press, is it, Carla?" He was talking mostly to the girls, but it was for Karen's benefit, as well. She hadn't been here in 2005, and she had no experience with the sort of shit the press could fling at you, or the mess they could make of your life, when murder was on the front page. "It's anyone outside the immediate band family. It's your friends as well, and casual hanger-on types backstage. And by the way, there will be no parties, not until this is all sorted out. We clear on that?"

"Oh God." Solange looked a bit queasy. "Dad, you don't think they're going to do what they did last time?"

"That's exactly what I think they'll do." He didn't sound happy, not at all. "So no parties, on your best behaviour, and no grist for their filthy little mill. If you think the fake axe job they did on you back then was ugly, try wrapping your head around what they'd do with real ammunition. If there's anything out there, they'll dig it up. Keep your tongues in your heads, all right? No talking to anyone outside about it. No arguments, either of you. And if there's anything at all that they're going to find by digging, you'd best sit down with Carla and let her know the worst now, so we can deal with it. Clear?"

The look on Suzanne's face was a dead giveaway. She opened her mouth, but right then, the suite phone went off, and here it was, the word from the lobby. Detective Genovese, NYPD, Homicide Division, had arrived. Since the lifts to both our floors were security card access only, did we want to send someone down...?

"Right." Ian hoisted himself up. "On my way."

He left the door open, probably so that we'd hear the lift coming back up. Nice clear message: with the cops in tow, we needed to shut our gobs. But he needn't have worried—no one said a damned thing, the entire time he was gone. I've never been in a room with that many people, with no noise at all. You'd have thought we were all stuffed, or something.

Bree got up and poured us each more coffee. I took my cup and blew her a kiss; off to one side, out of the corner of my eye, I caught a bit of byplay that left me wondering. Suzanne reached out and laid a hand over one of Solange's. She looked on the verge of tears. Solange didn't turn around to look at her stepsister, but she did use her free hand, and patted Suzanne's with it. I caught Bree's eye, and realised she'd seen it as well. Something to talk about, when we weren't about to be invaded and put through it by some burly cop with a badge and an attitude as wide as Broadway...

Ian was only gone a few minutes. We all heard the lift give its little ping, and then a murmur of voices, out in the corridor: Ian's, and a much quieter one.

Then he was back inside, leading the way for a youngish bloke. Bringing up the rear was a woman who might have been Sophia Loren's kid sister. She was Bree's age or thereabouts, and she was drop dead gorgeous.

"Right." Ian looked gobsmacked, and it was pretty obvious why. The entire room had been watching the door, and as an entrance, you couldn't top it, really. "Everyone, this is Detective Maria Genovese, from Homicide. She's handling the investigation into Phil's death."

Chapter Twelve

Don't ask me why it never occurred to me that Patrick's replacement might be a woman. I haven't got a clue.

Maybe I'm just a sexist old sod, all right? Whatever. All I know is, I was expecting a bloke. And even if I hadn't been, I wasn't expecting a homicide detective who looked like an Italian movie star. It was nuts.

I wasn't alone, either. Everyone was gawking, and that included Mac. Scary, you know? Gawking's not something I've ever seen him do much of. But yeah, Detective Maria Genovese really was that traffic-stopping.

"Good morning." Oh, bloody hell—the woman had a voice that matched the rest of her. She sounded like someone who knew she could run her own phone-sex business, but kept it damped down, and of course, that made it even sexier, all that smoke underneath. "I'm sorry to drag you all out of bed so early after your show last night, but murder won't wait."

I took a fast look round the room, trying to sort out reactions. It was split down the middle: the blokes were trying not to salivate like Pavlov's dogs, and the women were glaring.

Not all, mind you. Luke didn't look anything but cautious, and Ian was just being Ian. As for glaring, Bree wasn't, and Dom wasn't; I wasn't sure about Carla. The girls weren't letting on how they felt about it—in fact, Suzanne had gone back to hiding behind her hair.

But Katia's hands were balled up tight, and one look at Tony's face pretty much explained why. Cyn Corrigan had the look I always think of as 'frosty English rose' going on—she's very pale and pretty, and when she gets outraged, the cool blonde thing goes icy.

"Yeah, murder's really inconsiderate that way." I hadn't seen Mac move, but there he was, bowing over the lady's hand. Just behind me, one of the women muttered something; it sounded like *oh, please.* "And you've been dragged out just as early as we have. I'm Malcolm Sharpe, by the way."

"Yes, I know. I recognised you, of course." She glanced around the suite, looking, memorising, placing. She didn't seem to have any problem with letting Mac hang on to her fingers, so maybe we weren't suspects. "It's very nice to meet you. I know Blacklight's in the middle of a tour, so hopefully we can get this cleared up soon. If we can count on your cooperation -"

"Of course you can." That got my eyebrows up. He was seriously off-balance, Mac was, if he was lengthening his odds of getting into a pretty woman's knickers by interrupting her. "We're glad NYPD is on it. Phil was with us a good long time, over twenty years. If someone killed him -"

He stopped cold, because she'd met his eye. Her own were an amazing colour. You know the sort of trashy novel, the ones with the half-naked virgin on the cover, being half-crushed to death by a bloke with arms like tree trunks? Yeah, well, there you go. Our new copper in charge had that whole 'eyes like sapphires' thing happening. This was getting ridiculous.

"There's no 'if' about it." The beautiful Detective Genovese might not be making any move to get her hand back from him, but she wasn't about to waste time small-talking rubbish, either. "This is a homicide. Unless you have a theory as to how he or why he hid his car somewhere—we still haven't found it—walked up to Fort Tryon Park, broke his own neck, and lay down just off a path in the middle of the night, after he was dead?"

It was weird, all of us staying silent and letting Mac do the talking. Then again, maybe not; after all, he's the frontman and it's not just onstage. He's the one Carla usually has doing all the one-on-one PR stuff. He can charm the scales off a fish. I know, that makes it sound like he's full of shit, fake charm, calculating, but that's not it. It's the real thing, and Carla figured out years ago just how useful that can be.

"I don't think anyone here is stupid enough to think that." I wasn't hearing any of that famous charm, not at the moment. He was being totally straight with her, and their stares had locked up. "But until you said it, we had no details. All we knew was what Ian, here, told us: that Phil was dead, and that he'd been found up near the Bronx. And frankly, since this obviously is a murder, whoever did it ought to be hoping you beat us to it. Phil was family."

He let go of her hand about then, and she suddenly smiled at him. Oh, bloody hell. As if the eyes hadn't been enough. Detective Genovese was a bit of too much...

"You're loyal." She was still smiling, and he wasn't moving. That was also brand new: Malcolm Sharpe, probably the most kinetic human being I've ever met, was just pinned there by that smile. "I admire that. But please don't make vigilante threats, Mr.

Sharpe. It muddies the waters, and it's illegal, anyway. Just let us do our job, all right? The best way to do that is cooperation."

"Threat?" Ian had apparently remembered who was supposed to be doing the talking. He didn't seem particularly smitten with the lady—not dislike or anything, just not affected much. "I didn't hear a threat, Detective Genovese. Just an expression of how we all feel, pretty much straight across the board. You said you wanted our cooperation, and you've got it, no question. But we've got a show tonight, and the band needs some rest, so if you don't mind, let's get started. What's your preference? Who do you want to do first...?"

I'd already sussed that Genovese was on top of her shit, and the next few minutes gave me no reason to change my mind about that. She let us know who she wanted to talk to, and in what order; she seemed to think a quick statement from almost everyone would clear the ground and let her get into the details. That should have been reassuring, but something about the way she said it set my alarms ringing.

"I want to make it clear, right now—at the moment, we don't suspect anyone here of actual physical involvement in this crime." She was looking straight at the two Hedley girls, and my nerves had gone tight as an over-tuned guitar string. "I do have some additional questions for Ms. Hedley and Ms. McElroy."

"Like hell you do." Luke's voice was iron. "Not without me there. That goes for Mrs. Hedley as well. If you talk to our kids, you do it with their parents present. We clear on that?"

"Of course." She turned the amazing eyes his way. "I haven't had time to get too deep into details. Is either of your daughters underage, Mr. Hedley?"

"They're both twenty." Luke wasn't giving an inch. I couldn't tell if he'd noticed that neither girl was thrilled with the idea of talking to the cops with him there. Solange was biting hard at her lower lip, and as tense as she was, she had nothing on her stepsister. I caught a glimpse of Suzanne, peering out behind her hair; she was so pale, I thought she might pass out. "I don't know if that's underage or not. Doesn't matter. We're sitting in."

"Then I think we're all set." That smile again, but Luke wasn't falling for it. He just nodded. "We'll need a room to use—I really don't need to drag you all down to Homicide. And can we bring a couple of chairs in from here? Three, actually."

"Excuse me, but no. I don't think so."

That stopped the action, all right. Half the blokes in the room were on their feet, like a bunch of ageing Galahads looking to challenge each other to duels or something for the privilege of finding the lady her chairs, but Bree's voice got everyone's attention. She wasn't glaring, but she wasn't hurrying to find Genovese a chair, either. And she wasn't kidding: that *I don't think so* had been pretty damned definite.

"I'm sorry." Genovese turned towards Bree. "I don't have everyone's name straight…?"

"I'm Bree Godwin Kinkaid, John's wife. I don't want to sound inhospitable, but this is our suite, and you can't hold your Q&A session in here." Oh, crikey. My stomach tightened up—that particular tone, you didn't argue with, not in your right mind. "I don't mind giving everyone coffee and breakfast, but I'm not inviting anyone to play good cop-bad cop in our bedroom. John needs his sleep. There's a corporate suite one flight up, the Presidential Suite. It's a lot bigger than this one anyway. I suggest using that, or someone else's. But I need everyone out of here, as of now."

"Of course, Mrs. Kinkaid." Genovese looked at Bree, and my stomach did a flip-flop. "That's perfectly understandable. I don't want to inconvenience anyone, if it's avoidable."

Nice little speech. She understood, she was willing to move on, she got it, all about the compromise. And it was bullshit. Maria Genovese was a predator.

It was Patrick Ormand, the sequel, part two, whatever. The nice lady from Homicide might be setting Mac on fire, she might be gorgeous enough to turn the rest of the band's heads, but she was a hunter. Those dark blue eyes were trying to see straight into my wife, bones and all. I'd seen it before, with Patrick Ormand; I hadn't liked it then, and I didn't like it now.

I was trying for that odd little marital mind-reading thing Bree and I seem to get, during stressy moments: *don't buy it, she wants an answer and that's all she wants, it's all pants, there's blood out there somewhere and she smells it, don't give her a damned thing.* One fast look at Bree, and I let my breath out. She'd got it.

"Why don't I take both your statements first? Then we can relocate upstairs, and get out of your way." Genovese's voice was easy, casual, just the right note, and Bree wasn't buying a word of it. "We do try to be as unobtrusive as possible, at least I do. I'm aware that Mr. Kinkaid suffers from multiple sclerosis, and I don't want to add to his stress triggers."

"Good, because adding to his stress triggers is something I don't allow." Bree'd found a comfort zone, and she was sticking to it: no antagonism, but no compromise, either, not if she thought it would affect me badly. "Let's get this over with, so John can go back to bed. What do you want to know?"

So we ended up going back to bed for a couple of hours, after she'd turfed everyone out. That was good, I needed the sleep, but of course I didn't really get much kip at first, because I kept wondering what was going on upstairs.

Bree curled up next to me. I thought she was hoping to catch a bit of rest herself, but she was probably just making damned sure I stayed in bed. Didn't trust me not to slip away and find out what was happening—she knows about my morning paper jones, and she was afraid it would upset me. There are times she might as well be my bloody nanny, you know?

We did manage some rest, after I'd decided the best way to relax enough to sleep was obvious, especially since we were already in bed, and might as well let the big comfy mattress multi-task, you know? There's nothing like a good hard fast shag to knock a bloke out, and Bree was right with me.

It was pretty intense, mostly because I was using the sex as a way to shut down not only a worried mind, but an aching body, as well. The MS had backed off from the first hell of the morning, but it was making noise, letting me know I'd been up too early and forced to deal on too little rest. We probably had a better morning than the rest of the crew—they were all upstairs getting turned wrongside out by the Gorgeous Detective—but of course there wasn't any way to ask.

We stayed in bed until noon, with the Do Not Disturb sign on the suite door. No one rang us, not on either of our cells or on the room phone; there were no messages, not even from Ian or Carla, with updates about the press. Either Bree had scared people enough to not want to risk pissing her off by waking us up, or else there was no news yet. That surprised the hell out of me. Bree was ordering a room service lunch, and once she'd got off the phone, I said so.

"Maybe there's something in email?" Bree'd woken up achy as well; she'd dealt with it by unrolling a soft mat, getting down on the carpet, and doing yoga, stark. I know sod-all about yoga, really, but I'd watched her doing it long enough to know the names of the some of the moves she uses: head to knee, downward facing dog, things like that.

A naked woman doing yoga is something only a few fortunate men in this world ever get to see, and everything below the waist was doing its best to salute. That wasn't happening, we'd already been there that morning and I wasn't feeling energised enough to try for an encore, so I just sat down at the computer and watched her for a couple of minutes, enjoying the visual.

"John?" She was on her feet, doing a wheel posture. She's

really limber, Bree is. "Anything in email? Because there ought to be something, at least letting us know when we're being picked up for dinner. I want to confab with Katia, but not until I know what's going on. Anything?"

"Haven't looked yet—been looking at you instead. Give me a sec, yeah?" I powered up the laptop. I had mail, all right—Ian, Carla, David Walter from the London office, "Crikey, yeah, new messages, but I want to check Nial's blog, first."

"...As those of you who live local to the East Coast may already know, the Blacklight family is dealing with a tragedy. Sometime early this morning, our longtime head of security, Phil MacDermott, was killed. We've been asked by NYPD not to discuss the investigation, and of course, we'll honour that request.

We still don't know what happened, or why. But we do know this: the entire Blacklight family is devastated. Phil had been with us for nearly two decades, and he's going to be missed, in every possible way..."

"Anything we need to know?" Bree'd done with her yoga, and pulled on an oversized Blacklight tee-shirt. She had all her diabetes stuff out, and was taking her blood. "And what's your take on Detective Lollabrigida?"

"Who?" I'd opened my new email list. First one from Ian was just a recap, sent to everyone: investigation was proceeding, statements given to the media by Carla, no one in the immediate band family under any sort of suspicion, no restriction on continuing the tour, please be aware we might need to answer future questions, phone number for Blacklight's lawyers. "Oh, right, the Blue-Eyed Bombshell. What I think is, she's probably a very good copper, because she's got that same blood-smelling thing going on that Patrick's got. And honestly, Bree, I don't think she's making our Christmas card list any time soon. I'm not a big fan of people who light up when they smell blood -"

I stopped. Another email from Ian, just coming in. It was marked *Urgent—Missing Person.*

"John?" She was behind me, reading over my shoulder. "What is it?"

I wasn't saying anything, not yet. I clicked on the email, and opened it.

From: Ian Hendry

To: mac@knifesharpe.co.uk; scorrigan@irisheyes.co.uk; lukeh@blacklightband.co.uk; calwil@bunkerbrothers.co.uk; jpkinkaid@blacklightband.co.uk; tmancuso@bombardiers.net; Carlafanucci@fanuccipros.com; Ops; Production

Date: 17 August 2008

Subject: Missing Persons info

"Brand new problem. I told Detective Genovese about the three deaths on the first European tour leg. As you know, David Walter gave Pirmin Bochsler at Interpol a complete list of the local hires used at every show on that leg. She requested Pirmin Bochsler's number, and she rang him, in my presence. We have an update, and it's not good news.

Pirmin's people have spent the past month tracking down every name on that list. He talked to Maureen Bennett, and asked about who cashed their cheques and who didn't.

Five people on that list are unaccounted for. Three of them are officially missing: one hired door security in Moscow, one local stagehand in Helsinki, one local stagehand in Antwerp. They're trying to get information about the other two.

Something's going on, and whatever it is, it's bigger than we'd thought. Whatever it is, people are going missing and they're dying.

I'm asking you all: keep your eyes open, don't take any unnecessary risks, listen to your security detail. The minute I get any new information, you'll get it as well.

If you've never been swarmed by the media, you're lucky. Even as protected as we were, dealing with them was a drag.

The news about Phil had hit, and hit hard. I'd been pushing away remembering how bad it had got when Perry Dillon got nailed a few years back, but this was about a thousand times worse.

I shouldn't have been surprised at the way the media latched on, you know? I mean, we had the number one album in the world. We were out on a huge, record-breaking tour. We'd locked up the top three spots on the charts with the CD's first three singles. And of course, we were in the one place on earth where the media always has beat people ready to go.

I read Ian's email, with Bree reading over my shoulder, and said a few serious nasty words under my breath. I was already on the phone with Ian before Bree'd finished reading.

"JP, good, you're up." He sounded just as he always does, which was reassuring, somehow. "Didn't want to wake you—Bree sounded pretty cross this morning. You check your email?"

"Yeah, I did." I'd gone to the windows, looking out over the skyline. Nice view of the Chrysler Building, but that wasn't doing me any good, not just then; what I wanted was the view straight down to the street. "How bad is it down there?"

"What, the paparazzi?" He sounded disgusted. "Hip-deep, or maybe all the way to the chin. I'd planned on the band having dinner downstairs at 57—they'd have closed the place for us. But with the press out there, I said sod it, not up for risking a run-in or getting delayed. We're making do with the catered spread backstage at the stadium. Show starts at 8:15, so we want to be onsite around six."

"Cool. Ian—listen." It was a gorgeous day. If the weather held up, the fans were in for a nice evening. "Couple of questions, here. Detective Gorgeous—all she asked us was what we'd been up to last night. Nothing fancy. Same for you?"

"Yeah, same thing. I'll be talking to Jamil Corbin, once he gets some kip. No sleep last night, so he's not really coherent yet. But soon as he's rested a bit, we're conferencing."

"Good. Look, Ian, did Genovese get it, about the Euro leg? Those other deaths, how important they are? Because if they aren't part of what happened to Phil, then I'm Barry Manilow."

"She seemed to, yeah." He sounded surprised. "She's sharp, JP. I don't think anyone's likely to sneak anything past her. Tell you the truth, it's a weight off my shoulders. Let the bloodhounds cope with it—catching bad guys, that's their gig, not mine. I've got enough on my plate, dealing with the NFL people about the Super Bowl halftime show."

"The what? Did you say the Super Bowl?"

Of course, that got me off the subject of dead people, at least for a minute or two. Turned out some marketing genius at the NFL had figured it out: since they were underwriting what was officially being marketed as Blacklight's NFL stadium tour, why not use that PR tie-in and have us play the halftime show at their biggest event?

So we were going to be playing to a television audience of more people than I even wanted to try wrapping my head around. Nice, that was, and so was our price: Six million dollars for twelve minutes. Doing sums was never my strong suit, but that, I could do just fine, ta ever so.

"Okay." Bree was gesturing toward the bathroom, a nice clear signal—*do you need me for anything, or can I take a shower?* I waved her away, and she headed off to the towels and hot water. "Let's wrap this up. One more thing, and it's tricky. You'll proba- bly tell me to mind my own damned business. But I don't like landmines and I love Luke, and I want to know. Were you there when the girls were questioned? Solange and Suzanne?"

"No." He didn't sound surprised at me asking. "Luke gave us all the boot. It was just the family. Why?"

"Suzanne knows something. She was scared shitless, Ian. Be- fore you brought Genovese upstairs, Luke was telling the girls that if there was anything the press might find out, tell Carla about it now, and keep it manageable. I got a look at Suzanne's face and Ian, I swear, I thought she was going to faint."

"Yeah, I noticed." That didn't surprise me. Ian's as smart as they're made. "But I can't think of any way to get that out of Luke, if he doesn't feel like sharing. You?"

"No. Damn. Okay. What time do we need to be downstairs…?"

All things considered, that show was brilliant. No special guests, but the audience didn't seem to feel deprived. I wish I'd felt better, myself, but I seemed to be running a low-grade fever; I kept heating up and cooling down, all during the show. Not really crazy about the East Coast humidity, and whatever was mucking with my internal thermostat, that couldn't have helped much. It felt like someone had soaked about fifty pounds of cotton wool in hot water, and then wrapped me up in it.

Back in the dressing room between sets, I found a chair and just sat—I was limp as a rag. Bree took one look at me, found a clean towel, and headed for the drinks cooler. She came back over and handed me the towel.

"Here. I soaked it in ice water." She crouched down next to me. She had that concentrated look she gets, when she's worrying over me. "Are you okay? You're a really weird colour."

"Yeah, I'm fine. Just hot, is all." I draped the towel over my face for a few seconds. It felt fantastic. "Much better. Ta, love, I needed that."

I draped it round my neck, and looked around the dressing room. I never pay much attention to the backstage crowd, but right now, I had the feeling that being able to ID as many people as possible back there was a good idea.

So I was actually paying attention for once, which may be why I caught an interesting little incident. Suzanne had been standing off to one side of the catering table, hanging out by herself. She seemed to be doing just what I was doing: checking out the room.

Out of nowhere, she had two spangled headscarves and two pairs of big dark eyes with her, one at each elbow. One of the twins said something to Suzanne, and she ignored it, and I mean ignored it with her entire body. You couldn't miss it.

"Whoa." Bree was watching, as well. "Was that a snub?"

"Don't know what else you'd call it."

The second twin—I remembered their names for some reason, but I couldn't tell which was Azra and which was Paksima—laid one hand on Suzanne's arm. Suzanne jerked her arm away as if something nasty had landed on it, a wasp or maybe a snake, and walked off fast, heading for her mum. Karen was off talking to Barb Wilson. Both women turned, and smiled. It was like a door closing between Suzanne and the twins.

"Wow." Bree's hand was resting on my thigh. "Check it out. Detective Lollapalooza looks interested, doesn't she?"

Bree was right. I hadn't noticed Genovese, but I saw her now. She was interested, all right. She jerked her head, short and sharp; a bloke materialised, listened to her say something into his ear, nodded, and melted back into the crowd.

That little bit of theatre had a follow-up. Mostly, between sets, Mac will rest, do a couple of minutes of yoga, limber up for the second set. He doesn't bring stuff to anyone, they bring it to him, especially on this tour, because the second set opener was all him, burning it down with "Hammer It Home." Takes a lot of energy, that song does.

Things were different tonight. Maybe I hadn't been looking for Maria Genovese, but Mac had been, because there he was, with a plate of food. He offered it to her, looked like a schoolboy handing a posy to his best girl, or something. There was a look on his face I'd never seen there before.

"How pathetic is that shit?"

I jumped in my seat, and Bree started, as well. Dom had come up behind us. She was staring at her boss.

"Pathetic?" Bree got up and stretched. "God, I hate this diabetic circulation thing; I'm creaking when I move. Are you talking about Mac, Dom? Why is that pathetic?"

"He's in love, that's what." She was looking at Genovese, and there was nothing in her voice, or in her face, no way of telling what she really felt about it. "First time since I've known him. And he hasn't got a prayer, the dumbass. Going to get his heart broken."

"What?" Bree was blinking at her. "Why?"

Dom turned and met Bree's eye. Dom does the whole stone-faced thing very well, but right then, there was something flickering in there. I just couldn't sort out what it was.

"If you don't know, it's not my place to tell you," she told my wife. "Might want to take my word for it on this one. He can give her roses and chocolate and anything else, but that shit aint happening. The man's not getting any of that."

She spotted Ian in the doorway, one hand up. "Showtime, yo. Catch you later."

That entire second set, good as it was, I was distracted. The audience was really into it, going berserk, but I kept thinking about what Dom had said. I couldn't parse it out, and that annoyed the hell out of me.

Mac was really on, extra sparkle, extra anger in the lyric, extra movement, extra everything. Holding a crowd is what he does, but this was all the way up and over the top, even for Mac. I wondered how much of it was for Maria Genovese's benefit.

I seemed to be noticing all sorts of things I hadn't bothered with before. After the show, waiting for our limos, we let ourselves be herded into groups of six or less by the security detail. Ian had briefed us on how it was going to be handled for the night, just until Patrick got here and got a handle on it: where to be and when, and with whom. He wasn't taking any arguments, and no one was offering any. They'd given temporary charge of what Ian insisted on calling "detail movements" to Jamil Corbin, and Corbin wasn't enjoying it much. Not his thing, apparently.

We were in the first group this time, Bree and me plus the Hedleys. Each group had a security team member with them, in plain view. Nothing hidden about it, not now—if whoever was behind Phil's death was watching, Ian was letting them know we were being looked after. Genovese seemed to approve, or at least she wasn't interfering with the arrangements.

We were waiting for our limo to be brought round, when I caught another of those odd little moments. Luke and Karen had got into a nice natter with Bree. I wasn't really listening, just hanging out, listening to muscles bitch and nerve endings moan, reminding myself to take some extra anti-spasmodic if I fancied a decent night's kip.

Something had caught Suzanne's attention. I couldn't see her face, but I watched her shoulders hunch up, tight and hard, the way Bree's do when she's afraid something's about to hit. Solange was staring in the same direction, and there wasn't much love in that look.

Those stares were aimed at the Tahini Twins. They were about twenty feet away, and they'd scored, assuming that a male chew-toy was the object of the exercise. No clue who the kid was, but he had a twin on each arm, and he looked as if he couldn't believe his luck. I wondered if he was dim enough to actually think he'd done the picking up.

I looked back at Luke's girls, and out of nowhere, my own shoulders were as tight at Bree's ever get. It was the look on Suzanne's face that twigged me; she was staring at Azra and Paksima and there was something about that look that didn't sit well there. Panic? Hate?

One of the twins saw her, and waved. I watched those

hunched shoulders begin shaking, and her hands balled up.

Solange saw it, and bless the girl, she dealt. She'd been avoiding her new stepsister for quite a while, but she got a look at Suzanne and got one arm around her waist. She leaned hard, whispering into Suzanne's hair; Suzanne relaxed, not all the way, just enough for Solange to be able to turn her around completely, a one-eighty away from the twins.

"Bad company." Luke had stepped back, watching the girls, keeping his voice low. "I tell you what, JP, being a stepdad is a lot trickier than being just a dad. Thank God for my daughter. I'd be completely hosed without her helping."

"Bad company?" Something was trying to sort itself out in my head. "You mean the twins?"

"Yeah, the little party animals. They're bad company and bad news." The look he was giving them wasn't any warmer than his stepdaughter's had been. "Turns out Suzanne spent a month partying right along with them. Paris first, then they invited her back to their Dad's little hotspot in the Persian Gulf. We only found that out this morning; she came clean. Foam parties, the occasional gang-bang with an unconscious dollybird, bondage of course, heroin, lots of pretty boys to amuse themselves with. They really do believe in wretched excess, apparently."

"Jesus, Luke!"

"I doubt Jesus was invited." There was no humour in his voice, none at all. "Suzanne's been told she's going in for an HIV test tomorrow. If we're lucky, she hasn't caught AIDS, and her mum's heart won't be any more broken than it already is."

"Why are they backstage?" I took a fast look; they were giggling, and the kid they'd marked as theirs for the night was looking besotted. First time I'd seen them, they'd tried it with me: tag-teaming, cooing, giggling, talking to each other around me. "Who the hell keeps letting them back here? Why don't we just boot them out on their pampered decadent bottoms?"

"Damned if I know. I think their dad is a friend of Mac's, or something. Or maybe they've just got so much money, they buy the venue if they can't get in any other way."

The limo had pulled up, and the liveried driver was holding the door. I noticed Suzanne and Solange were the first ones in. Luke put a hand on my arm, holding me back.

"I've had enough, JP. All right, we blew it. I know that. We didn't want to treat the girls any differently. We made sure Suzanne had the same privileges Solange has—same credit cards, access, the lot. We didn't stop to think, either of us, and I should have known better. Solange has had all that since she was born. But Suzanne wasn't prepared. She had no clue how to deal with it. So of course she went overboard, overspending, partying too hard, trying to do it all at once. I swear, it's as if she was running a race, trying to catch up to where Solange has been her whole life. All she's managed to do is nark Solange, and get herself in deep shit. Her mother's a complete wreck over it."

He sounded exhausted, bitter, nothing like the relaxed bridegroom of the past couple of months. I kept my gob shut, and let him talk. Sometimes that's the best you can do, and anyway, it's not as if I had any advice to offer.

"You know what's worse?" He wasn't done yet. "I never thought about how Solange might be affected. Mac had to clue me in, do you believe that? Since Viv died, it's been just me and Solange. Now she's lost her dad to a new wife, and she has to get used to sharing everything that's always been just hers with a sister, who's a kind of Cinderella, or something. I can't believe I could have been so dim, but I just didn't think. We've had no idea what to do, Karen and me, or how to handle it."

"Wow." The women had climbed in, and the driver was waiting for us. I held up a finger—*wait*. "I don't know either, mate. But if it's any consolation, I think Solange is on top of it. She seems bored with the party contingent. You might want to trust

210

your daughter, Luke—she's solid. Remember, she's Viv's kid, as well. She got her mum's smarts, not just her looks."

"Yeah, that's true. And she doesn't hide things from me, at least I don't think she does. Not the big stuff, anyway." He grinned suddenly, a genuine Luke Hedley grin. "Well, okay, maybe about sex. She runs to her godfather for that."

"What, she asks for advice about sex from Mac?" I grinned right back at him. "Scary thought, mate."

"Better him than me." The driver was still standing there, and we headed for the limo. "You know, JP, I never thought I'd live to say this, but I'm going to feel a lot safer once Patrick Ormand gets here."

"Yeah." I swung myself into the limo, and settled in between Bree and Luke. "I know what you mean."

Chapter Thirteen

*"...Greetings from Virtual Days, and welcome to another install-
ment of Tales from the Road. I'm in Washington, DC, logging in from
the band's dressing room on night number two at FedEx Field..."*

"JP? You okay?"

"Yeah, pretty much." I turned around and looked at Patrick
Ormand. Ten minutes to showtime, the crowd was kicking itself
into ready mode, and even though it was going to be full dark in
about half an hour, it still felt like the waiting room for Hell out
there. The humidity in DC was even worse than it had been in
New Jersey, and my entire body was whingeing about it. Of
course, Patrick looked about as crisp as he always did; everyone
else was wilting, he looked like he ought to be sitting on a porch
swing and sipping a mint julep, or something. "I just hate this
bleedin' weather. That's the down side of doing outdoor gigs, no

control over the environment. Doesn't look like it's bothering you much, though."

"Well, I'm a Florida boy." He was talking to me, but his eyes were moving. He had the full Patrick thing going on, not missing a damned thing. Scary as hell, but of course, this time we were paying him for it, and we wanted him sharp. "This is nothing. Thank your lucky stars there's no cicadas. No one in their right mind plans anything outdoors when the seventeen-year cycle hits. Hello, ladies—excuse me. Back to work."

He turned and was gone, moving past Bree and Katia, who'd just come up together. He'd switched his attention entirely—it was visible, that shifting of gears. One second he was nattering about humidity and insects, the next he was muttering into his headset, probably not even seeing the people he'd just been talking to. Much as I hated to admit it, my idea, about getting him to sign on as security chief, looked to have been smart on my part. Life was a lot less stressy since he'd got here.

"...I've been hinting about a Big Announcement for awhile, and I know the rumours are hot and heavy out in the Blacklight fandom. I finally got permission from management to share: Blacklight will be playing the halftime show at this year's Super Bowl! We get a good look at the venue week after next, when we play Tampa..."

"Hey babe." Bree brushed a stray hair off her face, and both the hand and the hair were damp. She hadn't bothered with the usual face paint; it was too hot for that. "God, I hate this humidity. Do you suppose Patrick ever sweats?"

"I wondered that, myself." I slipped an arm round her, and pulled her close. "Oi, Katia. You getting used to this yet?"

"Getting used to what? The heat or the tour? Yes, to both, but don't bother asking me which one I like better. Hey, Dom!"

"...We've had a lot of mail querying upcoming dates. We'll be taking a few weeks off after this leg. Next up will be Japan, beginning in early December. For our fans down under, keep your eye on the offi-

cial site for updates…"

It took me awhile to realise it, but there was no mistaking it: ever since Patrick's arrival, all the talk about the deaths had stopped. Something about the way he was balancing things, being head of security as well as being the band's official liaison to Genovese and Pirmin Bochsler, had a side effect: everything became invisible. We'd stopped having to look at it. If anyone else had gone missing, we hadn't heard about it. If Genovese had questions, she wasn't asking us directly. If anything was happening on the case at all, we weren't being bothered. Patrick seemed to be making sure of that.

I can't speak for anyone else, but personally, I was damned glad of that. The way I saw it, that stuff was Patrick's job, the reason I'd put his name forward in the first place. He knew how it all worked, so why not let him cope with it? It's not as if I wanted to talk to Maria Genovese. And if I didn't have to spend my spare time wondering what the coppers in Europe were doing, just as well. I had enough on my own plate.

Of course, the investigation was still going on. One thing I'd learned was, an unsolved murder never closes. Genovese had been backstage at a few shows since Phil's death; she'd been here last night, in fact. For all the contact I'd had with her, the Gorgeous Detective might have been a fan, or someone's plus-one. I actually found myself digging it when she showed up; she had this intense effect on Mac, just kicked him up that extra notch. The fans in Charlotte and Baltimore owed her for the heat in those gigs, but of course, they never knew it.

I kept coming back to what Dom had said, about Mac being in love, and getting his heart broken. Truth was, I'd never seen him act quite this way with a bird before. He's not used to getting turned down, but it does happen. The few times I'd seen it, he'd grinned, bowed over the lady's hand, and moved on.

This time, though, he wasn't moving on. If she was around, he went straight for her—it was as if those dark blue eyes of hers had some sort of magnet in them, and he was like a fridge door, or something. And she wasn't showing any sign at all of giving a rat's arse. Curled up in bed next to me, Bree had remarked that for someone as oversexed as Mac was, she'd never seen him bother to do much in the way of chasing. This time, he was chasing, but he didn't seem to be catching. I told Bree it was Mac's problem, he was a big boy, and anyway, broken heart or no, it didn't seem to be messing up his fronting Blacklight, and that was all I cared about, right now.

That was true, too; the tour was pretty much absorbing my attention. Ian had been right, when he'd warned us that we might end up touring the CD into the ground. We had a month in Japan coming up, and after that it was going to be Australia and New Zealand, and probably South America as well...

"Five minutes." Mac had swapped out the sweater for this leg of the tour, for a black thing with half-sleeves. It fit like rubber or latex or something, but actually, it was cool and comfortable, since it was made of mesh. "God, it's close out here. You all right, Johnny? Thinner crowd back here than usual, isn't it? Nice to have some space to breathe."

"Patrick's orders." Dom was scanning the backstage, looking for trouble, not finding any. If she minded about Patrick being in charge, she wasn't showing it. "We've got about eight people the new bossman hired, but there's also a shitload of people who aren't getting backstage any time soon. Trade-off."

"Are you all right with that, angel?" Mac stopped his dancing in place. "Working with Patrick, that is? I've been meaning to ask you."

"Hell yes. He knows enough not to get in my way, I know my job doesn't extend past you. So we're good. We stay out of each other's way, and coordinate for group stuff."

She sounded nice and impartial, which was amazing, when I

remembered what she'd done to Patrick Ormand's eye, back in France. Right that moment, she was doing just what Patrick had done: talk to us, while her attention was scanning the crowd, looking for trouble. "Man knows his stuff, dude. It's always nice to work with pros."

The last part of what she was saying was drowned out; the spots on the stage had shifted colour, and the crowd knew what that meant. Mac grinned at us, turned, and headed up the ramp.

"Do a good gig, John." Bree got one hand between my thighs, and squeezed. I leaned in for a hard fast kiss, tongue tip to tongue tip. Business as usual, her version of the wife kissing the husband goodbye at the front door in the morning as he trotted off to work. I suspect the average commuter isn't sent off for the day with a full erection usually, but, well, there you go. This is rock and roll.

Another great gig, same high energy levels, same nonstop response from the crowd. And these were crowds, serious numbers here; before *Book of Days* had caught fire, gone mega-platinum, created the frenzy and demand for live shows that made doing the smaller gigs economically useless, we'd played hockey arenas. Those aren't exactly nightclubs, but they're not stadiums, either. We'd gone from playing for eighteen thousand people to playing for seventy thousand. You might not think that a stadium show is different from a smaller one, but trust me, it is.

Into the limos, heading for the airport. We'd changed hotels today, or rather, the invisible army of people who handles all that for us had done it, getting all our gear out of the Four Seasons in Manhattan and down to Miami. We'd be using that as headquarters for the next ten days.

The chartered jet was waiting for us. Patrick had got there before us—he was waiting at the foot of the ramp, doing a headcount, making sure everyone was accounted for. Thing is, no one seemed to even really see him—it was as if he'd perfected Bree's old trick, becoming invisible whenever he fancied it.

Good at his gig, Dom had said. A pro. I've got a tricky relationship with him, and have had from the beginning. Maybe it was because of that, or maybe I'd spent so long watching Bree do the whole invisibility thing. Whatever the reason, even though no one else seemed to even see him there, I was aware of him.

I was bone-tired. I was stretching my legs, wondering how long until I could get out of my clothes and take my meds and try to get some energy back, when he came over and sat down next to me.

"Hey, JP." He was keeping his voice pitched low, but I'd heard that tone from him before: sharp and official. "Got a minute? I've been talking to Ian, and there's something I want to give you a heads-up about, before we let the band know."

"Right." I twisted my head to stare at him. Bree had wandered over to where Tony and Katia were hanging out. "What's going on, then?"

"You remember that there were five people on your payroll unaccounted for, people that hadn't cashed their paycheques?"

"Yeah, of course I do." I was keeping my own voice low, even though there was no one too near. "Ian sent an email about it. What's going on, Patrick?"

"There's an email going out to the band family tomorrow." His face—I don't know how to describe the difference, really. But there was a difference. I'd got used to seeing that hunter look, blood in the air. He didn't look like that now. He looked more like a judge, like someone about to offer up the whole *may God have mercy on your soul* line: remote, detached. "Two of them were found, both dead. Three are still missing."

He stopped. I glanced around, but there was no one near us.

"Right." I was staring at him. "And...?"

"The details will be in the email, or the meeting, or however Ian decides to do it. Maria Genovese has been working the New

217

York angle, and she's got some information to share. But I wanted to tell you: we had a four-way phone conference, me and Pirmin and Ian and Maria. It occurred to Pirmin that no one had bothered checking past the Blacklight connection."

"Not sure I'm following, mate."

"Well, the connection with the band is obvious." He glanced up, and caught a look from Ian; I thought I saw Ian nod, a tiny movement of his head. "But no one had looked beyond it, and they should have. They found a few other missing persons, that had nothing to do with Blacklight."

"What are you -"

"They looked at the venues, where these people had been after the show, but before they died." The plane lurched a bit, then steadied. "James Morse, the Manchester victim. They traced his movements, where he'd gone after Blacklight's show. There was some kind of locked-down party at a nightclub there, invite only. Turns out that he worked as a bouncer at this place, on a freelance basis. According to Pirmin, the guy dispensing the drinks that night told the Manchester cops that the party was suggested by Morse in the first place. He said there were about seventy people there, as far as he remembers it."

"Right." Something, a bit of light, was beginning to break at the back of my head. What was it Mac had said about those parties...? "Go on."

"I will." He was looking me straight in the eye, and out of nowhere, every alarm bell I had was ringing off the scale. "You aren't going to like it. But you'll see why I wanted to let you know first. They've got most of the party on film. He didn't want to let go of it—you'd understand why if you saw it. We have a pretty good idea about what he intended to do with it. But when Pirmin explained the penalties for impeding a murder investigation, he handed it over."

He stopped. Bree had got up, stretching, laughing, saying

something over her shoulder; she was talking to Solange and Karen. Solange was laughing, and Suzanne was listening; I saw a little smile break across her face. She looked easy, relaxed. She hadn't looked relaxed in a good long while.

"Other people from the Blacklight show ended up there." He was choosing his words, but he'd seen Bree get up, and he was talking faster. "We've got positive IDs on eleven people who were also backstage that night, including James Morse. Azra and Paksima al-Wahid were present the entire evening, both at the show and at the party."

"What else?" There was more, and I knew it. I also knew I probably didn't want to hear it. Didn't seem I was going to get a choice. "And hurry up, Patrick, will you please? Bree doesn't need to hear this, not now."

"The twins came with James Morse. They actually arrived as a foursome; they had a friend with them." His voice was very quiet. "I'm afraid Pirmin is going to need to talk to Luke and Karen Hedley."

The email Patrick had mentioned turned out to be a voicemail instead, Ian telling us he wanted everyone together next morning for an emergency meeting and multi-city conference call, all band personnel and family, no exceptions and no arguments, at noon sharp.

That doesn't happen often, Ian flexing his muscle like that. It takes something major; when he does do it, we know he's not just crying wolf. So Bree and I headed up one floor, to the top of the Four Seasons Miami. Ian had set the meeting up for the Presidential Suite, the band's corporate headquarters.

That was also different, arranging it for upstairs. I couldn't help thinking that maybe Ian wanted this on his own turf, what Bree calls home court advantage. It was the obvious move; I mean, yeah, we'd got used to people gravitating to wherever Bree

219

was likely to be pouring coffee and offering hospitality. But there were a lot of people, and our suite was half the size of the corporate one. Even with all the extra room, we were too close together for comfort. Still, he'd made a point of not even giving our suite as an option.

Not that there was much comfort going round up there, not that day. That was about as uncomfortable a meeting as I'd ever got saddled with, during all my years with Blacklight.

Patrick might not have said anything to anyone else—I wasn't too sure why he'd told me, actually—but of course, rumours about what had gone down at the Manchester club had got out, somehow. No one was talking about it, but Luke's face gave it away. He knew what was being said, all right.

That look on Luke's face—damn. It had no business there, you know? He was still a newlywed, and he wasn't supposed to look that stony or that drawn. I saw Mac lean over and whisper something to him, and Luke nodded. That answered the question, about whether Ian had told anyone else. As tight as Luke and I have got over the years, Mac's his oldest friend, and always there for him. They both knew, I could tell.

And Luke might be stonewalling it, but Karen was a wreck. She had no clue how to deal. She came in right behind Luke; Bree took one look, and the next thing I knew, my old lady was on her feet, across the suite, and had got one arm round Karen's shoulders, bending down to say something. Karen said something back, and I saw Bree and Luke look at each other over Karen's head. They're both quite a lot taller than Karen.

I got a bit of a lump at the back of my throat just then. That look, between Bree and Luke? That could have been any two of us, covering someone's back. Bree's as loyal as they're made, and if anyone has reason to know that, it's me.

I noticed Patrick watching, as well. He looked at Bree for just a moment, then back around the room, managing to not catch my eye. He's very fond of telling me he doesn't fancy my wife, is Patrick Ormand. Makes a big point of it. I wonder if he's dim enough to believe it, or to think I'm dim enough to believe it.

I'd told Bree once before, during a very bad time for us, that Blacklight might not be the kind of family American telly liked showing, but we're a family. We look out for each other. She'd believed me then, and the band had proved me right. So it gave me a warm feeling, seeing her choosing that road, as well.

I'd switched my interferon shots from Mondays to Sundays, in case the travel schedule triggered anything unpleasant in the way of side effects and I needed the Monday to get over it. No side effects today, but my left arm was throbbing from the shot. At least I was hungry. Carla had arranged things with the hotel catering, and by the time we'd got up there, there were already steam trays full of food set out, and the entire suite smelled brilliant. Bree was looking queasy—she hadn't had anything with her morning diabetes meds, and they tended to upset her tum. She got herself some toast and fruit, loaded me up a plate of stuff, and we settled in.

"Okay." Ian wasn't wasting any time, not on polite natter or anything else. "The phone's going to ring at half past, and I want us on the same page and ready. Luke, where are the girls? We want everyone here."

"They're on their way." If Luke wanted to tell Ian to go to hell, he was biting it back. "Suzanne had a doctor's appointment this morning—we'd already set it up, and changing it wasn't on. Solange went with her. They're back, but Suzanne had some blood taken and she's feeling dizzy. They'll get here when they get here, Ian. Let's get on with it. What about this phone call? Who is it, and what's it in aid of?"

"Pirmin Bochsler in Marseilles, and Maria Genovese in New York. We've set this up through conferencing, and we're last on the list, so I want you to be aware, people, and watch what you

221

say. Under the circs, I don't think anything's going to be off the record. This is for keeps."

He stopped, looking for words. "I'm not sure how many of you know this. There was a party after the Manchester show, the night James Morse went missing. The bartender at the club is an enterprising type, apparently—he thought he might make a few quid by filming the party, which seems to have been pure X-rating all the way, and selling it to the paparazzi. And a handful of our people were there."

"We knew about the party, Ian. Suzanne told us the whole story." Luke's voice was rock steady. "We know what kind of party it was. We know what went down. She got into some bad habits. That's on me. It's my fault, for not knowing she was in trouble. That's what a dad is for, and I messed up. I know that, believe me. What does this have to do with James Morse? And what's this about a video?"

"Morse brought Suzanne to the party." Ian sounded rough, short of sleep even for him. "Sorry, Luke. But there's no dodging it. He showed up at the club with the Al-Wahid twins clinging to one arm and Suzanne on the other. It's all on the video. And the cops have it."

I saw Karen's eyes close, as if she were trying to blot out the world, maybe just long enough to get some courage. Out of no-where, I suddenly remembered Bree, sitting in her rocking chair in our bedroom at home, rocking, just wanting the world to sod off and leave her alone for a minute. She'd sat there when I'd left to take care of my first wife, sat there when her mum had acci-dentally spilled a secret that Bree'd kept from me for her entire adult life, sat there when she found out she had cervical cancer. I hoped Luke would see it, get it, understand it. I hoped he'd buy Karen a rocking chair.

"Karen, I'm sorry. I'm not trying to be an insensitive git, but the bottom line is, this is murder and there's no hope in hell of

222

dodging the facts." Ian was talking to her, but he kept glancing at the door. "You know, it's almost funny, but the cops getting their hands on that thing might be a stroke of luck. Hard to believe, isn't it?"

"Luck?" Tony sounded sick. Next to him, Katia was keeping quiet; while she quite liked Karen, she hadn't developed much sympathy for Suzanne McElroy. "Jesus, Ian. Is that some new meaning of the word? Because I'm damned if I can see how you'd call this luck."

"Tony, you're not thinking. Ian's right." Dom stretched her legs out, rotating her ankles. "Ask yourself. What sucks worse? Having our shit all over the internet? Or locked up in a police evidence locker?"

Luke reached out suddenly, and got hold of Karen's hand. She wasn't meeting anyone's eye, not just then. I remembered what Luke had told me, about Suzanne going in for an HIV test. Bad habits, Luke had called it; playing with fire when you've never got close enough to get burned before and haven't got the sense to know what heat means, was more like it. I'd survived that sort of stupidity myself, fire in the form of booze and snowballs. Remembering Bree coping, how much it taken out of her and how oblivious I'd been about it then, I had a pretty good notion of what Karen and Luke were going through.

Right round then, the door opened and the girls came in together. And there it was again, that family thing, loyalty. Solange may have been fed up with Suzanne, but the shit had hit the fan and she wasn't letting her friend, her sister, deal with it alone. I realised, I'd never believed she could be any other way, not for one minute. Luke might blame himself for not being a good stepfather, but he'd done a proper job raising Solange.

There wasn't any time to parse out what the reactions around the room were. The girls had barely walked in when the phone on the dining table buzzed. Ian glanced at the clock on the wall, and his jaw was tight. He let his breath out, and punched the button for the speakers.

Half past twelve. Showtime.

"Good morning." Pirmin sounded same as he always did; calm and organised. "Is everyone there? Detective Genovese?"

"Good morning, Pirmin." Her voice, all that smothered smoke, drifted out into the room. I glanced at Mac—I couldn't help it. It's not as if she was trying to make him crazy, or at least I didn't think so, but it was happening anyway. "Would you like to start? I'm expecting Jeff back with some information any minute now, but it isn't here yet."

"As you wish." He cleared his throat. "I must first make certain—Patrick? Are you there?"

"Yep." It was very weird; half the males in the room looked like ageing satyrs the minute they heard Genovese's voice, but Patrick didn't seem affected. It wasn't that he hadn't noticed the reaction, either. The day Patrick Ormand misses a trick, they'll screw down his coffin lid. "I'm in Miami, with the band. Let's wrap it up, Pirmin, okay? Maria, that work for you?"

"Wrap it up?" Mac had turned, and was staring at Patrick. His eyes had gone narrow. "There's something to wrap up? Got something you fancy sharing with the rest of us, Patrick?"

"I don't. Pirmin and Maria do." If Patrick was remembering that he was talking to one of his bosses, it wasn't showing. "I'm just along for backup. Besides, there's probably news I don't have yet—I'm not working for the officials anymore, remember? Pirmin, what's happening?"

Pirmin summed it up, nice and clear. He got the ground cleared away, leaving room for the smaller stuff: after-gig party, bartender on the make for an easy mark, filming the goings-on. He wasn't sparing anyone, but he wasn't piling on, either. He didn't go into details about the video, not then, and once it was obvious he wasn't narked at anyone, I saw Suzanne's colour get back to normal, and so did her mum's. Strange, though: Solange wasn't relaxing. Her shoulders looked just like Bree's on a bad day. I was so busy wondering about that, I nearly missed a major bit of information from Pirmin. Lucky for me, Patrick hadn't missed any of it.

"Just a moment, please." Patrick sounded like his old copper self; I thought, *right, so much for the whole 'not being official any-more' deal.* "Sorry to interrupt, but part of my job is liaison, and I do speak the language. You're saying this jerk with the digital camcorder took some street shots? To go along with the booze and dope and rough sex?"

"That is correct, Patrick, yes." Pirmin still sounded neutral. "During the course of the evening, he made four trips out to the front of the club. There are distinct sweeps of the street, includ-ing one automobile that was parked there for the entire party. They are very nice clear shots."

All of a sudden, his voice changed. It only took a moment to remember where and when I'd heard it before: Pirmin on the hunt for a murderer and a terrorist called Terry Goff, back in France. "That car, in particular, merited our attention."

The suite was absolutely quiet. Amazing, really. It's quite hard to keep musicians quiet, especially rockers. But no one was mak-ing any noise at all.

"Pirmin, hold on." Maria Genovese must have had her own speakers on, because I could hear the crackle of paper coming through the ether, a bloke's quiet voice murmuring in the back-ground. "I just got confirmation of something we'd been working for the last few days. About that car—Jamil Corbin initially couldn't remember anything about the car parked in front of the Lazy Eye Club, the night Phil MacDermott was killed, except that it was black and looked European in make. Of course, we told him that if he remembered any more details, to let us know. Yesterday, he did: there was something strange about the plate.

The colour wasn't a standard New York license plate. Neither was the way the information was laid out."

"I don't get it." That was Carla. She'd been pretty quiet so far. "Are you saying that the car, the one Phil was watching, had fake plates? How would that help? Any idiot can fake up a set of license plates."

"Not fake plates." There it was, finally—teeth bared, looking for blood. Of course it was going to show up eventually, if Maria Genovese was even halfway decent at her job. And since she was high up enough to do what Patrick used to do, she had to have a touch of predator in her somewhere. I wondered if Mac had heard it. "Specialty plates, designated for a leasing agent, conferring some unique privileges. What was sitting in Corbin's memory was the physical placement of the information. The person or persons who hired that car had diplomatic tags."

The penny dropped, right about then. Yeah, I know, I should have seen it sooner. But this stuff is different when it's happening to you, or people you love—I'd found that out, these past couple of years. Turned out I wasn't the only who'd just sussed it out, either.

"Son of a bitch!" Mac was on his feet, and I jumped—he was seriously narked. "Spit it out, Detective Genovese. Or are we expected to sit here like good little boys, with our hands all nicely folded in our laps, and wait breathless for you and Pirmin to clue us in? Because, fuck that, darling. You're not teaching a master class on how to be a detective—people are dead, quite a lot of people. Greg Maltin and Phil MacDermott were family. So let's get on with it. Who provided those dip corps tags? No more games, and no more guessing. Just dish."

"I don't play games when it comes to murder, Mr. Sharpe." Mac must have hit a nerve. "The tags came from the same source as the credit card used for the rental—by the way, it was rented for the exact length of Blacklight's stay at the Four Seasons. The tags were procured through the consulate of the Emirate of Manaar, and the name on the credit card is Almanzor al-Wahid. Does that name mean anything to any of you?"

"What in the world...?" Barb Wilson looked gobsmacked. "I know that name. Isn't he a friend of yours, Mac?"

I looked across at Mac. He didn't look to be any less angry, but he didn't look like he was willing to say a word, either. Not just yet, anyway.

"Our information is the same, Maria." It was Pirmin, precise as ever. "The Manchester automobile has diplomatic tags, as well: our identification matches yours. Almanzor al-Wahid is the emir of Manaar; he arranged for the hire of the Manchester vehicle. Now it seems he was responsible for hiring the vehicle implicated in the death of Phillip MacDermott. Manaar has been in the news recently, particularly in the financial section. Emir al-Wahid is building a billion-dollar resort on the Gulf, to compete with Palm Islands as a tourist destination."

"I've met him." Mac got his voice back. "He's contributed to causes I've done spots for, health issues in the Third World. We were at school for a year together—that is, we were there at the same time and knew each other. We filmed a spot together, AIDS awareness in Africa. But a friend? Not really. I've got very specific parameters before I call someone a friend. He's an associate, someone I know. His daughters have been wandering around backstage on this tour, as a matter of fact, generally getting in the way and hunting for pretty boys to play with. And just so you know, even if I wouldn't tap al-Wahid for an evening out on the tiles, if you're trying to tell me he's hired someone to kill Blacklight personnel who go to parties, you might as well save your breath. That's absolute bullshit."

"I am not saying that." That calm of Pirmin's was beginning to get on my last nerve. "At least, not yet. There is no benefit in speculation without facts. We do have two facts: the Emir is responsible for procuring at least two automobiles for someone's use. Those automobiles were present at two locations which are linked to homicides. Friend or not, Almanzor al-Wahid will have some questions to answer."

Chapter Fourteen

"...1 October, 2008—Waving from Seattle. It's late at night, post-gig, and I've got five spare minutes to catch up on my laptop while we wait for the weather to clear. Blacklight just did a brilliant show. The audience here had some incredible energy. Of course, the special guests during the second set didn't hurt—not to taunt, but right now I'm sitting less than five feet away from Anne and Nancy, and they're both talking vocal styles with Mac, complete with sound effects..."

"Uncle John?"

"Hmm?" I opened my eyes. I'd been doing that quite a lot, lately, catching whatever rest I could, whenever I could, and the dressing room, backstage at Qwest Field, felt nice and relaxed just then. The truth was, I was wiped out, exhausted. This leg of the tour still had a month to go, and the break before we began the Japanese leg couldn't come quick enough for me. "Sorry, I was just resting my eyes. Oi, Solange, what's going on, then?"

"...It's been fantastic having so many of the guest bands come play with Blacklight—so cool, in fact, that the band's been asking themselves why they didn't do this ages ago. We've been getting all sorts of mail about it. I'm not slacking, but this tour has just turned into such a juggernaut, and so much has been happening, that keeping up online has turned into quite the circus act. But Stu Corrigan has promised to do an online Q&A session, sometime between now and the Super Bowl gig, so keep your eyes open, all you aspiring drummers..."

"Can I talk to you?" Solange sounded very unsure of herself, not something I associate with our band baby. She looked it, too; Suzanne was across the room, watching us, not moving, and Solange wasn't meeting her stepsister's eye. "I mean—can I ask you about something? Just you, and Aunt Bree?"

"You got it." Under normal circs, we'd have been long gone by now, into the limos and off to the airport for the flight back to San Francisco. The band was using the Four Seasons there as the base for this part of the tour, which meant Bree and I got to go home, hang with our cats, sleep in our own bed. Tonight, though, there'd been a run of bad weather elsewhere, late season supercells over the middle of the country. Didn't matter that we weren't anywhere near the storms in question; cancelled or delayed flights are like dominos, even when you've got a posh private charter. Flights were backed up everywhere.

So our flight south, Seattle to San Francisco, was delayed ninety minutes, and probably more. Given the choice between waiting at the airport or chilling out in the dressing room, we'd opted for that. After all, it wasn't as if the limo drivers had other commitments. They'd wait for us.

"...We have a treat for you fans in the All-Access Club. Check the streaming video link marked "Bearded Boys." It's a little something from the 16 September show in Irving, Texas, where Luke and JP got to trade blues licks with one of the great local bands. Watch Mac get

230

*his best Sonny Boy Williamson on, keeping up with all the guitar play-
ers on his harp...*"

I got up, slow and careful. Little Queenie and the new JP
Kinkaid Signature Les Pauls were much lighter than the axes I'd
been playing since I first fell in love with Gibsons, back when
Harold Wilson was Prime Minister. But even with the much
lighter guitars, I still hurt from the waist up, pretty much con-
stantly. I was trying to not let Bree see it, because there was sod-
all she could do to fix it, and it would have made her nuts.

"Thanks. Could—can we do it now? And please, can you get
Aunt Bree? I really want her."

That got my attention back to Solange. Yeah, I know, I can be
dim, but her voice was a dead giveaway. I took a good hard look
at her, opened my mouth, and shut it again. The girl was freaked.
I mean, seriously freaked, on the verge of losing it.

"Right. Come along." Getting upright took some effort; I was
wincing, and trying not to show it. Of course, that didn't work,
not for a moment. Solange, even edgy and twitchy and worried
half off her nut, doesn't miss much.

"Uncle John?" She shot a fast glance toward where Bree was
sitting, talking to Katia. Bree saw us; I jerked my head, she said
something to Katia, and got up, heading our way. "Are you all
right?"

"Yeah, I'm fine, I'm just achy. Look, do me a favour—don't
mention that to Bree, all right?" I was talking as fast as I could;
Bree was coming toward us at a quick trot. "Doesn't take much
to get your aunt's knickers in a twist, not when it's about me and
my health stuff, and I'd rather not upset her—hello love, got a
minute? Solange wants a quiet word, just the three of us. Let's
get out of here and go find a corner somewhere."

We headed for my personal dressing room, stopping to tell Ian
where we'd be for the next few minutes. He'd have lost it if we
hadn't—not having us together when there's travel involved,

that makes him edgy as hell. He told us he'd ring us if we got the call to get to the airport, and waved us out.

Solange stayed dead silent, trotting along behind us. Not a word out of her, not a peep, nothing at all until I'd waved the women in—ladies first—and closed the door behind us.

"Right." There was still a fruit basket on the table, and some bottles of mineral water. Me and Cal, we're both ex-boozers and our private rooms never have alcohol; that's part of every contract rider. "Okay. Here you go, Solange, have some apple juice. No idea how long we've got before Ian rings, so best to get this party started. What's on your mind?"

"I think I'm in trouble." She'd sat down on the sofa and clasped her hands in her lap. She was trying to control her breathing. I suddenly remembered how young she really was—twenty seems like a baby to me, these days. "And I don't know what to do. I can't talk to Dad, or Mac, not about this."

"Trouble?" Bree sat down next to her. "Solange, honey, you know we've all got your back. What kind of trouble?"

"About that guy who was killed in Manchester." Solange has beautiful hands—they're a more slender version of Luke's hands, classic musician's fingers. Right then, her hands had balled together so tight, they looked deformed. "I think I've been withholding evidence, material evidence, I mean. I know something—more than one thing. I don't think the police know."

"Wow." Bree shot a fast glance at me. "And...?"

Silence; Solange had her teeth sunk deep into her lower lip. Bree threw me another look, and squared up her shoulders.

"Solange, look." She sounded reasonable, but also pretty damned definite. "You wanted to talk, right? You wanted to get it off your chest? Cool. We're here, just the three of us. But we can't help you avoid stepping in shit if we don't know where it is. You're twenty and you're more sophisticated than most of the adults I know. So stop acting like a debutante, and let's have it.

232

What are you worried about? That we'll tell the cops? Or that we'll tell Luke?"

"It's not about me!" Her lips were shaking. "I mean, I didn't—I wasn't—he wasn't with me."

"Oh, bloody hell." I'd sussed it out, finally. "This is about James Morse and Suzanne, yeah? Right. Solange, love, you're the nearest thing to a kid I'll ever have. Probably just as well, since I'd make a piss-poor father. So I'll just play at being your dad for a moment, and tell you to dish and be quick about it, because honestly, you're making me want to thump you. We won't tell Luke or anyone else unless we absolutely have to, and we'll talk to you first. All right? Good enough?"

She told us. And the first thing she said, she answered a question no one had even asked: how in hell no one had noticed that Suzanne and Solange hadn't made the plane ride back to London from Manchester, the night Morse died.

"That was the night where we had two planes, instead of one." She was sniffling—tension, easing up. Letting shit out can be as good as an old-fashioned Quaalude for relaxing the muscles, you know? "Remember? The 737 had some kind of engine trouble, and they rang Ian to tell him at the show? He was off his head and they said don't worry, we'll fix it, and they got us two smaller planes."

"Yeah, I remember." I did, vividly, in fact. Carla'd had to calm him down, and it had taken her a good long while to do it, especially since the responsibility was actually on her. "Bree and I were on the first one—so was your dad, and Mac."

"I know." She met my eye. "We told them we were taking the second one."

"Oh, for fuck's sake!" I shook my head, not at her, just at how dim I was. Oldest damned dodge in the book, and no one had caught it. "Yeah, it's a good thing I'm not anyone's dad. Of course you weren't on the second flight, were you? What did you do, the pair of you? Catch the first commuter flight in the morning, and slip into your room before anyone was about?"

"Yes. I'm sorry, Uncle John. If you feel you've got to tell Dad about it, I get it, I promise. But I can't hold this in any more. I just can't." Her voice had gone very tight. "What happened was, Suzanne wanted to go to this stupid party. I said I didn't. It was at some club halfway across the city, and I didn't know James Morse, and anyway, I don't like the al-Wahid twins—I think they're a couple of vampires."

"Good description." She was sharp, Solange was. Easy to forget that sometimes. "Did you tell her that?"

"I never got the chance to tell her. We were off to one side, and she flipped out. She wasn't crying, but she was saying all these things, about what I had and now I was trying to keep her from having it as well. It was insane."

"Oh, Jesus." Bree got hold of Solange's hands. "What did she do? Accuse you of being a snob? Or was it pure jealousy, the whole 'you're trying to keep me down' thing?"

"Both." Bree'd startled her. "But I swear, that wasn't it, Aunt Bree. She was wrong. I've never been a party girl. I mean, I'll go to the occasional do, but most people at parties really just want to hang with me because of Dad being famous. And who wants to do that? I mean, who wants to be surrounded by people who only care who you know? Boring and insulting, I call it."

"So do I." Bree hadn't let go of Solange's hands, but she was smiling, just a bit. "So Suzanne wanted to go to this party, and you didn't. But you ended up going. It sounds as if she did a really good job with the emotional blackmail."

"Well—not really. Because that makes it sound as if she was being all manipulative, and I honestly don't think she was." Out of nowhere, the blue eyes, so much like her mother's, were wet. "It would have hurt less, if she'd just been pulling my chain. But she meant it. She thought I was being a poncey snob. She said I resented her, and Karen, too."

234

"Well—she wasn't completely wrong." Bree sounded gentle, but not soft. "Was she? I don't mean the snob part— but about the resentment part? Hell, you wouldn't be human if you didn't resent them both. After all, you've had Luke to yourself since your mother died. It's been the two of you, Hedleys against the world. And here comes not only a new wife for your father, but a new sister. I don't want to sound like some damned shrink—I don't like shrinks—but I know what it's like, being an only child with one parent. My father was shot down in Viet Nam when I was maybe three. And honestly, if my mother had come home with a guy and announced she was marrying him, I would have freaked."

We've got a lot of shit we're never on the same plane with, me and Bree, but there's this occasional thing that happens: we look at each other, she smiles, and each of us knows exactly what the other one's thinking. It happened right then: I caught her eye, and she smiled, small and fast. The thought went through my head *not after you were sixteen, you wouldn't have freaked; once we got together, you wouldn't have even noticed.* And she knew just what I was thinking. I could see it, in the way her lip twitched.

Right then, though, her attention was on Solange. "Don't be so damned hard on yourself, okay? The reaction is normal. You weren't being a mean bitch, to feel that way—your whole life got turned upside down. You not only had to share Luke with Karen, you had to share him with Suzanne. So wanting them both to just disappear, that's natural. Adjusting to that must have sucked like a Hoover. Don't cry, not now. Cry later—shit, cry at your father. Let him know you get it. Then maybe he can stop blaming himself for Suzanne's problems. Don't cry now, there's no time. What is it you think you know, that the police don't?"

"It's about James Morse." She was hating this, hating every word. "I went back and read the email, the one Ian sent, after they found Morse's body. They said there were rope burns on his wrists. That was why they decided it was a murder."

She stopped. This time, at least, it wasn't only me being slow; Bree looked out to sea, as well.

"He—his wrists being tied up—that wasn't anything to do with him dying." She was very pale, as pale as Bree gets. "The rope thing—the twins did that. Azra and Paksima."

"Gordon *Bennett!*" What had Mac said, about those parties? His voice popped into my head, nice and clear: *I know that kind of party. What did they trot out for this one, Suzanne? Threesomes with blindfolds? Ropes and gags?* "He wasn't tied up by whoever was hanging out in the car with the diplomatic plates, he was tied up for some rough sex with the Tahini Twins. That it?"

She nodded. "I have to tell the police. Don't I?"

"Yeah, but you ought to trust your dad, love. No need to talk to Detective La Dolce Vita or Pirmin, if you don't fancy it." Her face went even paler. "Right, okay, not comfortable with that idea. Do you want me to tell Luke for you?"

"I think she should tell Patrick." Bree was watching me, and she wasn't smiling, not anymore. "That's his job, isn't it? Liaison? That's part of what you pay him to do. I say let him handle it. And Solange, if you want us there, we'll be there. But John's absolutely right. You really should trust your father. You're going to have to tell him eventually anyway, because he's going to be hurt if you don't."

"Okay." She wasn't meeting either of our eyes, and the hands were back to a single white-knuckled knot. "But there's something else. After they'd done their thing—the twins and Suzanne—it was all three girls, and him. And no, don't even think about asking me if I was part of that."

"I wasn't going to, believe me. I don't think John was going to ask, either. Hang on, I'm thirsty as hell." Bree rooted round in the fruit basket. "Good, plenty of bottled water. Here, take one. Go on. You said, something happened after?"

"They tied his wrists." She sucked down some water, and I

236

saw her shudder. Maybe it was too cold. "He let them—he seemed to like it. But when they were done, he said, untie me, and they wouldn't. Suzanne was freaked. I don't think she had a clue what she was getting into, not then. But the twins kept at him and they wouldn't untie him. He was getting more and more narked."

It was an ugly picture, uglier because I could put names and faces on the women involved. It's strange, you know? I haven't got much imagination. I'm a musician; that's where that part of me lives. But I could see this one in my head, and I wished I couldn't. I could have done quite nicely without that.

"Did they untie him eventually?" Bree had drained a bottle of water and started another one. Diabetes makes you thirsty, she tells me. "I suppose they must have."

"No, they didn't. He got loose by himself." The words were coming a lot easier now. "I have to make you understand. I was stuck, don't you see? I didn't want to be there in the first place and I was totally narked at Suzanne but I couldn't very well abandon her there, and anyway, where was I supposed to go? There weren't any flights down to London until early morning and I didn't want to look for a hotel. I didn't know what to do."

"Right. So what *did* you do, then?"

"I stayed as far away as I could, right up at the front of the club. I was miserable and cross and I felt a complete cow, letting Suzanne get into a mess, but I was furious with her too. So I don't know what set him off, but James Morse came right past me, fumbling with his trousers. He was absolutely livid. The twins followed him—they chased him out into the street."

She stopped, not hunting for words, but because my phone was buzzing. I flipped it open.

Text message: flight to SF cleared one hour to departure need you lot back in the green room now Ian.

"Finish it up, Solange. And do it fast." I was up on my feet, trying to ignore the trembles in both legs. "Cars are on the way and we need to get back. Keep it short. What happened?"

"They went out after him. They were doing their thing—you know how they flutter their hands, and throw dimples at people? And he wasn't buying it. His wrists were a mess, I could see that when he went past me. He'd rubbed them raw trying to get the ropes off." She was talking at hyperspeed, and somehow, that just made the mental picture that much clearer. "One of them grabbed at him, the way they do. She got hold of his wrist. He was about ten feet away and he yelped with pain. I heard him. He shoved her, hard—I mean, he knocked her down. And he stumbled off down the street."

"The car." Bree sounded urgent. "That black sedan, with the diplomatic plates?"

"It was there—it was parked." Solange was at the door, her face crinkled with tears. She looked miserable. "It pulled away from the curb, and followed him. I saw it. I'm going to have to tell them about it, aren't I? About all of it? About how we didn't go back to London that night, what they were all up to? About the rope marks on his wrists, how they got there? God, Dad's going to kill me."

I didn't answer that. Neither did Bree. No answer was really needed, and Solange knew that as well as we did.

This wasn't about sex or drugs or bad behaviour. It was about murder.

Usually, when Bree suggests a spur of the moment party, I just nod and say, *right, love, whatever you like*. This time, when she announced that she wanted to have the entire extended band family over to Clay Street the Friday afternoon after the Oakland show, I told her I thought she was out of her mind.

Of course, I knew why she wanted to play hostess. We'd been on the road for months, eating room service or catering meals, or hitting restaurants. On the road, it doesn't matter whether your suite is the one people wander into to hang out; it's still a hotel, not yours, and you really can't cook.

Bree gets incredibly territorial about hospitality, and 2828 Clay Street, that's been hers since she was eighteen. Good long time, you know? So yeah, she was aching to have a day at home where she could show everyone what they were missing, being out on the road: show them the hole, then fill it with nosh.

But this was a lot of people, and a lot of prep for it. Besides, I'd been getting used to actually being at home alone with her. So I put my foot down, and told her no.

She stuck her tongue out me.

"Too late. You haven't checked your email yet, have you? I already invited everyone. I asked all the Bombardiers, too, and Sandra and Katia said they'd come over early and help me set food outside. The weather's supposed to be nice." She patted my hand. "Stop glaring at me. Friday, two o'clock—pretty much everyone's coming. We'll feed them, let them relax, and shoo them off to the hotel by sunset. Stop *glaring* at me, damn it!"

"I'll glare if I bleedin' well want to." I wasn't joking, either; right that moment, I could have thumped her. "I ought to put you over my knee, you know? We finally get a day off and you've got to play Superwoman?"

"I know, I'm an evil brat." She leaned over suddenly, and kissed me, tongue tip to tongue tip. "You can put me over your knee any time you like, and you know it."

So Friday morning, instead of sleeping late, I was out of bed at nine, helping Bree neaten the house and set out dishes and whatnot. I ran the vacuum cleaner over the floors, on the slow side because for some reason, my whole body seemed to think this party was a bad idea. I couldn't even really whinge about how tired I was—after spending so much time and energy hiding it from Bree, I couldn't piss and moan about her not noticing, you know? I did let her cope with the food, though. After all, she's a cook.

People began turning up just after one, and it turned out Bree'd had a good idea, after all. The vibe at that party was really good, at least for the first part of it, probably because everyone was so glad to not be in a hotel room or backstage somewhere for a few hours. We ended up with an impromptu jam session out in the back garden, after we'd locked the cats in our bedroom to stop them getting out; me and Luke on a pair of acoustic guitars, vamping some old standards, with Mac singing and playing his harp. Every neighbour within visual distance had their head out a window. I spotted a few and waved, but they were mostly gawking and didn't wave back straight off. Like I said, most of the day, it was a nice mellow party.

Luke and Karen showed up, with both girls in tow, halfway through the afternoon. I wasn't sure how things were between the girls just then, but it was a relief to see them all looking so solid, as a family.

It had been dodgy there, for a bit. Solange had opted to tell Luke, rather than Patrick, and she'd been scared shitless. I couldn't sort out why—I mean, he's not a pushover, but he's never been anything other than a doting dad. It was Bree who clued me in, that what Solange was scared of was disappointing him, that she'd never had to face the possibility before, so of course she was freaked.

We'd offered her backup, and she'd taken it. So we got to sit there and watch Solange melt down, admitting what had gone on to Luke. Karen wasn't there for that one, just the four of us. And of course, Luke had got both arms round his daughter and let her cry herself out. Once she'd calmed down, he'd told her he loved her, he was proud of her coming out with it, and oh, by the way, loyalty's a damned good thing but using your brain was just as good and if she ever pulled a stunt like that again, she'd best wait until she was twenty-one. We left them alone, and left them to tell Patrick and Pirmin, as well.

The party had hit one of those lulls you get at every major gathering, people relaxing and just generally chatting, when the front doorbell rang. The fog was beginning to roll in, so we'd moved indoors. Bree'd been relaxing with a small glass of champagne; since the diabetes, she'd cut it almost completely out of her diet. She loves the bubbly stuff, but she'd dropped it without a blink. I'd mentioned that to Miranda, and before I knew it, there was Bree's mom, Super-Doctor, telling her that the occasional bellini or kir royale wasn't the Antichrist and wouldn't kill her, so no need to play martyr.

"I'll get it." She headed for the door, leaving me in the big double parlour with most of the band, and Patrick Ormand. I was just about to ask if everyone had what they needed—I'm bad at hosting—when Bree called me from the front hall.

"John?" Her voice was about as peculiar as I've ever heard it. "John, can you come out here, please? I need you."

The room went quiet. I'm damned if I know why—I mean, only our local friends from the Bombardiers really know her well enough to get how odd her voice was. But everyone went silent.

She was standing in the doorway, one hand on the knob, eye to eye with a total stranger, standing on our welcome mat on the other side of the threshold. Out on the street, a black Rolls was idling.

He was standing there, a dark bloke in a dark suit. There wasn't anything special about him, not that I could see. He looked familiar, though; there was something about him, a kind of arrogance. Just the way he was standing, he gave off the vibe that he thought he owned the place.

Whoever he was, arrogant or not, he had manners, I'll give him that. He waited for Bree to do the talking; maybe he thought he owned us and the house as well, and maybe he could

241

back up the arrogance coming off him in waves, but she was the lady of the house and he was waiting for her to say something.

"John." She was keeping her voice nice and level. "This is Almanzor al-Wahid. He says he was invited."

Right then, the penny dropped, hard enough to dent the maple floors. That explained the arrogance, all right. It also answered whether he had anything to back it up with. The answer was yeah, too right he did. He had his own bleedin' emirate.

"Yes." He sounded courteous, a bit formal. "I was told by my old friend and associate, Malcolm Sharpe, that this was where I might find him today. Perhaps I presume too much, to have arrived with no notice?"

"Excuse me a moment." Bree lifted her voice. "Mac? There's someone here to see you. I'm perfectly willing to let any friend of yours in, and of course you can invite anyone you like, but a little confirmation would be good."

What was seriously weird about all that was that al-Wahid never moved, not an inch. He just stood there, ignoring the fuss and the tension as if he thought we were ants, or beetles, or something. Not worthy of his attention, you know? First he was keeping his eyes on Bree's face, and then he wasn't, because he was looking over her shoulder.

Mac had come out into the hall, and he wasn't moving either. He was staying right where he was. Domitra was just off to his right; al-Wahid was watching Mac, Mac and I were watching al-Wahid, Bree was watching me. We were like a bunch of cats, everyone staring at each other; under different circs, it might have been funny. But there was something about the way Dom was standing that pretty much killed any idea I might have had about laughing. I'd seen that stance before. She was tense, and ready, and expecting some kind of trouble.

"Malcolm." He sounded smooth, very calm. I hadn't thought much about his accent before, but it occurred to me about then that he sounded Canadian, or American or something. Took me a moment to remember that Mac had said they'd been at school together, in England, so yeah, no surprise that he had almost no accent of any kind that I could sort out. "Am I not to be invited in? You told me you would be here—was I wrong in thinking that was meant as an invitation to talk?"

Mac stayed quiet. Bree stepped back suddenly, as if she couldn't take the tension as it was. Maybe she'd remembered all those nosy neighbours of ours, who were probably taking notes about the Rolls, and ringing Homeland Security. Maybe she'd just remembered she was the hostess and this was an invited guest, even though she hadn't invited him.

"Come in." She glanced at Mac. "I'm closing the door."

"Thank you. You are very kind." al-Wahid took a step toward Mac; he had one hand out, as if he was going to offer to shake. Out of nowhere, Dom wasn't next to Mac anymore. She was in front of him, blocking al-Wahid off.

"Ah." The emir might be arrogant, but he wasn't stupid, or suicidal, either. "The beautiful Domitra is still with you, I see. If you are angry with me, Malcolm, will you not do an old friend the courtesy of saying so? Why do you think you need protection from me? And why invite me, if only to issue a snub?"

"I didn't invite you—it's not my house. But I'm not surprised you came, and not sorry, either. And it's not my place to be angry with you, Ali." Mac's voice might as well have come from Mars, he sounded so remote. "I'm not the one you injured, not directly. I'm seriously pissed off that you damaged my friends and family, people I love. But if you want to be told about someone being narked with you and why, you're on."

He turned on his heel, and walked into my front parlour.

"Let me introduce my friend, Luke Hedley." He was talking over his shoulder. "Luke, this is Azra and Paksima's father, Almanzor al-Wahid. Back at school, I always called him Ali." He grinned suddenly, no charm anywhere. "Have at it, mate. Give it your best shot. Let it rip. After all, Ali said he wanted to hear it. Didn't you, Ali?"

It was a really bizarre situation. Luke and Mac obviously had a grip on what was going on, but me, I didn't have a clue. It was like watching a stage show, or something, where you're in the fourth row and the actors all know what's happening, and some of the people out there with you know too, because they've had a peep at the script. These were my bandmates, guests and friends, and I was a spectator in my own house, an audience member with no idea what the show was about.

Bree suddenly reached for my hand. The Bombardiers were watching, Cal and Stu weren't moving—no one was. On one of our two sofas, Karen Hedley was holding on to her daughter's arm. Solange, though, was up on her feet, right behind her father. She looked icy cold and drop-dead gorgeous, a perfect visual copy of her mum. Viv had been a nice woman, friendly and warm, but she could do pissed-off and parky like a Royal when she needed to. Solange was doing her mum's memory proud.

"You are Luke Hedley." If al-Wahid was feeling outnumbered or thinking his footing was chancy, being on our turf, it wasn't showing. Seemed nothing could rattle the bloke. "My old friend Malcolm would have me believe I have done harm to you, in some way. I would much prefer to know it, if this is the case."

"You're bloody right it's the case." Luke wasn't cold, he was blazing. I glanced over at Karen and Suzanne, and saw Suzanne's hair, swinging to cover her face. "In more ways than one, too. Your hired thugs damaged our band family, but I'm not the only one affected by that. I've got a different problem with you. You want me to tell you how you damaged me and mine? Oh, man, buckle up. I can hardly *wait*."

I heard Bree suck in her breath. I didn't blame her; I nearly said something, myself. Almanzor al-Wahid was about to be on the receiving end of something he apparently had coming. And Mac could tell al-Wahid he hadn't invited him, but that was pants. He'd invited him, all right, and this was why.

"Your girls, the pair we booted out and forbade entry to." Luke was shaking. This had been boiling up, eating at him, waiting for a time to blow, and the time was now. "They took my daughters along for their little games. Solange saw it for what it was, but Suzanne? It's a miracle she hasn't got AIDS, or isn't addicted to some of the trash your kids exposed her to. Fuck, it's a miracle she's not dead. Heroin, rough sex with strangers, doping the girls who didn't fancy being gangbanged by a bunch of bored little shits with no scruples and no ethics."

Al-Wahid opened his mouth. Something had got to him, all right, but he wasn't getting a chance at telling us about it. Luke hadn't done with him yet.

"Have you had your kids checked for AIDS? Or don't you give a damn about the damage done?" The words were wrung straight out of him. "What were you thinking, letting your girls run wild like that? What in hell kind of father are you?"

Almanzor al-Wahid went rigid; I could hear breath whistling through his nostrils. Except for that, you could have heard paint dry, it was so quiet.

Luke and the emir were locked up, eye to eye. Patrick Ormand watched from the hallway door, obviously ready to deal if things got out of hand. And Domitra hadn't moved an inch from her protective stance in front of Mac.

The tension in that room—well. You couldn't miss it, unless you were entirely dim. The thing was, I was still in the dark about a lot of where it was coming from. I mean, yeah, I got the bit about Solange and Suzanne. But what Luke had said about al-Wahid's two thugs damaging our band, that I didn't follow. And if everyone else had been given an update and I hadn't, there was going to be hell to pay.

245

"If this is true, what you say about Azra and Paksima, then my family has done dishonour and disservice to yours." He hated having to say it—every word of what he was saying made him twitch. An apology, any apology, that wouldn't sit well with that arrogance of his. "You have all right to be angry. I offer apology to your daughters on behalf of mine, their mother, the house of al-Wahid. I have been blessed with no children but my two daughters, and perhaps it is true that I have given them their way too much, and let them forget their honour, and mine. Perhaps there is some way in which I can make restitution?"

"That's a very pretty speech, Ali. Unfortunately, it doesn't change a damned thing." Mac had his hands on his hips. He has this thing he does, part of his stage moves—if you were out front of house during a gig, you'd think he might be about to jump off the stage, straight at you. Very catlike. In a small space like our front room, it was impressive as hell. "Luke was right, about it being a miracle that his girls are okay. But you've got something else to answer for. I know you probably can't be touched for any of it, but I want to know. And what the hell, since you've got your damned diplomatic immunity, you might as well dish. Satisfy our curiosity, Ali, will you? Those two murderers you kept hiring cars for. Why? We've got, what, ten people dead that we know about, and probably more. Pirmin Bochsler at Interpol is all over that. Why, Ali? You always struck me as being fairly civilised, no matter how spoiled you were for power. Why hire people to follow us about?"

"Oh my God." Bree whispered it, breathed it really, and I turned and met her eye. I tightened my grip on her hand; light was breaking, hard and fast, and we were both seeing it.

"They were not following you, Malcolm, or your band." First crack in the facade, or that's what it looked like; his voice had changed, and that smooth olive-skinned face had flushed. "They were hired by me specifically to protect my daughters, to make

246

sure they came to no harm. I gave no instruction at all, beyond making certain that no harm came to my girls, and staying out of sight, so as not to annoy them in any way. There was nothing to make them do what you—and your police friends in Europe and New York—have accused them of doing."

"So—what? They were just bodyguards? Nothing to do with us?" Mac hadn't relaxed at all. He sounded disgusted. "Oh, please, Ali. That's total bullshit. Try it on the dog. If you didn't tell them to nail anyone who rogered your little darlings, what were they doing? Why hire a pair of killers?"

"It was poor judgement." Yeah, the facade was breaking up, all right. Looked like he had one soft spot, and that was the Tahini Twins. "They came to me recommended by my own security people, highly so. I did not stop to consider how their low opinion of women might colour their view of my daughters. Azra and Paksima are Paris-educated, and sophisticated. My girls are modern girls. The men I hired came, perhaps, from a more traditional Muslim background. They have a more restricted view of how young girls should comport themselves."

"So they stayed out of sight and basically decided that the definition of 'no harm' was 'killing anyone who sullied the boss's daughters'? And all the time, they were probably thinking the twins were a pair of worthless little tramps, and despising them? And you paid them for that? Cor stone the bleedin' crows, mate, I'd ask for my money back, if I were you."

I heard myself say it, and jumped half a mile. I hadn't actually meant to say anything at all; I was just thinking it. But there it was, out in the room, and everyone was turning my way. Oh, bloody hell. I felt my ears get hot.

"And Johnny nails it." Mac was actually grinning at me, the cheeky bugger. The grin didn't last; he turned back to al-Wahid. "So you hired a pair of traditional Muslim men to watch over your daughters? Not the brightest thing you've ever done, Ali,

247

you know? And people are dead, because of it." His voice went stony. "Including two of our own. Greg and Phil were family, Ali. You fucked up taking care of your own family, and we lost two of ours because of it."

"So it would seem." Al-Wahid was bleached. No other way to describe it—he'd changed colour. Maybe it was a cultural thing or maybe just that Mac had punched a hole straight through his armour, but he was stiff and angry and hating this. "I have given you my profound apologies for this, all of you. It was not what was intended. What else would you have me do?"

"Turn them over." It was Patrick, and there it was again, that whole 'may the Lord have mercy on your soul' thing. "Waive diplomatic protection. Allow extradition, and let Maria Genovese have them. They killed a man in New York. Let the State of New York give them a fair trial."

"I cannot do that. The precedent that would set would be undesirable. But there will be restitution. Trust me for that." I had no idea what he was thinking, but he sounded pretty damned final. He turned, looking at the sofa; Karen had her arm around her daughter. "I share your anger. Again, in the name of all my house, I give to you my profound apologies."

He turned on his heel, stopped for a fraction of second to nod at Bree, and went.

Chapter Fifteen

"…So, Blacklight played the halftime show at Super Bowl XLIII yesterday, and just for a change, I had nothing to do except panic off to one side because, well, you know, Super Bowl. The production company did a scaled-down version of our three-ring stage. They adapted it beautifully to a performance that had to take five minutes to set up and tear down. Of course, having it on wheels didn't hurt. Might have to try that…"

"Oh wow, oh man!"

I turned round, and looked at Tony. This was the first time since the tour began that I'd seen him nervous, but he was nervous now.

"…The band's supposedly resting between the Japanese and Australian legs of the tour. That depends on your definition of 'rest'. Between the Super Bowl and their appearance at the Grammys next

week, 'rest' isn't the word I'd use. Speaking of which, having the kind of recognition that Book of Days has gathered—thirteen Grammy nominations, people! Completely amazing!—is really gratifying…"

"Everyone ready?" Mac was front and centre, all alone for a change—the arrangements at Raymond James Stadium hadn't left any way for Dom to stay near Mac. Last I'd seen her, she'd been heading up to the luxury box, to watch the show with the rest of the band family. She hadn't looked happy about it, either. "Great energy in here today. I love the idea that, what, eighty million people are watching. Tony, you look spooked. What?"

"What do you mean, what? Are you shitting me?" Tony was nearly drowned out in the roar from the seats. Tampa's stadium holds about 84,000 people, and at the moment, the entire world press was there as well. There were also enough satellite uplinks to scare anyone. "Eighty million people, is what. That and, oh yeah, it just happens to be the fucking Super Bowl!"

"And now, ladies and gentlemen, Super Bowl XLIII is proud to present the Halftime Show entertainment…."

"Here we go." Stu had come up beside me, flexing his wrists, getting ready. He had a pair of sticks, just moving them about, limbering up, getting his hands turned on. "Good thing Ian didn't cave on that pre-recorded rhythm section shite. I'd have stayed home and slept in, instead."

"Yeah, that was completely barmy." I had to raise my voice; the crowd was beginning to really make noise. "I just loved the excuse, didn't you? How it was all split-second timing, and forcing the band the synch up with a pre-recorded rhythm section would make us stick to the time limit? Surprised they asked us to play, if they thought we were such amateurs. Shit, we've been together, what, thirty plus years, and they honestly think we can't structure a bleedin' set to end at twelve minutes? I wonder if they tried that rubbish on the Stones?"

"I'm even more curious about what Mick told them, if they

did. I'll have to ask him, next time I see him. Or Keith." Mac was bouncing, foot to foot. "Come *on*, people, it's showtime, just bloody announce us, will you please...?"

"...*Blacklight!*..."

It was a killer, killer twelve minutes, and with a killer paycheque, as well: just under six million dollars. Five hundred grand a minute, not too bad, yeah? Especially since we only did two songs.

It had taken one short band meeting—five minutes—to decide what we wanted to do. We opened with "Liplock," five minutes of high intensity, every damned note of it aimed straight at the groin. When we'd first told the NFL people what we wanted to play, they'd had a look at the lyrics and started making the sort of noises I'd have associated more with nuns. Ian came back to us and said they were flipping their shit over it, we pointed out that the Stones had covered "Rough Justice" as part of their twelve minutes, and that the programming puritans might want to check out the lyrics to that one. Good call, since the song's got lyrics suggestive enough to have made them squirm. No clue whether or not they'd done that, but we got the green light for that and "Remember Me," so it really didn't matter in the end.

The nice thing about "Liplock" is that, besides the whole effect of melting the knickers on millions of women watching the show, the song showcases Tony's piano. Normally, I play Little Queenie on that one, but this was the Super Bowl and there was some scary number of eyes watching us, so I'd opted to risk my back and my insurance rates, and brought my Zemaitis pearl-top along, just for "Liplock."

Mac gave me my Zemaitis, Big Mama Pearl, as a wedding present. First time I'd ever played a Zemaitis, it had been one almost identical to Big Mama Pearl. The song had been "Liplock," and we'd nearly melted my basement studio at Clay Street with it; just jaw-dropping, yeah? The guitar is one of the world's rarest

251

axes, because Tony Zemaitis didn't go in much for a lot of fancy custom electronics. And it has effects that can make it sound like damned near anything, including the nether regions of a full-grown male lion in heat. A Stratocaster whines and twangs, a Les Paul wails, a PRS guitar croons. Big Mama Pearl does all of that, and she growls, as well.

When we walked onstage at Raymond James Stadium, it was the first time in a year that the lights down were already down, that we'd been announced to the crowd, that there were actual amps and monitors onstage. One thing I'd told Ian was a non-negotiable item in the contract rider was a security guard for Big Mama Pearl. She's worth easily a hundred thousand dollars just as a guitar, but belonging to me, that jacks up the value in the eyes of some loopy collector who might get a woody over the idea of owning her. I'd been ready to dig my heels in, but they didn't argue, and the security bloke, hand-picked by Patrick, stayed with one hand on the battered old case and the other near what was probably a fucking Uzi, or something. He was just offstage, eyes on the guitar—the official NFL production staff had sense enough to know just what was up, and they left all the handling of my gear to Jas, my guitar tech.

So both my guitars had a bodyguard. I was playing one of my hollow-body Pauls, the new JP Kinkaid signature models, for "Remember Me." If anyone managed to boost that one off its stand and out of the stadium under their coat, it was a minor issue; Gibson had sent me a dozen of them, and at the moment, there were two more just like it backstage, locked up in a roadcase.

It's funny, the way we remember things, notice things. In the middle of the longest tour I've ever done, that Super Bowl gig was a standout. There's a lot of snide stuff said by the music press, when an older band plays one of these, you know? *Oh, he hasn't got the pipes he used to have. Oh, he's got batflaps—remember when he was twenty and he was all muscle and skinny, now he's old and saggy*. Yeah, right, we'll leave out the fact that the skinny twenty-year-old was probably a junkie or a boozer or a cokehead, bourbon and cola for breakfast. But mostly, what the older bands get from the younger media is *oh, they just aren't relevant—pathetic old geezers, that lot.*

And of course, that rubbish wouldn't fly, not with us, not on this tour. Mac's voice was never the standard rocker's voice, and the bit of low-lying gravel in there, now that he was sixty, sounded brilliant and natural. He was still all toned whipcord, no particular batflaps anywhere, but that was metabolism and good health; he was never a druggie and he's worked out forever.

And the relevance factor? Yeah well. *Book of Days* had been out a year, and we'd had five number one hits off it. We were spoiled for choice, really. But the Young Turks or whatever they call themselves these days, they weren't talking about commercial relevance, and we knew it.

No, what stopped them cold was, the two biggest hits both take a good hard smack at world politics. The only reason we'd opted for "Remember Me" instead of "Hammer It Home" as the second song tonight was because the coin toss came up heads.

So the lights were down, and then they came up in a blaze and eighty-four thousand people went nuts. With the set-up being fast and uncluttered for the time issue, the video veil wasn't being used. It was as basic as it gets, us and our fans—just like old times, if you left off the invisible audience of eighty or so million people, watching round the world.

Twelve minutes. We started by slamming right into pure sex, me and Mac trading the heat between his vocals and the Zemaitis, letting Tony take the vicious little piano solo halfway through, pure barrelhouse, the kind of ivory-tickling rock music hasn't had for too long a time. Tony's one of the last great boogie rockers left out there; most of them have died over the years, and

253

there's a hole where most of them used to be. We and the Bombardiers, we'd got lucky, having Tony.

Having got the crowd to the edge of musical orgasm, Luke swapped his PRS for a Strat, I swapped the Zemaitis for my Paul, and we went into "Remember Me." It was a driving, wrenching version, different from the ones we'd been doing; this one had a kind of urgency to it. Not just the music—the vocal, as well.

Eleven minutes, fifty seconds. Arms round each other, bowing from the waist, audience stone fucking berserk, stamping and screaming—you'd have thought, honestly, that they'd forgotten there was supposed to be the second part of a football game, when we were done—and offstage, at twelve minutes on the nose. I was about as exhausted as I would have been after a full show, because that twelve minutes had got everything I could put out. When you're playing the halftime show at the Super Bowl, you don't have to save anything for an encore.

"Bloody hell." Mac was towelling off. He'd just sucked down a litre of mineral water in about eight seconds, and he was trembling with the adrenalin crash. "Johnny, your guitar sounded amazing. I'd forgot just how intense that thing is. Ian, how did we do? From the smile, I'm guessing we were at least decent…?"

"You joking? You lot were as good as I've ever heard you." From Ian, that was high praise. "Plane's on the tarmac—we've got clear skies back to Miami. There's a late supper waiting on the jet and the limos are here. The women are on their way down from the Commissioner's box. Anyone interested in the second half, you can watch it on the flight back."

Into the limo, the basic six-seater; me and Bree, Mac and Dom, Luke and Karen. The Hedley girls hadn't come along for this one—technically, we were on tour break. The women were all energised, we were all knackered. Very bizarre.

"Good gig." Luke sounded nice and lazy. We weren't talking much; Bree and Karen were nattering away, but Dom was sitting back with her eyes closed and the blokes were all getting our second wind. "Is that someone's cell vibrating?"

"Mine—no, it's yours." Mac sat up, and fished his out. "Someone's still buzzing. What the hell...?"

"That's me." I had mine out, and flipped it open. "Hang on— I've got a text message."

"Same here." Luke looked up, and stared at us. Bree and Karen had gone quiet; Dom had opened her eyes. "It's just a URL. JP? Mac? I don't get this."

"It's a link to the English language version of al Jazeera." Mac was completely still—all that energy seemed to have come to a full stop. "Dom, have you got your fancy phone with you? The Treo or Blackberry or whatever it is you've got? It can hit the internet, can't it? Access it?"

"Yes. Here." She had it open, ready to go. "What's the URL? Whoever's sending you hot porn links from Arabia, they don't love me, because I didn't get one. So I need to type it in."

Mac rattled it off, and Dom's thumbs moved. We were still purring along through traffic, following the official escort. The window between us and the driver was shut. Privacy's one of the underrated things about limousines.

"Whoa." We were all staring at Dom; something in her voice had the edge that generally means someone's about to get put on the floor with an arm twisted up behind them. "Mac, this is some scary shit, dude. All about dead guys and missing body parts. Here. You read it."

"Manaar, two hours ago: the mutilated corpses of two men were found by people leaving a nightclub in a popular tourist section. In what appears to be a gruesome execution-style slaying, both bodies were missing their right hand. The pathologist confirmed that the amputations were post-mortem. The men have not yet been formally identified, nor has there has been official comment from the Palace."

That was probably the quietest plane ride I've ever been on.

255

Of course, the rest of the band, as well as Ian and Patrick, had got the same message we'd got, and at the same time. You'd have thought we'd be talking, but no; none of us seemed to have one word ready, to say about it. The women were silent, as well. The plane's satellite television system stayed off. About the only thing that got said was Ian announcing that he wanted a band meeting, first thing tomorrow before anyone even thought about catching their flights home, to discuss it.

It didn't occur to me until we were in the limo, pulling up to the Four Seasons in Miami, that we didn't have a corporate suite for the one-night stay to do the Super Bowl. Cramming everyone into one of our rooms was going to make for a very crowded meeting. But as it turned out, we didn't need the meeting, after all.

We were walking into the lobby when the concierge saw us, and headed straight for us. Or, rather, it was Luke he was heading for, and he was nervous. Unusual, for a concierge; my experience is, there's very little rattles them. They learn how to cope early on, if they work for a good hotel.

"Mr. Hedley?"

"Yeah, I'm Luke Hedley." We'd all stopped behind him. His voice went sharp, suddenly; I saw Karen go pale. "Is there a problem? Something wrong?"

"No, sir, not a problem." He glanced toward the desk, and one of the staff nodded at him. "A package was delivered for you, about an hour ago."

Bree had hold of my hand. My own eyebrows had gone all the way up—no reason I could see for the bloke to look so nervous. Hell, he'd even spooked Luke, making him wonder if there was a problem with the girls. But the concierge was edgy as hell, and I couldn't suss out why.

"Really?" Luke looked to have relaxed a bit. "Who from?"

"I'm sorry, Mr. Hedley, but I don't know. We did try to get a signature for you." The bloke was watching his desk staff; the girl who'd headed off behind one of the nice discreet doors was coming back, holding a biggish box, very carefully, all the way out in front of her and away from her body. A weird little notion crossed my mind: she was walking like someone holding a live explosive. "But he declined to sign. And since he told us you were expecting this, we didn't want to insist."

"I was expecting it? News to me." Luke took the package, and peered at it. It didn't look like much, just a basic carton, carefully wrapped, with some stickers on it. "I wonder what -"

He stopped, mid-word. His face had gone the colour of dirty snow.

"Right." I don't know how he got it out, since he wasn't moving any muscles that I could see, but he did. "Thanks. Good night. Karen?"

We had one entire floor to ourselves that night, along with the lift lockout, and thank God for it. Bree and I took the last lift up; when we got upstairs, we found everyone waiting by our door. Maybe they knew they were going to want some comfort.

No one was saying anything, and the silence was beginning to get to me. Luke set the box down on the dining table, took a long breath, and looked around at us.

"Okay." He sounded steady as a rock. "Just to let you know, this thing's got "do not open diplomatic courier cargo" stickers all over it. Nothing about where it came from. But I can guess." He gulped, suddenly. "Pretty sure I can guess what's in it, too. Jesus, I hope I'm wrong."

"Oh, man." Bree had hold of my arm now, digging her fingers in hard. "Luke, don't. Don't open it. Just—look, can't we get someone up here to do it? Someone official?"

Yeah, I know, I'm dim. But the penny still hadn't hit the floor, believe it or not; I looked at Bree, and I wondered what she was on about. Unbelievable. Mac, though, he already knew.

"Bree, angel, do you really want the local law enforcement talent up here while that thing is opened? I mean, bloody hell, pretty obvious what it's got to be, and someone remind me to take Ali al-Wahid out behind the stage for a little talk, next time he shows up anywhere, all right?"

And there it was, finally, me catching up with the rest. There are days I wonder how many grey cells the years of boozing and blow killed off. It was all there: those simultaneous text messages, diplomatic immunity that had got the package through customs with no questions asked, addressed specifically to Luke, the man whose family he'd damaged. And I hadn't caught it. I had now; problem was, I wasn't letting myself believe it.

"Luke, man, you squeamish?" Domitra had left Mac's side, and moved up to the table. "Want me to do it?"

I jerked my head. She was holding her Swiss army knife in one hand. She looked calm, and competent, and impatient.

"Yes." Luke stepped back and away. "Yes to both. I'm very squeamish and I'd love for you to do it, thank you, Dom. Karen, outside please. Off you go. We're sure it's not a bomb, right?"

"Not a bomb." Mac was watching his bodyguard, and there was a muscle jumping along his jawline. "Ali has no reason to send you a bomb. If we're right, this is rather worse, just not as dangerous. Open it, Dom, would you please? Let's get this over."

"No, she isn't opening it. That's my job."

I think we'd all forgot about Patrick being there. But he was there, all right, stepping up to the table.

"Dom, can I borrow that knife, please? Thanks. And I agree with Mac, this is almost certainly not a bomb, but I'd like everyone out of here, out in the hall."

"I'm not going anywhere." Mac and Patrick had locked up, eye to eye. "This is on me, mate. I'm the connection between Ali and the band—his little starfuckers were let run rampant because everyone knew I know their dad. And that included Phil."

He sounded completely final. "So you're not risking your life or anything else while I wait safe out in the hall. And Dom, angel, just shut up. You don't get a vote."

"Works for me." She sounded bored. "What makes you think I was going to argue?"

In the end, we all stayed. Patrick didn't like it, but he worked for us now and he did what he was told, sliding the blade of Dom's little utility knife carefully around the wrapping. He was probably preserving it for evidence. It fell away, rustling, and Patrick stopped.

It wasn't a box. It was a styrofoam cooler, taped shut.

"Patrick. Hang on a minute." My own voice made me jump, and my tum was doing flip-flops. "Whatever's in there, it's on ice, or probably a cold pack. That's a cooler. My interferon comes packed in one of these, whenever it's shipped."

"Thanks. I already knew that much, but thanks. Confirmation is always good." He sounded perfectly calm. "Excuse me, I want to finish this."

He edged the knife into the heavy tape, found the slit between the top and bottom halves; I heard a hiss as the seal was broken. Then he had it free, and lifted the lid.

"Well." Still calm, but there it was, the predator look. "Everyone stay back, please. Domitra, I need a witness. Would you mind...?"

"Sure."

She peered down, over his shoulder. I thought I saw her face twitch, but that was probably in my head. She's pretty tough, is Domitra.

"Wow." She glanced at Luke. "This emir dude is major biblical. Eye for an eye—okay, maybe a hand for a hand. When he said he'd make restitution, he wasn't fucking around."

"Live from the Staples Center in downtown Los Angeles, CBS is proud to present the 51st Annual Grammy Awards..."

259

The house lights went down, and the crowd made some noise. Not the roar we'd got used to hearing the past year—the Staples Center isn't a stadium—but a decent roar anyway.

"Nice to be dry, isn't it?" Luke had edged close. "You all right, JP?"

"Yeah, not a problem. It's only one song." I shifted Little Queenie and tried to straighten my back. It hurt like hell; the Super Bowl gig had been about a week ago, other side of the continent. Both that show and this one had needed rehearsal and soundchecks on site. It was probably the one time during the tour when the tech and production staff got to rest, while the band worked. Nial, Ronan, Ian and Carla were here tonight, but they weren't working—they were all nominees for something to do with *Book of Days*. "And yeah, I'm sorry for the red carpet watchers. They'll be lucky not to come down with pneumonia."

"...*Performing 'Remember Me,' the first nominated song for Best Rock Song of the year...*"

Luke shook his head at me. He knew I was feeling seedy. He also knew I was in a worry over Bree.

I had good reason to worry; she'd stayed in San Francisco, saying she was exhausted. No surprise, since she'd been coughing since we'd got home from Tampa. Now she'd gone stuffy and feverish, as well. She'd offered to tough it out and come down, but I'd put my foot down. It was one show, on one night, and she had flu. It was typical February weather in California, pissing down rain. I wanted her warm and dry. I'd rung my mother in law, and asked her to look in. We were leaving for Australia in just over a week, and Bree needed to be healthy.

So she'd missed the Grammys. What scared me was that she hadn't argued about it, not a word. I'd been all ready to go to the mat with her over it, and she'd just taken it.

"Showtime." Mac danced past us, heading for centre stage. "Are you doing all right, Johnny? You look as if you've just gone down half a mile of bumpy road."

"I'm fine." They were taking their time about announcing us. Little Queenie was the perfect weight for a stage axe, but right then, she felt as heavy as one of my Pauls. "Not to worry."

Right then, the lighting changed, overheads all shifted, and all of a sudden, the stage and everyone on it was standing in the middle of the Blacklight logo.

"...BLACKLIGHT!"

The crowd exploded, and we went into "Remember Me."

A night to remember, that was; any time you set a record, do something that's never been done, it's worth remembering. We'd been nominated for thirteen Grammys, and designated for two more that had no competition, and we swept.

It got ridiculous after awhile. We trotted up the stairs to the stage to accept the first handful of awards. We sat and cheered as an opera singer read off the Previously Awarded list; Carla and Nial had got an award for Best Recording Package. Ronan, in full kilt, took his award for Best Engineered Album. Every category they read off that we were nominated for, the list ended with *and the Grammy goes to, Blacklight, for something or other to do with Book of Days*. It was nuts.

Halfway through the evening, we accepted a statue in one of the two categories we'd had no competition for. They give those out every year. One is the Hall of Fame award, for an old album that's shown extraordinary legs; the other one's called the Grammy Legend Award. It's designed to make you feel like the geezer you've got to be to qualify for one.

We'd got given the Hall of Fame award, for our album *Pick Up The Slack*, at a quiet lunch after rehearsals two days ago. But the Legend award was given during the actual show. Nice thing was, we each got to say a few words—they told us we each got one minute.

So everyone had prepared something, just a cheery sound byte.

I hadn't, though. I was just going to thank the band for letting me into the magic circle, all those years ago. I was still planning on saying that, when I stepped up to the mic, right up to the moment I opened my mouth.

I don't know where it came from. Maybe it had been sitting there, waiting for a chance to pop out; maybe it was *Pick Up The Slack*, talking about that particular album, because that was more than just my first tour as a member of Blacklight, it's the tour where I met and fell in love with Bree.

I looked out into the crowd, industry honchos, disappointed nominees, expectant faces, and out of nowhere, I remembered coming to San Francisco during *Pick Up The Slack*, doing a radio spot, asking the DJ if I could send a personal message over the air. And there it was: just a nice idea, right now, yeah?

"I just want to say hello to my wife, Bree. She's been there for me for going on thirty years, and she was too sick to come down for this tonight. Also, she thinks she's invisible, and I'm proving her wrong."

Everyone was hushed, watching. I blew a kiss at the cameras.

"Always on," I told her, and I knew she'd be watching. "Always burning. Cheers, love. And thanks to these nice people behind me, for letting me play with them, and covering my back."

What was really cool was, Luke followed me up to the mic, and he did the same thing. Whatever he'd planned to say got replaced with a simple thanks to the band, and a loving shoutout to Karen, for being willing to not only marry the cranky old sod, but also for adding Suzanne to the Hedley family. What the hell, it was a good spot for some honest sentiment.

As I say, Blacklight swept. Of course, there was one award we weren't in the running for, and that was Best New Artist. That led to a really funny moment backstage. I'd done a couple of photos and made some small talk with the press; I really was achy, though, so I excused myself and headed into the green room. I found both Luke's girls backstage. They hadn't bothered doing the Super Bowl—two English roses, they didn't give a rat's arse about that—but they weren't about to miss the Grammys. I walked in and found them staring up at the wide-screen TV. I opened my mouth to say something, but Solange hushed me.

It was the Best New Artist winners, four American kids who looked to be in their early twenties. One of them, a fresh-faced kid with a mop of curly black hair and wire-rimmed glasses, seemed to be the designated cliché dropper, except he wasn't dropping clichés. He was being genuinely funny.

"...in a Blacklight-free category. In fact, after the show, we were thinking about hitting all the after-hours clubs and parties with the Best Reggae, Best Country-Western, Best Rap or Hip-hip, and Best Classical category winners."

The audience howled. The lead singer grinned, hoisted his award, and the band headed offstage.

"Funny bloke." I was watching Solange; she really looked smitten. "Who is he? And who's the band?"

"That's Curtis Lind." Her eyes were still pinned to the telly. "He's the lead singer and guitar player. The band's called Mad At Our Dads. You must have heard them, Uncle John. They had a big pop hit last year, 'South For the Winter'. It sold some huge number of copies. The only reason it didn't go to number one on the charts was because Blacklight had the number one spot most of the year. I'm sort of surprised you don't recognise them, because they're from the Bay Area. They formed Mad At Our Dads when they were all students together at Santa Cruz. It's a very cool university."

"That's Curtis Lind?" I knew who he was; I'd heard the song, and the lead guitar work had caught my attention, nice hints of jazz influence, some interesting shimmering riffs on an old Telecaster that looked a bit like the one Andy Summers plays with the Police. I had no clue where the band had got its name, probably some pop culture reference, but it was a brilliant name anyway. "He's a solid player."

"They're a good little band." I hadn't heard Mac come in, but there he was, with Patrick and Dom in tow. He was grinning at Solange, and she was turning bright pink. Of course he'd seen the look on his goddaughter's face, and read it straight off; it's very hard to dupe Mac on the subject of sex. "Fancy the singer, do you? Good taste. Singers are the best."

Solange muttered something, and fled. Suzanne shot Mac a grin, and wandered out after her sister.

"Oh, good, it's all grownups." Mac was opening a bottle of mineral water. "Finally! I wanted to say something, but not with the girls in here. Johnny, I have to apologise. To Bree, really, and I will when I see her, but also to you."

"You do?" I blinked at him. "Right. For what?"

"That whole thing at Bree's party, when Ali al-Wahid showed up. I had no business inviting him. It wasn't my house, or my party, and I didn't ask Bree first. I know it narked her, and it put her in a rotten position. And I have to admit it, that was malice aforethought: I was counting on that, on her being furious but letting him in anyway, because, hell, this is Bree. I know how she feels about hospitality—such a fierce girl. But I wanted Luke to be able to nail Ali for what had happened, and I wanted it on our turf. So I let him know about your party. That was really cheeky of me. I'm sorry for it."

We hadn't talked about it, not since that night after the Super Bowl. I'm not a big fan of the Old Testament 'eye for an eye' thing, so I'd passed on looking into that styrofoam cooler, sent by the twins' daddy presumably, with the hands of the men who'd murdered Greg Maltin and Phil MacDermott in it. Not my thing, amputated body parts.

But it had crossed my mind more than once, that sending that cooler was almost criminally thoughtless. Suppose Karen had opened that thing? Or Solange? Almanzor al-Wahid was just as short-sighted in carrying out his nasty little apology to Luke as he'd been in hiring a pair of hard-line misogynists to bodyguard his brats in the first place.

"I'll tell Bree. I've been meaning to ask you something. How did you know the story behind the two guys in the rental cars? I mean, you told al-Wahid you knew. Did I miss an email?"

"I didn't know." He'd pulled up a chair. "God, my legs hurt. Too much time on my feet, these past months. I guessed, Johnny. I worked it out, and then I went to Patrick with what I thought must have happened. We were wrong about the reasons, but right about the basics."

"Not sure I'm following this, Mac."

"My first idea was that Ali had something in for us, maybe for me personally, or maybe he was narked at Luke's girls. Parents find it easy, blaming everyone around them when their kids behave badly, don't they? But all the pieces were there, Johnny. I thought about the car in Manchester, about what Solange said about the car Phil was watching the night he was killed. Plus, there was that thing from Pirmin, about a witness seeing two men dump Greg Maltin's body in the river in Zurich. So there it was: a black car with diplomatic plates, two blokes in it, different countries. I just did the math. But I really had no business involving you and Bree, not without asking you first. I'm sorry."

"It was nice solid deductive reasoning." Patrick had been listening, and nodding along. "Interesting for me, being out of the official end, for once. Pirmin's worked Interpol long enough to be philosophical about it, but Maria Genovese's really pissed off—American cops are trained to think no one is beyond the law. Ah well, she'll simmer down eventually. I'm betting Charlotte's giving her nonstop backrubs, to ease the pain. That's the nice thing about going home to a trained masseuse every night—she can work the knots out of Maria's back."

265

It was the casual voice that gave it away. Too casual, especially for Patrick, you know? Deliberate.

I looked at him, and then at Dom. Neither of them was meeting my eye. And they were both not looking at Mac. I did, just for a moment, and wished I hadn't. He's got that mobile, fine-drawn face. Pain doesn't look good on him.

It had never occurred to me. I'd thought it was vaguely amusing, ironic rather, that Mac had fallen in love with one of the few women on earth who looked to be immune to him. It had never even crossed my mind to wonder why she was so unaffected.

I remembered Dom in a dressing room months ago, watching Mac with Maria Genovese, saying he was going to get his heart broken. Bree'd been as puzzled as I was. At least I wasn't the only dim one, not this time: Bree hadn't sussed out that Maria Genovese was gay, either.

And neither had Mac. If the look on his face was anything to go by, Mac had realised it about ten seconds ago. Just goes to show, even the savviest bloke in the world can go blind when it comes to love...

Right then, my pocket began humming. They'd requested us to turn our cells off or put them on vibrate for the duration of the show. I was damned glad of a phone call right then; the last thing I wanted was a conversation with Mac. I flipped it open, and saw Bree's cell number in the ID screen.

"Bree?" Good, she was checking in. Nice to not have to worry. "You feeling better, love?"

"John?" Not Bree's voice. "This is Miranda."

My heart stuttered, and kept stuttering. My mother in law had her doctor's voice on: careful, neutral.

"Miranda! What is it? Where's Bree?" The others were staring at me. "What's wrong?"

"It's all right—she'll be fine." Calm, professional, neutral. I remembered sitting in a hospital waiting room with her, while Bree

266

was having cancer surgery. She'd sounded just like that, even then. "I didn't want you to get home and not find her there. I had her checked into the hospital. She was having trouble breathing. They've got her on oxygen right now, and they've started a course of antibiotics. The official diagnosis is pneumonia."

Chapter Sixteen

"...9 March 2009—Greetings from Huka Lodge, at Lake Taupo on New Zealand's North Island. The band family's having a two-week rest break between the end of the Oz-Kiwi leg and the beginning of South America. Normally, I wouldn't be here—most of the crew's already headed off to Buenos Aires, setting up for our first South American show, at River Plate Stadium—that's PLAH-tay, not the dish you eat your supper from. The senior staff, including yours truly, stayed behind for a couple of days. As gorgeous as this place is, I wish our reason for staying was happier...."

"Bree? You all right?"

Bree turned round and looked at me. She wasn't smiling—what we were doing out there didn't leave much room for smiling—but her face softened up. New Zealand in March, it was the end of summer, and the wind was lifting her hair around her face.

"I'm fine. Tired, but fine." She brushed the hair away. She'd lost weight, back in hospital, and she was even paler than usual. She got tired easily, much too easily, and little things that she'd normally be handling without a second thought seemed to be making her cranky and fretful. It scared the shit out of me, but I'd spoken to Miranda long-distance, and she'd told me this was normal for people who'd had pneumonia. "I'm pretty sure this is jet lag. Don't look so freaked. Didn't the lodge people say they were bringing out some chairs? I could use one."

"Right. You stay there, and I'll go get you one."

Heading across the lawn, I found myself thinking about the way things change. She'd spent half her life bullying people into making me comfortable. And now here I was, bullying people into making her comfortable. Ironic, yeah?

"...As most of you know, the band lost two of its extended family earlier in the tour. This break is our first chance for the memorial we all wanted, a chance to say goodbye to Greg Maltin and Phil MacDermott in our own way. That's happening today, we've flown in Phil's sister and Greg's parents...."

I found a staff member, and explained about the chairs. Turned out they were already on it; while the staff bloke and I were discussing it, chairs were already being set out, along with a long table full of nosh and beverages. I thanked him, turned round, and headed back, in time to see Tony setting out a chair, and Bree settling herself in.

Huka Lodge is what I call fantastic digs. It's out in the country, so far out that we'd come in by helicopter. We'd hired the entire place, twenty rooms and suites spread out between different buildings, with a pool leading straight out to the local falls. The place was gorgeous, close to perfect.

It was giving us the sort of break we needed to recharge. Huka's got a main lodge, and also a posh separate house, called the Owners Cottage, with four incredibly fancy private suites.

Bree and I were staying in one of the suites in that; Tony and Katia had another one, and Katia had been blissed since we'd got here, so I sussed out why Tony was looking so relaxed. Luke and Karen had the third one, and the girls were sharing the fourth.

When I got back to Bree, she'd sat down and she wasn't alone. Cal and Barb Wilson had come up, and Carla, and a woman I hadn't met before.

"John." Bree smiled up at me, a genuine smile, tired as hell, but bona fide Bree. "This is Kath MacDermott, Phil's sister. Kath, this is my husband John."

"Pleased." She held a hand out, and I shook it. She looked a lot like Phil: same strong jaw, same bushy eyebrows in a vee, and—I know it sounds strange—same voice. "It was very kind of your people to fly me here for this. What happened to Phil, hearing that, well—it was a shock. Phil was very much attached to you—he called you his second family."

I shook hands with her, and said something conventional and probably trite. Truth is, I didn't know what to say—I'm crap with things like that, funerals, having to let someone know what I'm feeling. Hell, it's taken me long enough to be able to do it with Bree. Doing it with strangers is beyond me.

I got lucky this time, because Mac came up, with Dom and Patrick. The day Mac doesn't know what to say in any situation at all, I'll know there's a snowboarding grand prix going on in Hell. While he was getting Kath MacDermott to smile and wipe her eyes at the same time, I pulled up a chair next to my wife and tried to get my head into the space for saying goodbye to a couple of friends who shouldn't have died when or how they did.

That afternoon turned out to be one of those things that stay with you, long after they're done with. I hadn't had anything to do with planning it—I wasn't really sure who had—and I'd expected it to be something I'd want to do and then forget. Mourning in public isn't my thing anyway.

270

But it turned out not to be sad at all—it was informal, and up-beat. Mac started it off, getting up and sharing stories about Greg and Phil. Both of his were warm, and light-hearted, and that got it moving; next thing I knew, Domitra was up and telling us about an incident where she and Phil had mixed it up with a pushy reporter. She did it in pure Domitra style, and it was so funny that Kath MacDermott let out a bark of laughter and then looked really surprised at herself. Patrick was standing off to one side, grinning; I suspect the story tickled up his memories of deal-ing with the media, back in his cop days.

I even got up and talked about Greg for a bit. His parents weren't much older than me, and that really was unsettling. It brought home a weird realisation: Greg could have been my kid, and he was dead, way too soon.

It went very quickly, which also surprised me. I remember my mum's funeral, a few months after Cilla and I'd got married; she'd had a heart attack, which hadn't done much damage, but she hadn't been home from hospital a week when she'd had a stroke, and that was it. Her funeral was sad and long and drag-ging, with Cilla in black next to me, fidgeting and edgy. I wonder now whether it was the coke making her hyper, or whether I'd read her wrong and she hadn't liked my mum, or if she couldn't deal with something that didn't put me in the spotlight. It was a bad day, and whenever it comes up in my head, I push it away.

This one was lovely. At the end, Kath got up and said a few words, about how much Phil had loved us all, and how, now, she could see why. I had a lump in my throat at that one, but it was a good lump, you know? And when Jack and Mary Maltin got up and asked if it was all right to read us bits from some of Greg's letters home from the road, we all got damp round the eyes.

So yeah, a nice memorial, very cleansing, with a sense of clo-sure. After all the talk, Carla got up and let everyone know there was food, and then maybe music, if anyone felt like playing. The

271

Huka staff had done up a good spread, and we spent the afternoon out on the lawn, talking, playing, singing.

Besides the chairs, the staff had also set out oversized hammocks. Bree and I climbed into one, side by side and hip to hip, with cold glasses of mineral water on little tables either side of the hammock. I closed my eyes, just relaxing. She was warm up against me, and it felt damned good.

She'd missed most of the Australia-New Zealand leg, thanks to the pneumonia. Those gigs had been especially good ones, musically—I spent three weeks missing the hell out of her and worrying day and night. That left me pissy and edgy, and it got into the music. I'd get her on the phone, worry over her, and then head off to the show and blow the floor off the stage at Melbourne or Adelaide or Auckland.

Six days in hospital, with a two-week course of strong antibiotics to follow, had left her limp and tired, and her mum had announced that Bree needed rest, needed to stay put with no getting on planes or changing time zones and suppressing her immune system. Since Miranda admits that she's probably the most hands-off mother on earth, Bree and I were both pretty startled by how fierce she'd been over it.

But she's a surgeon, and she knows her stuff. And I'd been grateful, because I'd been prepared for a huge fight over it—having Miranda as backup put the lid on any inclination Bree had to do the Brave Little Woman, and act as if I couldn't function without her there. The truth was, she'd been too worn out to argue. And being exhausted, that was how she'd got vulnerable to getting pneumonia in the first place...

"John?" She sounded peaceful and mellow. "When does this tour end?"

"Early September, sometime—the sixth, I think. Five nights, outdoors at Wembley, and then we get to go home, sleep for a month, hang out with the cats, and count the money, once Maureen Bennett deposits the royalty cheques." I turned my head sideways and looked at her. That's trickier than it sounds, in a hammock. "And speaking of the cats, you look like Farrowen when she thinks she's got away with something. What's up, Bree?"

"I just had an idea." She really did look smug. "My mom's birthday is in September. You know what I'd like to do? Give her an incredibly cool birthday present."

"Fly her to London for the shows, you mean?" I thought about sitting up, but decided against it. Across the lawn, Mac was playing his mouth harp. There were birds singing in the trees, songs I didn't recognise—the birds in New Zealand aren't much like the ones we've got in America, or Europe. "Get her a posh suite at the Four Seasons? Take her out for a fantastic birthday dinner or two, maybe shopping at Harrods, tea at the Dorchester? That it, then?"

"Wouldn't that be cool?" She sounded about as animated as I'd heard her since the pneumonia. "It couldn't be a surprise—she'd have to arrange time off from the hospital, and there would be plane tickets and stuff. But can we? Because I want to do something amazing for her, John. She may want to keep her nose all the way out of my business but you know what? She's been so *there* for me, every time I've needed her, and the only way I ever get to say thanks is by cooking her a meal. And that's just not enough. It sucks."

"I don't know that I'd say your cookery sucks, love." The more I thought about the idea of having Miranda over for a birthday prezzie, the better I liked it. "But I'm with you. I'd love to do something special for your mum. Let's coordinate it with Carla and Ian, all right...?"

So we finished out that rest break on a nice mellow note, with a proper goodbye to Phil and Greg, and the end of the tour coming slowly into sight.

273

We still had nearly six months left to go. The South American leg, up next, was going to be a bloodbeast, running to nearly the end of May. We'd be playing some of the biggest stadiums anywhere. Latin America has huge venues, the sort of numbers that make you blink: Mexico City seats some ungodly amount of people, a hundred and fourteen thousand. And in Rio, we'd sold out Maracanã, three nights with a hundred and twenty thousand people each night. If I thought about it too much, I got dizzy.

After we finished up in Latin America, Ian had scheduled us a nice rest break, a full month of doing sod-all at home. If we wanted to do interviews, that was our call, but he hadn't set up a damned thing. Then Europe for the final leg of this thing, playing stadiums from Barcelona just before Bree's birthday, all the way around to Russia and Athens and Zagreb and back to five nights at Wembley in September.

"John—can I ask you something?"

"What a peculiar question, love." She'd sounded uncertain enough to make me decide she needed a pair of arms round her, so I managed to roll over and gather her in; of course, that got the hammock creaking and swinging under us. "Bloody hell, who knew you could get seasick in a hammock? Anyway—ask away."

"After this tour is over, do you think maybe it could just be us for awhile?"

We were face to face under a good high sun, and I saw tiny little lines round her eyes and mouth. They hadn't been there six months ago, at least I didn't think they had. It did something odd to me, to my heart. Diabetes, pneumonia, that meltdown in Chicago when she thought she was extraneous, having to cope on her own with Wolfling getting sick: had this tour taken so much out of her that she'd broken because of it...?

"It's not that I'm not having an incredible time." *Shit.* I'd stayed quiet too long, and now she was worried, hurrying to justify it. "It's just that I want you all to myself for awhile. Once we're done with this, can we just take a couple of months, just us? Can I bolt the front door and keep the world away?"

"What, rebuild that magic wall of invisibility? Just for a few weeks?" I took her face between my hands. The breeze was soft, and warm against my back; someone, probably Luke, had picked up one of the acoustic guitars, across the lawn. I could hear it, lacing in and out with the breeze and noise of the falls. "Of course we can."

"We?"

It was a fair question. So many years, it was all Bree, building walls between us and the world, walls that kept us apart from each other, from getting things done, from moving forward a lot sooner than we had. I'd bitched and whinged and moaned and complained about those walls of hers; it had taken a death and a confession and a complete verbal arse-kicking from Domitra to show me what was wrong, not just with Bree, but with me. For way too long, those walls had been all hers.

"Yeah." I kissed her. "We."

"BLACKlight! BLACKlight!"

Early September in London, sunset's officially at eight. The weather can be anyone's guess, but the BBC weather service had promised a pleasant evening, clear skies, temperatures expected to hover near 17 Celsius, mid-sixties if you live in the States. It was a gorgeous evening to end the longest tour we'd ever done, and hopefully the not quite hundred thousand fans, chanting the band's name out in the big bowl of New Wembley Stadium, were digging it.

"Hey, baby."

I turned round, and smiled at Bree. Last I'd seen her, she'd been in the green room. She'd been hanging with her mum most of the past few days, but when Ian had given us the signal to start queuing up, Miranda was in the corner, having some kind of discussion with the doctor we'd had travelling with us, this leg.

"Oi, love." I shifted from one foot to the other; business as usual, really. I was surprised I wasn't more tired, but there you go—knowing I could go home the day after tomorrow and sleep in every morning for the next two years probably took the edge off. One thing the weather people hadn't mentioned was how unbreathable the air was. This air quality back in the Bay Area would have had a "spare the air day" warning attached to it. "Where's your mum? She having a good time?"

"BlackLIGHT! BlackLIGHT!"

"Wow, it's loud out there! I thought English fans were supposed to be polite and well behaved." She pitched her voice up a bit. "What were we—oh, right, Mom. Yep, she seems to be digging it. She and the tour doctor—what's his name, Eberleigh? They were comparing notes about something they both treated somewhere, no idea what it was, and anyway, I couldn't pronounce it. She'll come out when the show starts."

"Works for me." I wasn't saying what had popped into my head—*yeah, don't see you fancying squeezing my nuts with your mum watching*—but I didn't have to; she gave me that smile, the one we get to share when she's read my mind. It really is a trip, being together this long.

I wiped sweat off my face with the back of one hand. There'd be water onstage, hopefully; good job the only singing I do is backup, because I was dry as a bone. At the foot of the ramp, Mac was dancing in place. The way he was moving, you'd have thought it was opening night, not the tour closer. Luke was right behind him, and the Bunker Brothers were heading for us, getting in place in front of me, talking with their heads close together. Tony was just making his way up to us, getting in behind; he and Katia were holding hands.

"You lot ready?" Ian had come up, with Patrick and David

276

Walters from Fallow House. There was a huge crush of people backstage tonight, and had been for all the Wembley gigs. A lot of that was the London staff, getting to do the show at home, complete with full backstage perqs. "Remember, we're staying awhile after the crowd goes. The production and video staff have a prezzie for the band, something they've put together. There'll be a presentation, after the place clears out. So everyone take ten in the green room and stay put, okay?"

"They're putting out some amazing food." Bree was leaning against me, and I was rubbing her bottom lightly. She'd opted to close the tour they way she'd opened it, by wearing her wedding dress, blue velvet and buttons. She says it's good luck. "You know, I didn't think any stadium could make me look twice after Maracanã. But that arch just blows my mind. It's amazing."

It really was. We'd played the old Wembley Stadium, back in the day——first for Live Aid and then in '97, closing out the Jubilation City tour. I wasn't likely to forget it, since I'd been diagnosed with MS that summer. But the new design was fantastic, and the place had a whole new feel, at least for me.

"Man, I can't believe it's almost over." Tony was behind me, and for the first time since we'd queued up and waited in this same order at the Palais Omnisports in Paris, a year and a half ago, he sounded relaxed. "Hell of a ride. You okay, JP?"

"Yeah, I'm good." I shook my arms, trying to get rid of a couple of pins and needles. Nothing major, really, but the truth was, I was probably a lot more tired than I was admitting to myself. I took a long deep breath, or tried to. "London must be having an air quality control issue, that's all. Can't wait to get back to San Francisco."

"John?" Bree had stepped back. She was staring at me. "Babe, are you sure you're all right?"

"BLACKlight! BLACKlight!"

"Fine. A bit short of breath, is all. Nothing ten hours of sleep and getting back to San Francisco won't fix." I lifted an eyebrow at Bree. "You planning on wishing me a good gig from over there?"

She opened her mouth to say something, but the roar from the crowd carried the words away. Mac had hit the stage.

It was a fantastic show. I've said it before, you just can't touch the energy you get onstage during a tour opener or closer. We'd been staggering the set list, to keep it fresh for the tour—it's really easy to get stale. Blacklight's got a huge backlist of material, luckily, and we pulled out all the stops for this gig. I spent most the night perched on my usual stool; I was beginning to think I'd seriously underestimated how tired and shaky I was.

The break at the halfway point was ten minutes longer than we'd been taking for any other show on the tour, and I was damned glad of it. I actually hunted up the doctor we'd brought with us for this leg, and got him to point me at the oxygen. I'd never done that before—Mac uses it quite a bit, but of course he's a singer, uses a lot of breath. I'd never felt the need before, but I did tonight. The air felt thick, dirty maybe, and I couldn't quite get enough into my lungs to keep me at my best.

A few hits off the oxygen tank, and we were back on for the second set opener. No guests tonight—it was pure Blacklight, doing what we've always done, which is playing our asses off, giving the crowd a show they'd talk about for years to come. And we did it properly. The entire band rode that wave; we all knew that tonight was the end of it, no reason to hold back. Once we got back to the hotel, we could sleep for a week, go home, do whatever we fancied doing, because this was the end of the *Book of Days* tour. Tonight, the crowd got all of us.

Two encores, and during the break between them, something a bit weird happened. I'd gone back for another hit at the oxygen tank—that caught my mother-in-law's eye and she started asking me questions—when Solange and Suzanne cruised past. They

278

weren't paying attention to me, not beyond a quick wave, but all of a sudden, I heard singing. I mean, really good singing, the sort of voice that usually winds up fronting a band and getting rave reviews from besotted reviewers, about stuff like range and arpeggios and whatnot. I had the mask over my mouth, and didn't really want to take it off, but I did have a moment of wondering if oxygen can cause hallucinations, because it sounded as if that singing had come from one of Luke's girls, and I was damned if I'd ever heard either of them singing so much as a note. I finished up sucking down the oxygen, smiled at Miranda—she was watching me, and she wasn't smiling back—and headed back out.

There were damned near a hundred thousand people out there that night, and no one left early, not from the looks of it. Of course, they didn't have to, since the local transport agencies were running extra trains and buses. So everyone was still there for the encore: arms around each other's waists, deep bows, the lot. Same stuff we'd been doing for two hundred and sixty shows, in hockey arenas and soccer pitches and NFL stadiums.

House lights up, finally, and it was over, at least the part the public and fans got to see. Offstage, I found a road case and leaned against it for a moment, just trying to catch my breath, get my legs to work, figure out why I was feeling so damned weird…

"John? John, what's wrong? You're a very bad colour."

"Oi." I focussed my eyes on Miranda. "Half a mo."

"You're panting." She has these pale blonde eyebrows, very high arches, but right then, they were in as deep a vee as I'd ever seen Bree's go. She reached a hand out and got hold of my wrist. "My God, your pulse is off the charts! Come and sit down for a few minutes. I'm going to talk to Rick Eberleigh and get him to check you out. I think you should plan on an ER stop between here and the hotel."

"Casualty ward, you mean." My right arm was tingling, and I

rubbed it. "A & E ward. Maybe they can give me something for this headache? It just came on."

Back into the dressing room. Bree turned, saw Miranda first and then me, and of course, that was it, she was right there, finding a quiet place for me to stretch out, with a damp cold cloth over my eyes. That took some of the teeth out of the thunder in my skull, but the rest of me was pretty damned off.

Wembley emptied out, finally. It took the best part of an hour, and there were some press people still there, not in any hurry to go anywhere. So when Ronan and Nial came in to tell us that the entire crew wanted us somewhere where we could see the video veil, it was the band and extended family, about a dozen media types, and a handful of Wembley regular crew.

I followed everyone out, but only as far as the doorway at the back of the ramp. There were seats above us, up a flight of stairs, but I was damned if I was climbing anything just then, I was that light-headed.

"Hang on to me." Bree had her arm round my waist, and I was leaning against the doorjamb. "Here's hoping this is short, whatever it is. We're stopping at the nearest hospital—I don't know which one, but that's where we're going, and don't argue."

I started to answer her—*not planning to argue, love, believe me*—but just then, the video veil began to shimmer, and the stadium's sound system came on. And there we were, thirty-plus years of Blacklight, memories and people, all of us and all our history, dancing pictures on four transparent walls made of thousands of tiny lights.

You had your fifteen minutes, to strut and fret your stuff onstage—the time was right and you were right there in it, audience was ready for some noisy rage

"Oh, wow! Nice choice, picking 'Remember Me.' Is that tonight's version they've got going?" Tony had come up, and he was peering up at the nearest video veil. "Ugh, that's making me want to hurl. JP, don't look at that shit, look across stage at the front veil. This one's too close—it's totally distorted. Vertigo central. Man, are you okay? You look terrible."

"Not sure." Crikey, I felt dizzy. "Bree, is there a chair anywhere?"

But now that's past, it's time to go, you did your bit, you're off the show—maybe it'll help to know: We will remember you

"Here." She had the chair behind me, under me. I sat; I was watching the screen, and there was Mac up there, moving at warp speed and made out of light, looking not much older than Solange was now, wearing the flash gear we all wore back in the seventies. "I'm getting the doctor, and Mom. Hang on."

"Okay."

Lights, movement, things gone long ago, so many. A shot of Cilla, jutting a hip at the camera, pouting for whoever'd been holding it. There was Solange, maybe three years old, in the front garden at Draycote with Meg Fallow, playing with a baby goat, Solange giggling, stopping suddenly, looking lost and almost panicky, her face crinkling up, and Meg gathering her in. I wondered if she was suddenly realising her mum was gone, not coming back...

You were good, you had no reason—you twisted up that gift so bad; talent marries hate, I call that treason to all the music you once had

I was rubbing my right arm, and the headache was back. Weird thing was, I couldn't really make myself feel involved with anything just that moment. Not being able to breathe all the way in, that was worrying, but even that, I couldn't really care too much—the feeling reminded me of my drinking days, when I'd have the occasional brandy. I was watching the pictures up there, dancing and moving, old faces, gone faces, people I'd cared about, people who were still there for me, but everything seemed to have got detached, or maybe I had.

I don't know how you found that hole I don't know how you lost your soul But I can't deny it's true: We will remember you

There was Bree, twenty feet tall, on my arm in the same blue dress she was wearing right now—it was after our wedding, back at the Bellagio, stopping in the doorway to the high rollers suite where we'd held the reception, and there was Mac and a few of our guests, doing an a capella version of "I Knew The Bride When She Used to Rock and Roll." There were Stu and Cyn, dancing at their own wedding back in 1985, Cyn looking like the angel off the top of the Christmas tree, until she did a twirl and showed some serious leg.

"John? John! Oh God –" Bree's voice, but was it onscreen or next to me, I couldn't tell... "Mom! *Mom!* I need you!"

We never know just what might happen, we never know how high to fly maybe we get to keep each other, or lose it all in the blink of an eye

The screen was gone, or maybe they'd moved it, because out of nowhere I was looking at the night sky, stars, the lights of London setting up an under-glow, the arch of stars holding up Wembley's roof. I had my head in someone's lap, somone's hands on me, soft and sure. My legs were all over the place but my back was stiff, and I was jerking about because something was going on in my chest; no air, no breath, and I had to close my eyes because I was so damned dizzy, but I couldn't puke all over Bree's wedding dress, she was holding me, not letting me go, hanging on, keeping me safe...

And now I lay me down to sleep you're everything I want to keep

"Get his shirt open—where's that AED? Bree, honey, lower him all the way down to the floor, and you can't be touching him anywhere. I know, but let go, darling." Miranda, that sounded like. Things were getting farther away, I wasn't sure how or why, I just knew I didn't like it. "No, of course I can't say for sure, but it's not the usual arrhythmia. Symptoms match up with ventrical tachycardia—if he starts fibrillating, we'll lose him. Where the hell are those paddles!"

"John." I could hear her, my wife, her voice nice and low but it cut straight through the band, the voices around me, all the shouting and feet pounding and the world that seemed to be slipping away from me. I forced my eyes to focus, for just a moment, and there she was on her knees, her face close to mine. "Listen to me, okay? Remember how I told you once, that I never ask you to do anything, and I never ask you not to do anything? John, can you nod if you remember?"

If you should wake and find me gone, feel free to live, and carry on

I nodded. Of course I remembered—her asking that, that was silly. She'd gone missing, rung me up, asked me to trust her…

"Okay." Clear, warm voice, the voice I loved the best. I always said she had music in it. "I said I never ask you to do anything or not do anything, but I'm asking you now. To do something, to not do something."

So much to do, so much to see, I only ask one thing:

There were warm hands on my chest, undoing the shirt, very fast and competent. Bree was going, she was fading out, her voice and her green eyes and all the rest of it. I was so damned tired, ready to let it go, but she wanted to ask me something and I could do that much…

"Clear!"

"Don't die." I couldn't hear anything, it was getting very far away, but I could hear her. She'd never let me down, not once. "I'm asking you to do that. Stay alive. Don't die."

Please, remember me

Noise, pain, all my breath was going, electricity crackling near me, Miranda was rubbing gel or something against my chest. I had no words left, no air, but damn it, Bree'd asked me something and I had to answer somehow.

"*Clear!*"

"Always on." I thought I said it, but I wasn't sure, because there wasn't enough of me left in the body her mum was shocking to be sure. I tried, one more time. "Always burning."

Eyes closing, too heavy, no way to keep them going, no way to hold on. I thought I heard her say something, voice and music, and then she was gone, and so was I.

Epilogue

October in London, the end of British summertime starts getting really close. The days get short, and the autumn doesn't seem to want to hang about. Winter's right there waiting, just the other side of Guy Fawkes Day. Not a lot of daylight left.

18, Howard Crescent, London NW1, was pretty much the last place I expected to be settling into right now. We should have been back in San Francisco long since. I mean, yeah, all things considered, I was quite happy to be settling into anywhere at all, and I got why we were staying in London for a while; the cardio people at Whittington Hospital, up the road in Highgate, wanted to keep an eye on my fancy new hardware.

"John?" The limo had stopped, and Bree had one hand on the door. She wasn't waiting for the driver. "We're here."

"Yeah, I know." I turned to grin at her. It was a real grin; I'd

285

been doing that quite a lot since Wembley. The only time the grin got a bit wobbly, and made me have to think about faking it, was when I looked at what the past six weeks had done to her. The damage was visible, you know? There was no way for me to pretend it wasn't there. "Let the driver get the doors, love, okay? It's part of what we pay him for. Besides, I like watching people wait on you."

"Okay." She brushed hair away from her face, and I felt the grin want to fade off and disappear. Two months ago, that hair had been red, a dark auburn slowly beginning to fade in tiny streaks. Now it was mostly grey—six weeks was all it had taken, six weeks of what had to have been non-stop terror on her part, basically. And now, this afternoon... "I just wanted to make sure we were in before the rain hits. It's going to pour tonight. I know the weather service said probable, but my knees are talking to me. There's a storm out there."

She wasn't meeting my eye, and I knew why. Something that had happened earlier today, on our last pre-release visit with the resident heart expert. One more thing between us, that needed to be dealt with.

I shifted in my seat, feeling the ICD move and settle. It was taking me a good long time to get used to having the damned thing under my skin. The thing's actual name was a mouthful; it was called an implantable cardioverter defibrillator, but bollocks to calling it that. Far as I was concerned, the square bulge just under my left collarbone was a tickybox. No sign of problems with it, the cardiology specialists had done a stellar job, and I hadn't even had to deal with being awake for the procedure; they'd done it while I was out, after the ambulance had got me to the A&E at Northwick Park Hospital, Bree and Miranda with me in the back. It wasn't ideally placed for a guitarist, mind you—I was going to need some custom straps made, because the straps I've got hit it dead on, and that was uncomfortable as hell, you know? But no problems otherwise.

"We've arrived, Mr. Kinkaid." The driver had got my door open. Bree was already out, and around my side of the car.

"Ta." I got my legs out, feeling a tiny tremor. The MS had been well-behaved through all the heart stuff. That was just as well; turned out having an ICD put in came with a side issue, and I wasn't going to be able to get MRIs in the future. I'd told Bree that almost made the entire miserable episode worth it, but she didn't seem to find that funny.

The driver wasn't offering a hand, maybe because Bree was already there, close enough to hang on if needed, far enough to let me do it myself if I wanted to. I wasn't moving too quickly these days—the first couple of days out of bed, I'd been using a cane to get about, but I'd dumped that in a hurry. I'd switched over to Whittington Hospital, up in Highgate, partly because they had a fantastic cardio department and partly because, once I realised where Bree was taking me to recuperate, it seemed the obvious choice.

The doctors had been at me about pacing myself, getting into some sort of very light exercise regime, something I could take back to the States and keep up with once I got home. Bree thought that was brilliant, and she'd got really good at nagging me about it. She was already dropping little hints about the pair of us getting into a PT program, once we got back to San Francisco. But that wasn't going to happen for a while, yet.

The house—yeah, well. I'd really thought, last time we'd been through the front door, that was the last time. We'd set a lot of history to rest, burying Cilla's ring in the back garden, me coming clean with Bree about how hard I'd been boozing when I'd been away from her, just getting it all out between us.

And Bree hated the place. She's got damned good reasons— for one thing, this was Cilla's house, and Bree was never going to feel comfortable in it. I'd tried giving it to her, and she'd basically backed off, hissing and spitting. Plus, she'd got the scare of her life here, injured on Cilla's old works. That led to an AIDS test, and a Hep C test. Not a good two days.

So, what with one thing and another, she'd have been happy to have never seen 18, Howard Crescent again. I'd been meaning to sell it; the house is worth a couple of million easily. My idea was to put the money I got for it into the addiction recovery clinic I was funding in Cilla's name.

But of course, *Book of Days* had become a monster and the tour had followed. And then there was me, going into something the cardiologists called V-fib, which, apparently, would have killed me in about eight seconds if Miranda hadn't been there, hadn't known my medical history, hadn't known to shock the heart directly. Doing that, she'd shocked me back to life again.

So 18, Howard Crescent was still ours, and maybe that was the luck Bree's blue velvet wedding dress had brought us. While I was unconscious for four days after the heart attack on 6 September, Carla and Ian had told Bree to give them a list. They wanted to know what she'd need in the way of a place suitable for rehabbing a cardiac patient with a shiny new ICD making damned sure the ventricles of his heart didn't spark out again.

Bree—I got this from Carla—Bree never hesitated. She'd looked at them as if they were bonkers. She'd told them, we already had a suitable house for an invalid. She'd told Ian to hit the surgeons up for a list of anything medical the house might need, and told Carla to please hook her up with the local markets and restaurants, and make sure there was power and water and that the place was stocked with basics. And that was that.

I was weak as all hell. Recovery from the V-fib had been hampered by an infection I hadn't known was there, and what should have been maybe a week in hospital after I woke up had turned into a month, while they got that under control. I'd expected that to kick the MS into high gear—I mean, what the hell, it's all immune system stuff, you know? But the MS laid back and let my immune system get on with it. Nice of it.

So everything had been coming along. I had this arrhythmia, it had got out of control and messed with the ventricles of my heart, the arrhythmia had become tachycardia and then something called ventricular fibrillation. Miranda had explained it to me, and truth to tell, it put a picture in my head I couldn't quite shake: the lower chambers of the heart, quivering out of time like a bad drumbeat. It's a bad one, V-fib is. It'll kill you if you don't shock the beats back to normal pretty quick. And of course, there was the infection, piling it on.

Then that last meeting with the surgeon, just a few hours ago, and here we were, with everything on the edge of falling apart, and Bree's red hair gone grey...

I tipped the driver, and leaned on Bree, heading up the path. She had the keys to the house in her hand. Every time I'd been here, I'd seen ghosts: me on my own, me and Cilla, young and just married and the entire world mine if I fancied it. Today, though, the ghost I knew was waiting was different.

The two of us, me and Bree, just a few hours ago, had been sitting on one side of about half a mile of polished desk, listening to the heart bloke going on. He had a lightboard up behind him, with x-rays of my chest and heart. Creepy, that was. It reminded me of my neuro's office back home, with the MRI shots of my brain.

"Interesting, about this scarring." He'd been up, pointing at something I couldn't really decipher. "You know, we requested your records from San Francisco—apparently you had a minor cardiac event a few years ago, in Boston?"

"Yeah, I did." I'd had Bree's hand in mine, warm and easy. "Not a bad one—it felt bad, but that's because the MS was roaring at me. The doctor at Mass General said it wasn't too bad, anyway."

"Going by his notes, I'd have to agree." He tapped the light-board again. "But what about your first heart attack?"

"Sorry?" I blinked at him. "Only had the one, until this last charmer at Wembley. Not sure what -"

"Here. This scarring." Both his brows were up. He was about my age, but a lot rounder. "I want to be clear about this, Mr. Kinkaid, because it's puzzling me. You've got what's known as monomorphic ventricular tachycardia, a classic case. The most common cause is scarring, dead tissue, from a previous heart attack; the natural electrical current that regulates the beats jumps the scar tissue, goes around it. It can't self-regulate. Well—you've got the scarring. But it's very old, from the looks of it. Thirty years, maybe more. Could you have had a heart attack you weren't aware of? Something that caused your heart to stop, and leave this mass of scar tissue?"

Bree's hand, resting in mine, was suddenly rigid. I heard the tiny intake of air, and felt her sway beside me.

Shit.

Thirty years, he'd said. Yeah, there was something, all right. Thirty years ago, I'd rung Bree up from a cheap hotel in San Francisco, cold turkey on snowballs, flipping my shit, hallucinating, begging for help. I didn't remember that night, just the re-sults of it: Bree, barely sixteen, stealing what she thought I'd need from her mother's locked drug locker, bringing it to me, trusting me to know how much was safe.

I hadn't. I'd done all of it, except for the stuff I'd made unus-able by bleeding into it when the razor slipped and sliced into my hand instead of cutting lines of blow. And the blow—pharmacy grade—had been ten times the strength of the cut stuff I'd been using before.

It had stopped my heart, all right—kick like a horse. Bree had done compression and CPR, and started it going again, same as her mum had done for me a few weeks ago, except she'd been sixteen, terrified off her nut, and she hadn't had paddles.

"Doesn't matter." I heard myself say it, nice and easy. Next to me, Bree didn't seem to be breathing. "How it got there, I mean. Now we know it's there, we deal with it. Knowledge is power, yeah? Question is, will the ICD take care of it?"

Reassurances, instructions on coping with this thing they'd put in under my skin, requests to please stay in London for a month or so, so they could monitor how I adapted, making an appointment. Bree, silent next to me, not saying a word. I wasn't letting go of her hand until I had to, but I caught a look at her face and what I saw there killed any hope that she might not have sussed out what had come to light, up there in the expert's office.

The first drops of rain hit the brick path behind us just as we got inside. I hadn't even got the door closed all the way behind me before the sky went yellow, there was a long rolling boom of thunder, and the clouds opened. It was a lot of sudden noise, which may be why it took me a second to realise that, behind me, Bree had her face in her hands. She was sobbing.

I turned, and gathered her in.

I didn't say anything, not then. What was there to say, you know? I couldn't knuckle her under the chin, tell her to stop playing Bree d'Arc, say, *knock it off, this wasn't your doing*—it was her doing, and we both knew it. I couldn't tell her it was no big deal, even though that was no more than the truth. I couldn't make soothing noises. She wouldn't buy it.

The bottom line was, she'd brought me the drugs all those years ago, the pure pharmaceuticals that had stopped my heart for nearly a minute, long enough to leave the scarring that had left me vulnerable to the tachycardia. The fact that I'd asked her to do it, that my jones had put a girl too young to have to be that strong in the position of power over life and death—my life or death—that wouldn't matter to her, or hold any weight. All she could see was that she'd damaged me.

291

But I had to say something. This was us, it was me and Bree, and I didn't know what I was going to say, just that there were words, truth, something, and I'd best just let them fly.

"Bree."

She was shaking and silent, no noise along with the tears. I could feel the strange little box that was my new lease on life, just under the skin; she'd already learned to shift automatically, so as not to press up against it. "Bree, listen. Just listen to me, all right?"

She nodded. No words, no sound. But she nodded.

"A few weeks ago, you asked me to do something for you. I was almost gone, almost over and out, set closer, but you asked me not to go, and I listened to you. Didn't I?"

Another nod, the hair that used to be red moving against my cheek.

"Okay." I had one hand up, stroking her hair. "I'm asking you to return the favour. Let it go."

She pulled back then, and faced me, opened her mouth. But I just kept talking. It was coming, and I let it come.

"Let it go, love. Yeah, I know, I get it. Without that night in the Saturn Hotel, things might be different. But you aren't thinking. I'd have been dead by morning if you hadn't come. I'd have hit the streets, found what I wanted there. I was a junkie, Bree. And I'm not asking you to pretend it didn't happen, or pretend there wasn't collateral damage. That would be tricky enough. I'm asking you to do more than that, a lot more. Just let it go."

Not a word. She just stood there, her teeth sunk into her lower lip, staring at me. I was even skinnier than normal, and getting my weight back up to something useful was going to take some doing. And she wasn't the only one with a lot more white in her hair than had been there before 6 September.

"Please. For me." I leaned forward, using that free hand, bringing us face to face. "For us. Let it go?"

"Okay." She nodded. "I'll try."

She meant it. It was all right there in her face: how hard it was going to be to not beat herself up over it, take the blame, burn herself at the stake every minute of every day. But she understood, you know? She got it.

She was doing it for me, knowing that watching her struggle with it, making herself suffer for it, would hurt me, as well. I don't know that I would have understood that a year ago, but I did now.

"Good," I told her, and kissed her, long and deep, tongue tip to tongue tip, the way we'd always liked it best. It was the first time I'd done that since Wembley, one small step on our road back from the shadowy places in our own personal book of days.

JP Kinkaid

Photo by Nic Grabien

Deborah Grabien can claim a long personal acquaintance with the fleshpots—and quiet little towns—of Europe. She has lived and worked and hung out, from London to Geneva to Paris to Florence, with a few stops in between.

But home is where the heart is. Since her first look at the Bay Area, as a teenager during the peak of the City's Haight-Ashbury years, she's always come home to San Francisco, and in 1981, after spending some years in Europe, she came back to Northern California to stay.

Deborah was involved in the Bay Area music scene from the end of the Haight-Ashbury heyday until the mid-1970s. Her friends have been trying to get her to write about those years— fictionalised, of course!—and, now that she's comfortable with it, she's doing just that. After publishing four novels between 1989 and 1993, she took a decade away from writing, to really learn how to cook. That done, she picked up where she'd left off, seeing the publication of seven novels between 2003 and 2010.

Deborah and her husband, San Francisco bassist Nicholas Grabien, share a passion for rescuing cats and finding them homes, and are both active members of local feral cat rescue organisations. Deborah has a grown daughter, Joanna, who lives in LA.

These days, in between cat rescues and cookery, Deborah can generally be found listening to music, playing music on one of eleven guitars, hanging out with her musician friends, or writing fiction that deals with music, insofar as multiple sclerosis—she was diagnosed in 2002—will allow.

Visit her website at www.deborahgrabien.com

CPSIA information can be obtained at www.ICGtesting.com
Printed in the USA
LVOW091449130911

246117LV00002B/53/P